SILVER WINGS, SANTIAGO BLUE

The jocular voices and the back-slapping camaraderie going on didn't include her, as pilots milled about the ready room, playing cards or chatting idly, puffing on endless cigarettes. She wanted to be part of the living world, not an onlooker.

Mary Lynn couldn't put a name to the force that made her turn around so that she saw Walker when he came in. His officer's cap was raked to the back of his head, showing the heavy brown hair that grew with such unruly thickness. His leather battle jacket hung open and the tails of the white scarf draped around his neck were dangling loose.

Walker paused to draw a match across the abrasive strip of its match cover and cup the flame to his cigarette. Over the fire, he caught sight of the small, silent woman watching him from a corner of the room. Her dark eyes were on him, rousing him fully.

For an instant, she became the only living thing in the room for him. Slowly, he lifted his head, staring at her as he shook out the match. Steadily, she returned his gaze, not looking away or showing reluctance.

There was a message in that – one he wanted to explore . . . to be sure of its meaning.

Also by the same author,
and available in Coronet Books:

THIS CALDER RANGE
STANDS A CALDER MAN
CALDER BORN, CALDER BRED

SILVER WINGS, SANTIAGO BLUE

Janet Dailey

CORONET BOOKS
Hodder and Stoughton

Copyright © 1984 by Janet Dailey.
First published in Great Britain by
Hodder & Stoughton Ltd in 1985.

Coronet edition 1985.

British Library C.I.P.

Dailey, Janet
    Silver wings, santiago blue.
    I. Title
    813'.54[F]   PS3554.A29

ISBN 0-340-37770-4

─────────────────────────────────

Printed and bound in Great Britain for
Hodder and Stoughton Paperbacks, a
division of Hodder and Stoughton Ltd.,
Mill Road, Dunton Green, Sevenoaks,
Kent (Editorial Office: 47 Bedford
Square, London, WC1 3DP) by
Cox and Wyman Ltd., Reading, Berks.
Photoset by Rowland Phototypesetting Ltd.,
Bury St Edmunds, Suffolk.

To Jerry, my flight instructor back in 1968 when I earned my private pilot's license,

and to Frank, the F.A.A. pilot who gave me my "up check,"

and to Bill, my husband, manager, friend, and lover, but more important in this case, the man who showed me the skies and encouraged me to fly in them myself. Now I know what it's like to be high above the earth, rocking a plane and singing at the top of your lungs from the sheer joy of solo flight.

With special thanks to former WASP Harriett "Tuffy" Kenyon Call, for her memories and mementos of those years.

Author's Note

The parodies of song lyrics appearing on the pages delineating the Parts of this book are the actual songs the Women Airforce Service Pilots (WASPs) sang while they marched to and from the flight line, their classes, and their barracks. In their own way, the songs tell much of the girls' story.

HIGH FLIGHT

Oh! I have slipped the surly bonds of earth,
   and danced the skies on laughter-silvered wings;
Sunward I've climbed and joined the tumbling mirth
   of sunsplit clouds – and done a hundred things
You have not dreamed of – wheeled and soared and
   swung – high in the sunlit silence.
Hov'ring there, I've chased the shouting winds
      along,
   and flung my eager craft through footless halls of
     air.
Up, up the long, delirious, burning blue, I've topped
  the windswept heights with easy grace,
Where never lark or even eagle flew.

And, while with silent, lifting mind I've trod the high
   untrespassed sanctity of space,
Put out my hand, and touched the face of God.
John Gillespie Magee, Jr.

In December 1941, Pilot Officer Magee, a nineteen-year-old American serving with the Royal Canadian Air Force in England, was killed when his Spitfire collided with another airplane inside a cloud. Discovered among his personal effects was this sonnet, written on the back of a letter at the time he was in flying school at Farnborough, England.

PROLOGUE

She sat amidst a framework of canvas and piano wire, her long skirts tied around her knees and her legs extended full length in front of her. No doubt her thudding heart competed with the reverberations of the 30-horsepower motor spinning the two propellers. When the wire anchoring the Wright Brothers flying machine to a rock was unfastened, the *Flyer* was launched five stories into the air, and in that wildly exhilarating moment Edith Berg nearly forgot to hold on to her seat.

Beside her Wilbur Wright was at the controls, dressed in his customary high starched collar, gray suit and an automobile touring cap. The flight over the Hunaudières race track in Le Mans, France, lasted two minutes, three seconds, and Edith Berg entered the pages of aviation history as the first woman to ride in a flying machine. It was all a publicity stunt to promote the reliability of the new Wright flyer, an idea concocted by her husband, Hart O. Berg, a sales representative for the Wright Brothers.

The year was 1908 and Edith Berg was an instant sensation, her courage and daring applauded. The press loved the stunt. The French shook their heads and whispered among themselves, 'That crazy American woman! And imagine her husband's letting her do it!'

She wore a stunning flying suit of plum-colored satin, from the hood covering her raven hair to her knickers and the cloth leggings, called puttees, which wrapped her legs from knee to ankle. It was understandable that the all-male members at the Aero Club of America's headquarters on

11

Long Island would look at twenty-seven-year-old Harriet Quimby with open mouths, especially when she asked to be licensed as an aeronaut – a woman! (The government had not gotten around to accepting responsibility for licensing pilots and wouldn't until 1925.)

The green-eyed writer for *Leslie's Magazine* suggested the members let her demonstrate her flying skills. With considerable skepticism they watched Harriet Quimby climb into her gossamer biplane and take off. She flew over a nearby potato field, then banked the plane back to the field and set her aircraft down within eight feet of her takeoff point – setting a new record for the club in landing accuracy.

The date was August 1, 1911, and Harriet Quimby became the first woman to be licensed as an aeronaut. In a wry comment to reporters she said, 'Flying seems easier than voting.' Not until 1920 would the Nineteenth Amendment be ratified, giving women the right to vote.

She sat cross-legged in the doorway of the fuselage while the flame-red, tri-motored Fokker airplane with gold wings, the *Friendship*, floated on its pontoons in the harbor off Burry port, Wales. Her short-cropped hair was the color of the dune grass on Kill Devil Hill, site of the Wright Brothers' first powered flight.

Captain Hilton Railey rowed alongside the *Friendship* and shouted to her, 'How does it feel to be the first woman to fly the Atlantic? Aren't you excited?'

'It was a grand experience,' Amelia Earhart replied, but she knew she hadn't flown the Atlantic. Bill Stultz had been the pilot and navigator on the flight. 'I was just baggage. Someday I'll try it alone.'

That was June 18, 1928.

Four years later, on May 21, 1932, Amelia Earhart landed her red 500-horsepower Lockheed Vega in a farm meadow outside of Londonderry, Ireland. Exhausted, she crawled out of the cockpit and said to the staring farmhand,

'I've come from America.' It was five years after Lindberg had made his Atlantic crossing.

On January 12, 1935, Amelia Earhart accomplished another first in aviation history by becoming the first pilot, male or female, to successfully fly from Hawaii to the continental United States, landing her Vega at Oakland Airport in California. That feat was immediately followed by the first non-stop flight to Mexico City, then from Mexico City to New York.

As a women's career counselor at Purdue University in Indiana, Amelia Earhart advised a group of female students, 'A girl must nowadays believe completely in herself as an individual. She must realize at the outset that a woman must do the same job better than a man to get as much credit for it. She must be aware of the various discriminations, both legal and traditional, against women in the business world.'

Amelia had already encountered them in 1929 when Transcontinental Air Transport, later to become Trans World Airlines, asked her to become a consultant for them along with Lindbergh. While he flew around the country checking out new air routes, she traveled as a passenger, talking with women and lecturing various women's clubs on the safety and enjoyment of flying.

At the Bendix Transcontinental Air Race in May of 1935, Amelia Earhart had the chance to meet newcomer Jacqueline Cochran, whose story would rival any tale by Dickens. As an orphan, her birth date and parents unknown, she was raised by foster parents in the lumber towns of northern Florida. It was a hardscrabble existence, and little Jacqueline often went shoeless. When she was eight years old, her foster family moved to Columbus, Georgia, to work in the local cotton mills, and Jackie worked, too, on the twelve-hour night shift. A year later, she had charge of fifteen children in the fabric inspection room.

She left the cotton mill to go to work for the owner of a beauty shop, doing odd jobs. A beauty operator at the age of thirteen, Jackie was one of the first to learn the technique of giving a permanent wave. She began traveling to demonstrate the technique in salons through Alabama and Florida, until a customer persuaded her to go to a nursing school even though she only had two years of formal education.

As a nurse, she worked for a country doctor in Bonifay, Florida, a lumber town, so much like the places where she'd been raised. A short time later, after delivering a baby under wretched conditions, she abandoned her nursing career and went back to the beauty business. She became a stylist for Antoine's at Saks Fifth Avenue, both in his New York and Miami salons. In 1932, at a Miami club, Jacqueline Cochran met Floyd Bostwick Odlum, a millionaire and a Wall Street financier. She told him of her dream to start her own cosmetics company. Odlum advised her that to get ahead of her competition and to cover the kind of necessary territory she would need wings. Jackie used her vacation that year to obtain a pilot's license, and subsequently the equivalent of a US. Navy flight training course.

At the same time that Jacqueline Cochran Cosmetics, Incorporated, was born with Odlum's help, Jacqueline Cochran aviatrix came into existence. In 1934, this striking brown-eyed blonde made her debut in air-racing circles with the England-Australia competition. Engine troubles forced her to land in Bucharest, Rumania.

In the Bendix Transcontinental Air Race of 1935 which saw both Earhart and Cochran competing, Earhart took off in the middle of the night with the rest of the starters. Cochran's Northrop Gamma was next on the ramp for takeoff, when a heavy fog rolled over the Los Angeles airport. The plane ahead of her roared down the runway and disappeared into the thick mist. The sound of a distant explosion was immediately followed by an eerie light that backlit the fog. Her reaction was instinctive, her nurse's training taking over. Jackie jumped in her car and followed the fire truck down the runway. Both arrived too late to do the pilot any good. By the time the fire was put out, the pilot was dead.

Jackie stood beside her aircraft while the tow truck dragged the burned and twisted wreckage off the runway. The fatal crash left everyone a little stunned, including her. A government aviation official was standing not far away from her and she heard him say he thought it was suicide to take off in that fog. The realization that she was next in line sent her running behind the hangar so no one would see her when she vomited.

When her legs quit shaking, she placed a long-distance call to New York and talked to her ardent backer and now her fiancé as well, Floyd Odlum. 'What should I do?'

But Odlum couldn't tell her, ultimately advising her that it came down to 'a philosophy of life.' At three o'clock that morning, Jacqueline Cochran made a blind takeoff, her fuel-heavy aircraft barely clearing the outer fence which ripped off the radio antenna hanging below the plane's belly. She spiraled up through the fog, flying by compass only, to gain altitude to clear the seven-thousand-foot mountains inland from the coast.

Amelia Earhart came in fifth in the race, but an over-heated engine and dangerous vibrations in the tail of the Northrop Gamma forced Jackie back to the starting line at Los Angeles.

May 10, 1936, was the wedding day for the slim-built, sandy-haired Floyd Odlum and the glamorous and gutsy blonde Jacqueline Cochran. The homes she'd never had as a child became a reality as they purchased an estate in Connecticut, a ranch near Palm Springs, and an apartment in Manhattan overlooking the East River. Aviation had long been a love of Odlum's, so his interest went beyond being merely a supporter of his wife's career. Among his many holdings were the Curtiss-Wright Corporation and the Convair Aircraft Company. So it wasn't surprising that the Odlums helped finance Amelia Earhart's around-the-world flight.

On June 1, 1937, they were in Miami to see her off

on that last, fateful trip. Before she left, Amelia gave Jacqueline a small American flag made of silk – which became a symbolic 'transfer of the flag,' in military jargon, when Amelia Earhart vanished without a trace. Speaking at a tribute to the famous woman aviator, Jacqueline said, 'If her last flight was into eternity, one can mourn her loss but not regret her effort. Amelia did not lose, for her last flight was endless. In a relay race of progress, she had merely placed the torch in the hands of others to carry on to the next goal and from there on and on forever.'

That year, Jacqueline Cochran won the women's purse in the Bendix Air Race and finished third overall. On December 4, 1937, she set a national speed record, traveling from New York to Miami in four hours and twelve minutes, bettering the previous time set by the millionaire race pilot Howard Hughes. The following year, Jacqueline Cochran won the Bendix Race, covering the distance of 2,042 miles in eight hours, ten minutes and thirty-one seconds – nonstop! Her plane was the P-35, a sleek, low-winged military pursuit-type aircraft. She set a new cross-country record for women, and in 1939 broke the women's altitude record. She received her second Harmon Trophy, the highest award given to any aviator in America, presented to her in June by the First Lady, Eleanor Roosevelt. She kept flying, setting records, and testing new designs and new equipment.

But events in Europe were dominating the world scene. The Axis held control over Czechoslovakia, Albania, and Spain. In September, Hitler sent his German Panzers into Poland. On the 28th of September, the day after Warsaw fell, Jacqueline Cochran sent a letter to Eleanor Roosevelt, expressing her view that it was time to consider the idea of women pilots in non-combat roles and implying a willingness to do the advance planning for such an organization. Beyond expressing gratitude for the suggestion and stating her belief that women could make many contributions to the war effort should they be called upon to do so, there was little Eleanor Roosevelt could do.

16

Throughout 1940 and the first half of 1941, Jacqueline Cochran continued to expound on the idea of establishing a women's air corps to free male pilots for war duty. After she had lunch with General H. H 'Hap' Arnold, Chief of the US. Army Air Corps, and Clayton Knight, who directed the recruiting of pilots in America for the British Air Transport Auxiliary, General Arnold suggested she should ferry bombers for the British and publicize their need for pilots. Knight thought it was a splendid idea.

But the Air Transport Auxiliary headquarters in Montreal wasn't as enthusiastic. Their response was, 'We'll call you,' and they didn't. Undeterred, she got in touch with one of her British friends, Lord Beaverbrook, who just happened to have recently been appointed minister of procurement, formerly called aircraft production. During the second week of June, Montreal did indeed call and ask her to take a flight test – Jacqueline Cochran, the holder of seventeen aviation records, twice recipient of the Harmon trophy, and the winner of the 1938 Bendix Race.

After three days of grueling tests that seemed more intent on determining her endurance than her flying skill, Jackie made the mistake of joking that her arm was sore from using the handbrake when she was accustomed to toe brakes. The chief pilot stated in his report that while she was qualified to fly the Hudson bomber, he could not recommend her since he felt she might have a physical incapacity to operate the brakes in an emergency situation.

His objections were deemed petty and overruled by ATA headquarters, and Jacqueline Cochran received orders to ferry a Lockheed Hudson bomber from Montreal to Prestwick, Scotland, with a copilot/navigator and radio operator as her crew. But her troubles weren't over. Vigorous protests were made by the ATA male pilots, who threatened to strike. Their objections ranged from concern that ATA would be blamed if the Germans shot down America's most famous woman pilot to complaint that an unpaid volunteer – and female to boot – flying a bomber across the Atlantic belittled their own jobs. A compromise was ultimately reached whereby Jacqueline Cochran would be pilot-in-command for the Atlantic crossing, but her copilot would make all the takeoffs and landings. On June 18, 1941, Jacqueline Cochran became the first woman to fly a bomber across the Atlantic Ocean.

On July first, she returned from England. In her Manhattan apartment, with its foyer murals showing man's early attempt at flight and a small chandelier designed to resemble an observation balloon hanging from the ceiling, she held a news conference and talked about her trip to Britain. After the reporters had gone, Jackie received a phone call inviting her to lunch with President and Mrs Roosevelt.

The next day, a police escort drove her to the estate at Crum Elbow, the famous Hyde park mansion with its majestic columned entrances. She spent two hours with the President. The meeting resulted in a note of introduction to Robert Lovett, Assistant Secretary of War for Air, in which the President stated his desire that Jacqueline Cochran research a plan creating an organization of women pilots for the Army Air Corps.

Her subsequent interview with the Assistant Secretary early in July resulted in Jackie's becoming an unpaid 'tactical consultant,' with office space for herself and her staff in the ferry Command section. Using the Civil Aeronautics Administration's files, she and her researchers found the records of over 2,700 licensed women pilots, 150 of them possessing more than 200 hours of flying experience. When contacted, nearly all were enthusiastic about the possibility of flying for the Army.

Jacqueline Cochran put forward a proposal to her former luncheon partner, Army Air Corps General 'Hap' Arnold, to utilize not just the 150 highly qualified women pilots but to give advance training to the more than two thousand others. Hers was not the only proposal regarding women pilots the Army received. Nancy Harkness Love, a Vassar graduate and commercial pilot for the aviation company she and her husband owned in Boston called Inter-city

Airlines, had also contacted the Ferry Command of the Army Air Corps with a plan to use women pilots to ferry aircraft from the manufacturers to their debarkation points.

But in July 1941 such drastic measures seemed premature to General Arnold. The United States was not at war, and there was an abundance of male pilots. He wasn't sure that it ever would be so dire that they would need women.

Then Pearl Harbor happened. By the spring of 1942, the Army was 'combing the woods for pilots,' and the plans of the two women were resurrected. Jacqueline Cochran was in England recruiting women to fly for the British ATA when she learned that Nancy Love was putting together an elite corps of professional women pilots, ranging from barnstormers to flight instructors for the Ferry Command. Jacqueline Cochran raced home to argue with the Army Air Corps commander, General H. H. Arnold, for her training program, offering him more than a few pilots – promising him thousands, and assuring him she'd prove they were every bit as good if not better than men.

The situation *was* dire. The Allies were losing the war on all fronts in September 1942. General Arnold agreed to Jacqueline Cochran's proposal. The following month, she was busy locating a base where she could train her 'girls.' Facilities were finally provided for the first two classes of trainees at Howard Hughes Field in Houston, Texas, but it soon became apparent that the Houston base wasn't big enough to hold her plans.

Her girls were learning to fly, and they were doing it 'the Army way.'

Part One

We are Yankee Doodle pilots
Yankee Doodle do or die.
Real live nieces of our Uncle Sam
Born with a yearning to fly.
Keep in step to all our classes
March to flight line with our pals
Yankee Doodle came to Texas
Just to fly the PTs.
We are those Yankee Doodle gals.

CHAPTER ONE

In her parents' Georgetown home, Cappy Hayward sat on the sofa cushion, her shoulders squared, her hands folded properly on her lap, and her long legs discreetly crossed at the ankles. On an end table sat a framed photograph of her father wearing his jodhpurs and polo helmet and standing beside his favorite polo horse. The picture of the proud, handsome man smiling for the camera bore little resemblance to the career military man confronting her now. Her face was without expression, emotions controlled the way Army life had taught her, while she watched her father's composure disintegrating in direct proportion to his rising anger.

Dropped ice cubes clattered in the glass on the bar cabinet. The golden leaves on the shoulders of Major Hayward's brown Army jacket shimmered in the January sunlight spilling through the window. Major Hayward was not accustomed to having his authority questioned, and certainly not by a member of his family.

'I thought we had discussed all this and it was agreed you were not going to pursue this highly experimental program. It is a damned stupid idea to train women pilots for the Army.' He pulled the stopper out of the whiskey decanter and splashed a liberal shot of liquor into the glass with the ice cubes.

'You "discussed" it and reached that conclusion,' she corrected him smoothly. Her shoulder-length hair was dark, nearly black, a contrast to the startling blue of her eyes. Her poise was unshakable, giving a presence and authority and an added sense of maturity to this tall, long-legged brunette.

'Now, don't go getting smart with me, Cappy.' A warning finger jabbed the air in her direction.

As a small child, she'd always begged to wear her father's hat. He'd been a captain then. Subsequently, she had been dubbed his 'little captain,' which had become shortened to Cap, and eventually expanded to the nickname Cappy.

'I'm not,' she said evenly. 'I am merely informing you that I have been accepted for this pilot training program and I'm going.'

'Just like that, I suppose.' Displeasure made his voice harsh. Its lash could be much more painful than any whipping with a belt. 'What about your job?'

Wartime Washington, DC, paid high wages for moderately skilled typists, but Cappy didn't consider the work to be much of a job. It demanded nothing from her, and provided no challenge at all. There was a war on and she wanted to make some meaningful contribution, no matter how trite it sounded. She wasn't doing that, typing inter-office memos nobody read, in some dreary 'tempo' – one of more than two dozen prefabricated office buildings the government had erected for temporary quarters. After sweltering all summer inside the gray asbestos walls, Cappy couldn't face an entire winter shivering in them.

'I've already given them my resignation.' She glanced down at her hands, then quickly lifted her chin so her father wouldn't get the impression she was bowing under the dictatorial force of his arguments. 'I'm not going to change my mind, sir.' She slipped into the childhood habit of calling him 'sir,' a throwback to the days when a gangly, white-pinafored, pink-ribboned little girl had trailed after her tall, handsome 'daddy' and been sternly ordered to call him 'sir.'

With a sharp pivot, he swung away from Cappy to face the meekly silent woman anxiously observing the exchange

24

from the cushion of a wing chair. He lifted the glass and poured half the contents down his throat.

'This is all your fault, Sue,' he muttered at his wife. 'I never should have allowed you to persuade me to let Cappy move into an apartment of her own.'

'Don't blame this on Mother,' Cappy flared. 'She had nothing to do with it.'

Not once during her entire life could Cappy recall her mother taking a view opposing her husband. She was always the dutiful Army wife, ready to pack at a moment's notice and leave behind her friends with never a complaint. With each move to a new post, her mother painted, papered, and fixed up their housing into beautiful quarters, only to leave them for someone else to enjoy when they moved again. She observed all the Army's protocol, treating the colonel's and the general's wives with the utmost kindness and respect, and taking their snubs without a cross word. Her mother was either a saint or a fool, Cappy couldn't decide which.

'Women in the cockpits of our military aircraft is positively an absurd idea,' her father ranted. 'It will never work. Women are not physically capable of handling them.'

'That's what they said about welding and a half dozen other occupations supposedly only men could do. Rosie the Riveter has certainly proved that isn't so,' Cappy reminded him. 'You should be glad about that. If it weren't for women like Rosie, you wouldn't have all your war machinery coming off the assembly lines now.'

Rosie the Riveter's occupation was the antithesis of what her father saw as suitable for a female. If they had to work, women could be teachers, nurses, secretaries, and typists. In truth, her father wanted her to get married and give him a grandson to make up for the son he'd never had, Cappy being their only child. Dissatisfied with her choices, he'd even picked out a future husband for her – Major Mitch Ryan.

Cappy hated the Army – the way it submerged personal-

25

ities in its khaki sea and imposed discipline on almost every facet of her life. As far as her father was concerned, the Army was always right. The Army was right to move them every four years, never allowing attachments to people or places to form, and it was right to discourage socializing between officers' families and those of enlisted personnel. When she was nine years old, her father had caught her skipping rope with a sergeant's daughter. Cappy still remembered how much fun Linda was and all the variations she knew. But the Army caste system had been violated, and Cappy had been forbidden to see her little friend again, and had her skip-rope taken away. And her mother had not said a word in her behalf – accepting, always accepting.

Cappy had been too well trained by Army life to ever openly rebel. But the minute she reached her majority and legally could live apart from her parents, she had moved out. It was a case of serving out her hitch. From now on, she made her own decisions and her own friends. And if they happened to be someone like Rosie the Riveter, she didn't care even if her father did.

'Don't cloud the issue,' he answered contentiously. 'Learning manual skills does not mean a woman is capable of the mental and physical coordination required to fly long distances. Why on earth would you even entertain the idea?'

'Maybe you shouldn't have taught me how to fly,' Cappy murmured with a small trace of mockery.

It was the one time she'd felt close to her father, that summer of her seventeenth year when she'd been going through that awkward, coltish, long-legged period. She and her mother had been watching from the ground while he performed beautiful and exciting aerobatics in the sky. After flying he had always seemed relaxed, more approachable, and less the stern disciplinarian. A few questions from her had led to a ride in the plane.

Suddenly her childhood god began to look upon her with favor; her father taught her to fly. For a while they'd

26

had something in common, experiences to share and things to talk about – until the novelty had worn off for him. It had been cute to teach his daughter to fly, like teaching a dog a new trick. Later, he hadn't understood why she wanted to continue such an unfeminine pursuit. Always she'd been a disappointment to him, too tall and striking to ever be the petite, pink-and-white little girl he envisioned for his daughter, and not the son she knew he wanted.

Typically, he ignored her reminder of his role in her flying as his jaw hardened, his blue eyes turning steel-hard, so similar in color and quality to hers. 'Young women on military bases are going to be ogled by every noncom around. How can a daughter of mine subject herself to that kind of leering humiliation?'

'I was raised on military bases,' she reminded him. 'I can't see that there's any difference.'

'There damn well is a difference!' His neck reddened with the explosion of his temper. 'You are my daughter. If any man so much as looked at you wrong, they answered to *me*! A single woman on base is just asking to be rushed by every man jack there.'

'It doesn't say very much for the men, does it?' Cappy challenged.

'Dammit, I want you to be practical,' he argued. 'If you're determined to make some use of your pilot's license, join the Civil Air Patrol instead of traipsing halfway across the country to attend some fool training in a godforsaken Texas town.'

'That's a joke and you know it,' she retorted angrily. 'You've told me yourself that it's ridiculous to even suppose there will be an invasion of the East Coast. And the chance of any long-range bomber strike is equally remote.'

'No daughter of mine is going to take part in any pilot training program for women! I won't have you getting involved with any quasi-military organization that is going to send unescorted females to male airfields around the country. Why, you'd be regarded as no better than tramps.'

27

Outwardly, she showed a steely calm, all those years of disciplining her emotions coming into play and keeping her from giving sway to her anger. 'You no longer have any authority over me. You may still have Mother under your thumb, but I'm not there any more. I came to inform you of my plans. Now that I have' – Cappy picked up her coat and scarf from the chair back – 'I see no reason to stay any longer.'

'Cappy.' Sue Hayward sprang to her feet, dismayed by this open break between father and daughter.

'Let her go, Sue,' Robert Hayward ordered coldly. 'If she has so little respect for her parents that she would deliberately go against our wishes, then I don't care to see her again.'

Briefly, Cappy glared at her father for demanding his wife's undivided loyalty, then she started for the door, knowing well whose side her mother would choose. She caught the silent appeal in the look her mother gave her unrelenting husband before she turned to Cappy. 'I'll walk you to the door.'

Waiting until they were out of earshot, Cappy said, 'I'm not going to apologize, Mother. I'm not sorry for anything I said.'

'He meant it, you know that.' She kept her voice low as they paused by the front door. 'Don't go into this program just to spite him, Cappy.'

'It's what I want to do,' she insisted. 'I don't think you ever understood that. I don't deliberately do things to upset him. There are things I want to do because they give me pleasure. Haven't you ever done anything that you wanted to do? Has it always been what he wanted, Momma?'

'I love him. I want him to be happy.' Every discussion on the subject brought a look of vague confusion to her mother's face.

'Haven't you ever wanted to be happy?' But Cappy didn't wait for an answer. Her mother was too much a reflection of her husband, even to the extent of reflecting

28

his happiness. 'What do you have, Momma? You have no home, no friends – you haven't seen your family in years.'

'It hasn't been possible. The Army –'

'Yes, the Army.' Cappy struggled with the toe-tapping anger she contained. 'It's no good, Mother. I won't change. I won't be like you.' She sensed the faint recoil and realized how her thoughtless remark had hurt. 'I'm sorry.'

'This is what you want?' her mother asked quietly. 'To fly?'

'Yes.'

There was a moment's hesitation while her mother searched Cappy's face. 'Then go do it,' she said.

The encouragement, however reluctantly given, was totally unexpected. Misty-eyed, Cappy gave her a brief hug. 'Thank you,' she said softly, then became knowingly wary. 'But I promise you, I'm not going to set foot in this house again until *he* invites me.'

From the living room came the harsh, commanding voice, calling, 'Sue? Susan!'

'I'm coming, Robert,' she promised over her shoulder, then exchanged a hug with Cappy.

Cappy tucked the ends of her loosely knotted long wool scarf inside her coat and reached for the doorknob. 'Goodbye, Mother,' she said.

Outside, Cappy paused a moment on the stoop, then walked carefully down the snow-shoveled steps to the sidewalk. The visit had turned out almost the way she had expected it would. She had anticipated her father's anger, his lack of understanding. She breathed in the cold, sharp air and started off.

With head down, she turned at the juncture of the main sidewalk and walked in the direction of the bus stop. At the crunch of approaching footsteps in the snow, she lifted her glance and tensed at the sight of the Army officer in a long winter coat – Major Mitchell Ryan.

'Hello.' His breath billowed in a gray, vaporous cloud as he smiled at her in puzzlement. 'Am I too late? I thought the Major told me dinner would be at six this evening.' It was typical of her father to invite the bachelor major to dinner without mentioning it to her. She had been foolish enough to go out on a few dates with him after her father had introduced them. Now both of them seemed to believe Mitch Ryan had some sort of proprietary rights over her.

Cappy reluctantly stopped to speak to him. Dusk was gathering, sending lavender shadows across the white townscape. She looked out across the snow-covered lawns and bushes rather than meet the narrowed probe of his dark eyes. 'I wouldn't know. I'm not staying for dinner. Father and I had a falling-out over my decision to join the training program for women pilots.'

'General Arnold's new little project. Yes, I remember you mentioned it to me.' His head was inclined in a downward angle while he studied her closed expression. 'There is some skepticism toward it.'

'I've been accepted.' She tilted her head to squarely meet his gaze, since he was a head taller than her five-foot-seven-inch height. The rich brown shade of his eyes had a velvet quality, and there always seemed to be something vaguely caressing about the way he looked at her, a definitely disconcerting trait – all the more reason to stay clear of him now that these last few months had shown her she could like him. Major Mitchell Ryan was career Army.

'Are you going?' His eyes narrowed faintly.

'I report to Avenger Field in Sweetwater, Texas, next week.' She started walking and Mitch Ryan swung around to fall in step with her, the wool Army coat flopping heavily against his long legs. Like Cappy, he looked straight ahead.

'For how long?'

'Twenty-six weeks, if I make it the full distance.'

'What then?'

'Then I'll be assigned to the Air Transport Command, I expect, ferrying planes around the country,' she said.

'And where, exactly, does that leave us, Cap?' His head turned in her direction, the bill of his officer's hat pointing down.

'I wasn't aware there was any "us."' Her mouth was

30

becoming stiff with the cold, but it seemed to match her mood.

His leather-gloved hand caught her arm, stopping Cappy and turning her to face him. 'Don't go.' He held her gaze, their frosty breaths mingling.

'Why?'

The line of his mouth became grimly straight. He was struggling to conceal the frustration and annoyance he was feeling. 'Surely the Major advised you of the negative image associated with women and the military.'

'Yes, I heard the whole lecture, but this happens to be a civilian group.' She stayed rigid in the grip of his hands.

'I suppose I can't change your mind about going.' The muscles along his jaw stood out in hard ridges.

'No,' Cappy replied evenly, without rancor. How many times had she seen Mitch since her father had introduced them three months ago? A half-dozen times maybe, but no more. Yet she must have turned down thrice that many invitations from him. Her rejection only seemed to add to his determination. It was just as well she was leaving before his persistence wore her down and she became involved with him despite her better judgment.

Through the thickness of her winter coat, she could feel his fingers digging into her arms. 'There's a war on, Cappy.'

'Washington is loaded with man-starved girls. You aren't going to miss me for long, Mitch. Not in this town.' The approaching rumble of a bus was a welcome intrusion on a scene that was becoming very uncomfortable to Cappy. 'Here comes my bus, Major. I won't have a chance to see you again, so we might as well say goodbye to each other now. It's been fun.'

He flicked an impatient glance toward the oncoming bus, then brought his attention back to her face. 'Fun. Is that all it's been to you?'

'Yes.'

For an instant longer, his dark gaze bored into her while his mouth tightened. With a roughness he'd never shown her before, Mitch dragged her closer and bent her head backwards with the force of his kiss. It was hard and short, briefly choking off her breath. When he abruptly released her, Cappy gave him a stunned look.

'Go,' Mitch ordered roughly with a jerk of his head toward the braking bus.

'That achieved nothing, Mitch.' The tactic was so typically military – to overpower and control. Cappy wanted him to know it had failed. He might be like her father, but she was not like her mother.

'Then there's nothing to keep you here, is there?' The hard gleam in his eye challenged her.

Behind her, the bus crunched to a full stop next to the snow-mounded curb. Cappy hesitated only a split second. Long ago she had resolved not to let herself be open to hurt. It was better to know what she wanted. In the long run, it would spare her a lot of pain and heartache. She waved for the bus to wait for her and left him standing in the snow.

The clickety-clack of the iron wheels clattered in the background as Cappy gazed at the Texas buttes to the south. They were the only landmarks in an otherwise monotonous landscape of mesquite and dull red earth beneath a gray sky. Yet she observed it all with a controlled eagerness.

There was a movement in her side vision, followed by an outburst of raucous laughter. Cappy let her attention stray from the dust-coated train window to the group of servicemen at the front of the car. It was a motley assortment of passengers on board, weighted heavily on the side of soldiers either heading home on leave or reporting for duty.

Everybody was going somewhere. It had been that way for over a year – ever since Pearl Harbor. Cappy glanced at the family from the Arkansas hills, seated across the aisle from her. The woman and her three children were on their way to California. She had confided to Cappy earlier in the journey that her husband had 'gotten hisself a right fine job at one of those aeroplane plants.' Cappy had surmised from the woman's wide-eyed look of wonder that he was making more money than his family had seen at one time before.

'Momma, I'm hongry.' The oldest child made the hushed comment which carried to Cappy's hearing. The girl looked to be about seven although the mother didn't appear to be much older than Cappy's twenty-two years.

Cappy's head bobbed slightly with the rocking sway of the train while she observed the family with idle curiosity. For all the woman's apparent inexperience of the world, the blue eyes above those hollow, boned cheeks possessed a knowledge of life's more basic realities.

The woman removed a wax-paper-wrapped sandwich from the satchel at her feet without disturbing the toddler sleeping on her lap. The middle child, a five-year-old boy, stared at the sandwich with big eyes, but didn't say a word. When the woman pulled the sandwich into two more-or-less equal halves, the older child made a faint sound of protest.

'Now, Addie, you share this with your little brother,' the woman admonished with a warning look that silenced the girl, but Cappy noticed the resentful glance she gave the boy.

The sandwich didn't appear worthy of a fight. The thick slices of bread almost hid the thin slice of cheese trapped between them, yet the children ate it slowly, savoring every mouthful, and carefully picking up any crumb that fell. The woman bent across the sleeping child again to rummage through the satchel, and this time came up with a small, slightly withered-looking apple. As she straightened, she noticed Cappy watching her. She darted a quick, self-conscious glance at the apple in her hand.

'Would ya care fer an apple?' the woman offered hesitantly. 'They're right sweet ones growed from our own tree in the back yard. They kept real fine in the cave this winter.'

'Thank you, no.' Cappy noticed the faint show of relief

in the woman's expression. 'I'm getting off at the next stop.'

Cheese sandwiches that were more bread than cheese, old and wrinkled apples – Cappy mentally shook her head in a kind of wry pity. She couldn't recall ever eating plain bread and cheese in her life. Army life had insulated her from much of the Great Depression. Food had always been plentiful in her family, purchased at PX prices. They had never lacked for anything.

A man in a Marine uniform approached, deliberately catching her eye. He paused by the aisle chair next to the window seat she occupied and braced his feet against the rock of the train.

'Anyone sitting here?' He indicated the vacant aisle seat.

Cappy gave a negative shake of her head. 'Help yourself.' Such advances had occurred so many times during her long train ride, they had acquired a certain monotony. As the young marine dropped into the seat, she asked, 'Are you heading home on leave or on your way back?'

'Reporting for duty in California,' he said. 'Rumor has it we'll be shipping out in a few weeks. Destination – some "nowhere" in the pacific.' His mouth twisted in a rueful grimace, intended to elicit sympathy.

'Somebody has to go, I guess.' Her sidelong glance mocked his pity-me look.

He laughed shortly, unsure whether she was joking or making fun of him. He eyed her, faintly puzzled by the aloof poise she maintained, so at odds with the vibrant image of her long dark hair, curled at the ends, and her vivid blue eyes.

'My name's Andrews, Benjamin T. Ben to my friends.' He tried to smile. Usually the uniform did the trick for him with girls but he could tell she wasn't at all impressed by it.

'Hayward, Cappy.' She mimicked his military phrasing.

'Cappy, eh.' He seemed to search for a topic that would give him control of the conversation. 'Well, where are you bound . . . Cappy?'

34

The clackety-clack of the train became louder as the connecting door between the passenger cars was opened. The conductor entered and started down the aisle. 'Swee-eetwater! Next stop, Swee-eetwater!' He made the rhythmic announcement as he walked through the car.

'This is where I leave you – Avenger Field, Sweetwater,' Cappy said to the Marine and glanced briefly out the window. The flat-topped mesas to the south that had dominated the landscape since Abilene were gone. All she could see now was flatly undulating country beneath a gray and bleak sky.

The train began to slow as it reached the outskirts of the Texas town. Another young woman in the front of the passenger coach stood when Cappy did and took her suitcase from the overhead rack. Their glances met across the heads of the other passengers, and recognition flashed between them – recognition of the shared purpose for which they'd traveled to this west Texas town.

'I'll get that for you.' The Marine reached for the blue suitcase bearing Cappy's initials and lowered it down.

'Thanks, I can manage.' She started to take it from him, but he eluded the attempt.

'No doubt you can,' he agreed with a rare show of humor that put them on equal footing. 'But my mom taught me to carry heavy things for a lady.'

Unexpectedly liking him, Cappy shrugged and laughed. 'Suit yourself.' They made their way to the end of the coach with Cappy gripping each passing seat-back to retain her balance against the slowing lurch of the train. The grinding screech of the brakes put an end to any further conversation as the train rumbled to a stop. 'Good luck to you, Ben.' She stuck out a friendly hand to say goodbye to him.

'Yeah.' He looked at her hand for a second, then at her face, and leaned forward to plant a kiss on her surprised lips. Grinning, he handed her the suitcase. 'A fella never knows if he'll get another chance to kiss a pretty girl.'

Cappy smiled widely. 'Liar,' she mocked the trite sentiment, as a barrage of wolf whistles rose from the other servicemen in the car.

Wartime had a crazy effect on people, a fact she had noticed before. It became an excuse for them to throw aside convention and do what they pleased – and they usually did.

The door opened and Cappy turned to leave. Her glance locked with the other girl also waiting to disembark. There was a bold and reckless quality about her – an earthy zest. Cappy had a distinct feeling this girl would do anything on a dare. About the same height as Cappy, maybe an inch shorter, she had sand-colored hair, bobbed short into a mass of loose curls that needed little attention, and her eyes were an unusual gray-green, very frank in their gaze.

The conductor took their luggage and carried it down the steps. He left it sitting on the platform of the Texas and Pacific train depot and came back to give them a hand down. A raw wind lashed at their cheeks as Cappy followed the other girl. She looked down the track, but no one else had gotten off the train. All the townspeople seemed to have been chased inside by the blustery wind of this gray, February day. Their glances met again as they reclaimed their respective suitcases.

'I heard you tell that private you were bound for Avenger Field.' The girl's voice had a pleasant rasp to it, husky and warm, yet as bold as she was. 'Since we're both going to the same place, we might as well share that lone taxi.' She nodded in the direction of a navy-blue sedan that had just driven up to the train station.

'Why not?' Cappy couldn't argue with the practical suggestion.

The numbing wind chased away idle chit-chat and hurried them both to the waiting taxi. The driver stepped out, his collar turned up, a cowboy hat pulled low over his forehead. He angled his body into the wind while he took their suitcases.

'Reckon you two are wantin' to go to Avenger Field with the rest of those females,' he surmised, sizing them up with an all-seeing glance while he juggled their luggage and opened the trunk.

'That's right,' came the whiskey-rough reply as the girl didn't wait around for the car door to be opened for her, but bolted into the rear seat. Cappy followed and shut the door. Finally sheltered from the bitter wind, the long and lanky girl suppressed a shudder. 'It's cold out there. I always thought Texas was warm,' she grumbled.

'Texas is infamous for its "blue northers."' Cappy opened her purse and removed a cigarette from a pack. 'Want one?'

'No thanks.' Gray-green eyes were on her as the match was struck and the flame held to the tip of the cigarette. 'Are you from Texas?'

'No, but I've lived here.' Exhaling a cloud of smoke, Cappy settled into her corner of the back seat. 'My name's Cappy Hayward, by the way.'

'Marty Rogers, from Detroit, Michigan.'

'My last address was Washington, DC.' She flipped open the car's ashtray, glancing at the driver when he slid behind the wheel. 'I'm an Army brat, so – you name it, I've lived there.'

When the taxi pulled away from the depot, the Rogers girl leaned forward to ask the driver, 'How far is it to the field?'

'Not far.' He shrugged as if to indicate the distance was of little import and not worth his time figuring.

'A couple of miles.' Cappy supplied the information she had gleaned from inquiries within the Army system.

'How do you know? Have you been to this air base before?'

'Actually it isn't a military air base. It's a municipal field converted to military use to train pilots.' She took a drag on her cigarette and exhaled the smoke while she added, 'The town named it Avenger Field last year – to train pilots to "avenge" the attack on Pearl Harbor.'

'You're a veritable fountain of information. I thought I'd done well merely locating Sweetwater on a Texas map.'

The husky gravel of her voice had a taunting pitch of self-mockery, a wry humor always lurking somewhere to poke fun at something.

'We had some British flyboys out there. Last of 'em left last summer.' The driver volunteered the information, tossing it over his shoulder to his passengers in the back seat. 'Got some American boys out there now,' he told them in a voice that was thick with the local twang.

'They only have a few more weeks before they finish their training. Then, rumor has it, Avenger Field will be strictly female.' Cappy sensed the questioning look and acknowledged it. 'I did some checking after I received my telegram from Jacqueline Cochran ordering me to report here. Only half of our class will be training at Avenger Field. The other half is reporting to Howard Hughes Field in Houston.'

The taxi had already passed the last buildings on the edge of town. From the little she'd seen of Sweetwater, it hadn't struck Marty Rogers as being a place filled with action, whereas Houston at least conjured up images of a big town. Oh, well, she decided with a mental shrug, she had come here to fly, not to party. A good thing, too, because about all she saw out the window was a heavy gray sky and a lot of desolate country.

'I don't care. I just want to fly,' Marty asserted a little more strongly than was necessary.

'Don't we all,' Cappy murmured and stabbed out the fire in her cigarette.

'I suppose your father's a pilot in the Air Corps.'

'He has a desk job in Washington. He's been posted to the Pentagon – the new building in Washington they built to house the military command. He flies, but strictly for his own pleasure.'

'Is that how you learned?'

'Yes.' Cappy didn't elaborate on her answer to the first truly personal question put forth. She could have told this Rogers woman that her father now rued the day he'd ever taught her to fly. Sharing information was one thing, but giving confidences to strangers – 'telling all' in the space of five minutes – was another.

Over the years, she had lost count of the number of new homes she'd lived in, new towns, new friends – the pathetic eagerness to be liked. She had made the mistake of confiding things about herself to those she thought were new-found friends only to have them blab it all over school. She'd learned the hard way to keep things to herself – problems, fears, and desires. It was better to be self-sufficient; then people couldn't hurt you.

'How did you learn to fly?' Cappy switched the focus to Marty Rogers.

'When my older brother, David, took up flying, I had to give it a whirl. One time up and I was hooked.' Her wide mouth quirked in wry remembrance. 'My folks bought David a plane, a little Piper Cub. I mean he's the number one son so he gets everything, right? I turned out to be an afterthought in more than one way.'

David had always had center stage from the time she could remember. She had grown up in her older brother's shadow, worshiping him sometimes and violently resenting him other times. The competition between them was strong – as strong as the sibling love that bound them.

'Anyway –' Marty took a deep breath and plunged on. 'David let me use his plane as long as I paid for the fuel. It was a helluva good deal for me.' She swore naturally and casually, managing to make it inoffensive. 'You should have heard him when he found out I'd qualified for this flight training program the Army's giving us. He was so damned green with envy.'

'Why is that?' Cappy knew she was expected to ask.

'With that plane of his, he thought he was going to have a leg up on everybody when he joined the Army. He figured with all his hours and experience he'd be a shoo-in for pilot training, but he couldn't pass the physical.'

'I think we all sweated that.'

'Yeah, well, David's on his way to Fort Bragg in North Carolina for paratroop training. He decided if he couldn't fly planes for the Army, jumping out of them was the next best thing. Hell, I'm twice the pilot he ever thought of being and I know it.' Marty bragged without apology. 'Not that my parents are ever likely to notice anything I do.' She paused a second, an indignant anger surfacing. 'You know, David left a couple of weeks ago for camp, and for his last night home my mother used all of her meat-ration coupons on a steak for him! You know what I had my last night? Macaroni. It isn't fair.'

'I know what you mean,' Cappy said with empathy.

'Do you have any brothers?'

'No, I'm an only child.'

'Lucky you. Your parents probably think anything you do is wonderful. Do you know how my father reacted when I told him I was going to take this training? I got this whole lecture that proper young women should be content to stay on the ground. He just couldn't get it through his head that I'm twenty-four years old. I don't need his permission.'

'I was forbidden to come,' Cappy replied.

'You're kidding! I figured an Army father would be all in favor of it. Isn't that something?' She sat back in her seat. 'You ought to hear my folks carry on about the way I smoke and drink and date guys. Their precious son certainly is no saint. Where do they think I learned everything? Hell, I'm probably not an ideal daughter.' She hit a flat note. 'But I can't be what I'm not. Besides, there's a war on.' Marty came back to her old form, husky and uncaring. 'It isn't fair that David gets to go and have all the excitement while I'm supposed to sit around and twiddle my thumbs.'

The driver slowed the taxi and Cappy glanced out the window at the guardhouse marking the entrance to the field. 'Looks like we're here.'

The taxi stopped in front of a long, slant-roofed building, squatting low to the ground and painted gray as if to match the clouds overhead. Military paint came in only three colors: battleship gray, olive drab, and khaki brown. Beyond were the barracks buildings, six of them marching by twos facing each other lengthwise in a north-south line. The hump-backed roofs of two hangars were visible. Atop one there was a tower of sorts that reminded Cappy of a widow's walk, a flight of steps leading to it from the outside.

In addition, the recreation/dining room and ground school classroom buildings made the third side to the triangular layout of the field buildings with the hangars for a base line. A long stretched-out building ran parallel to one of the two intersecting runways. Windows lined the front of one end where the pilot's 'ready room' was located, the place where the trainees would await their turn to fly. The other end was divided into classrooms for their ground school courses. All the wooden, gray buildings were huddled by the runways, intertwined by taxi strips linking the ends of the runways with the flight line and hangars as well as with each other. From the air, Avenger Field resembled a crudely drawn map of Texas.

The driver set their suitcases on the hard-packed ground spotted with a few tufts of tenacious buffalo grass. Splitting the fare, Cappy and Marty each paid their share. He pocketed the money and gave them a wondering look. 'It beats me why you gals would think you could take up this flying business. It ain't natural, ya know.'

'I guess we're all just a little crazy,' Marty informed him with mock seriousness at his male prejudice against females and flying.

It sailed right by him as he turned away, shaking his head. When Marty glanced at Cappy, she was wearing the same slightly exasperated expression. The common bond brought a smile to each of them. A feeling of adventure and excitement ran high in Marty's veins. As the taxi rumbled away, it suddenly ceased to matter how cold and forlorn the day was. This was the chance of a lifetime and there wasn't a damned thing that was going to stand in her way. She could tell Cappy Hayward felt the same way.

'This is it.' Marty looked at the administration building before them.

'Let's go in.' Cappy hoisted her heavy bag and started for the door, her deeply blue eyes agleam.

Accustomed to being the one in the lead, Marty faltered a second before she followed the calmly assertive brunette. As Cappy opened the door, the cold wind rushed inside to announce their arrival to the large group of women already gathered in the big room. The sudden draft swirled through the blue-gray smoke hanging in layers close to the ceiling. Heads turned toward the door to protest the gust of cold air, then remained in the same position to eye the newcomers. But the lull in the conversation didn't last long as Cappy and Marty were quickly absorbed and the buzz of female chatter reached its former level.

It seemed natural that since they had arrived together, they would stay together. They worked their way through the massed clusters of women until they found a patch of unoccupied floor and set their suitcases on it.

Throughout the room, luggage was put to a variety of uses – racks for coats to be draped on, backrests for those seated on the floor, and narrow seats for others to sit on. Marty shed her heavy winter coat and laid it across the top of her suitcase while she glanced at a trio of women only a couple of feet away.

'Hi.' She wasted no time getting acquainted, untroubled that Cappy Hayward exhibited no such eagerness. 'Marty Rogers from Michigan.'

'Hey, I'm from Chicago,' piped up a girl with dark hair. 'Whereabouts did you fly?'

'Out of Detroit mostly.'

'Where are you from?' The question was directed at Cappy, acknowledging her presence on the periphery of the group.

'Cappy Hayward, Washington, DC.' She identified herself with the close-mouthed crispness Marty had already begun to expect from her.

'Is that where you did your flying?'

'No. I logged most of my hours out of Macon, Georgia,' she replied.

'Oh?' The dark-haired woman nearest to Marty had been an interested listener, half sitting and half leaning on her suitcase. Marty blocked her view of Cappy, so she straightened to look around her. 'Are you from there originally?' The girl's soft, drawling voice revealed her southern upbringing, silky and sweetly refined. But it was her size that startled Marty – she was so much shorter than the rest of them.

'I'll be damned,' Marty exclaimed under her breath. 'You must have just made it above the minimums.'

'I squeaked through by an eighth of an inch.' She laughed. 'Five foot two and five-eighths. It was a good thing they measured me in the morning or I wouldn't have made it.'

'How do you see over the control panel? Hell, for that matter, how do those short legs of yours reach the rudder pedals?' Marty poked fun at her in a jesting manner. 'You must sit on a stack of pillows.'

'Only two.' She pointed to a pair of cushions, secured with a strap to her suitcase handle.

Noticing the initials *MLP* on the suitcase, Marty couldn't resist asking, 'What does MLP stand for – Mighty Little Pilot?'

'Mary Lynn Palmer,' she corrected, offering an apple-cheeked smile at Marty's razzing yet managing to convey a ladylike air.

'Hello, Mary Lynn.' With her handshake, Cappy managed to inject a modicum of manners. 'My father was stationed in Macon five years ago. He's career military, a major in the Army Air Corps.'

'In that case' – Chicago spoke up – 'let me officially welcome you to the Three hundred nineteenth Women's Army Air Forces Flying Training Detachment – more familiarly known as the Three hundred nineteenth WAAFFTD.' They were designated as Class 43-W-3, meaning they would be the third class of women to graduate during the year 1943.

'God, what a mouthful,' Marty commented, then informed the others,' If you want the lowdown on anything, just ask Cappy here. She knows just about everything.'

'How soon do you think they'll make us a branch of the military? They're talking of bringing the WAACs in – and the Navy women, too.' The girl from Chicago took Marty at her word.

It was on the tip of Cappy's tongue to say, 'When hell freezes over if my father is to be believed,' but she suppressed that urge and responded with military tact. 'So far, we're only an experiment. The two classes that started ahead of us three months ago in Houston haven't graduated yet. On paper, it looks good to train women pilots to ferry aircraft so men can be released for combat duty. Until we prove we are capable of doing that, the jury is out.'

'It gripes me the way men think we can't fly as well as they can, given the same training,' Chicago complained, but there was a hint of reservation in her voice, as if she might have some misgivings of her own.

'Don't you know it's because all females are scatter-brained, too flighty to fly?' Marty retorted.

'Well, I'm just glad an airplane doesn't know whether it's being flown by a man or a woman,' the third member of the trio said, a comely blonde who slouched in an attempt to diminish her nearly six-foot stature.

Just then, Marty's eye was caught by the sight of a tall, very fashionably dressed woman threading her way through the lounging clusters of females. Marty had always believed that she carried her height well, but this auburn-haired woman moved with an almost regal grace.

'Who is she?' Marty discreetly gestured toward the stately redhead with a small nod of her head.

'She's really something, isn't she?' the shy blonde replied with a trace of envy in her voice.

'She looks like she stepped out of the pages of a Paris fashion magazine,' Marty murmured.

A second later, the woman stopped beside two huge steamer trunks set next to the wall. A full-length leopard-skin coat was draped negligently across one of them. The woman used it as a cushion to sit on and crossed her long, silk-clad legs.

'Good God,' was Marty's stunned, blasphemous comment. When the woman slipped a cigarette into the end of a long silver holder, it was too much for Marty. 'I've got to meet her. She can't be for real.' She looked expectantly at the others. 'Are you coming with me?' she challenged them, but didn't wait for a reply.

Curiosity prompted all of them to trail after her, assuming a guise of nonchalance. A wide bracelet glittered with jeweled brilliance around the woman's wrist, and the blonde whispered to Chicago, 'Do you suppose those are real diamonds?'

No one, not even for a minute, believed anything about her was phony. When she noticed them strolling so casually her way, her glance slid away as if to snub them. Then she turned back, her chin lifting a fraction of an inch while a cool smile edged her red, red lips.

'Hello.' A very cultured and smooth voice greeted them.

'Hi, I'm Marty Rogers. We couldn't help noticing you sitting over here by yourself.' Her glance went to the big trunks in obvious question.

'I'm Eden van Valkenburg from New York.' She extended a slim, manicured hand in greeting. Her long nails were painted the same bright red shade as her lipstick.

For a second, Marty wondered if she was supposed to curtsy over the proffered hand. But when she shook it, the returning pressure was firm and definite. It gave Marty a second's pause.

'Let me introduce you around. This is Cappy Hayward. We arrived on the same train,' Marty explained. 'Her father's an Army man so if you have any questions, just ask her.' There were no more handshakes, just exchanges of polite and curious smiles. 'Mary Lynn Palmer is from

45

Mobile, Alabama. And – Chicago, I don't know your name.'

'Gertrude Baxter, but everybody calls me Trudy.' She ran a hand over her limp hair, a self-conscious gesture in reaction to the stylish and obviously very sophisticated woman before her.

'I'm Agnes Richardson – Aggie.' The awkwardly tall blonde bobbed her head in quick introduction, then couldn't keep from gushing, 'I just love your outfit.' She gazed enviously at the powder-blue wool dress with its padded shoulders and full, draping skirt.

'Thank you. Actually, I feel slightly overdressed.' The frank admission caught them all by surprise.

None of them thought she would say what they were all thinking, but the proud gleam in Eden's brown eyes should have warned them. She knew it was better to verbalize their thoughts for them than to let them talk behind her back.

'Do you?' Marty replied, always quick with a whiskey-voiced retort. 'It's the cigarette holder. It's a bit too much, don't you think?' It was a gibe meant to sting. Marty had never cared for people who thought they were somehow better than everyone else. The air crackled briefly with a sparking antagonism.

'Are both these trunks yours, Miss van Valkenburg?' Cappy quietly inserted the question between them.

She was slow to turn her attention away from Marty. 'Yes, they are.' She met the pleasantly interested look and found nothing threatening in the inquiry. 'I felt I should bring only what I absolutely needed.'

For a stunned second, no one could say anything. Even Marty waited for the redhead to smile at the little joke she had made, then realized the woman was dead serious. The discovery seemed to hit them all at the same time. Beside her, Chicago choked on a gasp of laughter that brought on a coughing spasm.

'You did bring an evening gown, didn't you?' Marty asked with a straight face.

46

'No.' Eden van Valkenburg appeared taken aback by the question as she warily searched the faces of the other women. 'Will I need one?'

'Oh, God,' Marty muttered, and she swung away, missing the flare of anger in the redhead's expression.

A hush was spreading across the long rec hall. When it reached their small group, they all turned to find the cause of it. An officer in an Army uniform had entered the building. Once he had the attention of the entire room, he introduced himself as the base commander, and told them what to expect over the next twenty-six weeks while they learned to fly 'the Army way.' It wasn't a heartening speech as he ominously warned that two out of three would 'wash out' – fail to graduate. It became very clear they were going to be subjected to military rules and disciplines, with demerits issued for any infringements.

As he briefly listed some, he came to '. . . profanity will not be tolerated . . .'.

'Oh, damn,' Marty murmured under her breath, and the blond-haired Aggie Richardson tittered with laughter.

CHAPTER TWO

By the time the five girls retrieved their luggage and joined the queue at the linens window, they were near the end of the line. In a definite break with what Cappy Hayward regarded as Army tradition, the women were being allowed to choose their roommates – or bay mates, since the barracks were divided into bays, each with six bunks. The five of them – Cappy, Marty Rogers, Mary Lynn Palmer, Trudy 'Chicago' Baxter, and Aggie Richardson – had decided to share a bay and take potluck on who would make up the sixth.

'I guess we have to get used to shuffling in these damned lines,' Marty muttered.

'That's the Army way,' Cappy replied.

Aggie inched closer. 'I wonder where that rich van Valkenburg girl is?' She looked down the line of females to see if she could find her.

'She's probably trying to find a bellboy to take her trunks,' Marty joked, then shook her head. 'Can you believe her? If it wasn't so damned funny it'd be pathetic.'

'You didn't give her much of a chance.' The accusation was made in the softly drawling Alabama accent of Mary Lynn Palmer.

From anyone else, Marty might have bridled at the reprimand, but from this dark-haired, dark-eyed woman, she didn't take offense. Despite their brief acquaintance, Marty was ready to swear there wasn't a mean or spiteful bone in Mary Lynn's body.

After thinking it over, she conceded, 'Maybe I was quick to judge her. But I wasn't really trying to make fun of her.'

'Oh, weren't you?' Chicago chided.

'Maybe I was, but the situation was so damned comical.' Marty defended her behavior while hinting that she sometimes went for the joke without considering the feelings of the person who was the butt of it.

'Maybe she plans to write a book on what to wear when you go to war,' Chicago suggested with a quick laugh.

As the line moved along, they each had their turn at the linens window and received their sheets, pillowcases, and blankets. Loaded down, they headed for the row of barracks.

'All the bays are alike,' Cappy Hayward informed them. 'Anybody have any preference for location?'

'It doesn't make any difference to me,' Marty said and the others nodded their agreement. 'Lead on, Cappy,' she declared, then shivered. 'And get us out of this damned wind.'

'You're going to have to start watching your language,' Cappy advised her. 'They start issuing demerits tomorrow.'

The barracks were new, hastily constructed frame buildings, covered with cheap clapboard siding, and roofed with asphalt shingles, painted a dingy Army gray. Red dust clung to every groove, evidence of the pervasiveness of the dry Texas soil. A narrow, roofed walkway fronted the long buildings, pairs of double-hung windows alternating with bay doors.

As they neared the end of a long walkway, Cappy opened the door to an empty bay and the others trooped in behind her. They stopped inside and stared at the austere quarters. The plasterboard walls had received a coat of white paint, but gouges, scuff marks, and telltale yellow water stains warning of a leaky roof took away any sense of newness, although every building on the field, except for one hangar, had been constructed within the last year.

Six narrow Army cots roughly three feet apart stood one end against the wall in a long line. A thin mattress covered with blue-and-white-striped ticking lay atop each metal-framed bed together with a lumpy-looking pillow in the same material. At the foot of each was a large-sized foot-locker, taking up more room on the bare wood floor. A wall switch by the door turned on the overhead light, housed in a dark green metal shade. The windows also sported green window shades, but no curtains.

'Be it ever so humble' – Marty walked to the cot nearest the end wall to dump her linen on it and set her suitcase on the floor – 'there's no place like home sweet home.'

Cappy made no response as she chose a cot of her own, taking the next-to-last on the other end. She laid her things on it in advance of settling in. The other three followed suit more slowly.

'These cots aren't even as wide as the studio couch in my apartment back home,' Chicago offered in a distant voice.

'You hadn't better roll over in your sleep at night or you'll wind up on the floor,' Aggie predicted. All of them could feel the grittiness of the floor beneath their shoes, that fine dust pulverized into the boards.

'Mighty little Mary Lynn is the lucky one,' Marty surmised. 'These cots are just her size.'

'I'm not that small,' she protested, claiming the second cot, next to Marty's.

But Marty was already investigating the footlocker that would serve as closet and bureau, and paid no attention to the reply. A raspy laugh came from her throat, a brief burst of humor. 'Can you imagine that van Valkenburg dame trying to fit her two trunks of clothes into this?'

Her question was met with faint smiles as each tried to adjust to her spartan environment. All five of them came from different parts of the country, different backgrounds. Yet, the fact that they were at Avenger Field meant it was likely they had all enjoyed a measure of affluence in their lives or they never would have been able to attain a pilot's license nor accumulate the number of hours necessary to meet the requirements. Flying was an expensive hobby. Few women had the desire to fly and even fewer had the opportunity.

Choosing to explore her new surroundings rather than unpack, Marty closed her locker and straightened to look around the room. A door was at the other end.

'Where does that lead?' she asked, already heading down the length of the room to find out.

'It's probably the bathroom,' Cappy guessed and followed to see if she was right.

Marty entered and came to an abrupt stop, startled by the sight of a strange female washing her hands at one of the two white porcelain sinks protruding from the wall, their pipes exposed below. 'Sorry, I –' she started to apologize.

'No problem. I'm finished.' The girl shook the excess water from her hands and reached for a towel to dry them.

Besides the two sinks, the small, communal lavatory contained two showers and two stalls, lighted again by a ceiling fixture with a green-painted metal disc. Marty noticed the second door and frowned. 'I thought this was our bathroom.'

'It looks as if we have to share it with the girls in the next bay,' Cappy said.

'That's what we were told.' The gangly brunette finished drying her hands and cast a wry glance at the limited facilities.

'You're kidding!' Marty protested. 'Twelve girls sharing *one* bathroom – and *one* mirror?'

'It's absurd, isn't it?' the other girl said in a commiserating tone as she walked through the door to the adjoining bay.

'Absurd isn't going to be the word for it when tomorrow morning comes and we're all trying to get in here at the same time.' Marty foresaw the room would become a battleground with each girl fighting for her turn. Cappy didn't disagree as they re-entered their bay. 'Better set your clocks early if you want a crack at the bathroom before the stampede starts in the morning,' she warned the others.

They were all busy unpacking or getting their beds made, but Marty didn't feel like tackling hers yet. She sat on her cot and spread her fingers across the blue-striped mattress to test its softness. Mary Lynn Palmer had taken the cot next to hers. Her suitcase lay open atop it while Mary Lynn transferred her clothes to the footlocker. Marty spied the framed photograph lying among some lingerie.

'Who's the picture of – your fella?' she asked.

'You could say that.' Mary Lynn lifted it out to show Marty the photograph. 'It's my husband.'

Belatedly, Marty noticed the gold wedding band on Mary Lynn's left hand. The gold-edged frame held a photo of an Army pilot, an officer's cap sitting jauntily on his head, thick dark hair waving close to his ears. He had on a fleece-lined leather flying jacket, unzipped at the throat, and dark, smiling eyes stared at Marty from a lean, handsome face.

'Is he ever damned good-looking.' Marty read the inscription scrawled across the bottom of the picture: 'To my darling wife, Mary Lynn, All my love always, Your adoring husband, Beau,' then passed the picture back to Mary Lynn. 'He flies, too,' she observed.

51

'Beau is a B-17 pilot – stationed in England.' She spoke in a very low and soft voice that managed to convey the strength of a deep emotion. 'He flies the big four-engine bombers they call the Big Friend.'

'Lucky guy. I'd love to crawl into the cockpit of one of those someday.' Marty rested her hands on the edge of the cot and casually leaned forward, noticing the caressing way Mary Lynn touched the photograph.

'Flying is how I met him.' She laughed softly and corrected herself. 'Well, that isn't exactly *how* I met him. A big air show was held at a field outside of Mobile and my daddy took me to see it. That's where I saw Beau for the first time and found out he was a flying instructor. I persuaded my daddy to let me take lessons so I could meet him. You have no idea how hard it was to fly an airplane when he was talking in my ear.' Her laughter invited Marty to join in. 'After we were married, Beau used to tease me that it was the flying bug that bit me – not cupid's arrows.'

'How long have you two been married?' Marty guessed they had to be newlyweds since Mary Lynn hadn't lost that dreamy-eyed look. Sooner or later she'd wake up, Marty knew. With the war on, it was likely to be later, though.

'Ten years.'

'Ten . . . Wait a minute. How old are you?' Stunned, Marty frowned in disbelief. 'Were you a child bride or something?'

'No. I was seventeen when Beau and I were married.' Mary Lynn smiled at Marty's reaction and set the free-standing frame upright on the footlocker. 'But I knew from the start he was the only man for me.'

'It must be nice to know you belong like that to somebody.' Long ago Marty had become resigned to her single state. She'd been born without the nesting instinct, lacking homemaking skills and the yen for a settled existence. She craved action and excitement too much. Once, during her early college years, she'd let a man try to tame her wild streak and show her a sample of domestic bliss. The only part that hadn't bored her was the bedroom. Within a week they were at each other's throats, he insisting that she settle down and stop carousing and Marty refusing to change her nature. After they split up, she had joked to her friends that she should have known it would never work. Even as a child, she had enjoyed playing doctor, but hated playing house.

So Marty had fun. Looking at Mary Lynn, Marty knew she could never be like her. Petite, dark-haired and softly feminine, she was the type men wanted, not Marty.

'I miss him.' Mary Lynn traced a finger across his picture. 'When Beau was sent overseas I couldn't stand being in the house without him, and I moved back home with my parents. That was a mistake, I'm afraid.'

'You don't get along with your parents either?'

'It isn't that exactly. I mean, my daddy is a sweetheart. He insisted on driving me to the train station in his car when I could have taken the bus and saved him precious gallons of gasoline. And he knew I had to pay my own fare here to Sweetwater, so he slipped me five dollars to be sure I had spending money on the train. He spoils me.'

'Must be nice.'

'It is.' Her dark, lively eyes sparkled with the admission, a smile highlighting her cherub-round cheeks.

'Then what was your problem living at home?' Marty asked curiously.

'My mother and I had trouble getting along. I guess I'd lived away for too long. I didn't always do things the way she wanted them done.' Her shoulders lifted in a vague shrug. 'And I was restless. I wanted to do something – to contribute in some small way to the war effort – to do my part. Outside of being a wife, the only skill I had was flying. I knew how badly they needed pilots . . . so I decided that if they'd take me, I'd go. Mother thinks I'm foolish.'

'Why?' Marty demanded.

'She felt I could contribute a lot more by going to work at one of the defense plants and get paid better for it too.' Sometimes Mary Lynn felt her mother hadn't wanted her to leave because she didn't want to lose the money Mary Lynn paid for her share of the household expenses. She knew what a struggle financially it was for her parents and she felt bad for having such mean thoughts about her mother. 'She couldn't understand that flying makes me feel close to Beau. When I'm up in a plane, I feel that I'm near him.'

'What does Beau think of all this?' Marty wanted to know.

'He's in favor of it,' Mary Lynn assured her. 'He knows how much the Army needs good pilots, and naturally he knows I am one since he taught me. He feels as I do –' Her drawling voice took on an earnest tone, catching Chicago's attention in the next cot. 'We all must do what we can to shorten the war and bring our men home sooner.'

'That's true,' Chicago inserted while Aggie, in the adjacent cot, listened in. 'The more women we can put in the air, the more men can be sent overseas and the more planes can be sent over Germany. What we're doing here is vital.'

'I know all this is important to the war effort.' Tall, gangly Aggie glanced at her fellow baymates somewhat hesitantly, unsure of her welcome in the conversation. 'But for me, it's the flying – the chance to do something I really love. Up there, with the sky and the clouds – the exhilaration – the sense of power – it's like nothing else.' She became caught up in the struggle to express her feelings. 'There's nothing to hold you back. You're free, totally free. It's a kind of delirious joy and awe all mixed up together. Flying is a physical, emotional, and spiritual experience.' When she paused, she noticed the silence and the way everyone was staring at her. Her chin dropped quickly in a self-conscious gesture. 'I guess I sound crazy.'

It was a moment before anyone spoke. 'No, you don't,' Mary Lynn said quietly. 'I think we all share those feelings you just described. But some of us have never heard another woman say them.'

'Oh, I don't know. I think Aggie did get a little carried

away,' Marty suggested wryly. 'She's made flying sound better than kissing.'

The atmosphere immediately lightened as smiles spread across their faces. 'You're right, Marty,' Chicago agreed. 'It's the next best thing, maybe, but not better.'

They laughed dutifully at Chicago's small joke, but underneath her soft laugh, Mary Lynn felt a twinge of guilt. No matter how much she justified her decision to enlist in the training program the underlying reason was the same as Aggie's – she loved to fly. How a blue sky beckoned to her, tugged at her soul and urged her to come away and experience the ecstasy of its heights. She knew the power of its call, that wild sense of freedom that was so exhilarating, and the feeling that Beau was with her – right beside her, flying through the same clouds. When she was up in that sky, nothing else existed – not the war, not her fears for Beau, her parents' problems – nothing. She could leave them behind when she flew, but they were always waiting for her when she came back down on the ground.

Next to the end of the row of bunks, Cappy Hayward stood up. 'Let's get unpacked and the beds made,' she said, prompting the others to return to their tasks, then she went back to the opened suitcase lying on her cot. The precisely folded clothes were arranged in an orderly fashion. She'd had ample experience at packing in her lifetime.

Cap. There was such irony in the nickname she'd been given. But, of course, the others didn't know of her abhorrence for the military, its cold impersonality and demand for unquestioning obedience. Never would she live the life her mother had. She had hated it, never having any sense of roots, any friends, or any control over her existence. Perhaps the latter was what had addicted her to flying. In an airplane, she possessed that control. And Aggie was right – there was no sensation like it.

The hard rap of a hand rattled the bay door in its frame. Aggie made a start toward it, then glanced at Cappy.

'There are some guys in uniform out there. I noticed them a minute ago through the window. Do you want to get the door, Cap?'

Cappy's hesitation lasted only a split second as the knock sounded again. 'Sure.' She replaced the folded blouse on the pile of clothes still in the suitcase and crossed the room to the door. She scanned the khaki uniform of the man standing outside, noting the chevrons on his sleeves. 'Yes, Sergeant?' Standing to one side of the door, out of sight of the others, was the tall redhead in the leopard coat. One steamer trunk was sitting on the walkway while a second soldier waited by it, his breath clouding in steamy vapors.

'Is there room in this bay for another occupant?' The sergeant's broad, flat features wore a thin-lipped expression that suggested his patience had been tested. The redhead didn't appear to be in a much better mood.

'We have an empty cot.' It was the last one in line, next to hers and closest to the bathroom, a dubious advantage since it was like sleeping next to an elevator. The barracks' thin partitions did little to mask the sound of clanging water pipes, flushing toilets, or chattering occupants. Just as Cappy started to move out of the doorway so they could enter, Marty Rogers shouldered her way in.

'What does he want, Cap?' A second after she asked the question, Marty noticed the auburn-haired female huddled deep in the warm fur of her coat.

'If you'll hold the door open, we'll carry this trunk inside.' The sergeant ignored her question as he signaled the waiting soldier to pick up his end of the trunk.

Eden van Valkenburg's hands, gloved in expensive black leather, bunched the collar of the leopard-skin coat tightly around her neck as she took one look at Marty Rogers and turned to the sergeant. 'I want to check another . . . bay.' It took her a second to recall the proper terminology.

'The accommodations are the same in every one, miss.' Exasperation threaded the sergeant's voice as he picked up an end of the trunk.

'I think it's the company, not the accommodations, that she wants to change,' Marty suggested wryly.

The sergeant wasn't interested in their clash of personalities. 'Please move out of the way, ladies.' There was a strained politeness in the order as he backed toward the doorway lugging his end of the trunk. Marty had no choice but to move out of his way or be bowled over.

With a grudging acceptance of her fate, Eden followed the trunk-toting men into the barracks. Her dark challenging gaze made a sweep of the other faces in the room, making it clear that she liked the idea of sharing the quarters with them no more than they did. Cappy could empathize with that feeling of alienation, of being an outsider, unwanted and unwelcomed. How many new school classrooms had she entered, looking at cold-faced strangers who stared back? Too many.

The two men deposited the large trunk on the floor next to the empty cot. As they turned to leave, Cappy noticed the van Valkenburg woman open her purse and riffle through the contents. When the sergeant walked past her, she stopped him and pressed something into his hand. 'Thank you,' she said, snapping her purse shut, missing the man's initial start of surprise at the folded bill he held.

'Keep your money, miss.' He pushed it back into her hand with a look of vague disgust. 'This isn't a suite at the Waldorf.'

He was shaking his head as he walked out the door. A flush darkened her cheeks with hot embarrassment. Cappy could well imagine that the wealthy socialite was so accustomed to tipping bell-boys and porters for carrying her luggage that she had passed the money to the sergeant out of habit. While the enlisted man might have accepted it, the sergeant appeared to have had a bellyful of high-toned females.

When the door shut behind the sergeant, a heavy silence overtook the room. The staccato click of Eden's heels seemed to punctuate it as she walked briskly to the trunk, peeling off her leather gloves, finger by finger.

'What happened to your other trunk?' Marty made a sauntering foray over to the vicinity of her Army cot.

'I made arrangements to have it shipped home.' She swept the hat off her titian hair and lifted the ends with a push of her fingers, not bothering to look at Marty. 'It seems there were a great many items that I regarded as necessities which weren't required here.'

'That must have been tough to do,' Marty suggested in a faint taunt.

Anger was seething just below that cool surface. That vague self-mockery was all a pose to conceal how painfully foolish she had been made to feel. Granted, she had made a rather large mistake but she had no intention of letting this tawny-haired, raspy-voiced female rub her nose in it.

'Actually, it wasn't difficult at all,' she retorted, smiling sweetly. 'One of the staff helped me go through my trunks and weed out the nonessentials.' The leopard-skin coat joined the hat, purse, and gloves already adorning the bare mattress.

'Some weeds,' Aggie murmured, staring at the coat that was again serving as a cushion for its owner as Eden sat down on the narrow Army bed. Cappy moved past Marty and returned to her cot, situated between Aggie's and Eden's.

'All this reminds me of a fairy tale,' Marty declared with a sweep of her hand in Eden van Valkenburg's direction. 'I have a feeling the princess is going to wake up in the morning and complain to us about sleeping on a pea.'

Eden opened the black leather purse and removed a gold cigarette case. Determinedly ignoring Marty, she took out a cigarette and tapped it on the metal to more firmly pack the tobacco. 'Does anybody have a light?' she inquired. Cappy tossed her a book of matches. Eden took one and raked its sulfur head across the sandpaper-rough strip. She carried the naked cigarette to her mouth while she held the match flame to it, the fancy holder abandoned. Making a face, Eden picked the loose bits of tobacco from her red lips.

Because of her gross misunderstanding of both the training situation and the type of accommodations available, Eden knew she was off to a bad start, both with the flying staff and her fellow trainees. But it only made her all the more determined to stick it out. Besides, roughing it for a while would be a lark. It wasn't as if she had to live under these spartan conditions forever. She took another puff of her cigarette, then crushed it out while she tried to pick the shreds of tobacco off the tip of her tongue.

As the flurry of interest her arrival had created faded, the others went back to their work. At the next cot, Cappy was drawing her sheets tightly across the mattress. Eden watched her a few minutes, then smiled to herself. She had never made a bed in her life . . . nor unpacked a trunk and put away her own clothes, for that matter.

'Hey, Cap.' Chicago frowned as she watched the brunette tightly tucking the ends in. 'Did your father teach you to make a bed like that? I bet you really could bounce a coin on it.'

'You can, I promise.'

'Would you show me how to do mine?' she asked.

Eden watched while Cappy instructed the others in the art of making beds the 'Army way,' then made an attempt at doing her own. The results were less than encouraging.

'Want some help?' Cappy asked, offering but not forcing her assistance on the redhead.

Eden straightened, faintly surprised by the friendly yet reserved gesture. 'Yes. Thank you, Miss Hayward.'

A wry smile quirked Cappy's mouth. 'Better make that Cappy, or plain Hayward. In the Army, manners and formality go by the wayside about as fast as privacy, so you'd better not wait for someone to pull out your chair or hold the door for you,' she advised as she showed Eden how to pull the bedsheets and blanket taut.

'I'll remember that,' Eden replied with a determined nod and worked to make the precise fold in the corner ends.

After some initial mistakes and ineptitude, Eden stepped back from the cot in satisfaction, the dark wool Army

59

blanket stretched tightly, the covers turned precisely back, and the pillow situated squarely in the middle. She reached for her purse, now sitting atop the trunk with her fur coat and hat.

'Let's see if a coin will bounce on it.' She took out a dime and dropped it onto the cot. It hit the blanket and bounced into the air, then landed again with a small hop. The sense of triumph was followed by the sobering thought, 'I suppose we'll be expected to make the beds every day.'

'Every morning and checked before every inspection. The Army loves inspections,' Cappy warned dryly. 'Their motto is "A place for everything and everything in its place." And the Army doesn't have any place for personal mementos – photos, little keepsakes, or the like. They'll expect this bay to be spotless, and they'll inspect with white gloves to find out if it is.'

'I don't suppose they have –' Eden paused in mid-sentence as she looked around the narrow confines of the long bay, then responded to her own unasked question. 'No, I guess the Army wouldn't have cleaning ladies that come in and tidy up. We are they, I suppose.' She smiled in irony and joked, 'And Mother complains about the shortage of servants since the war started. They keep quitting to go to work in the factories.'

Cappy's mouth curved in a warm line, liking that self-mocking humor and what it told her about the redhead's character despite her privileged and affluent life style. 'Everyone wants to do their bit for the war.'

'God, don't I know it. Mother was always volunteering me for some new war project of hers,' she declared. 'Whether it was rolling bandages for the Red Cross, collecting "bundles for Britain" or . . . once, I even helped her haul wheelbarrows of dirt up to our penthouse apartment so she could have a victory garden on the balcony.'

'No blood donations?' Cappy grinned.

'Oh yes. Me, and every one of my friends as well as a few distant acquaintances,' Eden assured her. 'Dear Ham

60

insisted he was becoming anemic from giving so much blood.'

'Ham?'

'Hamilton Steele.' Eden had an instant image of the unprepossessing man nearly twice her age with dark, thinning hair and gold wire glasses. The scion of an old established New York banking family, he had much to recommend him, no matter how staid and conservative he was. 'He's a dear man and a good friend. I probably would have married him if I hadn't met Jacqueline Cochran at the Christmas party my parents gave. At twenty-five, what else is left? I've done practically everything. Made my society debut, attended Vassar, and toured Europe. The only occupations someone of my social status is supposed to seek are marriage and motherhood – in that order. I was nearly bored and desperate enough to take the plunge.'

It was an empty life Eden described. Cappy could well understand her dissatisfaction with it. 'Is that how you found out about this flight training program for women – from Jacqueline Cochran?'

'Yes. As a matter of fact, her exploits are what prompted me to get my pilot's license. Flying is about the only thing that makes me feel alive.'

'I think all of us feel that way.'

For Eden, it was a feeling to which she clung. Her life had become much too riddled with cynicism, living as she did in a moneyed world. Everything, it seemed, had a purpose other than the one purported – even where the war was concerned. Like the 'Buy Bonds' drive, which was not really an attempt to fund the war. The intent of the Series E bonds, as her father was wont to assert, was to absorb the 'little man's dollars' and curb inflation. She saw the way the big businesses profited from defense contracts because they had the factories, the assembly plants, and the workers already in place to grind out the war machinery. The government had to make pragmatic decisions, and Eden could see that the rich got richer and the poor did a little better than before.

'Jacqueline Cochran painted an exciting picture of her program at the party,' Eden recalled while casting a disparaging glance at her stark quarters. 'But she did mislead me. She indicated I would be taking my training in Houston instead of some cowtown in the middle of nowhere. Our chauffeur is arriving with my car next week. Where will I go in it?'

'I don't know. But you can always look at it another way. Without the car, you'd be stuck here,' Cappy suggested, a small smile edging the corners of her mouth.

'You're absolutely right,' Eden agreed, laughing and liking the woman she'd be sleeping beside for the duration.

By late evening, nearly all talking had died. It was a travel-weary group that lounged on their cots. From the shower, Eden entered the bay wearing a rose satin robe with matching mules.

Cappy was the only one in the group not busily scribbling a letter. 'Not writing home?' Eden sank onto her cot and picked up a nail buff to shine her long, professionally manicured fingernails.

'No one to write to.' Cappy shrugged with apparent indifference. She had dropped her mother a short note, informing her that she had arrived safely, but she had no longtime friends.

'No one?' Eden frowned, vaguely curious. 'I thought you had a father in the Army.'

'I have a father but he doesn't have a daughter,' she replied, then paused to meet Eden's confused glance. 'He disowned me.'

'Good lord, why?'

'Because I came here.' Cappy hesitated, then with false indifference, continued. 'No daughter of his was going to fly for any quasi-military corps. Never mind that he taught me how to fly himself.'

'He'll get over it. Parents always do.'

'You don't know my father,' Cappy dryly countered. 'He couldn't have been more horrified if I had told him I was joining a traveling bordello.'

62

A smile briefly twisted Eden's mouth. 'That attitude isn't confined to your father. I've often heard mine say that intelligence is wasted on women. I suppose it harks back to that old belief that we can't be taken seriously – as pilots or anything else. Men might teach us how to fly as a cute novelty – rather like training a dog to sit up and beg – but they only want the trick performed when they say.'

'How true,' Cappy murmured with a very clear mental image of her father.

'And as for the military,' Eden continued, 'it's obviously a corrupting influence, because from what I hear in New York, a woman in uniform is somehow immoral.' Her dark eyes were agleam with mocking laughter. 'You put those two things together and this *is* about the equivalent of a traveling bordello in a lot of people's minds.'

Cappy laughed in her throat, losing some of her bitterness over the situation with her father. Still, the clash of personalities had been inevitable. Both of them were too strong-willed, and her father was too accustomed to imposing his authority. It was a long time since she had been the blindly obedient daughter, never questioning his orders.

From her cot, Marty paused in her letter-writing to watch the friendly interplay between Cappy and Eden down the row. They were talking in low tones so she hadn't heard what they were saying. What a group, Marty thought. Three cots down, Aggie was tying her hair in rag curlers, using a mirror propped on her cross-legged lap. This side of her, Chicago was lying on her back atop her cot, a knee bent and one leg bobbing in the air, matching the rhythm of her popping gum while she added pages to the voluminous letter she was writing home.

Eden van Valkenburg, Marty noticed, had slipped out of her satin robe and tossed it carelessly on top of the footlocker. As she turned back the covers on her cot, she kicked off her feathered mules. The matching rose satin nightgown could easily have passed for a low-cut evening gown. When Marty saw her slip on a ruffled sleeping mask in the same rose satin material, she couldn't help but shake her head.

'What a well-dressed trainee wears to bed,' she murmured under her breath, untroubled by her own plain blue pajamas.

In the next cot, Mary Lynn Palmer, petite and feminine in her baby-doll pajamas, looked up from the writing pad balanced on her knee. 'Did you say something, Marty?' She frowned.

'No.' The strong north wind sifted through the cracks around the windows and door, creating sudden drafts of cold air. 'God, this place is drafty,' Marty complained, suppressing a shiver.

'When summer comes, we'll probably be glad of that,' Mary Lynn predicted.

'Listen.' Marty cocked her head as the wind carried the sound of deep, singing voices. 'Do you hear that?'

'Yes.' Mary Lynn listened a minute. 'It must be those cadets in the next barracks.'

'I guess,' Marty agreed.

For long seconds, they listened to the indistinguishable melody until it trailed away on the wind. 'So far away from home,' Mary Lynn murmured in a subdued tone. Marty wasn't sure if she was referring to her husband overseas in England, the trainees next door, or themselves, but it didn't seem important.

'Yes,' she said simply and turned her attention back to the half-finished letter to her brother.

CHAPTER THREE

The sudden shrill blast of noise woke Eden from a deep sleep.

She sat bolt upright in bed and ripped off the satin

sleeping mask that covered her eyes. For an instant, the completely alien surroundings threw her; she didn't know where she was. Someone hit the light switch, and a pillow went sailing across the room at the culprit as Eden shielded her eyes against the sudden glare.

In the next cot, Cappy Hayward threw back the covers and swung her feet to the floor. 'Come on, you guys. Reveille. Rise and shine.'

When Eden tried to move, muscles stiffened by sleeping on the wretchedly uncomfortable cot ached in protest. Blinking at the still bright light, she forced her body to turn so she could sit on the side of the cot. Behind the green shades, the window panes were black.

'It's still dark outside.' The sleeping mask dangled from her hand. 'What time is it?' She flexed her shoulders and neck, arching them to ease the stiffness.

'Six fifteen,' someone answered, but Eden's mind wasn't functioning well enough to identify the voice.

Her groan was involuntary. Under her breath, she muttered, 'This is uncivilized.' Either no one heard her comment or else they all agreed with it.

'The bathroom!' It was Chicago who issued the panicked reminder of the facilities they shared with six other women. As she and the tall blonde charged the bathroom in their pajamas, Eden couldn't help thinking that the pieces of cloth tied in Aggie's hair resembled little white propellers all over her head.

'Better start getting dressed,' Cappy advised her, when Eden continued to sit on the edge of her cot, waiting for the grogginess to leave. 'We have to get the beds made and the bay cleaned up for inspection.'

'What time is that?' With a weary effort, Eden tilted her head back to blearily gaze at the brunette who seemed so knowledgeable about the routine.

'Breakfast formation is at six forty-five.'

She was slow to calculate the time. 'A half hour?!' Her eyes opened wide. 'But it takes me an hour just to put on makeup and do my hair!'

'It can't anymore,' Cappy replied with a look of sympathy.

With an effort, Eden stifled the impulse to declare it was barbaric to expect anyone to function at this hour of the morning, and pushed herself off the cot. No one else was complaining, so it seemed wisest to keep her own mouth shut.

In the mess hall proper, the women trainees filed by the steaming service troughs for their cafeteria-style breakfast, and proffered trays, sectioned by indentations to separate the food, to the kitchen help. As Aggie Richardson carried her trayful of food to one of the long tables, she paused to let the shorter Mary Lynn Palmer catch up with her. 'Real butter,' she marveled to her baymate. 'There's no rationing in the Army.'

'I know. I think I've forgotten what it tastes like.' Mary Lynn set her tray on the table and stepped over the bench to sit down.

The others in their group were only a few steps behind them. There was a lot of scraping and table-bumping before all of them were seated. Chicago looked around at the corps of female trainees occupying the mess hall.

'I thought we might see some of those cadets at breakfast this morning.' Disappointment edged the curiosity in her remark.

'Yeah. Where do you suppose they are?' Marty swept the mess hall with a frowning glance.

'You have about as much chance of seeing them as you do of catching a snipe,' Cap declared with indulgent mockery for their wishful thinking.

'Why?' Aggie wanted to know.

'Because the staff is going to arrange the schedules to keep us separated. You can bet if we're at one end of the field, they'll be at the other,' Cap predicted with a knowing light in her keen, blue eyes.

'I've never heard of anything so damned ridiculous.' The gravelly protest had escaped Marty's lips before she realized what she'd said. She cast a quick, guilty look around to see if she'd been caught swearing, but there was no one in authority within hearing. Marty continued with her thought. 'It doesn't make sense to make such an effort to keep us apart. Good heavens, their barracks are right across from ours.'

'But it's a no-man's-land in between,' Cap cautioned.

'Or maybe you should say "no woman's,"' Chicago suggested with a short laugh.

'Ha. Ha.' Marty forked a mouthful of scrambled eggs from her tray. Eden van Valkenburg was sitting across the table from her, nursing a cup of coffee and ignoring the lone piece of toast on her tray. 'Is that all you're eating?'

'I'm not hungry in the mornings.' She shrugged indifferently and fingered the unappetizing slice of toasted bread.

The tall, big-boned Aggie Richardson gazed at the sleekly fashionable redhead with undisguised envy. 'Gosh, you look fabulous this morning.'

Eden smiled in pleased surprise at the compliment. 'Thank you.'

'It's no wonder,' Marty inserted. 'You should have seen the mess she left in the sink when it finally was my turn to use it.'

'Sorry.' Her apology was slightly abrupt. Cleaning dirty sinks had always been the maid's job. She was expected to do more than make her own bed, she realized, and sobered at the thought of how much adjusting she had to do.

No dawdling over breakfast was allowed as the day began in earnest. At breakfast formation, the seventy-five women trainees were split into two groups, called flights. From their ranks, a flight lieutenant and section marchers were elected for each group. It was a flight lieutenant's duty to call her flight to breakfast formation in the mornings and command the section marchers who drilled them in columns, marching every place they went on the field.

Individuality was further smothered by the issuance of regulation flight gear. In addition to the leather battle jackets, the parachutes, flight caps, and goggles, they received standard Army knaki flight coveralls.

When they returned to the barracks later that day, Eden shook out the jumpsuit given to her and looked at the inside tag. 'These are men's coveralls,' she protested to the rest of her group.

Aggie had already unzipped the front of hers to try it on. As she stepped into it and pulled it up so she could put her arms through the sleeves, the others stared at the way it fit her six-foot frame. The shoulder seams extended two inches past the width of her shoulders and the material sagged around her legs and hips like a deflated balloon.

'It's too big,' Aggie said in surprise, while everyone else hastily tried on their own.

'Good grief, they look like those outlandish "zoot suits" the Mexicans are wearing in California,' Marty complained as she watched Eden struggle to tighten the belt on her flight suit so it would at least look as if she had a waist.

'Do you suppose they'll shrink?' Mary Lynn suggested hopefully.

'Maybe they will –' As Marty caught sight of the petite brunette, laughter exploded from her. The sleeves were so long they hid her hands, and the crotch hung down around her knees. Mary Lynn tried to take a step and tripped on the bottoms of the pants.

'They don't really expect us to wear these, do they?' Eden wondered for all of them.

Only Mary Lynn's appeal for a smaller suit was granted. The rest had to make do with what they were issued. The smaller-sized coveralls didn't improve the baggy fit of the style when Mary Lynn tried them on.

'Just call us the glamour girls,' Eden joked feebly while she fastened the straps of her parachute, which ran uncomfortably between her legs.

For the time being all they could do was grumble about the fit of the jumpsuits as they were again called to fall into formation. In ragged columns, they marched toward the flight line, slowly making the transition into a military unit.

A large, circular pool was located in the middle of the base. Its low sides were constructed of stone with a cement cap around the lip. In the center of the reflecting pool of water, a fountain rose out of a stone base. Word spread through the ranks identifying the pool as the Wishing Well. A scattering of coins shimmered in the bottom where the sunlight caught them. The male trainees here before them had tossed the coins for luck to ensure a satisfactory check ride.

But it was the planes parked along the flight line that generated the most excitement. The ready room, where they gathered to wait for the instructors to call them individually, had windows all along the front, facing the parked planes. A motley assortment of tables and chairs was scattered about the room for the use of the thirty-plus women trainees in the flight group, and a Coke machine stood in the corner to ease their dry-mouthed excitement. Marty's heart thumped against her ribs, betraying her eagerness. She'd never flown anything more powerful than her brother David's Piper Cub.

'Martha Jane Rogers!' A deep, male voice boomed her name, and she came to her feet, flinching at the dreaded use of her given name.

'Martha Jane?' Chicago laughed and slapped at Marty's leg when she passed by.

But it seemed unimportant as her legs stretched into long, eager strides to carry her across the ready room to the huskily stout man who had called her name. He was standing by the door with a clipboard in his hand, chewing on an unlit cigar. The earflaps on his cap were turned up, the straps dangling to create a comical sight, but the tough and unrelenting expression on his round, bulldog features didn't invite a smile.

'You Rogers?' He swept her with cold eyes.

'Yes, sir.' Marty pushed her chin out, refusing to be intimidated by his gruffness. 'Everyone calls me Marty.'

'I'm not everyone, Rogers,' he said flatly.

'No, sir.' She lowered her chin a fraction while her jaw

tightened and she struggled to contain the quick retort she wanted to make.

His attention appeared to shift to the clipboard. 'How come you sound so hoarse? Have you got a cold or something?'

'No, sir. I always sound like this,' Marty informed him.

He gave her a hard, short glance, then looked back at his clipboard. 'My name's Turner Sloane, and I'm going to be your instructor for this primary phase of your flight training. Any objections?'

'No, sir.' But she pulled in a deep breath to hold on to her patience and forced a pleasant smile on her mouth when he looked up.

'It wouldn't do you any good if you did.' He tucked the clipboard under his arm, then pushed his hands into his pockets.

'That's what I thought.' Marty's smile grew wider and lost its pleasantness as in silent disgust she watched him manipulating the fat cigar to the other side of his mouth. All the instructors were civilians, mostly pilots who were too old to qualify – like Turner Sloane – or who couldn't pass the stiff Army physical.

'That smart mouth is going to get you in trouble, Rogers.' He tilted his head back, his gaze narrowing, and Marty realized she was a good inch taller than he was.

'Yes, sir.' It was very difficult to keep her mouth shut. Even that response had a hint of sarcasm. Marty had a strong suspicion that he was deliberately needling her.

'Are you ready?' That cigar held between his teeth made every sentence come out in a kind of sneer.

'Yes, sir.' Her own militarily correct responses were beginning to grate on her nerves. But she wanted to fly, whether this man wanted to teach her or not.

He took the cigar out of his mouth to bark gruffly, 'Then get going.' As if this whole conversation had been her idea.

Swallowing the hot rush of temper, Marty used that fire of energy to push herself out the door ahead of him and into the coolness of a west Texas winter day. Outside, she

70

pulled up to wait for him, her gaze running impatiently to the rows of nose-high aircraft parked on the hangar's apron, nearly thirty that Marty could see. The area was astir with activity, planes taxiing while instructors and trainees made their walk-around, or ground inspection to visually check the plane's airworthiness.

With a wave of his hand, Turner Sloane singled out the trainer they'd be flying. Marty suppressed the urge to run ahead and shortened her stride to keep pace with her slow-walking instructor, but her gaze devoured the plane.

That spurt of antagonism she'd felt toward her argumentative instructor was forgotten as she listened intently while he described the features of the Fairchild PT-19, its takeoff and landing speeds, its stalling characteristics, its cruising speed, fuel consumption and range. Marty stared at the low-winged plane with its open cockpits, the forward one for the pilot and the rear cockpit for the passenger, or in this case the instructor. A high charge of nervous excitement had her stomach churning and her hands itching for the feel of the stick. She trailed a hand along the edge of a wing. The metal almost seemed alive.

'Are you going to stand here gawking at the plane all day or what?' Sloane challenged her belligerently.

Stung by his mockery of her awe for the plane, Marty made a sharp denial. 'No.'

'Well, what are you waiting for? Climb up there in the front seat.' He jerked a hand toward the open cockpit.

Closing her mouth, Marty climbed onto the low wing and walked forward to the front seat. Awkwardly, she maneuvered herself into it, hampered by the bulky flight suit and the parachute straps between her legs. By the time she had buckled herself in, Sloane was standing on the wing. After he had shown her the location of the instruments and gone over the operations with her, he made sure she had on a helmet and earphones so she could hear his instructions from the rear seat above the engine noise.

'But what if I want to talk to you?' There was no microphone for her use.

'I am the teacher and you are the student. I do the talking and you do the listening,' he stated and didn't crack a smile. Marty held her tongue and stared at the instrument panel. It was becoming clear that this was not going to be fun. But if Turner Sloane thought that was going to dampen her enthusiasm for flying, he was greatly mistaken.

Within seconds after Turner Sloane climbed into the back seat of the open cockpit, he was barking in her ear. When the 175-horsepower engine roared to life, so much more airplane than she'd ever flown before, the vibrations added to the excited trembling of her own nerves. All her senses were alive, her perceptions heightened.

As they taxied away from the apron under Sloane's pilotage, Marty felt the movement of the jointly controlled rudder pedals under her feet. The tail-wheel aircraft had a typically nose-high attitude which made it next to impossible to see anything in front. He S'ed the plane down the taxi strip, curving left and right in order to have a view of what was ahead of them.

The hammering voice in her ear constantly reminded Marty that she wasn't along for the ride. But she was all concentration as he aimed the plane down the center of the runway. The roll was begun, the engine thundering with full throttle and the wheels bouncing roughly over the ground as the plane gathered speed. Her throat tightened as she kept watching the airspeed indicator.

Then came that moment when the vibrations stopped and as the plane lifted off the ground the engine roared smoothly. All the anxieties and tensions seemed to fall away from her. Marty smiled with the utter calm and confidence that filled her.

The sensation of speed abated as the plane climbed effortlessly into the high, gray sky, staying well below the cloud ceiling. The altimeter needle rotated, marking off the altitude they gained in hundreds of feet. The small, dusty town of Sweetwater lay to the east. Marty spied the gypsum plant and a small refinery, highly visible landmarks in this west Texas terrain of mesquite and greasewood.

The stick pressed against her knee as the plane banked to the north. Below her, all the roads seemed to have been laid by a compass, running either north-south or east-west. It was a country meant for flying, with a lot of open sky.

After the plane had attained the desired altitude, Turner Sloane leveled it out. They had reached one of the practice areas. Two other PT-19s were already in the vicinity, doing maneuvers.

'All right, Rogers, you take the stick,' ordered the rough voice in her earphones. 'I want you to make a simple, slow turn to the right.'

There was a surge of adrenaline through her system as her hand gripped the stick between her legs. That exhilarating sense of power was nearly all-consuming when Marty gently banked the plane to the right and felt its instant response. When the turn was complete, she smoothly brought the wings back level with the horizon.

'What's the matter, Rogers?' came the caustic voice. 'Was that too hard for you? You lost thirty feet in altitude, and the ball never saw the center of the turn-and-bank indicator. Try it again, and this time use some rudder.'

So it went, with Turner Sloane finding fault with everything she did. Marty felt as green as a raw beginner. It was one of the most frustrating experiences in her life.

Less than an hour later she heard, 'That's enough for today, Rogers,' ordered in a voice that sounded riddled with exhausted patience. 'Take a heading back to the field.' For a split second, Marty froze. Her head swiveled in panic while she tried to get her bearings. 'What's the matter, Rogers? Are you lost?'

'When he said that to me' – Marty's hands were doubled into fists as she recounted the story to her baymates – 'I wanted to take those earphones and jam them right up his –'

'Careful, Marty,' Mary Lynn cautioned her.

'– butt,' she offered as a concession.

'Did you know where you were?' Aggie questioned.

'I knew the field was somewhere to the south, so I just turned the plane in that direction and crossed my fingers. Luckily, I saw the smoke from the refinery and managed to zero in on the field after that,' Marty explained with a rueful expression for the whole misadventure. 'I think I would have flown in any direction before admitting to Sloane that I wasn't sure where the field was. I don't know why I ended up with such a hard ass for an instructor.'

'My instructor made it quite clear that I shouldn't expect any special treatment just because I'm a woman.' Cap tapped the ash off her cigarette. 'They're probably going to go to the opposite extreme to make sure they aren't accused of it.'

'Do you think that's it?' Eden curled a leg beneath her as she sank onto her cot. 'I wondered if the problem was the fact that we aren't paying for our own training. If we were customers hiring them to train us, we'd be treated with more respect.'

'But it wouldn't make them like us any better,' Marty pointed out.

'I don't know.' Chicago frowned and shifted uncomfortably, appearing slightly self-conscious. 'I didn't have any trouble with Mr Lentz. He was real nice to me.'

'Yeah, I saw you two when you taxied back to the hangar.' Aggie poked the short-haired brunette in the ribs. 'He helped her down off the wing and everything,' she told the rest of the girls with a big wink.

'Look! Chicago is blushing.' Marty drew everyone's attention to the dots of color in her cheeks.

'Come on,' Chicago protested. 'He was just being polite.'

'You seemed to have an awful lot to talk about,' Aggie teased. 'You stood out there in the cold a good ten minutes.'

'He used to live in Chicago when he was a little boy – in the same suburb where I live. He was just asking me about some of the old places he remembered.'

'Is he married?' Marty asked.

'No –' Chicago stopped abruptly when she saw the glints of laughter in their expressions. She reddened even more. 'He just happened to mention it,' she insisted.

'Just happened to mention it,' Marty repeated with teasing mockery. 'What does this paragon of gentlemanly virtue look like? Tall, dark, and handsome, I'll bet.' When Chicago showed signs of reluctance, Marty urged, 'You tell us, Aggie.'

'Well, he's about five foot eight or nine. He's got a good build, not too skinny and not too stout,' Aggie began. 'With that cap on it was hard to tell, but I think his hair was brown. His eyes were brown, too . . . or were they blue? I can't remember. Which were they, Chicago?'

It was an obvious trap. Chicago glanced around the room, then a faint smile touched her lip corners. 'Blue,' she said and they all laughed. 'But for all the good it does, they might as well be purple. They made it pretty plain to us today that we aren't allowed to socialize with our instructors.'

'Rules are made to be broken, honey,' Eden inserted in a silken voice. 'The trick is, don't get caught.'

'Is that the voice of experience talking?' Marty challenged.

'Of course.' Eden tipped her head back, exposing the creamy arc of her throat, and blew a stream of cigarette smoke upwards.

'Getting into trouble is a lot easier than getting out of it . . . I suppose, unless you can buy your way out of it,' Marty retorted with acid sweetness.

'Don't be so testy, Marty,' Cap inserted grimly.

'How come you're always sticking up for her?' Marty demanded.

'I'm not,' she retorted impatiently, then noticed Mary Lynn pulling on her flight suit. She took advantage of the chance to change the subject. 'What are you doing?'

'I'm going to find out whether this thing will shrink.' She zipped the oversized garment all the way up to her chin, and looked at the others. 'Anyone for the showers?'

'Hey! That's a great idea!' Chicago seized on the suggestion and hauled out her own flight suit to put it on.

Before it was over, six pairs of coveralls were hanging on the clothesline in back of the barracks. Judging by the number of dripping wet khaki coveralls already hanging on other lines, the idea wasn't a unique one.

CHAPTER FOUR

Four days later bay doors were standing open, crowded with female trainees. More women were hanging out the double-hung windows, bottom sashes fully raised. Their low, laughing voices had a conspiratorial sound as they made jocund comments, looking across the Texas-red ground, sparsely covered with scrub grass between the long gray barracks.

A deeper rumble of voices came from the direction of the opposite barracks. The roofs were extended into wide overhangs that shielded the concrete walkways abutting the buildings to create a military version of galleried walks. A straggly male group of enlisted trainees shuffled toward their assigned bays, dressed in their flight suits with parachute packs slung over their shoulders. There was a dragging tiredness about them that didn't stop them from smiling and flirting across the distance with the bevy of women who were making their own assessment of the men.

'Say, girls!' A tall, lanky airman with a thatch of light brown hair all askew from his helmet and goggles called to them. The long white scarf tied around his neck gave him a somewhat dashing air. 'Why don't you come over?' The invitation was seconded by a chorus of his buddies.

'Yeah, birds of a feather should flock together,' another shouted.

Another one added his voice. 'Wanta flock?'

'Can't.' Marty's distinctive voice lifted in answer. 'We aren't allowed to socialize.'

'That's a rotten shame,' the first retorted.

'it sure as hell is,' she agreed. Beside her, Cap groaned under her breath.

Then, suddenly, a stern voice was saying, 'You just earned your first demerits, Rogers.' A quick pivot and Marty found herself confronted with a staff officer. With a stern clap of the hands, all the trainees were called to order. 'Okay, girls, fall in. Volleyball time.'

As they trudged into marching columns, stifling groans, Marty glanced across the way at the tall cadet who lingered in his bay doorway to watch. Her shoulders lifted in a barely perceptible shrug of resignation. His mouth curved upwards at the corners.

By the conclusion of the first full week, a grueling pattern had begun to take shape. The new trainees attended five hours of ground school daily, the primary phase consisting of courses in mathematics, physics, aerodynamics, engine operations, and navigation. They also spent four hours daily on the flight line. And their spare time was taken up with a regimen of calisthenics, volleyball, or baseball.

Exhaustion was dulling some of the shiny newness of the adventure, but their enthusiasm for flying was undampened. It was a quiet group that lounged about the bay preparing for an early night, their hangar-flying talk finished. The initial discomfort about undressing in front of each other was a thing of the past; Chicago pattered around the bay in her underclothes and bare feet, carrying the robe she had intended to put on and forgot. Mary Lynn was curled up on her cot, busy writing her nightly letter to her husband.

Sitting cross-legged on her cot, Cappy was sectioning off strands of her silky brown hair and wrapping them around her finger into tight curls, then securing them to her head with one of the war-precious bobby pins she held clamped between her lips. Eden gathered up her towels and cosmetics case with its jars of creams and lotions, and headed for the bathroom for her nightly beauty routine.

Marty observed her departure. 'She's so soft and squeaky clean, I don't know how she stands the rest of us.' Her arm was hooked around her upraised knee, pulling it to her chest while she puffed on a cigarette. Then her thoughts drifted to another pet peeve. 'I thought this was supposed to be a civilian organization, so what's all this Army discipline about?' she grumbled, indirectly grousing about what was rapidly becoming known as Marty's 'damned demerits.' 'We march here and we march there; it's regulation this and regulation that. Orders, all the time.'

'How else are they going to keep control without a punishment system?' Cap reasoned, removing the bobby pins from her mouth long enough to talk. 'We've got them outnumbered. They need something to hold over our heads to keep us in line.'

'I hate logic.' Marty, already in her pajamas, flopped backwards onto her pillow and blew smoke at the ceiling.

There was a rustling of sound outside the window, soft scurrying and whispering. Marty sat up on her elbows to stare at the door, her head cocked at a listening angle. The others, too, had heard it and strained to identify it. There was a very faint, light tap on their door, a single knuckle knocking. Marty was on her feet in an instant, pulling on her robe as she strode to the door, the half-smoked cigarette dangling from one side of her mouth. With her hand on the knob, she leaned close to the door jamb.

'Who is it?' she demanded in a low murmur.

'Turn out the light and let us in,' came the roughly whispered response.

'Lights out, everybody,' Marty warned before she plunged the bay into darkness. Aggie squealed in protest. 'Shh,' she hissed, then carefully opened the door a crack. Three figures sprang out of the darkness and slipped in quick succession through the narrow opening.

'Who is it? Who's there?' Chicago demanded and pulled

out her flashlight to shine it on the trio who had dropped down to hug the wall just inside the door.

The beam illuminated the dirt-darkened faces of three grinning cadets, centering on the lean-faced ringleader with his shock of sun-bleached brown hair. 'Don't get scared, girls. We thought with all this training we ought to practice a little nighttime reconnoitering in case we find ourselves bailing out over enemy territory.'

'Good thinking.' Amusement riddled Marty's voice.

'It's lucky that we found friendlies straight off, wasn't it?' His audacious smile broadened, creating parenthetical grooves in his lean cheeks. 'I'm Colin Fletcher. The guy on the right is Art Grimsby, and the other one's Morley Tyndall.'

Their initial surprise over, the girls crowded around the door next to which the men squatted. There was a confusion of hand-shaking as they introduced themselves, talking over each other in a jumble of voices.

'We raided the kitchen before coming here,' Colin said, and he produced a cloth-covered basket. 'Since you couldn't come over for drinks with us the other day, we thought we'd share this little snack with you.'

The cloth was turned back and a warm smell drifted upwards. Chicago breathed it in. 'Hamburgers,' she declared in a mock swoon.

The basket was ceremoniously passed around for each to help herself. 'Where did you get them?' Marty asked, taking the first bite.

'Mom fixed them for us,' the dark-haired, pale-skinned Art Grimsby replied. 'She's a sweet old lady. Calls us her "boys."'

'A regular dear heart,' Morley agreed. 'Even gave us some Cokes. I'm afraid we'll have to drink it out of the bottles, though. She wouldn't spring for any glasses.'

'Here you go.' Colin opened one of them and handed it to Marty. His hazel eyes seemed to single her out from the others. It piqued her interest as she made a closer study of his face in the dim pool of light cast by the flashlight. A

79

shock of wheat-brown hair fell across his high forehead, nearly hiding it. The straight bridge of his nose was long and narrow, matching the high ridges of his cheekbones. But she was more attracted by the devilish glint in his eyes than by his aristocratic features.

'Do you do this sort of thing often?' Marty wondered if other bays had entertained these cadets.

'We had no reason until you girls moved onto base,' he acknowledged. 'We couldn't believe our luck. How many cadets get to share an airfield's facilities with female trainees?'

'Right. We celebrated when we heard you were coming,' Art Grimsby asserted.

They lapsed into a discussion of planes, flying techniques, instructors, and ground school courses, with the cadets warning the girls of the difficulties in the advanced stages of training. When their eagerness to share knowledge and show experience had passed, the conversation took a personal turn, delving into lives and backgrounds.

'I'm from Pensacola,' Colin said in response to a question. 'My parents still live there . . . in a big old house on the Gull. That's where I learned to fly. But you know the Army. They sent me over to England, had me on a ground crew, then decided maybe they could use my flying talents and sent me back here for training.'

Mary Lynn spoke from the shadowed edge of the light pool. She leaned into view, her features subdued. 'My husband is assigned to a squadron stationed at an airfield somewhere in England. He's a bomber pilot. B-17s.'

'What's his name?' His thoughtful look narrowed on the petite southern woman, a hint of compassion showing in its depths. 'Maybe I know him.'

'Beau. Beau Palmer.' In a breathless rush, she gave him the squadron group.

He let it run through his mind, then slowly shook his head. 'Sorry. I don't think I met him.'

All week Mary Lynn had seemed subdued, spending most of her time gazing at the photo of Beau. Of the whole lot, Mary Lynn was unquestionably the most lonely. But, then, she was the only one who had a husband far away. No one else in the group had a steady boy friend, except Eden, if Hamilton Steele could be called that.

The connecting door to the bath opened, spilling light into the bay. The tall, shapely form of Eden van Valkenburg stood silhouetted in the opening, motionless at the blinding darkness of the room.

'What is this? Who turned out the lights?' she demanded.

'For godsake, keep your voice down.' Marty rasped the warning. 'Hurry up and shut the door.'

As soon as Eden shut out the light from the bathroom, Chicago directed the flashlight beam at her so she could see to cross the room and join the group. Her face was bare of any makeup and a turban was wrapped around her head, hiding her russet-red hair. Marty groused to herself over the way Eden could look so wretchedly perfect, so nakedly beautiful in her shimmering satin robe.

'Well, well. Why didn't someone tell me we had visitors?' Eden remarked, smiling vaguely as she sank gracefully onto the floor beside an Army cot, using it as a back rest. Introductions were made, then apologies rendered since all the hamburgers and Coca-Colas had been consumed. Stories were reiterated, including Colin's. 'You were in England?' Eden remarked.

Colin nodded. 'Yes.'

'I adore London.' When she took a pack of cigarettes from her cosmetic case, the three Army cadets scurried through their pockets in search of a match.

'Have you been there?' Art Grimsby scored the victory, struck the match and suddenly illuminated the semidarkness.

Eden bent her head to the flame, then straightened to blow aside the inhaled smoke. 'Dozens of times. Not recently, of course. I think the last time' – she paused to recall – 'was shortly after I almost eloped with Nicky, our chauffeur. I used to go to a great nightspot – some crazy pub on the waterfront along the Thames. It was called the Boar and Hound, or some such thing. Do you know it?' she asked Colin, a nostalgic gleam in her eye.

'The one with the stuffed boar's head behind the bar, a huge tusker?' At Eden's affirmative nod, he said, 'I believe it was called simply the Boar's Head.'

'What an incredible coincidence! You've actually been there, too!' she said with amazement. 'I used to close that place nightly –'

'*Was* called the Boar's Head?' Marty picked up on Colin's past tense usage and the solemnness of his expression. Eden paused to stare at him as the significance of Marty's comment penetrated.

'That whole section of the waterfront was bombed out by the Jerries,' he stated.

The bay fell into silence. Eden suppressed a shiver at the icy cold finger that ran down her spine. The war suddenly had a reality beyond the headlines and the newsreel footage, or even her mother's many war-related social activities. So many ecstatic memories had been wrapped up in that English pub. To learn it no longer existed, the entire block destroyed, never again to be visited, leaving only mental images which would eventually fade from the mind, was sobering. War killed – people, places, feelings.

Colin looked at his watch. 'It's getting late.' He glanced at his buddies. 'It's time we were getting back.'

'Yes, before they do a bed check and discover we're missing.' Morley tried to inject some levity into an atmosphere that had grown heavy.

Marty untangled her long legs and pushed to her feet. 'Let me check and make sure it's all clear.'

They doused the flashlight as Marty opened the door and stuck her head outside. The sky was ashine with stars, thousands glittering on a velvet blue backdrop. The night's silence had settled on the column of barracks. She looked up and down the long row of buildings that faced each other. The only visible signs of life were the yellow patches of light gleaming from the windows, isolated spots of brightness in the dark shadows of the covered walkways. Nothing stirred.

Marty motioned for their forbidden male guests to join her at the door. With silent stealth, they came to her side and took their own cautious look out the door. One by one they squeezed through the narrow opening and immediately ducked down to hug the shadows. Colin was the last to leave. His narrow features were a blur in the darkness, but Marty sensed he was looking at her when he paused half in and half out of the doorway.

'Be careful,' she urged in a hoarse whisper.

'We'll do that,' he murmured. 'With your permission, we'll pop over again some time.'

His buddies were hissing at him to hurry. 'Sure.' Marty gave him a little push out the door, then rejoined her quiet baymates still huddled on the floor. She eyed Eden curiously. 'Were you serious about eloping with your chauffeur?'

'Unfortunately, yes.' Her mouth curved with a faint smile. 'I was going through what my father called my "plebeian" phase.' Her self-mockery was so evident, it encouraged the others to smile along with her. 'Luckily I realized that I was only marrying him to make an anti-money statement. But the more I thought about it, the more unwilling I became to give up my charge account at Saks . . . so I changed my mind about running away with him.'

'What happened?' Aggie was all agog over this peek into Eden's past.

'Daddy found out and fired him.'

'How insensitive can you get?' Marty demanded in mild outrage. 'A man loses his bride and his job all in one blow.'

'Anyway' – Eden liked a shoulder in a dismissing shrug – 'after that sobering experience, Daddy sent me off to Europe.'

'Alone?' Chicago asked.

'Yes.'

'I'm surprised he trusted you,' Marty murmured dryly.

'We flew to London first –' Eden began.

83

'Wait a minute,' Marty halted her. 'You just said you went alone. Who is "we"?'

'My maid and my secretary, of course,' she replied very matter-of-factly, as if it should have been obvious. A second later, Eden realized how very snobbish that sounded. 'I always traveled with a small retinue . . . until I came here. I haven't been very successful at getting you girls to wait on me.' She laughed at her own joke.

'It isn't all that funny,' Marty asserted when the others laughed with her. 'Thanks to her, our bay hasn't passed inspection yet, or have you forgotten? She's always leaving things lying around somewhere, expecting one of us to pick up after her.'

'Old habits die hard.' Her light response made a joke out of Marty's criticism. 'As I was saying, we flew to London, where I met Rinaldo, my expatriated Italian count. Three days later he proposed. It was another abortive engagement, however, but great fun while it lasted.'

'You were engaged to a real count?' Again it was Aggie who asked, expressing a typically American awe at a title.

'Yes. In this case, the tables were turned though. You see, Rinaldo's properties and bank accounts had been confiscated by the Italian Fascist Government for some trumped-up reason. And he wanted to marry me so he could live in the style to which *he* had become accustomed.' Eden dropped the burning butt of her cigarette into a Coke bottle, hearing it sizzle when it encountered the scant liquid in the bottom.

'That was a bit cheeky of him, wasn't it?' Cappy suggested dryly.

'The last I heard he was consort to one of Britain's titled ladies, who shall remain nameless,' Eden jested.

During the next week, Eden's chauffeur arrived with her car, a canary-yellow roadster with a convertible top and white leather interior. Unfortunately they weren't permitted off the field yet, so they couldn't take it out for a ride. And the cadets made two more late-night visits to the bay, staying later each time. After the last, Mary Lynn stumbled to her cot, weak with fatigue.

'The next time, tell your midnight Lotharios to come earlier,' she complained to Marty. 'Some of us would like to get some sleep.'

When reveille sounded the next morning, Mary Lynn pulled a pillow over her ears. It seemed as though only a few minutes had gone by before Cap cracked one eye open to look at the clock. She yelped the alarm as she sprang out of bed. But it was too late. All of them were late for formation.

As far as Cappy was concerned, the day went downhill after that. She wasn't prepared for the physics exam, which she was certain she failed. And there were no letters for her at mail call. Her mother had written once but that was all. It was a lonely feeling not to be remembered while others were exclaiming over their letters from home. But she didn't let it show, and if anyone guessed, it was Eden. The two of them stood off to one side and smoked, listening while others read aloud snatches from their letters.

Things seemed just as bleak when she took to the air. She was either using too much rudder in her chandelle maneuvers or not enough. She was not quick enough applying throttle in her stall recoveries. All she heard from Rex Sievers, her instructor, was criticism; never once did he raise his voice to her, but his grim tone of disapproval couldn't have been more crushing. When he cut the session short and ordered her to make a full stop landing, Cappy knew her incompetence had finally exasperated him. Utterly dejected, she taxied to the hangar area.

With the switch off, the spinning propeller blade slowed its revolutions to a stop. Cappy made slow work of going over the checklist to shut down the plane, dreading the moment when she had to literally face her instructor.

When he walked up the wing to the forward cockpit she occupied, Cappy didn't give him a chance to tell her what an abominable job she'd done. 'I don't know what's the matter with me,' she said in self-disgust. 'I can fly better than that.'

'I know you can, Hayward,' he agreed. 'And you're going to have to do it, starting now.'

'I know,' she murmured, her head still hanging low.

'From this moment, Hayward,' he re-emphasized his last phrase.

She lifted her head to stare at him, hardly daring to believe the implication. 'Solo?' The smiling glitter in his eyes confirmed her guess. All the poise that usually protected her disintegrated to expose her insecurities.

'You can do it, Hayward.' He winked and slapped the edge of the cockpit. 'She's all yours.'

A wide smile broke across her face as she unconsciously snapped him a salute. 'Yes, sir!'

Minutes later, she was skimming through the skies in the sleek, low-wing trainer. The blood in her veins pounded with the roar of the engine as the singing wind rushed by the open cockpit. All alone with the clouds, Cappy was filled to bursting.

It was like a dream. Right rudder down, stick back and eased to the right, the PT-19 soared into a steep climbing turn. At the top of it, when the wings grew heavy with a near-stall, Cappy gently straightened out of the turn and let the nose come down, and again, she and the plane were sliding effortlessly through the air. Chandelles. Lazy eights. Soaring and swooping in graceful turns like a leaf curling in the wind. Up here in the open-cockpit trainer, she was alone, completely alone with the wind and the sun on her face while she touched the sky. The solitude felt good and full, not lonely. An intimacy existed between her and the plane, the sleek trainer responding to her slightest touch. There was an ecstasy in it that could not be explained, only experienced.

When the runways of Avenger Field came in sight, Cappy contained a sigh and entered the traffic pattern. Her hands grew sweaty on the stick, and she wiped first one, then the other, on the baggy pants of her zoot suit. As she turned on her base leg, perpendicular to the runway, a family of tumbleweeds rolled onto the strip. She extended her turn onto final rather than risk fouling her landing gear or prop with the errant tumbleweeds.

The windsock sat at an angle to the runway, indicating a crosswind. The runways at Avenger Field did not seem to be laid out with the prevailing winds in mind. Takeoffs and landings were rarely made squarely into the wind. It seemed to always come at an angle, as now. On her final approach, Cappy crabbed the plane into the wind to hold a straight line to the runway. She kept her eyes alert for the appearance of a dust devil, those tiny cyclones capable of tipping a wing. The wheels of her landing gear touched down and rolled smoothly onto the ground while her tail slowly settled until its wheel met the ground in a textbook-perfect landing.

Back at the hangar area, Rex was waiting for her. His freckled face was split with a smile that went ear to ear. Hardly able to contain her own excitement, Cappy scrambled out of the plane and hopped off the wing, taking off goggles and helmet to shake her dark hair out to the wind. With swift, running strides, she hurried to her instructor, beaming with that inner thrill of accomplishment.

'I did it.' She stopped in front of him, her body straining with the urge for physical contact.

'You sure did. Congratulations, Hayward.' He took her hand and squeezed it between both of his, then held on to it. 'You are one of the best damned natural pilots I've ever seen. You try too hard once in a while, but you're going to be one of the best.'

Tears stung her eyes. For a minute, she couldn't see. She turned her head aside, lowering it while she blinked to clear away the blur.

It hurt that she had no one with whom she could share that compliment or the elated pride she felt. It would mean nothing to her mother, and her father wouldn't care. Yet, if she'd been a boy, right now he would have been bursting with pride. It wasn't fair.

'Thank you.' But her voice rang hollow. With her head

lifted once again, Cappy pushed her chin out and managed a distant smile. Puzzlement flickered across Rex's expression. But doors always closed when anyone saw too much or came too close to Cappy.

Mary Lynn soloed that same afternoon. When the rest of the trainees learned of their milestone, the two girls were dragged from their bay and hauled to the Wishing Well for a baptismal dunking.

Cappy was the first to be thrown into the three-foot-deep water, dumped head first, zoot suit and all. 'Grab some money!' one of the girls shouted as Cappy was going under. According to custom, the coins thrown into the pool for luck could be retrieved by those who had earned the privilege of being dunked. She surfaced, gasping with the shock of the cold water. When she opened her hand, a copper penny lay in her wet palm. Shivering, she scrambled out, aided by Eden's helping hand, which had also pushed her in. Then it was Mary Lynn's turn. In her letter to Beau that night, she wrote:

. . . They wanted to throw my two pillows in the pool with me, but Marty rescued them before they got wet. I managed to scoop up a dime and a British pee or pence, I guess they call it. One of the cadets from the UK must have thrown it into the well before a check ride. It immediately made me feel I was sharing the moment with you, darling. I'm going to keep the coin for luck – luck for me and for you.

Tomorrow we're finally going to be allowed to go into town. They've had us confined to the Field. I have some shopping I want to do, and I hope I can find some little souvenirs of Texas that I can send home.

I miss you, Beau.

All my love,
Mary Lynn

CHAPTER FIVE

Downtown Sweetwater, Texas, was only a few streets wide. The women trainees from Avenger Field flooded the business district of the small cattle community, splintering into groups composed of baymates.

'Lord God above, please let there be a hairdresser in this town,' Eden murmured as the six of them piled out of her bright yellow car and headed down the street.

'To hell with a hairdresser,' Marty retorted. 'If you're going to ask for something, make it worthwhile.'

'Like what? A drink?' Chicago suggested with a laugh.

'This may be a dry county, but you can bet there's some bootleg to be had if you know who to ask,' Marty declared. 'Colin's hinted as much to me.'

'I want to go in here.' Mary Lynn headed for the entrance to a small shop, and the others trooped along with her. 'You don't have to come with me, if you don't want to.'

'Maybe the clerk will be able to tell me where I can find someone to fix my hair,' Eden said.

All six of them invaded the shop, splitting to go down the aisles and investigate the merchandise. On the street outside, a big truck lumbered to a stop at the corner, pulling close to the curb. The trailer of the semi was fitted with long board seats to haul its human cargo and its slatted sides for ventilation earned it the nickname 'cattle truck.' As it disgorged its occupants, Marty recognized the tall sandy-haired cadet.

'Colin's in town.' She nodded to direct Cappy's attention to the handful of cadets coming their way.

Colin was in the middle of the boisterous, laughing group as it drew level with the gift shop. His hands were hitched in the side pockets of his trousers. Marty rapped on the glass window that separated them, attracting his attention, and waved. Given to impulsive behavior, she never thought twice about the possibility that a friendly gesture might be considered too forward. This nonsense about waiting for the man to make the first move had never made sense to her.

When Colin saw her, a crooked smile immediately broke across his features. He came up short, back-pedaling a step or two while the group flowed around him. Voices were raised in razzing comments that Marty couldn't quite hear when Colin separated from the group and approached the shop entrance.

The bell above the shop door tinkled when he entered. Marty turned expectantly to meet him, but before he could take a step in her direction, he was intercepted by the brown-haired salesgirl.

'Colin Fletcher, I was hopin' you'd stop in.' Her voice fairly gushed with delight, its nasal twang thickening with the dripping sweetness.

Quickly recovering from his initial start of blankness, Colin flashed her one of his winning smiles. 'Hello, Sally,' he said warmly, but his glance flitted by her to Marty, his eyes betraying a dry patience at the interruption. Marty's eyebrows arched in amusement over his situation.

'Momma would like you to come over tonight for supper.' All that eagerness in the invitation was positively cloying, as far as Marty was concerned. It was all she could do to conceal her reaction, steadfastly looking away so she wouldn't break into chortling laughter. 'We're havin' some friends over for homemade ice cream. I . . . Momma . . . knows how much you like it so she said for me to be sure and ask you over if I saw you today.'

'That's most thoughtful of your mother,' Colin acknowledged, and Marty glanced sideways so she could see how he was going to handle it. That dry, dashing charm was in evidence as he smiled at the girl. 'Unfortunately, some of us have already made other plans for the evening.'

'Oh.' Disappointment seemed to sag through her. 'You

90

will come to Sunday dinner tomorrow after church, as usual, won't you?'

'Naturally, I will.' He inclined his head in an affirmative nod, warmly polite but sufficiently aloof to discourage too much familiarity. 'I couldn't let a weekend pass without enjoying your mother's cooking, now could I?'

'No.' But it was plain, his explanation was not the one she wanted to hear. After a short hesitation, she added, 'If you change your mind about tonight, you're welcome to come anyway.'

'Thank you.'

There was an awkward moment while the sales clerk waited for Colin to say something more to continue the conversation, but he remained silent, regarding her with obvious forbearance. Mary Lynn stepped over to the cash register, giving the girl an excuse to move away. Colin looked after her for a moment with an expression of amused indulgence before he leisurely strolled over to Marty.

At the counter Mary Lynn was asking, 'Do you have a box or something I can pack these in for mailing?'

There was an attractive glitter in his hazel eyes when Colin stopped in front of Marty. 'We finally meet in broad daylight,' he remarked softly. 'With no dark corners the flashlight can't reach.'

'No slinking through the shadows.' Marty went along with his thought, but she was conscious of the hotly jealous look she was receiving from the sales clerk. Obviously Sally regarded Colin as her property, and Marty was poaching.

'The sunlight becomes you.' His mouth slanted with a crooked smile.

'Enough flattery, Colin, or I'll start to believe you.'

'Since this is your first trip to town . . . ladies' – he expanded his comment to include her other baymates within earshot – 'you should have an escort to show you the sights.'

'Sorry.' Eden was the first to turn down his invitation. 'I have the name of a woman who fixes hair. If I'm lucky, she'll

91

be able to do something with these nails of mine, too.'

Mary Lynn begged off with the excuse she had more shopping to do. Aggie and Chicago had some errands to finish, which left only Marty and Cappy to accept the invitation. Eden submitted to arm-twisting and promised to catch up with them later at the Bluebonnet Hotel.

'Where is it?' she asked.

'You can't miss it,' Colin replied. 'It's the only hotel in town.'

With Cappy on one arm and Marty on the other, Colin went swinging out of the shop as the little doorbell tinkled merrily. Their tour of the town, what there was of it, was periodically delayed by groups of cadets or other female trainees they met along the way. The size of their party fluctuated as others joined them for a block or two, then parted for some other destination.

The downtown businesses were grouped around the courthouse square – Sweetwater was the seat of Nolan County. Once they had strolled the square's perimeters and wandered its peripheral feeder streets, they stopped at the USO Club, but Marty and Cappy were refused entrance. All three of them left and ventured into more residential areas. After Colin had pointed out six of Sweetwater's ten churches, Marty suggested they save the remaining four for another time. He took them to the city park located at the north edge of town on Lake Sweetwater. He assured them they would hallucinate about this man-made body of water when the mercury soared to one hundred degrees in April and stayed there until September. Where the scrub growth encroached on the park, he regaled them with tales of dark-of-night assignations with the local bootlegger, a seedy old granny, as his story went.

The sun was resting on the lip of the horizon, igniting the sky with its copper-pink glow, when they arrived at the Bluebonnet Hotel. One of the cadets had rented a suite at the Bluebonnet where they could all congregate. The suite, as it turned out, consisted of two adjoining rooms with a connecting door.

Word spread of a party in progress. Soon there was a constant flux of trainees and cadets flowing in and out of the rooms and spilling into the outer hall. Cigarette smoke thickened the air while Coca-Cola bottles clanked. A cadet from Colin's barracks arrived with a bottle of clear liquid tucked inside his jacket. He produced it with a little flourish amidst the cheers of those who recognized the illicit liquor for what it was. While the bottle made a cola-spiking circle of the room, the cadet told them the spooky story of his eerie meeting in the mesquite brush with the lady bootlegger.

As many as eight or nine crowded onto the hotel beds at one time, virtually the only sitting area in the rooms. More camped on the floor, sitting cross-legged or with knees pulled up to their chests, while others leaned against walls. There was no clear pathway, so any movement meant stepping over bodies. Competition for the softer seats on the bed was keen. To leave the bed was to lose your place and free-for-alls erupted intermittently as others vied to claim space.

The roisterous clamor of loud, laughing voices filled the smoke-heavy hotel rooms. Marty was one of the lucky ones to have a seat on the bed, curled at the top with the headboard at her back. The pillow was long gone, in use somewhere as a cushion against the hard floor. Colin had a narrow edge of the bed near her, his long legs drawn up under him.

Marty poked a finger into her cigarette pack but it was empty. 'Damn.' She crumpled the pack with a mixture of irritation and disgust. 'I never smoked so much until I came here,' she said to Colin. 'My mother would have a hissy-fit if she saw the way I puff on them. She's very midwestern. According to her, nice girls don't smoke. 'Course, according to her, nice girls don't do a lot of things.'

'Parents are like that. They'd like us to believe they never did anything improper.' He dug into his breast pocket and took out a stubby, thin, hand-rolled cigarette, the paper ends twisted. 'Want to share one of these?'

'Sure.' Marty watched him place the crude cigarette between his lips, her glance lingering on his strong mouth. They were close, their bodies brushing, his back and shoulder pressing against her thigh as her arm hooked her legs and pulled her knees up under her chin. Neither attempted to carve out more space on the bed, preferring the physical contact.

With typical self-honesty, Marty recognized the wayward direction her thoughts were taking, which had nothing to do with the potent spirits that laced her Coca-Cola. Passion was a natural stirring of her body in response to the closeness of an attractive male. Her physician father had been frank in his early talks with her about sexuality so she had always regarded her own urges as normal. If she liked and respected a guy, she did not believe in holding back. As long as a consenting couple took the necessary precautions to prevent pregnancy, she saw no reason why they shouldn't make love and satisfy those natural urges. So after enjoying Colin's company for the better part of the day, it seemed logical for her to wonder whether she'd enjoy the embrace of his arms.

After the match flame had ignited the paper-wrapped tobacco, Colin pulled the smoke deep into his lungs and held it while he passed the cigarette to Marty. A smile twitched her mouth as she inhaled it. She was reminded of an old Bette Davis movie she'd seen once. This seemed a variation on the corny romanticism of that scene.

As the smoke's cloyingly sweet smell infiltrated her nostrils, Marty drew her head back to frown skeptically at the homemade cigarette. 'What is this?'

'Hemp weed.' His hazel eyes studied her with a certain bemusement. 'One of the cowboys from a ranch outside of town put me on to it. It makes you feel all loose and relaxed. It's a great tension-easer on those nights before a check ride.'

94

'Really?' Beyond the acridly sweet taste, Marty felt no soothing effect.

'The trick is to hold it in your lungs and slowly exhale it.' Colin took the cigarette from her fingers and demonstrated the procedure.

Marty tried it again, wrinkling her nose at the taste. She made the mistake of trying to swallow the smoke, and a spasm of racking coughs convulsed her as she waved a hand in front of her face to clear the smoke from the air she breathed. Laughing at her attempts, Colin persisted. Finally, squeezing the last drag out of the cigarette Marty managed it and nearly burned her fingers in the process as the fire neared the end of the butt.

With an air of expectancy, Marty sat quietly and mentally checked out her system. Beyond a deliciously liquid sensation, she didn't feel a thing.

'What did you say that was made from? Hemp weed?' she questioned Colin.

'Yes. It's a plant that grows wild around here.' He gazed steadily into her unusual gray-green eyes.

Soon the party began breaking up. They left in groups of threes and fours, segregated by sexes, some assisting their slightly inebriated friends. Cappy paused beside the bed where Marty and Colin were sharing another hand-rolled cigarette.

'We're leaving now, Marty. Are you coming with us?' She attempted to prod her baymate into action.

'I'll be along.' Marty impatiently waved her away.

Cappy turned to the others and shrugged. Together, Cappy, Eden, and Mary Lynn made their way to the hall door. The crowd in the connecting rooms had thinned to only a handful of people. Colin swung around to sit next to Marty, using the headboard for a backrest. He passed her the cigarette and she took a long drag, not paying any attention to her departing friends.

'This isn't very sanitary.' She gave him the cigarette that had just been between her lips and watched Colin carry it to his mouth.

'Neither is kissing,' he pointed out.

She chuckled. 'Now I know what this has all been about. You're trying to fuddle my thinking so you can take advantage of me.'

'You've found me out.' He acknowledged his guilt with a properly remorseful expression, but a wicked twinkle gleamed in his eyes. 'What a damned shame – and just when things were looking so good, too.'

Marty turned her head to study him. 'Did you really believe you'd have to resort to such tactics with me, Colin?'

'You're so damned forthright, I don't know for sure how to handle you,' Colin remarked with a rueful smile.

'I'm no simpering Sally, that's for sure.' After the oblique reference to the girl in the gift shop, Marty dropped the smoldering butt into her spiked drink.

'I guess that's it.' He tilted his head back and stared absently at the ceiling. 'I'm not interested in becoming some woman's husband, which is what the Sallys of this town are seeking. A few of the guys in my class want wives they can impregnate to ensure their immortality before they go off into enemy skies.'

'But you don't want marriage and all the things that go with it.' Marty studied his profile in a sideways glance, her head, like his, resting against the headboard. A long, patrician nose and slightly receding chin were his prominent features beneath that thatch of sand-brown hair.

'With you, Marty, I don't feel I have to pretend that I do,' he said, turning his head slightly to bring her into his vision.

'When I was in college, the girls who *did it* always seemed to convince themselves they were wildly in love with the guy. It was as if they needed the justification to avoid any feelings of guilt or immorality.' She sighed as her fingers made a slow trail up and down the slick sides of the squat pop bottle. 'As far as I was concerned, it was enough if I liked the guy and we respected each other.'

Marty had never bewailed her lost virginity, nor wept over the man who had taken it. To her, it seemed neither wrong nor unusual. After all, her brother certainly didn't practice celibacy. Whenever David could make it with a girl, he did. Her sexual urges weren't that much different than his, and if he could do it, so could she, albeit more selectively. She felt sorry for David with his indiscriminate ways, having discovered for herself how much more pleasurable it was to make love to a person than a body.

With a turn of her head, she looked into his eyes. 'I respect the hell out of you, Colin.'

Uncertainty kept him motionless while he tried to decide whether her choice of words had been deliberate. She took pity on his wary confusion and, with a laugh, she leaned over to kiss him. His fingers glided into her hair to cup her head and keep the pressure of her lips on his mouth.

'It's almost curfew,' he told her in a half-muttered complaint. 'We don't have much time to get back to the field.'

'Mmmm.' It was a conceding sound, made while she nuzzled his smoothly shaven cheek. 'It would be awful if we were late.'

Colin knew he was being mocked. When she slipped off the bed, he stayed, uncertain what her next move would be. Everyone had cleared out of the hotel suite with the exception of two cadets who were arguing vociferously the merits of the Spitfire over the Thunderbolt in a sky duel with a Focke-Wulf or Messerschmitt. With the long-legged stride of an athlete, Marty crossed to the connecting door and closed it. She also shut and locked the hallway door before she turned to face him, the suggestion of a lazy smile barely touching the corners of her mouth. Colin had the impression of a stalking lioness, all sleek and purring with power.

'On the other hand, it would be a shame to let this bed go to waste,' she suggested huskily.

His mouth quirked. 'A damned shame.'

When she came to him in the darkness seconds later, her nude, long-limbed form gliding against him, Colin recognized she was a rare woman. Bold and assertive, Marty was sure of what she wanted. While their bodies

97

strained together in passion, it escaped Colin that it required a rare man not to be intimidated by her aggressive instincts.

In the bay, Mary Lynn sat on her cot, a pillow propped behind her and a writing pad angled on her legs. She had written no more than two sentences in her nightly letter to Beau. The words simply wouldn't come. She read his last letter over again, hearing the intonation of his voice, that familiar speech pattern coming through the written words. The lonely ache inside her grew stronger.

Tonight had been the first social evening she'd spent in the company of other men since Beau had left. She had laughed and talked and been flattered by their attentiveness, always feeling safe with the gold wedding band around her finger.

When she tried to tell Beau about it in the letter, her pen hovered over the paper, making no marks. It had all been so innocent yet there was a sense that she had betrayed him by having a good time with other men. She had enjoyed herself, but now that the night was ending, she felt emptier and more alone.

She heard a scuffle outside the bay door. It opened quickly as Marty darted inside, laughing and breathless from running. The lively glitter in her silver-green eyes seemed to match the vibrancy she exuded.

'You lucky devil.' Cappy shook her head in mild disbelief. 'You just made it by the skin of your teeth.'

'I know.' Marty crossed the room and flopped onto her cot, winded yet subtly exuberant. 'Some tobacco-chewing cowboy gave us a ride in the back of his pickup. We had to keep ducking every time he spit out the window. It was the wildest ride I've ever had.'

No one asked who her companion was, all silently guessing it was Colin. As Mary Lynn studied the silkily contented look on Marty's face, loneliness and frustration welled in her chest. She knew that look, recognizing it from the times she'd seen her own reflection in the mirror after Beau had made love to her. Desire was a feeling she had suppressed, successfully, until this moment. She ached for Beau's touch, for the play of his hands on her body and the warmth of his mouth on her skin.

She flipped the tablet closed and attempted to push aside the urges clamoring within. With unreasoning logic, she blamed them on the evening she'd spent surrounded by other men, as if such needs had not been simmering below the surface for some time. Beau was her first and only lover.

'Hey, how come you aren't finishing your letter to Beau tonight?' Marty noticed the break in Mary Lynn's nightly ritual.

A dark flush stained Mary Lynn's cheeks while a tautness claimed her expression. 'I'm tired,' she asserted stiffly, and put away the tablet in preparation for bed.

Marty reclined on her cot, stretching languidly, like a satisfied cat. 'So am I'

Mary Lynn made no response as she slid under her bed covers away from Marty and rolled onto her side.

The next morning, many a cadet and trainee sat in church pews around the town and winced at the heavy-handed playing of an organ or piano, their heads splitting from too much celebration the night before. Most of the cadets were invited to the homes of local residents for Sunday dinner, but few of the women trainees had such invitations. Most regrouped after attending church.

Word of the party did not elude the field staff. The trainees were sternly lectured about their conduct and reminded that they were, at all times, representatives of the flight training program for women. How they comported themselves would affect the entire program's reputation.

Again, there was an attempt to strongly discourage any socializing with the cadets. Their classes and activities at Avenger Field were so well segregated they rarely saw each other. They didn't even have the chance to mingle on the flight line since the men did all their flying out of an auxiliary field in Roscoe, a small town not far away. This stepped-up attention to the problem severely curtailed Colin's visits to the bay. Others didn't understand and Marty didn't try to explain her lackadaisical attitude about seeing him less often. She and Colin were good friends who had become lovers; romance had very little to do with their relationship, so she wasn't thrown into a mope when she didn't see him.

After the weekend's respite, it was back to training full tilt. Ground school had their heads awhirl with carburetors and manifolds, learning, memorizing and transcribing the International Code, which was changed monthly, discussions and tests, as well as map and chart work. Then it was out to the flight line for dual instruction, two and three of the open-cockpit PT-19s taking off at a time, piggyback, and solo flying, the best-loved time of all in the air. Sandwiching the training were physical games and body-conditioning calisthenics, and evenings in the rec hall were filled with hangar talk.

After the evening meal one night, they dragged their bone-weary bodies back to the bay. Inside they sprawled on their cots and made a stab at conversation.

'Did you think the stew tasted funny tonight?' Chicago put the question to the group. Her hands were clasped behind her head, ruffling the ends of her short, brown hair.

'Not that I noticed,' Eden replied, reclining full length on her cot with a hand draped over her eyes to shield out the light. Her nails were short and unpolished and her red hair was hidden under a bandanna turban – the stylish socialite of three weeks ago had been absorbed into the group. 'But I don't think it was intended to tickle the palate. Ragout, it is not.'

'What's the matter? Isn't stew good enough for you?' Marty, tired and irritable, was quick to issue the taunting inquiry.

'A change would be nice.' Unmoving from her languid pose, Eden failed to rise to the bait, as usual.

'I heard' – Chicago paused to garner their attention, and sat up on one elbow – 'that they put saltpeter in it.'

There was an instant of silence while everyone digested the outlandish rumor, not fully disbelieving it. Eden removed her hand from across her eyes and lifted her head to stare at Chicago. 'Are you serious?' she said.

'Forget it.' Humor was laced in Cappy's mildly derisive tone. 'They don't have to do that. Just look at us. We're all too tired to even contemplate anything remotely strenuous. If a man held me in his arms, I don't know about the rest of you, but I'd probably fall asleep.'

Agreeing sounds of laughter came from the row of cots, not too loud and not too forceful. Smiles required less energy.

CHAPTER SIX

Flying was the all-consuming focus for the girls; anything else became relegated to the background as of minor importance. Their world was the sky above Avenger Field. When they weren't flying in it, they were looking into it, taking automatic note of wind directions and ceiling heights, or watching fellow trainees in the traffic pattern making touch-and-go landings while they waited for their turn in the air.

After almost a month, they had become familiar with the routine occurrences around the field. When a jeep from the motor pool went dashing off to the old hangar, everyone knew the line dispatcher was making a check of the anemometer to find out the wind velocity. The actual control tower was still under construction, and the temporary one, located atop the hangar next to the office building, housed little equipment in its second-story cubicle.

The grumblings of the maintenance mechanics enroute

to right an airplane that had ground-looped on landing were largely ignored. Little attention was paid, as well, to the firing of the biscuit gun. Construction always seemed to be in progress somewhere, rendering runways and taxi strips inactive. Sometimes the construction made landings dicey, but usually it was merely the frustration of blowing red dust that choked the lungs and coated the skin and powdered everything in sight.

There were rare interludes in the middle of the hectic pace when all seemed perfect. The sky would be that incredible blue, stretching to forever. A beatific stillness would claim the land, hushing everything except the bursting song of the meadowlark.

In the sky, aircraft performed lazy and graceful aerobatics, climbing high into the blue and spiraling down out of a full stall, then sliding into level flight. Pilots picked out the navigationally straight roads to practice their 'S' curves against, snaking along a line and changing their angle of bank in a turn to compensate for the changing push of the wind. Many a rancher's windmill was selected as an imaginary axis for seven-twenties, also called turns-around-a-point, consisting of two complete three-hundred-sixty-degree revolutions. The aerial patterns always appeared to be effortlessly executed, a series of slow, lazy curves, circles, and spirals, flowing languidly one to the other. Yet all of them were potentially lifesaving maneuvers.

All this practicing and honing of skills these past nearly six weeks was in preparation for that 'check ride' day. They were at the end of the primary phase of training. Their individual instructors had flight-tested them, but to advance to the next phase of basic training and fly the more powerful BT-13, they had to go up with Army pilots who would 'check' their skills. If they failed that test, they were through. There was no second chance – no next phase of training. They were dropped from the program.

As the time neared when they were either ready or they'd never be, the tension became palpable along the flight line, charging tempers and numbing senses. When the Army check-pilots arrived, anxiety levels reached their peak.

In the ready room, cigarettes were virtually chain-smoked. It was a subdued group of trainees who massed inside, conversing either in mumbles or in voices grown shrill with nerves. Their glances kept straying out the windowed front of the building to watch the takeoffs and landings of the planes piloted by their fellow trainees. Soon they would be up there, but the agony was in not knowing when your name would be called.

As Eden tore the paper off her pack of Lucky Strike Greens, her fingers trembled. She lit the cigarette with an unnatural clumsiness. She exhaled the smoke in an impatient rush while her thumbnail resumed its nervous flicking of her fingernail, making little clicking sounds.

'For crissake, will you stop that?' Marty Rogers snapped. 'It's getting on my nerves.'

'Sorry.' She stilled her thumb, but the ticking went on inside her. Her auburn hair was caught in a confining snood at the back of her neck, its richly deep red lustre toned down. The flight suit bagged all over her slim figure, creating a shapeless silhouette. Never had anything fit her so atrociously, yet she had become so accustomed to wearing it every day that she never gave it a thought.

On occasion, Eden was conscious that her standards were changing; she was judging people less from their outer appearance and more for their inner qualities. All her life, things had been hers for the asking; wealth and privilege gained her access to the most prestigious schools; name and position granted her entry into elite circles; money and power allowed her to indulge in nearly any whim. This was the first time she'd ever had to work for something – the first time she'd ever been treated the same as those around her – and she liked it.

The marching, the drills, the military inspections were a bore. It still didn't make sense to her why demerits were given because there was litter in the wastebasket; where else was she supposed to have put it? Yet the camaraderie, the closeness, the sharing of desires with her baymates, more than made up for the sacrifice of creature comforts and the hardships she'd endured.

She had worked hard to reach this point, so she appreciated the struggle some of the other trainees were going through. Eden knew she was a damned good pilot. Yet, while she had confidence in her ability, she wanted to pass this check ride so badly, she was a bundle of nerves. It was the first time in her life anything had meant so much to her.

Only minutes ago, she had watched the pale-faced and drawn Mary Lynn walk out of the ready room behind an Army officer. The petite woman had lost the natural color that usually highlighted her round cheekbones. Her dark eyes had become haunted with apprehension. But Eden looked with envy at the two pillows Mary Lynn had clutched to her breast like a shield.

'There goes Number Thirty-seven lifting off,' Chicago observed in a low, taut voice, referring to the aircraft number of the low-winged PT-19. 'Isn't that the plane Mary Lynn's flying?'

'I think so.' Cappy was the only one of the group who didn't appear to be a victim of the intense pressure weighing on them all. Looking calm and unflappable, she puffed on a cigarette. Eden grinned to herself when she noticed there was already a cigarette burning in the ashtray. Cappy wasn't as poised as she looked.

Earlier in the day, they'd all paid their ritual visit to the Wishing Well and thrown their coins into the pool, making a wish for an 'up-check.' Some even added a prayer to Fifinella, the Disney-designed, female gremlin who was the mascot for the women pilot trainees.

At the time, Eden had joked about the half dollar she had tossed into the pool, laughing at her own extravagant gesture and declaring that she was buying the fulfillment of her wish.

'Van Valkenburg.' A flat, deep-toned voice called her name.

Her head jerked around, and her heart plummeted

104

to her toes, turning her legs into rubber. Somehow she managed to crush out her cigarette despite the shaking of her hand, and scrambled to her feet, the parachute pack banging against her legs.

The military officer at the door was searching the room for a response to the name he'd called. When Eden stood up, his gaze stopped on her. With a cold, cocky arrogance, he looked her over. How much would it take to bribe him? Money, power, prestige, all the commodities that had cushioned Eden all her life had no value in this situation. It was a chastening thought to one accustomed to acquiring what she wanted through one means or another.

With her head held unnaturally high, she unknowingly made a comical sight as she crossed the room. All the grace inherent in her regal carriage looked gauche and ridiculous in the flappy, out-sized flight suit. Her long, leggy strides were reminiscent of a galloping giraffe. The amused smirk on the officer's face was understandable when she stopped before him.

'I'm Eden van Valkenburg,' she said.

When she followed him onto the flight line, she was a quivering gel of nerves. As she made her walk-around ground check of the assigned aircraft, Eden knew she was going to make some stupid mistake. All his questions seemed snide and tricky while all her answers sounded uncertain, even when she was positive of them. Was he trying to trip her up, or was it merely her imagination?

In the forward cockpit of the trainer, Eden wiped repeatedly at her sweaty palms before she pulled on her gloves. She was so scared, she was close to tears. As she went through the preflight checklist, anger started to build in her. Who did this man think he was, intimidating her in this manner? She had studied and trained long hours for this moment. She'd gone through too much and worked too hard to blow it now. Dammit, she was a fine pilot!

Later, when she crawled out of the cockpit and hopped off the wing of the primary trainer, she confronted the close-faced military inspector. She took off helmet and goggles along with the hairnet. She shook her head with a exhilarating sense of freedom and brought her hands to rest on her flight-suit-padded hips in an unconsciously challenging stance.

'Well?' Eden prodded him for a reaction. Despite all her confidence in her ability, she needed to hear the confirmation from an unbiased – or better yet, negatively biased – source. 'How did I do?'

'I'm giving you a satisfactory mark.' Although he made it sound as if he were doing her a favor, rather than giving her a mark she had earned, he couldn't diminish the importance of it.

With an unrestrained squeal of joy, Eden left him standing on the flight line and sprinted for the big fire bell that hung outside the administration building. She yanked on the rope, ringing out her triumph in the tradition of the successful trainee, laughing and crying in elation.

Not long afterwards, Eden learned that Mary Lynn had rung the bell before her. One by one, over the next two days, her baymates went up for their check rides. On the second afternoon, Marty charged into the bay like a crazy woman and did a mock war dance in the center of the room, whooping and carrying on.

'I flew that little baby the best that I knew how. Not even the big, bad Army can stop me now!' She sang while she danced around an imaginary point on the floor, then stopped, out of breath and elated, to share her victorious moment with them. 'I made it!! It's the old lucky thirteen for me.' She had advanced from the Fairchild PT-19 to the more powerful BT-13 aircraft.

But when she finally looked around the room, she noticed that none of her baymates' faces mirrored her jubilation. Instead, they looked uncomfortable and their glances skittered away in a grim and almost embarrassed fashion. Marty briefly had the feeling Eden would have enjoyed throttling her but her look didn't last long either before it was directed to the side and downward.

Bewildered by their reaction, Marty felt the silence

weighing on the room. Chicago shifted her position, enabling Marty to see behind her. Aggie was sitting on her cot, dressed in a skirt and blouse. Her curly blonde head was bent over the handkerchief she was twisting in her lap. Marty opened her mouth to tease Aggie about wearing civilian clothes. Then the significance hit her and her shocked gaze flashed to Mary Lynn. A small nod confirmed that Aggie had failed her check ride.

'Aggie –' Overwhelmed with guilt, Marty struggled to find the words that would make up for the salt she'd unknowingly rubbed on Aggie's wound. '– I'm sorry.' It sounded so inadequate. 'I didn't know,' she finished lamely.

'How does your foot taste, Rogers?' Eden asked angrily.

Marty turned on her, lashing out in anger. 'How the hell was I supposed to know she washed out?'

'God, I don't believe it.' Eden sent a heavenward glance at the ceiling.

'Somebody could have warned me when I came in,' Marty protested, still guilt-faced while she searched for a way out of the awkward situation.

'Why don't you just shut your mouth?' Chicago suggested.

It seemed the best advice. Marty's lips came together in a straight line. Sniffling loudly through her nose, Aggie stood up slowly, her six-foot frame all hunch-shouldered.

'It's all right. Marty didn't mean anything by it.' Her eyes were red-rimmed and swollen from crying. 'She has a right to be glad she made it. You all have. But . . .' Aggie blew her nose, and the sobs began to sound in her throat when she finally finished the sentence. '. . . I can't help feeling sorry for myself. I wanted so much to –'

The rest was choked off as Aggie abruptly turned away from them. For a minute, none of them moved, trapped by an awkward embarrassment. Finally, Mary Lynn went over to console her.

Marty sank onto her cot, thinking how odd it was that Mary Lynn had gone to Aggie's side rather than Chicago, who had been Aggie's best friend. An unnatural silence hung over the room while Aggie removed her belongings from the footlocker and packed them in her suitcase. Like all of them, Agnes Richardson had paid her own fare to Sweetwater and she'd pay her own way back home.

When the moment of leave-taking came, they all felt an odd reluctance to get too close to her, as if they were afraid her bad luck would rub off on them. They had trouble looking her squarely in the eye. Aggie understood and didn't linger. She didn't belong there any more.

The empty cot in the bay haunted them for days after Aggie had left. There were empty cots in other bays, too. Roughly twenty percent of their class had washed out in the first cut, beginning the weeding process. At the end of the week, Eden switched cots, occupying Aggie's former bed and vacating the noisy location next to the shared lavatory. It helped.

Only one letter came for Mary Lynn. Mail from England was spotty at best. Sometimes two weeks would go by without her getting a single letter from Beau, then a half dozen would come in one day with pieces snipped out of them. For a long time it had bothered her that their mail was being read and censored. But there was a war on, even if it did seem far, far away from Sweetwater, Texas.

She read her letter for the third time while she sat at a table in the recreation hall. The trainees often gathered there in the evenings to study, write letters, hangar-fly, socialize, and escape the small, stark bays, so militarily uniform and devoid of personality. It was strictly informal, chairs pulled around in casually formed clusters, girls wandering around with their hair wrapped in curlers, dog-eared magazines scattered around. The March issue of the *Sweetwater Reporter* was opened to the latest list of sinkings of Allied ships in the Battle for the Atlantic. The much-frequented Coca-Cola machine stood in the corner, wooden cases for the empty bottles stacked beside it. On the wall, a bulletin board posted announcements of church events and other activities, pertinent newspaper cartoons, and pinned messages.

A hot Ping-Pong match was in progress at one end of the rec room, Marty and Chicago against a pair of trainees from another bay. The slap-pop of the paddles and ball punctuated the chatter in the room as the game grew intense in a battle for match point. Marty's low-driven slam-shot won it.

Flushed and exhilarated, the pair of them returned to the table where Mary Lynn sat with Cappy and Eden. The five of them were rarely apart. Since Aggie's departure, they had taken to calling themselves 'The Inseparables,' hoping in some superstitious way it would mean they'd stay together through the completion of their training. Aggie's failure had sobered all of them. Their training was taken more seriously than before and their resolve to succeed deepened.

Marty pulled out a chair and plopped onto it, kicking back to rock the chair on its rear legs. 'Hey, kid, what are you reading?' she said to Mary Lynn.

Although Mary Lynn was the oldest, she was treated as the baby of the group, partly because of her size and cherub-cheeked face, but mostly because of her inexperience. She had married so young she'd never been on her own before.

'A letter from Beau.'

'I should have guessed,' Marty declared.

Cappy looked up from her meteorology textbook and glanced at the tablet in front of Mary Lynn. All this time she'd been hearing Mary Lynn's pen scratching across the paper, she thought Mary Lynn was taking notes from her own book, but she could see it was a letter. 'Hey, you're supposed to be studying,' Cappy reminded her. She was the unappointed captain of the bunch, naturally taking charge and handling everything from making sure their bay was ready for inspection to getting all of them up and ready for class on time.

'I will – as soon as I finish this letter to Beau. I'm telling

109

him about the new planes we're flying now.' She needed to tell him all the small details of her life, to share with him the things that were happening to her so she could feel their lives were still linked no matter how many miles separated them.

So she told him all about the basic training aircraft, the BT-13. Like the PT-19 they'd been flying, it was a low-winged, tail-wheeled airplane. But at that point the similarities ended. Called the 'Valiant' by its manufacturer, the Vultee Company, the BT appeared enormous with its powerful 450-horse engine. It had a front and rear seat, but unlike the open-cockpitted Fairchild, it had an enclosed canopy top. Another major difference, Mary Lynn wrote, was that the BT-13 had a radio. For the first time, the trainees were in communication with the control tower.

The operators in the tower gave the pilots their taxiing instructions and takeoff and landing positions. Mary Lynn told Beau that although some of the trainees had to learn a new language in communication, none of them minded being told what to do and when. They finally had a microphone attached to their headsets, and they could talk back.

'Leave her alone, Cap.' Marty could be counted on to defend Mary Lynn, invariably sticking up for the loyal, trusting girl she idealized. She seriously doubted that there was a mean, unkind bone in Mary Lynn's small body. No one dared say a thing against her in Marty's presence. 'A wife is supposed to write her husband every day when they're apart.'

'I'm not stopping her.' Cappy shrugged, but it made her think about how the Army separated couples, and not just during a war. When she married, her husband was going to come home to her every night. Under no circumstances were they ever going to live apart.

'Are you going to see Colin this weekend, Marty?' Chicago wondered.

'Sure.' She took it for granted. On weekends there was a casual mixing of the enlisted cadets and the women trainees in town, but mainly it was a friendly group thing.

110

Few routinely paired off the way Marty and Colin did. A wicked light danced in her silver-green eyes as Marty looked sideways at Chicago. 'Are you going to see Mr Lentz this weekend?' Always the agitator, she couldn't resist stirring up a little trouble by mentioning Chicago's former instructor in primary training. She knew her bay-mate had a crush on the man.

'No.' Chicago turned red.

Restless with this inactivity, Marty set her chair down hard on all four legs. 'Let's do something besides study,' she urged.

'You're right. This place needs some livening up.' Eden unexpectedly agreed with her.

'Her highness has spoken,' Marty said mockingly. 'Someone fetch the court jester.' She gibed at Eden, her favorite target when she wanted to pick a fight, because Eden was the only one who fought back.

'You do such a good job of it, Marty, we don't need another one,' she retorted coolly and closed up her study papers. Standing, Eden paused to motion them to follow her. 'Come on.'

After a second's hesitation, Cappy shrugged and put away her papers, too. The rest followed suit and trailed after Eden as she crossed the room to the upright piano. Used to commanding attention and occupying center stage, Eden sat down at the keys and began rumbling out a boogie-woogie beat that gathered a crowd.

By the time the weekend rolled around, the girls had discovered the basic training phase had a few twists besides new ground school courses, more powerful aircraft, and radios. But the most grueling and mentally strenuous was the concentration required to fly the plane by instruments alone. A black curtain enclosed their cockpit, shutting out any visual reference point. It was brutal on the nerves and on the senses.

'I could have sworn I was in the steepest right turn you've ever seen.' Marty was slumped in the chair, fatigue etched in her features. Colin listened sympathetically, his chair across from hers at the table in the hotel's restaurant, where they usually met on weekends. 'Those damned instruments showed straight-and-level flight, but it felt so real that I was sure they were wrong. Then that flaming Frye started yelling in my ears.' A tired sigh broke from her, heavy with self-disgust.

'Vertigo is something you just have to learn to ignore. You'll overcome it,' Colin insisted calmly.

'Yeah.'

'I agree.' Cappy was at the big table, too, along with Mary Lynn, Eden, and Chicago. 'Flying blind is no picnic. After two hours of it, my eyes feel like they're connected to my head with little springs, and they're going to pop out.'

'You girls better get used to it,' Colin advised. 'One of our guys got a look at your curriculum. You're going to be flying more instrument time than the cadet training calls for.'

'That isn't fair,' Marty protested.

'As ferry pilots, you'll potentially be flying in worse weather conditions than we will as combat pilots,' he reasoned. 'We have more emphasis on aerial acrobatics. It's natural.'

There were skeptical murmurings around the table. Instrument flying was definitely not a favorite among them, the five who had once believed anything connected with flying was a joy. Over the course of the last months, they had changed, too, but the determination remained, growing stronger as flying got tougher.

Seeing their expressions, Colin added, 'Wait until you do some night flying. Then you'll really find out what disorientation is like.'

'We start this coming week,' Cappy said.

'I haven't figured out when we're supposed to sleep yet,' Eden complained.

'And without her beauty sleep, Eden reverts to a witch,' Marty taunted, never able to resist a gibe at her rich baymate.

'Have any of you had your trainer into a spin yet?'

Chicago asked, uninterested in the ongoing but minor feud.

'It scared the hell out of me.' Marty confirmed her experience with it, while the others nodded a mutual agreement. 'I thought the plane was going to shake apart. I mean, it shuddered so violently I thought this was *it*.'

'I used up more than two thousand feet of altitude before I could level her out,' Cappy admitted.

'Instead of the Valiant, they ought to call her the Vultee Vibrator,' Eden suggested dryly, tapping her cigarette on the ashtray in the middle of the table. A black-haired woman in a tight-fitting dress walked by their table. The exaggerated sway of her hips caught Eden's eye. An eyebrow arched in dry, cynical humor. 'Speaking of vibrators,' she murmured.

Marty turned in her chair and looked over her shoulder. 'She really thinks she's a hot number, doesn't she?' It wasn't the first time she had noticed a member of that woman's profession in the vicinity, especially at the Bluebonnet Hotel.

'It's a pretty dress,' Mary Lynn said admiringly. 'It's a pity it's so tight.'

There was a slight break as everyone looked at Mary Lynn to see if that softly drawled remark was meant seriously. Her dark eyes blinked innocently back at them.

A staccato laugh came from Marty. 'For a married lady, Mary Lynn, you have certainly led a sheltered life. Can we blame it on your magnolia-white upbringing.'

Mary Lynn looked around the table, feeling ignorant but unsure why. 'What did I say wrong?'

In exaggerated mimicry, Marty copied her southern accent. 'Honey, I believe you would refer to that woman as a "lady of the evening," or perhaps a "soiled dove."'

Mary Lynn's dark eyes rounded as she craned her head to stare after the woman, then she paused to look at the group long enough to ask, 'Is that what they look like?'

Amid the laughter that followed, Marty declared, 'We'll corrupt you yet.'

Avenger Field wasn't equipped with runway lights. As the long shadows of twilight stretched over the field, it became customary to see the truck loaded with flare pots drive down the runway, depositing the burning oil pots at regular intervals.

What with 'flying blind' beneath a black curtain, hours spent on the ground boxed in the Link trainer to simulate instrument flight, and night flying, the girls were convinced the basic training courses were designed to test their sanity and their endurance. Cold showers and pots of Mom's black coffee kept them going – the showers taken before reporting for night flights and the coffee consumed in the ready room while they waited for their turn to fly – usually until two in the morning.

On takeoffs, Mary Lynn had still not gotten used to the sensation of charging down the midnight-dark runway, the yellow flames from the burning pots flashing in her side vision while she watched her airspeed indicator to know when to pull back on the stick. After liftoff, all was instantly swallowed into the blackness. It unnerved her every time.

Landing was equally tricky, the darkness lousing up her depth perception. She had to depend on her altimeter, virtually to the point of touchdown, and watch her airspeed to keep the plane above stalling speed. She couldn't remember making a smooth landing. Invariably, she hit with a thud and a bounce before skittering onto the runway like a wounded duck.

Endless time was spent in the traffic pattern around Avenger Field, making touch-and-gos – landing, applying full power, and taking off again. Other planes were mere pinpoints of light – the red and green navigational lights on their wings and the white beams of their headlights shining like sightless eyes on final approach to landing.

Once they left the traffic pattern to practice navigation by radio beam, Mary Lynn's infatuation with night flying surfaced. There was a magical quality in the utter blackness of a Texas sky sparkling with stars. Beneath the moonlight the airplane's wings appeared dusted with silver. The glass canopy over her cockpit sometimes seemed to reflect the moonbeams, bathing her in the silvery glow.

The odd ranch light shining in the bottomless black below her plane became an eye-catching sight. Mary Lynn filed away its location, so she could find the friendly source in the daylight. Passenger trains, with their many windows of lights crawling through the dark void, reminded Mary Lynn of caterpillars. In her ear the steady hum of the signal, beamed from the navigational radio beacon, confirmed that she was on course. If she strayed off the transmission quadrant, the sound changed to Morse Code beeps. *Da-dit*, which was the letter *A*, was repeated if she was to the left of her course; and *dit-da*, which was *N*, if she strayed to the right.

Each radio beacon had its own assigned frequency on which it transmitted. Its location was marked on maps so a pilot could fly from one beacon to another, changing from one frequency to the next. When a pilot flew directly over the transmitter, there was a cone of silence, allowing her to pinpoint her exact location on the map. The cessation of sound lasted for only a short interlude. An ear always had to be attuned to it or it would be missed.

The droning stopped for those ticks of seconds. Mary Lynn changed the frequency and made the turn toward the second beacon, following orders previously given by her instructor. Above the *da-dit, da-dit* that was beeping in her ears the instructor barked, 'What do you think you're doing, Palmer? I told you not to fly to the second beacon until you'd flown over the first. Haven't you got ears?'

The sarcasm made her bristle on her cushion of pillows. 'Yes, sir, and I heard the cone of silence.' Very sweetly, 'Didn't you?'

His failure to respond immediately was immensely satisfying. Marty had told her some of the instructors had only a few more hours in the BT-13s than they themselves had. 'The blind leading the blind,' she had joked. Mary Lynn had suspected Marty of exaggerating but it was beginning to ring true. On two other flights, she'd followed his directions and they'd wound up lost.

Finally, her instructor came back to claim defensively, 'I was just testing you.'

With a warm feeling of satisfaction, Mary Lynn headed the BT into the star-studded blackness. Minutes later, a sense of unease stole over her. The engine wasn't running right; it was a feeling rather than an actual change in its rhythm. She began checking the gauges.

The roughness began as a vibration. Her instructor started yelling at her. Then a tongue of flame leaped out from the whirling propeller, dancing, darting, and disappearing. Then it came again. Fire. The engine was on fire! The instructor screamed obscenities and yanked the controls from Mary Lynn; the stick banged against her knee. Mary Lynn was fighting her own waves of panic at the sight of that deadly yellow fire spilling backwards from the nose of the plane toward the front cockpit where she sat.

It was after 2 a.m. when Marty and Chicago staggered into their bay, physically exhausted, their heads whirling, still seeing the streamers of light from the flare pots in their side vision. Cappy was just climbing into bed, and Eden was already stretched out on her cot, the satin sleep mask over her eyes.

'I could sleep for a week,' Marty complained. She flopped onto her cot, letting her tired head sink into her hands.

'Couldn't we all.' Cappy pulled the covers up around her shoulders and turned onto her side, snuggling into the pillow.

With an effort, Marty raised her head. The cot next to hers was empty, the blanket stretched tautly across it. 'Where's Mary Lynn?' She frowned.

'I guess she isn't back yet,' Cappy said without bothering to open her eyes.

Chicago had wasted no time shedding her flight suit and

climbing into her pajamas. Late-night conversation was the last thing she was interested in.

'Good night.' She hauled her tired body onto the cot and slipped under the covers.

Marty was now the only one still up. She eyed the empty cot for another several seconds, nagged by Mary Lynn's absence. Then she shrugged her shoulders and announced to no one in particular, 'That stupid instructor probably got her lost again.' She reached for the zipper of her flight suit. 'You know, I don't know why we should bother to undress. We'll be getting up again in four hours.'

Eden, who had given every semblance of being sound asleep, finally said, 'Shut up, Rogers.'

The next morning the cot was still empty. Mary Lynn's absence could no longer be shrugged aside. Worry was a knife in each one of them.

'What do you suppose happened?' Marty probed each of their faces with her hard glance, afraid but unwilling to show it.

'I don't know.' Cappy shared the anxiety written in the expressions of her baymates, although it glimmered only in the blue confusion of her eyes. 'Like you said last night, Marty, they might have gotten lost. They probably landed at another field and decided to wait until daylight to fly back,' she reasoned. Until they were told differently, she felt it was wisest to maintain a positive outlook. She smiled to encourage optimism. 'We're all probably worrying for nothing.'

'Yeah.' But Marty wasn't convinced.

After reporting for morning formation, they skipped breakfast and went directly to operations. Marty shouldered her way to the front of the quartet and demanded to know what had happened to Mary Lynn Palmer.

'Please. We're her baymates,' Cappy said, attempting to temper Marty's belligerence.

There was a telling hesitation on the part of the establishment officer. 'I'm sorry, but the wreckage of her BT-13 was found this morning on a ranch north of here. The plane appears to have exploded on impact. A search is under way for the bodies now.'

'No.' The small negative came from Marty, who went numb with shock. It wasn't possible. They had made some mistake, her mind kept insisting. Mary Lynn couldn't be dead. Not her. Marty met the news with a raw and wild disbelief.

While the others reeled from the news, Cappy retained her presence of mind. 'Thank you,' she murmured to the solemn-faced woman. They walked out in a close bunch, shoulders rubbing, arms supporting waists, all of them needing the physical contact with one another. Chicago was the only one crying, sobbing softly while tears slid down her cheeks.

Outside, the sun shone down out of an incomparable Texas sky. Spring was bursting around them, birds trilling. It was a perfect day for flying, a gentle wind blowing, but the four were too stunned by the news to notice.

'I don't believe it,' Marty repeated.

Her expression was stark with the shock of it, her face drained and pale. Marty was taking it the hardest of all of them; she had been the closest to Mary Lynn.

They stood huddled together, grieving in silence. Beyond the loss of a baymate, there was the shock of coming face to face with their own mortality. Regardless of the cause – instrument malfunction, engine failure, pilot error, it could have happened to any of them. Chicago started crying again, smothering the sobs with a hand clamped over her mouth.

If they stood around much longer, Cappy feared they'd become paralyzed. 'Come on,' she urged quietly. 'We have to report to the flight line.' Her reminder seemed to fall on deaf ears, so she added, 'Have you forgotten? There's a war on.'

The stony look left Marty's eyes as she glared at Cappy. 'Hayward, you make me sick! You can take your stiff upper lip and shove it!' She stalked away, rigid and hurting,

118

unable to find a release for the pain that clutched her throat.

Later, Marty cut off her instructor Bud Hanson's expression of sympathy as she walked with him to the airplane parked on the ramp. She didn't want to hear the words, more confirmation of Mary Lynn's death.

'I don't want to talk about it, Bud,' she informed him in a hard, cold voice.

His glance skidded over her. 'Sure.'

Climbing into the cockpit of the trainer and buckling in was a strange sensation. She caught herself wondering what Mary Lynn had felt when the plane was going down. Had there been time for fear . . . or pain?

'FF eighty-one.' She depressed the microphone button to call the tower. 'This is sixty-two on the ramp requesting taxi instructions. Over.'

A tear slid down her cheek, followed by a second, and a third. Marty heard the reply, but she just couldn't seem to act. The tears turned into a steady stream, washing down her face and into the corners of her mouth.

'Marty?' Bud Hanson's voice came over the earphones. 'The tower gave you clearance to runway seventeen. Didn't you hear it?'

'Yes.' She sniffed loudly. 'I'm going.' With a check on either side for other aircraft, Marty pushed the throttle forward and stepped her foot down on the right rudder.

It was the poorest job of flying she'd ever done. She almost resented the patience Bud exhibited with mistakes usually made by beginners. Inside, Marty felt sick and dulled. On the ground, she paused to look at the chubby-cheeked man without quite meeting his eyes.

'I'm sorry, Bud,' she said.

'We're all entitled to our bad days.'

Her legs seemed to be made of lead as she headed across the concrete apron to the hangar. She spotted Chicago standing by a jeep parked near the hangar and immediately bent her head, not wanting to give any sign that she had noticed her baymate. The pain and grief were too fresh and too new. She didn't want to face any of them and listen to them talk about Mary Lynn. It hurt too much.

'Hey! Marty!'

It was too late. Chicago had seen her. Marty considered ignoring the shouted call, then grudgingly turned her gaze toward the girl and altered her direction when Chicago waved her over to the jeep. The knot in her throat got thicker as Marty guessed Chicago probably wanted to tell her the bodies had been recovered. Doll-sized Mary Lynn, all broken up and battered.

'Marty!' A familiar voice called her name.

All at the same time, Marty observed the short, baggy-suited girl waving at her, the crumpled parachute in the back of the jeep and the wide smile on Chicago's face.

It was Mary Lynn – very much alive despite the scratches from being dragged by the parachute when she had landed. Laughing and crying, Marty broke into a run. When the hugs and the laughter subsided, Mary Lynn explained how she and her instructor had both bailed out of the burning plane before it crashed. The wind had carried her slight weight farther, separating her from the instructor, who had broken his leg in the fall. After shivering through the night's cold, Mary Lynn had set out walking at dawn and met up with a cowboy.

'When he hauled me onto the back of that horse and it started bucking, I thought I was really doomed.' Mary Lynn laughed in retrospect. But the laugh faded as she glanced at the handle to the parachute ripcord, a souvenir she still gripped in her hand. 'I guess this makes me an official member of the Caterpillar Club, doesn't it?' This was an exclusive club whose membership was limited to pilots who had bailed out of an airplane and had the parachute handle as proof.

'It makes you the luckiest devil on earth,' Marty retorted.

'I know.' It would be a long time before she'd forget the sensation of that night – cracking the canopy and shoving it back, the rushing push of the wind and fiery heat from the flames blowing on her, hurtling into that black void and feeling that abject terror, pulling on the ripcord and waiting those agonizing seconds for the chute to open, the crack of the billowing silk and the sight of the burning plane spinning in its death throes. A long time.

'Hot damn! This calls for a party!' Marty declared, unable to blink back the tears in her eyes. 'Let's round up Cappy and Eden and go to the canteen. The Cokes are on me!'

'Yeah, we need to celebrate,' Chicago agreed. 'The Inseparables are all together again!'

CHAPTER SEVEN

Her neck and shoulder muscles ached with tension, but Cappy couldn't spare the few seconds it would take to relax them and ease some of the painful stiffness. All her concentration was focused on the instrument panel in front of her. Her hands gripped the stick between her legs and her feet operated the rudder pedals as she performed the maneuvers instructed by the voice on the headphones. The air inside the closed cockpit was becoming suffocatingly close. It seemed to add to the dull throb in her head.

'Okay, that's enough for today,' the voice said, then added, as an afterthought, 'Good job.'

All the instruments went dead, but Cappy was slow to loosen her grip on the stick. It seemed a permanent part of her. Sighing, she arched her shoulders and back, turning her neck into them in a flexing maneuver, then reached up to unfasten the hatch.

Whenever she first stuck her head out of the cockpit she always experienced that disoriented pause. She felt she'd been flying a plane this last hour, but she was climbing out into a classroom. Cappy swung over the side of the Link trainer and stepped down to the floor. The 'voice' was sitting at a table. He could communicate by phone with the 'pilot' and observe the pilot's performance as it was recorded by the automatic stylus.

With her feet on the floor, Cappy looked at the flight simulator that had tricked her once again into believing it was real.

The Link trainer was such an absurd sight – a boxlike structure with stubby mock wings and a ridiculous tail. It always reminded Cappy of a cartoon caricature of an airplane, something that belonged in a carnival. All it lacked was a fake propeller. But she supposed for all its comical appearance it accomplished its purpose, which was to give the trainees plenty of practice in instrument flying.

At the end of a Link class, Cappy always felt frazzled and worn out, as if her brains had been fried and scrambled. This time wasn't any different. It had been raining steadily since morning, so there would be no flying. With the day's classes over, the trainees were at loose ends.

Like herd animals, the five from Cappy's bay naturally coalesced into a group as they headed for the door. They all wore that same sense-dulled expression and that blank look in their eyes.

'Hell has to be a Link trainer,' Marty declared. 'It got so stuffy in there today I thought I was going to suffocate. Can you imagine what it's going to be like in the summer when the temperature hits a hundred in the shade . . . and us trapped in that sweatbox for hours on end? There isn't a muscle in my body that doesn't ache. And my head – the damned thing is pounding so, I'd just as soon cut it off.'

'Please do.' Eden's smlle was thin with sarcasm. 'Then the rest of us wouldn't have to listen to you bitch all the time.'

Marty curled a lip at her but didn't respond as they filed through the door. The rain was coming straight down in obscuring sheets. They huddled under the overhang of the building with the steady drum of the falling rain above them and the runoff from the roof creating a water screen in front of them. An incongruous evergreen, short and squat, stood beside the post, one of a scattered row that dotted the front of the classroom building. Evergreens seemed out of place in this red Texas landscape.

'Hell, I need a cigarette. Let's go over to the canteen for Cokes and smokes,' Marty suggested and looked to Cappy for agreement.

'Okay, but somebody has to go back to the bay and empty the pans.' Their barracks was not only notoriously drafty, but the roof also leaked. They had scrounged up a half-dozen containers and strategically positioned them to catch all the drips. Cappy had organized a system where they each set their alarm clocks for a different hour of the night so the pans would be emptied at regular intervals.

'I did it last,' Marty asserted. 'It's Chicago's turn.'

With a grimace, Chicago accepted her fate. 'I'll see you all later.'

'Aren't you going to join us at the canteen?' Cappy asked.

'Nawh. I got some washing I need to do.' There was a troubled and sad look in Chicago's eyes before she turned away and raised the collar of her battle jacket up around her head. 'See you later.' With her head down, she dashed into the rain. Cappy felt a twinge of pity for the girl as she watched her leave.

'What's the matter with her?' Marty frowned.

'I think this instrument flying is giving her problems.' Cappy shrugged to indicate it wasn't really any of their business.

'Some days it gets to all of us.' Mary Lynn hunched her shoulders and looked out into the downpour. Water was already pooling on the ground, the pelting drops splattering when they hit. 'A gloomy day like this naturally makes you moody.'

'It's definitely ruining my hair.' Eden hooked her finger

around a limp strand and let it fall. 'Look at the way it's drooping. Do you know what I keep fantasizing about? Getting a hot oil treatment for my hair, and a facial, then stretching out on a massage table and sipping twelve-year-old Scotch while trained hands rub away all the muscle aches and tension.'

'It sounds wonderful,' Cappy murmured.

'Especially the Scotch,' Marty agreed in her raspy, amused voice.

'This rain isn't letting up a bit. Why are we standing here?' Mary Lynn wanted to know.

'She's right. Come on.' Marty loosened her jacket and pulled it up over her head.

In follow-the-leader style, they all ducked their heads under their raised jackets and splashed across the compound toward the canteen. The rain drenched them.

'Hey, look!' Marty pointed to the administration building while water dribbled down her face. The local taxi was parked in front while its well-dressed, umbrellaed passengers waited to claim their luggage from the trunk, their heads turning in every direction as they gawked at everything they saw. The women looked bewildered, decidedly out of place, but eager to belong. 'It's the new class of trainees. Do you suppose we looked that green?'

'Probably,' Cappy replied, smiling faintly. That gray day almost a month and a half ago when they arrived at Avenger Field seemed years away.

'I think we need to show them the ropes.' There was a devilish glint in Marty's eyes.

'What does she mean?' Mary Lynn turned her head to look up to the taller Cappy, and got a faceful of rain in the process. Cappy tried to hide her smile at Mary Lynn's inexperience.

Come sundown, the clouds rolled away and a rainbow came out to compete with the fresh-washed brilliance of a scarlet sunset. The containers were emptied for the last time and stored away for a future rainy day. Then the Inseparables waited until Marty decreed the time was ripe.

Outside they joined other trainees of the first Sweetwater class and sloshed through the red mud to the barracks of the new recruits. Mary Lynn was swept along with the pack as they burst into the first bay. Marty was at the front of the assault, barking out orders and acting tough.

'Attention!' she shouted to the startled trainees, who were lounging on their new beds, writing their first letters home. After they scrambled off their cots, the giggling started as they realized they were being hazed by their 'upper classmen.' 'What's so funny?' Marty demanded without cracking a smile, but her light-colored eyes were gleaming with wicked humor. 'Stand up straight. Shoulders back, chest out, stomach in!'

The raucous spirit of the initiation went against everything Mary Lynn had been taught about kindness and courtesy, all the mannerly things that should be done to make a new person feel welcome. But the new trainees seemed to take the harassing and the sometimes cruel ridicule all in good fun. Obediently they marched to the confusing set of orders and attempted to sit in chairs they knew would be pulled away at the last second. When a few of them were selected to be thrown in the showers, they squealed with a kind of laughter.

At first, Mary Lynn wasn't certain she liked this brand of fun; it seemed a little too much. But gradually, as the hazing flowed from one bay of trainees to the next, she got the hang of the new game and joined in the mischief. In the last bay, she succumbed to an impish urge and turned off the cold water tap to the shower spray. Someone shouted the warning, and the fully clothed and saturated trainees managed to elude the scalding hot water that came from the shower head.

When it was over, they tramped back to their bay, laughing gleefully. Mary Lynn sprawled on her cot, mindless of the mud splattered on her slacks and caked on her shoes. She felt gloriously relaxed, all the pent-up frustrations and tensions gone.

'Did you see the way they jumped when I reached for

that cold water faucet?' She laughed in remembrance and looked at Marty, one of the instigators of the night's outing.

'It was the damndest sight I ever saw.' Marty snorted with laughter.

But it wasn't so funny the next morning when their entire class was sternly reprimanded for their sophomoric antics. The base commanding officer announced that any future hazing of new trainees was expressly forbidden. A girl from one of the other barracks had suffered a fractured tailbone after falling on the floor when a chair had been pulled out from under her. It was too soon to know if the injury would wash her out of the program.

'My momma always told me no good ever comes out of taking pleasure from making someone else miserable,' Mary Lynn remembered, too late.

'No one was supposed to get hurt,' Marty insisted in a subdued defense of their action.

'Zero thirteen, you are cleared to land.'

Eden compressed the mike button. 'Roger, FF eight one. Zero thirteen is cleared to land.'

Below the low-winged trainer, mesquite and scrub cedar dotted the ground. Eden lined up her BT-13 with the runway and adjusted her rate of descent. The ground seemed to rush up at her, blurring as she flew lower. Her wheels greased the runway, and the tingle of satisfaction she felt at the textbook-smooth landing was something that couldn't be bought.

As she braked to make the turn onto the taxiway, a voice came over the radio. 'This is Jacqueline Cochran.' Eden was instantly alert. 'I'm coming in for a landing. Clear the area,' the woman's voice ordered.

Eden taxied to the hangar, watching the sky. Planes swung out of the flight path of the stagger-winged Beechcraft approaching the field, climbing to circle at a respectful distance while the director of their women's pilot training program made a straight-in approach.

When the plane touched down, Eden had climbed out of the cockpit and jumped to the ground. After two hours of solo work, her time in the air was finished for the day. Eden made no move to walk to the hangar, waiting instead to greet her famous commanding officer and wondering whether Jacqueline Cochran would remember their meeting at that party the previous December.

With the airfield and the skies above it virtually empty of traffic, Eden couldn't help being amused. Long ago, she had been taught the value of making an entrance. There was no doubt that the director of the Women's Flying Training Detachment had accomplished it in style.

The big plane taxied by her, its propeller nearly touching the concrete. After braking to a stop, the engine was cut. Eden approached the Beechcraft, unconscious of the grime on her face and the ratty pigtails of auburn hair, as the familiar blond aviatrix emerged from the cockpit.

'Hello, Miss Cochran.'

Her greeting barely rated a glance as the director headed toward the hangar. 'Carry this for me.' She tossed a full-length mink coat to Eden.

Eden came to an indignant stop, stunned at being treated as some sort of servant. Outrage bubbled as she looked down at the mink coat in her arms. But she also saw the wrinkled clothes and dusty grime that covered her. She touched a hand to her absurd pigtails and broke into a laugh.

At the sound, Jacqueline Cochran slowed her steps and swung around to regard Eden with a commanding hauteur. 'Do you find something amusing?'

'I just realized my own mother probably wouldn't recognize me,' Eden replied, unabashed.

A finely drawn brow arched in question, creating a furrow in the smooth forehead. 'Have we met?' she asked, then immediately broached an explanation that was polite and aloof, fitting her rank as commander. 'I have interviewed many girls. I can't be expected to remember all their faces. I'm sure you understand that.'

127

'Of course, Miss Cochran.' Their meeting had been memorable to Eden, but it had been merely one of a multitude for the blond aviatrix. 'I'm Eden van Valkenburg. We met last December in New York at a party my parents were giving.'

'Yes, of course.' The significance of the name registered although Eden seriously doubted that Jacqueline Cochran actually remembered her.

And Eden's social equality with her commander had little effect but to temper her supercilious attitude into something a shade more condescending. She turned and headed again toward the hangar, expecting Eden to follow, her strides long and smooth, almost leisurely compared to her previous sweeping rush.

'Tell me, Miss van Valkenburg, how are you getting along?' she asked. 'Any problems or complaints?'

'No.' There was a whole list, from a leaky barracks roof to harassment by a rare few of the instructors, but Eden guessed she didn't really want to hear about it. Still relegated to carrying the mink, she absently burrowed her fingers into the dark fur, stroking its sleek softness and savoring the almost forgotten sensation. 'Besides, Miss Cochran, I've already learned the Army response to complaints is a very simple "That's tough."'

A low, melodic laugh came from Cochran's throat. 'How very true,' she agreed, and paused to face Eden when they reached the hangar. The smile softened her features and harked back to her southern upbringing. The look in her eyes when she studied Eden was both serious and sincere. 'If you ever do have a serious problem, I want you to come directly to me. You, or any of the other girls.'

'Yes, ma'am.' But it made Eden curious about the purpose behind this visit, although she was well aware their director regularly called on the base to check on the operations. 'What brings you here this time, Miss Cochran? Is it just a routine stop?'

'Not quite.' A self-satisfied gleam came into her eyes. 'You girls are going to have more company. We'll be shutting down the Houston operation and moving the entire training program here to Avenger Field. The demand for qualified pilots is outstripping the supply, and more men need to be released for combat duty, which means more women in the air. Houston doesn't have the facilities to allow an expansion, so we're taking over here.'

'The whole field?' Eden stared. The war. She'd almost forgotten about it. Flying, flying, all the time it was flying. The war, it was some remote thing that didn't really mean much to her. Newspapers – who had time to read them? Oh, sure, she knew Marty got letters from her brother, a paratrooper in the 101st Airborne Division stationed in North Carolina, and Mary Lynn heard regularly from her bomber pilot husband in England. She knew it, yet it didn't really touch her.

'The last class of Army cadets will be leaving next week, and we'll move in – lock, stock, and airplanes.' She smiled with a hint of pride. 'I can't stress enough the important contribution you girls will be making, stepping in for the men so they can go off and fight.'

'Yes.'

'I'll take my coat.' The prodding statement snapped Eden out of her reverie.

'Of course.' Unwittingly, she had been clutching the mink so tightly in her arms that the fur was being crushed. She attempted to smooth it with a caressing stroke of her hand while she reluctantly returned it to its owner. 'It's funny. At home I have a mink stole, a mink bolero jacket, and a coat like this, but I'd almost forgotten how soft they feel.'

Jacqueline Cochran took the coat and merely smiled at the comment. 'Good flying,' she said and walked away.

The light from a full moon spilled through the window of the darkened hotel room and cast a diffused glow over the interior. Colin lay in bed on his side, one arm crooked under his head on the pillow while the other rested along his length. The bedsheet covered his hips and left his chest bare, the muscled flesh gleaming pale in the moonlight.

Lying next to him, Marty broke into a mocking song, 'The stahs at night . . . are big and bright . . .' She clapped her hands. '. . . deep in the haht of Texahs!' She had deepened her voice to mimic his earlier singing.

'Enough.' Colin clamped a hand over her mouth to smother any future mangling of the song.

Her shoulders shook with the laughter he smothered. The husky chuckles continued in her throat when she finally pulled his hand down. The sheet slipped, exposing her breasts, but Marty felt no need for false modesty with Colin. His hands and lips had fondled them often. She brought his hand down to the valley shaped by the rise of her breasts, not to be provocative, but simply because it was the natural place to let it rest.

'I can't believe you actually sang that song to the towns-people. It took a helluva lot of nerve.' Her voice continued to croak with humor. 'It's practically been adopted as the national anthem of Texas.'

'I think they were rather pleased by our gesture,' he informed her, the corners of his mouth pulled in, suggesting a smile was lurking somewhere in warning of retribution to come.

'Oh, were they?' Marty mocked him again.

'Yes.' A warm, admiring glint appeared almost reluctantly in his eyes. 'They recognized we were expressing our appreciation for the way they've taken us into their homes –'

'And into their beds,' Marty interrupted.

'Ah, but gentlemen don't speak of such things.'

'How interesting.' Marty turned her head to get a better look at him. 'What do gentlemen speak about?'

'Other things,' he said. He withdrew his hand from beneath the slightly pinning weight of her hands and reached up to smooth the toasted gold strands of her hair against the white pillowcase. He curled the end of a lock around his finger, testing its silkiness. 'Your eyes remind me of the color of the water in the English Channel.' A certain drollness touched his mouth. 'I expect I'll be taking a dunking in it sooner or later. I'll write and let you know if it's the same shade up close.'

'I wish I could go in your place.' More than once when she was out flying alone, Marty had wondered what it would be like to be locked in the throes of an aerial dogfight.

But it was an experience she was denied, because she had the misfortune to be born female. She was allowed to make brief forays into the male world, but only with its permission. It had always rankled her to see how much more her brother, David, could experience and do than she could. It wasn't fair. Right now he was in training at Fort Bragg, jumping out of airplanes as one of the 'Screaming Eagles' – the 101st Airborne Division.

'I'll bet you do.' Colin chuckled and rolled onto his back, smiling at the shadow patterns on the ceiling.

With a turning lift of her body, Marty propped herself up on one elbow, facing him. The sheet slid down to her waist. 'I suppose you think I couldn't do it.'

'You? You could probably be the Joan of Arc of the skies, the warrior maiden with wings,' Colin retorted smoothly and caught her hand, carrying it to his mouth to kiss the center of her palm. His look became slightly serious as he gazed at her. 'I'm going to miss you, Marty. I didn't expect to say that, but it's true.'

'Please, let's don't get all sloppy and sentimental and spoil everything,' she urged.

'I'm not. I promise you.' He turned his lazy, smiling glance on her. 'No emotional entanglements for either of us – just good friendship. But I will miss you all the same.'

She leaned down to kiss his mouth. 'I'm going to miss you, too. These last weeks have been fun.'

The hanging fullness of her breasts invited the caress of his hands. Colin cupped the weight of one in his hand and rubbed his thumb back and forth across the hardening nipple.

'You're a rare one, Marty,' he declared. 'I doubt I shall

ever have the good fortune to meet a woman like you again.'

'We've been damned good together, haven't we?' She stroked the ridge of his shoulder with her fingers. 'I'm glad we've had this last time together for – what shall I call it? – our farewell fuck?'

Laughter rumbled from deep within as Colin caught her by the waist and twisted her back onto the mattress while he hovered above her. A wide, laughing grin split his face.

'Has anybody ever told you that you have a definite way with words?' he chuckled. 'You cut right through all the drivel and get straight to the heart of it.'

Her hands slid down his torso and under the sheets, gliding over his pelvic bones and continuing downward into the springy nest of hairs. 'In that case . . .' Marty peered at him through her lashes with deliberate provocation while her fingers deftly encouraged his hardening with caressing strokes. '. . . why has there been so much conversation tonight, and so little action?'

'Is that right?' Colin asked with a deepening smile. His hand pushed at the bend of her knee to open her legs, then he filled the opening with his body and lowered himself onto her. 'Well, if it's fucking you want, babe, it's fucking you shall get,' he promised in a voice husky with affection and desire.

Her hand cupped the back of his head to drag his mouth down onto hers. Marty kissed him, secure in the mutual respect and admiration they shared. Theirs was a caring relationship in which neither would be hurt. Marty sought nothing deeper than that, and, for once, she had found a man who wanted the same. Yes, she would miss him.

Later, the big April moon rode high in the sky, silvering the landscape and silhouetting the two, who faced each other outside the gates to Avenger Field. Marty gazed thoughtfully into the eyes of the lanky airman.

'I probably won't have a chance to see you again before we leave,' he said.

'I know.' There were no tears, just a twinge of regret at

the necessity of parting. As there was no need for tears, there was also no need for clinging embraces or a flood of words. Yet some final gesture, some appropriate remark, some hint of contact seemed to be required. After a long minute's pause, Marty offered him her hand. 'Good flying, Colin.'

He took it, gripped it warmly, and smiled. 'Same to you, Marty.'

CHAPTER EIGHT

In straight lines, the column of baggy-suited trainees marched toward the flight line. Out of step, Chicago skipped to get back into stride with the others while the section marcher called out the cadence.

'Hup, two, hree, hor. Hup. Hup.'

Someone started the singing, picking out the tune to 'Bell-Bottom Trousers.' It had become routine to sing while they marched. And they had a whole medley of songs to which they'd made up their own lyrics.

> Zoot suits and parachutes
> And wings of silver, too.
> He'll ferry planes like
> His mamma used to do!

While they were singing the fourth and last verse to the song, Marty noticed the formation of Army BT-13 aircraft approaching the field from the south. She missed the line about never trusting 'a pilot an inch above your knee' as she watched the basic trainers peel out of formation to enter the traffic pattern.

By the time they reached the flight line, everyone in the column had noticed the outsider planes preparing to land at their field. The column broke up and waited in front of the ready room for the arriving planes.

'It must be the Houston trainees,' Cappy said, the five of them grouped together again. 'I heard they were getting to fly their BTs here so they could have a taste of cross-country flying.'

'What an experience that must have been,' Marty grumbled with envy.

One by one, the planes roared in, the pilots showing off with their wheel-greasing touchdowns. 'I'll bet they think they're something.' No one disputed Marty's disparaging comment as the planes taxied up to the flight line and the women trainees tumbled out. They all unconsciously disassociated themselves from the arriving trainees, even though they were members of the same class, trained at different fields.

The invasion of strange faces wasn't at all like the arrival of the new trainees a couple weeks ago. Those had been novices, under-classmen so to speak, but these women were their equals, the other half of 43-W-3. While Houston had been the site where the women's flight training program had begun, with the very first two classes remaining there to complete their training, the Sweetwater half of the third class had been the first occupants of Avenger Field. They had a proprietary feeling toward it. Now they were expected to share it with strangers – outsiders. A sense of rivalry was inevitable.

Jimmy Ray Price, Cappy's instructor in the basic training phase, paused alongside their group, giving them a glowering, long-jawed look. 'Ya better quit gawkin' and get yourselves into the ready room. You're here to fly. Remember?'

Dragging their attention away from the tired but ecstatic Houston trainees greeting each other on the ground after their long flight, Cappy, Eden, Mary Lynn and Chicago filed into the ready room with the rest of their flight group. The flying side of them wanted to know what it had been like to make that cross-country trip from Houston to

Sweetwater, yet there was also a matter of pride which made it difficult to admit the Houston trainees had done something they hadn't. Besides, all the cliques were already formed, so that didn't leave much room for outsiders.

While the Houston group went through the orientation process at Avenger Field, the Inseparables flew with their instructors, getting in more instrument practice. The new arrivals were nowhere around when they landed, but their BT-13s were parked by the hangar, evidence of their presence on the base.

They were called into formation and marched to their barracks, then dismissed. They fell out of formation in a chatter of voices, disassembling and assembling into bay groups.

'It was really a sight to see – those two formations of planes barreling through the sky,' Chicago declared to the others.

The door to the bay was pulled open and they began filing through. Mary Lynn didn't notice the pile-up ahead of her and ran right into Cappy's back. Behind her the door swung shut, hitting her in the rump.

'Hey, what's going on?' she protested.

There at the back of the group with all their bodies blocking her view, Mary Lynn couldn't see what was causing all this consternation. Finally, Marty, who had been the dam-block, moved, and Mary Lynn saw a tall, slim woman sleeping on the far cot that Eden had once occupied. Her shoulder-length hair was a pale shade of blond, all touseled and mussed.

'What the hell is she doing here?' Marty wondered in a stunned outrage.

Her gruffness caused Mary Lynn to snicker behind her smothering hand. At the accusing look she received from Marty, she explained, 'This sounds like Goldilocks and Who's been sleeping in my bed.'

No one else seemed amused by her analogy. Mary Lynn decided they hadn't read that particular bedtime story as many times as she had, or they would have seen the humor

135

in it. For the moment, however, they were intent on the stranger in their midst.

'She's probably one of the trainees from Houston,' Cappy guessed as they drifted toward the cot.

'Well, that doesn't explain what the hell she's doing here.' Marty purposefully stalked to the cot and roughly shook the woman's shoulder. 'Wake up, Goldilocks.'

A violent toss of the arm threw off Marty's grip and a female voice snarled, 'Leave me alone.'

'Just what the hell do you think you're doing here?' Marty appeared incensed at the opposition she was getting as she hovered beside the cot.

This time the blond head moved a fraction. 'Sleeping. What the hell does it look like?'

'All right, *who* are you?' Marty challenged with hot sarcasm.

'One damned tired Woofted.' The woman made an attempt to burrow deeper into the cot and huddle into a smaller ball.

'A Woofted,' Marty repeated, then looked blankly at the others, still sarcastic. 'She's a Woofted, whatever the hell that is.'

The woman on the cot appeared to give up. In long, fluid moves she sat up on the edge of the narrow Amy bed, her shoulders bowing in tired lines and her head drooping with weariness. But there was plenty of fight in her voice, and her eyes were so violet as to appear almost purple-black.

'Women's Flying Training Detachment, stupid,' she said to Marty. 'Woofteds. W-F-T-D, Woofteds, that's what we call ourselves.'

'Woofteds, I should have guessed,' Marty said mockingly. 'We go by a much simpler term – trainees.'

The blonde raked Marty with a scathing glance. 'It figures.'

Marty was ready to claw those unusually dark eyes out of her head, but Cappy stepped in. 'Would you mind telling us what you're doing here?' Her tone had an authoritative ring, which didn't appear to sit any better with their Houston counterpart.

'I was assigned to this bay and this cot. Believe me, I don't like it any better than you do,' she stated flatly.

'I suppose the place isn't good enough for you,' Marty retorted.

'As a matter of fact, this place is the Taj Mahal compared to some of the living quarters we had in Houston. We lived in moldy, bug-infested tourist courts before they finally got barracks built for us. The food they served us was fit only for the garbage can. They finally installed a rest room. Before that, the nearest one was half a mile away. We wore the same clothes from dawn to dusk, because there was no place to change, so we walked around all day, dusty, dirty, and stinking with our own sweat.' Her sweeping glance encompassed all of them. 'You don't know how good this place is.'

'Isn't it wonderful, girls?' Marty piped sarcastically. 'Now we have our own resident expert. Instead of our parents telling us how rough *they* had it, we have a Woofted.'

'You don't like me and I don't like you,' the woman informed Marty. 'Let's leave it at that. Now I happen to have flown practically across the whole state of Texas, so if you don't mind, I'd like to get some rest.'

Marty backed away from the cot in mock deference. 'Forgive us for disturbing you. Just because this happens to be our bay it's really of little consequence. Why should we care who's sleeping in it?'

'Rachel Goldman from New York. Do you feel better?' she said sarcastically.

'New York,' Chicago repeated and nodded toward Eden. 'Eden's from New York, too.'

'Yeah?' She eyed the redhead, sizing her up with a wary, yet interested look.

'We live on Fifth Avenue just across from the park at Seventy-fifth,' Eden volunteered.

'Well, I'm from the Lower East Side,' she said and began

shifting in preparation to lie down again. She had slapped away the friendly hand that had belatedly been extended to her. Again, she stretched her long, feline body on the cot, and turned her back to them. In her stockinged feet, she missed being six feet tall by a fraction of an inch, so there wasn't much room left at either end of the cot.

Slowly they all moved toward their own Army cots, unsettled by this sudden intrusion of a stranger among them. The five of them had been a complete unit; they hadn't needed or wanted another.

'Someone probably had the bright idea of integrating the two classes,' Cappy suggested in an undertone.

'Well, it stinks!' Marty declared.

Mary Lynn winced at the loudness of her friend's remark. 'Marty, keep it down,' she advised quietly. 'She's trying to sleep.'

'So? I'm not going to tiptoe around here because of her!' Marty belligerently made no attempt to lower her voice, but the figure on the cot didn't appear to care.

It wasn't that Rachel Goldman was not used to defending herself. She had the sharp claws required to do it. They had been honed over the years of being picked on. As a Jew, she had often been made to feel unwanted, the victim of subtle persecutions and sometimes not so subtle ones.

There were only two things that had ever enabled her to escape, even briefly, from that. Dancing and flying. Despite her natural talent and years of training, there simply weren't many male dancers capable of lifting a six-foot ballerina, and her height made it equally difficult to get a job on a Broadway chorus line. So, mostly she had worked in nightclubs as a showgirl.

The first time Rachel had ever been in an airplane, it had been a transatlantic flight to Austria to visit her grandmother in Vienna. Of course, that was years ago, before Austria was occupied, when Hitler was merely a pompous-sounding fanatic, spouting his theories about the master race.

She'd spent a glorious month with her grandmother.

After corresponding for so many years, first at her parents' insistence, then because her grandmother seemed to really understand her love for the classic theater. Her grandmother had been wardrobe mistress at the Vienna opera house. At first, communicating was difficult; her grandmother's English was not good. Rachel's Yiddish was equally faulty, and her German nonexistent.

She had been fresh from flight when they met, enthralled with the sensation of it. She had talked about the experience for days on end until her grandmother had finally proclaimed, 'If you love flying so much, learn to do it yourself.' That, unfortunately, required lessons, which required money, and Rachel already had a big investment in dance.

Her parents had never been enthusiastic about her theatrical career, but her grandmother's support had always swayed the balance. When it came to flying, they had been even less thrilled to let their daughter try it. 'Marry, settle down, raise children. Forget all this nonsense,' her mother had urged. But Rachel had preferred her grandmother's advice. Ultimately, her parents had thrown up their hands, and Rachel had earned her own money for the flying lessons.

Along the way, she had learned some things, some bitter truths. If you want to be accepted outside your own community, don't be Jewish; if you want to get a job in a nightclub, don't look Jewish; if you want friends and lovers outside your faith, don't act Jewish. In some circles, it was even claimed the Jews were responsible for starting the war so they could profit from it. Some of the things 'Lucky Lindy,' Charles Lindbergh, had said still made Rachel cringe when she thought about them.

Since that awful day in 1938 when Austria was virtually handed over to Hitler on a platter, communication with her grandmother had become sporadic. A letter smuggled out of Europe by a fleeing family shortly after Warsaw fell was the last her family had had. Later came the vague stories of persecution, properties confiscated, arrests, roundups, then the work camps – some said death camps.

Way back in the beginning her father's group had lobbied Congress and the State Department in Washington to allow more Jewish refugees into the country. Hitler had offered to send the Jews to whatever country would take them, but almost no one had accepted – not even the United States.

Bitter – yes, she was bitter. And she hated, too, with a passion that would have made the Zealots proud of her. So when she had slapped away the one friendly overture made by Eden, it had been with the wariness of a cat many times burned, who now circled the beckoning flames but stayed well away from the warmth. Rachel's features had a hardened look to them that suggested all of her twenty-six years hadn't been easy ones. But Rachel was wiry and tough – a survivor. And right now, she needed a cat's short sleep.

The following day the last class of Army cadets left Avenger Field, Colin Fletcher among them. Just as their daily schedules had been regimented to keep the cadets separated from the trainees, so it was with their departure. The girls had no opportunity to wish them 'good luck and good flying.' They never actually saw the cadets leave. They were simply gone.

After an afternoon on the flight line, they returned to the bay to shower and change before evening mess. The vacant barracks across from theirs seemed faceless and forlorn. There had always been that underlying excitement of knowing men slept just across the way. Now that presence was gone, and with it, the little forbidden thrills it had conjured. The bays wouldn't be occupied until the next class of female trainees arrived in a couple of weeks.

'I'm going to miss those guys.' Chicago sent a glance in the direction of the opposite barracks as she opened the door to their bay.

'Yeah,' Eden agreed. 'No more late night visits from Colin and his cohorts. No more conversation by flashlight.'

Halfway through the doorway, Cappy stopped and bent to pick up a note lying on the floor.

'What is it?' Marty crowded ahead of Mary Lynn and Chicago.

'It's a note.' Cappy's curiosity was aroused as she moved into the long room and studied the small envelope in her hand. 'Addressed to all of us,' she added with a sweeping look.

'I'll bet it's from Colin. Hurry up and read it, Cap,' Marty urged impatiently, unzipping her flight suit the rest of the way down.

The connecting door to the bath facilities opened and the new baymate, Rachel Goldman, came in. Fresh from the shower, she was wrapped in a long blue chenille robe. Her wet hair had a silvery look to it as she rubbed the dripping ends with a towel. There was a slight break in her motion when she saw the five of them, then she continued toweling her hair dry as she walked to her cot.

Cappy removed the feather-thin note paper from the envelope, effectively directing the group's attention to it. 'It's from Colin, Grimsby, and the rest,' she said after a quick glance at the signatures at the bottom of the short message. 'We wanted to thank you' – she read – 'for all the nights you made less lonely for us, and for the warm memories we will be taking with us. Mary Lynn, we promise we'll keep an eye out for your Beau if we get to merry old England. We'll hope he understands when we give him your love.'

'Those rats,' Marty interposed with a chuckling laugh.

'They wouldn't?' Mary Lynn wasn't sure whether to laugh or not. No one answered her.

'To prove we aren't four-flushers, not by half, we have left one last treat for you to enjoy, a last cup of kindness.' A frown creased Cappy's forehead as she and the others tried puzzling out the meaning. 'Since we couldn't say goodbye to you, we won't say it now. Just "Good flying." . . . Signed, Colin, Arthur, Morley, and Henry.'

'What last treat?' Chicago asked, as they all looked

around the bay to see if something had been left – a package or a box. There was nothing in sight.

'Hey, Goldman?' Marty called, somewhat combatively. 'When you came in, was there anything sitting out here?'

'It'd still be there if it was,' she retorted.

'I'll bet they've hidden it somewhere,' Eden surmised. She gazed about the room for a logical hiding place.

"'A cup of kindness' . . . you drink it for Auld Lang Syne.' Distracted by Eden's musings, Marty started putting pieces together. 'You don't suppose?' she began, then a gleam of an idea spread the beginnings of a grin across her mouth. 'Half of a four-flusher – I think I know where they put it. Come on.'

'Where they put what?' A bewildered Mary Lynn followed the group, led by Marty, as they charged into the bathroom.

Marty went straight for the two stalls, unoccupied at the moment. She lifted the tank lid of the first commode, but it was the second one which contained the bottle of bonded whiskey. She held up the wet bottle in triumph while the others gathered around her.

'I can't believe it.' Eden almost fondled the bottle of aged liquor. 'Who did they bribe to get this?'

'How did they smuggle it in here – that's what I'd like to know,' Cappy murmured.

'Who cares?' Marty replied.

'But if we get caught with it on base, we're automatically thrown out of the program.' Mary Lynn saw nothing to rejoice about in that.

'That's true,' Marty agreed, but there was a wild sparkle in her olive-gray eyes. 'We don't have a whole lot of choice, girls,' she said. 'We'll just have to drink the evidence.'

Mary Lynn was the only one skeptical of the solution; the rest heartily endorsed the plan. Chicago was dispatched for a round of Cokes. Half of each bottle was poured down the sink to make room for the whiskey. In a conspiratorial huddle, they re-entered the bay carrying their spiked

Cokes. The capped whiskey bottle was tucked inside Marty's flight suit.

As they passed Rachel's cot, Marty nudged Chicago and stopped. In their absence, Rachel had dressed in slacks and a blouse. The thick mass of her blond hair was nearly dry.

'Thirsty, Goldman?' With a wide-eyed look of absolute innocence, Marty extended the extra Coke bottle to her, seemingly in a peace offering. 'You're welcome to drink this. Mary Lynn didn't want it.'

On the verge of refusing, Rachel appeared to reconsider and wavered for a skeptical minute before wanly accepting the bottle. 'Thanks.'

'Cheers.' Marty lifted her own bottle in a mock toast and watched with barely disguised glee as Rachel tilted the bottle to her mouth to take a swig of the Coke.

A second later, Rachel was choking on burning whiskey, coughing and spitting up the liquid her convulsing throat muscles refused to swallow. Despite her cupping hand, some of the liquid dribbled onto the clean blouse she'd just put on.

They all tittered with laughter, even Mary Lynn. Rachel Goldman was the only one who didn't see the humor in the prank. Anger glittered in her indigo-violet eyes as she shoved the bottle back into Marty's hand.

'Very funny.' Her voice still rasped on the edge of a coughing spasm.

'We thought so.' Marty's voice naturally matched the sound. 'The drink's yours, if you want it.' She offered her the Coke again. 'Mary Lynn doesn't drink anything but mint juleps.'

'Keep it.' Her look swept them all with contempt. 'You might have come here to party, but I'm here to fly.'

As Rachel stalked from the bay, Marty quirked an eyebrow, unperturbed by the denunciation. 'Little Mary Lynn isn't the only tee-totaler in our midst.'

Chicago looked apprehensively after their departing baymate. 'What if she reports us?'

'She won't,' Eden replied coolly. 'She wouldn't dare.' The implied threat in her remark was unmistakable.

'Here's to our guys.' Marty lifted her glass. 'May they never drink the water in the Channel.'

By the time lights out came, the 'evidence' had been consumed and the bottle was broken into non-incriminating pieces. All that remained of the label was a charred, curled mass of ashes. None of them had gotten drunk; they had more sense than that. But they slept deeply and soundly that night.

Too soundly. They missed reveille. And if Rachel Goldman hadn't yelled at them as she was heading out the door, they would have missed breakfast formation. Heavy-eyed, they staggered into line and tried to shake off the drugged sensation of sleep. They looked at Rachel, so alert and impassive, with a mixture of gratitude and resentment.

Outside morning mess, they dawdled to grumble before joining the cafeteria line. But the aroma of freshly made doughnuts invigorated their senses.

'I'd kill for them,' Marty declared as she piled four of them onto her tray.

As they reached the end of the line, Chicago stopped. 'Look. They've taken our table.'

Stunned by the announcement, they stared at the far end of the long table they had occupied since their very first meal at the base.

Part of the Houston class, including Rachel, was now seated in the space they considered reserved for them. Others in their class had always respected their right to it.

'I'll handle this,' Eden asserted and strode to the front, leading them across the room to the table. Their arrival barely rated a glance. 'Excuse me. This is our section.' Her cool hauteur implied all would be forgiven if they would vacate immediately – a tone guaranteed to make a *maître d'* bow, very low.

'What's your name?' Helen Shaw, a doe-eyed woman with a set of dimples carved in her cheeks, asked the question.

144

'Van Valkenburg. Eden van Valkenburg.' The self-importance was evident.

'Funny.' The woman looked around the table. 'I don't see your name anywhere.' The others in her group laughed to themselves.

A tremor of anger stiffened Eden. 'Very funny indeed,' she retorted. 'This happens to be our table. We have always sat here in this corner.'

'I guess you'll have to find another place this morning,' Rachel stated. 'Because this one is already occupied.'

Marty pushed her way to the forefront. 'You wanna bet, cookie?' she threatened.

'Forget it.' Cappy laid a restraining hand on Marty's arm.

'Why should we forget it?' Marty shook it off. 'We were here first. They're the ones who don't belong.'

'I think you have that turned around,' Rachel coldly corrected her. 'Maybe you came to Sweetwater before we did, but the Houston classes before you pioneered this whole program. We Woofteds were the guinea pigs.'

'That makes you something special, I suppose,' Marty answered mockingly.

Their dispute was attracting the attention of the other trainees in the room. Cappy could tell the Houston group would vacate the table only through force. There was no diplomatic solution to the situation.

'Come on, Marty,' she urged quietly. 'You can't afford any more demerits.' For the time being, they had to retreat.

But the battle lines were drawn. Possession of the table became the symbolic center of their dispute. Eden, Marty, Cappy, and the others regarded the Houston class as interlopers on the base, while their Houston counterparts saw themselves as heir apparents of the very first classes in the pilot training program for women.

What had begun as a personality conflict in the bay between Rachel and Marty became part of a larger rivalry. The Sweetwater half of the class assumed a proprietary attitude toward everything on the base, and the Houston half contested it.

Having Rachel in their bay made the situation more awkward. An armed truce existed; her presence was tentatively accepted. But for Marty it was a case of accepting under strong protest.

CHAPTER NINE

The day was glorious; sun-drenched skies stretched lazily to the flat horizons. On the ground the air was hot and dry, but at four thousand feet it was pleasantly warm. Bored with her solo practice of the requisite maneuvers, Eden decided to play a little aerial hooky and enjoy some of this afternoon sunshine.

She pushed open the canopy of her BT-13 to let in the day. In preparation, Eden trimmed the aircraft until it was practically flying itself. The skies around her were empty and blue when she unbuttoned her blouse and shrugged out of it, taking care not to bump the stick held between her knees.

The lacy brassiere supporting her breasts was one of those 'nothing' creations that barely covered her rose-brown nipples. It was designed to be worn under garments with plunging necklines, but Eden had found the flimsy and scanty bra ideal since its softness never chafed and its brevity allowed more freedom of movement. It was also perfect for sun-bathing.

With her blouse neatly folded and tucked behind her, Eden leaned back and closed her eyes against the sun shining on her face. The enveloping warmth was blissfully relaxing. The pleasant heat seemed to caress her bare skin; it was so soothing and sensuous. She basked in the cockpit, unconcerned, listening to the reassuring level pitch of the engine and the steady rush of air spilling over her aircraft.

Suddenly, a roaring noise intruded. Eden opened her eyes to scan her instruments, but her side vision caught the

146

reflection of sunlight on metal off her left wing. Another trainer was flying beside her, piloted by a grinning cadet. With a sudden shock, Eden realized he had a clear view inside the cockpit of her trainer and the lace brassiere revealed much more than it concealed.

She ducked lower, trying to make herself small, and banked the plane away from him. She had expected his pursuit, but she hadn't counted on the additional support he picked up. Within minutes, it seemed, she was surrounded by a swarm of buzzing aircraft, all vying for a glimpse inside her cockpit.

Her usually unshakable poise was fast forsaking her. Desperate, Eden tried to hold the plane steady with her knees while she struggled with her blouse. The whipping wind kept tugging at it and defying her efforts to find the opening of the sleeves. She had to keep grabbing the stick to straighten the erratic weaving of the airplane. Suddenly, the wind tore the blouse from her hands. She tried to grab it before it went sailing over the top of the canopy but failed. She swore she could hear the surrounding pilots cheer at the sight.

Hot with embarrassment, Eden crouched low in the cockpit and swung her plane into a steep turn, making a mad dash for the 'off-limits' safety of Avenger Field. As she neared her destination, one by one the pursuing aircraft peeled away.

Touchdown signaled the end of that ordeal and the start of another. With all the mechanics and instructors on the flight line, how on earth was she going to make a dignified exit from the plane when she was half naked?

Sneaking looks, Eden taxied to the hangar area and shut the plane down. When she peered cautiously out the side, she noticed a group of trainees in front of the ready room. Swallowing a big chunk of pride, she called to them. 'Hey! Will one of you bring me a jacket or something?' She risked one more look to see if they had heard her, then ducked back down.

In short order, someone was climbing the wing of her

trainer. As a shadow fell across her cockpit, Eden looked up with relief. Her expression froze into a kind of stiffness when she found herself looking into the almond-shaped eyes of Rachel Goldman. Any hope she'd had that this humiliating incident could be kept quiet died.

Later, in the bay after evening mess, Eden fumed at the unfairness of it. 'It was bad enough that it had to be one of those damned "Woofteds," but Rachel?!' she ranted to the barely disguised but sympathetic amusement of her four baymates. 'You should have seen the way she gloated when she handed me that blanket.'

'At least she gave you the blanket,' Mary Lynn pointed out. 'Come on, Eden, you have to admit there's some humor in it.' Marty had seen the regal redhead when she crossed the flight line, swathed in the blanket as if it was some royal robe, her head held unnaturally high and her cheeks flaming. If Eden hadn't already been the butt of all the Woofteds' comments, Marty would have poked some fun at Eden herself.

'Oh, it's very funny,' she returned sarcastically. 'On top of everything, that blouse happened to be one of my favorites. It cost the earth, too! Now some mesquite brush is probably wearing it.'

As Rachel entered the bay, there was an instant silence. The tall, supple blonde moved into the room, a catlike gleam in her dark amethyst eyes as they swept over Eden.

'How's the sunburn?' she queried maliciously.

'I don't have one.' Eden pushed the sweetly voiced comment through her clenched teeth.

'Really? Your face seemed very pink at mess tonight,' Rachel replied with feline slyness. 'I thought for sure it was because you had too much sun today.'

Eden found herself caught in one of those irritating moments when she wanted to make some really scathing response, but her mind deserted her. She simply couldn't think of anything. It would come in the middle of the night, when it was too late.

A new facet was added to the instrument-flying phase of their basic training when the trainees were informed they would be flying with a 'buddy' of their choice. The pairing was almost a natural selection. Mary Lynn and Marty elected to fly together while Cappy and Eden teamed up to make a unit, and Chicago paired up with Jo Ann North, a fellow trainee from the adjoining bay.

As they walked to their BT-13, Cappy thought nothing about the arrangement until she was strapped into the rear cockpit seat. Then the jitters shook her. All her instrument time under the black hood had been under the supervision of her instructor. Now she would have to trust Eden to correct any mistake she might make and to keep watch for any aircraft in their immediate vicinity to avoid a midair collision. She was literally trusting Eden with her life.

After taking off, Eden flew the plane to the designated practice area. Cappy fought the flutterings of unease in her stomach when Eden volunteered to go first. While the black curtain was being pulled in place, Cappy took the controls. As soon as Eden was ready, she surrendered them to her again.

Nervously, Cappy scanned the instruments and the skies around their plane, and kept an eye on the attitude of the aircraft's nose to the horizon while Eden practiced turns, descents, and climbs. She felt a strange urge to override the controls before Eden could unwittingly put the plane in a dangerous attitude where it might stall and spin out, but gradually, Cappy came to recognize her buddy's competence. Instrument flying was a precise skill, requiring the utmost in concentration. A calm began to settle her raw nerves as Cappy saw that Eden could fly as well as she could.

When it came time to switch, Cappy pulled the hood over herself without any reservation. She was confident of Eden's ability in an emergency. It was a rare experience to place her life in someone else's hands – to rely on another to keep her safe – yet that's exactly what she was doing. What's more, it filled her with an elated kind of relief.

149

After that first flight when they tumbled out of the aircraft, they looked at each other with new eyes. 'Has anybody ever told you you can fly, Hayward?' Eden remarked with a hint of amazement.

'So can you,' she replied.

A second later, they were laughing and companionably hooking an arm across each other's shoulder as they headed back to the ready room. Cappy felt near to tears. These last weeks they had eaten together, studied together, griped together, and shared the same sleeping quarters, but nothing had forged the closeness she now felt. It was respect and admiration, coupled with a hard-won trust.

Spring storms raised havoc with the flying schedules. The trainees were forced to fly when the weather permitted in order to get their required time in the air, which meant they gave up most of their April Sundays.

In May, the base command was thrown into a turmoil by the news that General George C. Marshall, Chief of Staff of the United States Army, as well as General Henry 'Hap' Arnold, Commanding General of the United States Army Air Forces, would be visiting Avenger Field on an inspection tour. The rumor of their impending arrival swept the barracks like a fire storm.

'I don't understand what all the fuss is about,' Eden shrugged, unimpressed by their titles.

'The Commanding General of the Air Forces and the Chief of Staff, no less. How blasé can you get?' Marty threw her arms in the air in a show of exasperation.

'You have to talk to Eden in terms that she understands,' Cappy said, good-naturedly ribbing her friend. 'You see, it's like this, Eden. Generals expect to review the troops – and we don't have a thing to wear.'

'What do you mean?' Eden asked cautiously.

'While the government was issuing us our battle jackets and zoot suits, they failed to include a Class A – in civilian terms, a dress uniform,' Cappy explained.

'Can you see us parading past the reviewing stand in our fatigues?' Mary Lynn laughed.

For the rest of the week, rumors abounded that frantic phone calls were being made to obtain a standard outfit for all the trainees. A short three days before the generals were to appear, the outfits, consisting of tan slacks, short-sleeved white blouses, and boat-shaped flight caps, arrived. Alterations had to be made in order to ensure proper length and fit, and with so little time left, the girls had to do it themselves. They were all in a mad rush to get it done.

Perched on her cot, Eden struggled with a needle and thread, trying to hem the legs of her tan slacks. The tip of her tongue was poked out the corner of her mouth, a study of concentration, as if facial contortions could assist the wayward needle.

'Ouch!' She jabbed herself in the thumb and quickly raised the injured finger to her mouth to suck on it.

Exasperation was showing in her expression as she studied the wound for any red dots of blood. Her bay-mates, all busy with their own alterations, barely gave her more than an amused grunt.

'My thumb has more holes in it than a pincushion,' Eden announced bitterly, then looked at the slacks on her lap. No more than a half-dozen stitches had been sewn. Yet, for all her painstaking care, they were irregular and uneven. In disgust, she tossed the pants aside and swung off the cot. 'This is ridiculous. I have no business taking a needle and thread in my hands. I've never done any sewing in my life and I'm not about to start now.'

'There aren't any maids here,' Marty reminded her dryly, struggling with her own ineptitude at anything more than the cursory sewing of a button on a blouse.

'Somebody has got to help me,' Eden insisted and looked around the room for a candidate, but all heads were bowed over their own tasks. She zeroed in on Mary Lynn, the only one of their group who had any skill with a needle. 'Mary Lynn?'

'I'd do it for you but I have to finish my own.' Mary Lynn's work entailed a major alteration of the waistline, length, and hips in order for the slacks to properly fit her petite frame.

At the hint of possibly forthcoming assistance, Eden crossed to Mary Lynn's cot to press her appeal. 'Please,' she urged. 'I'll pay you five dollars. Ten.'

'Don't say anything, Mary Lynn,' Marty advised. 'Maybe she'll make it fifteen.'

'Fifteen, twenty – I don't care,' Eden declared impatiently. 'These pants legs practically drag the ground. I'll stick out like a sore thumb.' The remark reminded Eden of her many-times poked thumb and she made another biting suck on it.

They all looked sympathetic to her problem and slightly amused by it, too. Then, from the last cot, an unexpected offer was made. 'If you want, I'll hem them for you.'

They had been for so long in the habit of ignoring the sixth member of their bay that when Rachel Goldman reluctantly offered to help, initially they could only stare at her. The ongoing feud between the two factions prompted Eden to question the offer before she jumped at it.

'Can you sew?' She retrieved her pants from the cot and warily approached Rachel, who was putting the finishing touches on her own slacks.

'My grandmother taught me.' With a series of dexterous flicks of the wrist, the needle flashed through the cloth. Rachel tied the thread in a knot, and bit the thread in two with her teeth. Eden was impressed with the entire process.

But her skepticism returned when Rachel, having neatly folded her slacks by the creases and laid them aside, reached for Eden's. She held on to them. 'Why are you doing this for me?' She had absolutely no reason to trust Rachel.

'For *you*?' The pronoun was stressed with contempt. 'I personally don't care how you look, but we march in the same squad, and I'm not going to have you drag all of us down because you look like a sad sack of shit.'

The response made perfect sense, but Eden's mouth thinned just the same as she handed over her slacks. 'They're already marked for the proper length.'

After surrendering the pants, Eden stayed by the cot to watch, playing it safe. With her shoulders pressed against the wall and one leg bent while the other braced her, Eden folded her arms in front of her. She kept an eye on the darting needle as it stitched the thread with precision. Her own proven ineptitude gave her a greater appreciation of the skill.

'Is your grandmother a seamstress in New York?' She considered passing the information to her mother. It could be worth knowing, especially now that no more designs were coming out of occupied Paris.

'No.' The sylphlike blonde didn't let her attention stray from her work.

'Where does she work?' Eden stubbornly persisted in the quest for information, mostly to irritate the uncommunicative Rachel.

'Vienna.'

The answer sounded so preposterous, Eden laughed. 'You're kidding?'

The blond head lifted, and those intensely violet eyes, like pansies with black centers, focused on Eden with cold challenge. 'She was the wardrobe lady for the opera company there.' She returned to her sewing.

Sobering, Eden realized that Rachel was serious. 'Was?' she said with a slight frown.

'My grandmother is in one of the Nazi work camps in Poland.' Rachel didn't look up.

The others had been listening in on the conversation. Rachel's last remark roused Mary Lynn's curiosity. 'What's this about work camps? I don't remember hearing anything about them before.'

'From what I've read, they're Hitler's version of our detention camps for Japanese,' Eden replied, then belatedly turned to Rachel. 'Isn't that right?'

'Maybe they look alike,' Rachel conceded derisively.

'Both have high barbed-wire fences and guards with dogs and machine guns. But the Jews who have escaped have told us they go there to die. The ones that don't starve to death, the Nazis slaughter.'

'That's absurd,' Marty scoffed from the other end of the room.

'Why?' Rachel was quick to challenge. 'In the last two thousand years, many countries have made some kind of attempt to do away with the Jews. Why should it come as any surprise that Hitler intends to try?'

'I think you're taking an extreme view,' Eden suggested.

'I am?' Her needle seemed to fly more swiftly in and out of the material, stabbing and surging. 'What do you call the White Shirts, the Lindberghs, the Henry Fords? What about Father Coughlin and his Christian Front? Or didn't you hear about the attacks on Jewish school children after the Irish Evacuation Day exercises in Boston just two months ago in March? Don't you think their anti-Semitic views are extreme?'

Her impassioned words prompted Cappy to inject some calm and reason in the heated air. 'Eden never meant to offend you.'

'No one ever does.' Her voice was quieter, flatter. 'Jews just make a good scapegoat. You can take all your fears and frustration out on us; blame the Jews for the Depression, the war – everything.'

At the end of her bitter words, there was an awkward silence. Her head remained bent to her task. Uncomfortable, Eden watched Rachel's hands and avoided the blonde's face.

'I'm sorry,' Eden voiced the feeling in the room, the phrase seeming inadequate.

'Being sorry is worthless.' A knot was tied and the thread was broken with a small snap. Then Rachel lifted her glance to Eden. 'When I was a little girl, I remember listening to my father during his morning prayers. One of the Old Testament verses he sometimes recited said, "Blessed art Thou, O Lord our God, King of the universe, who hast not made me a woman." l used to be sorry I was a girl because there were so many things I couldn't do. Being sorry doesn't change anything. If I can't be a soldier and fight the Germans, then I'll fly planes so a man can go. In my own way, I'll fight.'

'We all will,' Mary Lynn agreed in a low, tight voice.

Rachel handed Eden the finished pants. 'Thanks,' Eden said as she took them from her. Rachel's hand remained outstretched.

'Ten dollars is what you said you would pay,' Rachel reminded her coolly.

For a shocked instant, Eden was stunned that her offer had been taken seriously. Her reaction became tempered with cynicism. 'So much for *esprit de corps*,' she murmured and went back to her cot to fetch the money from her purse.

With the impending visit of the big brass, they managed to fit into their free time between ground school and flying not only the uniform alterations but also hours of drilling. Marching to and from the flight line, or mess, or the barracks took on a new significance. They practiced until their columns were as knife-straight as the creases in their new tan slacks. Then the word came.

'They aren't coming?' Mary Lynn wailed. 'After all I went through to get these damn pants to fit me!'

'Tsk, tsk, such language,' Marty said mockingly.

'There was a change of plans at the last minute,' Cappy informed them. 'That happens often in the Army.' Cappy knew this well, but she'd been all caught up in the excited furor, too.

'Is that it?' Eden demanded. 'I mean, they simply aren't coming – no apologies, no explanation, nothing?'

'That's it,' Cappy replied, then shrugged. 'Oh, there was talk of some low-level officer being sent around in the next few days to look around.'

Eden pulled off the turban that had enwrapped her red hair and slammed it on her cot, then flounced down beside

155

it, simmering. 'I feel as if I've just been stood up by my date. No one has ever dared to do this to me before.'

They all shared the feeling, and none of them liked it any better than Eden did.

The hush of the classroom was broken by the scratch of lead pencils on the test sheets, the rub of erasers to strike a reconsidered answer and the soft shuffle of papers. Cappy was bent over the essay-type meteorology quiz, the tension throbbing in her temples.

Define the difference between cirrostratus, cirrocumulus, and stratocumulus and the type of weather or associated fronts related to each. Cappy read the question and wanted to groan aloud.

As the lead pencil-point touched the paper, the door to the classroom clicked resoundingly into the near silence. Briefly, the class was distracted by the opening of the door.

It lasted long enough for most of them to surmise that the rather good-looking officer, escorted by one of the training staff, was the Army major sent on the unofficial inspection tour. Rumor had reported his arrival at Avenger Field earlier in the morning, so his appearance wasn't totally unexpected.

Except by Cappy. She stared at him, indifferent to the meteorology instructor, who joined him by the door to converse in whispers. That angled profile and strong jaw-line, that proud way of carrying himself, she'd know them anywhere. Cappy didn't need to see the confirmation of the name tag, on his breast pocket. It was Major Mitch Ryan.

Her throat felt tight and strangled by an emotion she was reluctant to name. Until she saw Mitch standing there, in the same room with her, she hadn't realized how home-sick and lonely she'd been. Cappy felt the excited rush of her pulse, the joy that soared inside her. Mitch was a slice of home. The remembered warmth in his dark eyes and the hard feel of his arms came rushing back.

Her fingers released their grip on the pencil and it

clattered onto the tabletop. Impulse nearly pushed Cappy out of her seat to cross the room to Mitch, but it died the instant he turned his gaze in her direction and she saw the hard, impersonal look in his expression. She realized how wide her smile had been and felt the sting of a rebuke for allowing her emotions to be seen in public. He was here in an official capacity, she reminded herself, and quickly lowered her gaze.

Her intense dislike for the requisite military discipline resurfaced as Cappy picked up her pencil and attempted to concentrate on the meteorology test, but she was conscious of all that went on at the classroom doorway. She recognized the familiar tread of his footsteps as he wandered into the room and strolled behind the test-taking trainees.

When Mitch paused by her chair, all her nerves went tense. Her pencil remained poised above the paper the whole time he was there.

Her mind refused to function or come up with a single, intelligent answer to any of the easy questions. In the edges of her vision, she could see the sharp creases of his trousers and the polished brown of his shoes. He stood next to her for so long that Cappy wondered if he expected her to acknowledge his presence. She started to look up, but he resumed his leisurely pace, moving by her.

A few more hushed words were exchanged with the instructor, then Mitch left the classroom. Cappy stared at the door for a long time, feeling hurt without being sure why.

Later, on the floor of the ready room, Cappy sat hunched over her bent knees, subdued and silent in the afternoon bustle of the flight-line area. She listened to her more talkative baymates with only half an ear.

'I don't know why we couldn't have multiple choice,' Marty complained. Then brightening, 'Now, if I'd been given my choice, I would have picked that rugged-looking major. I wouldn't have objected if he wanted to make a closer inspection of the troops.'

'Marty, you're incorrigible,' Mary Lynn protested with a laugh.

'Attention!' A voice barked the command that sent all the trainees scrambling to their feet.

As Mitch Ryan walked into the ready room with his entourage of base personnel, Cappy kept her gaze to the front, resisting the urge to look at him. 'As you were.' His richly timbred voice released them to return to their former casual informality.

Despite the order, Cappy couldn't fully relax. Her glance kept darting to locate him as he wandered through the room, smiling aloofly at the eager and admiring looks that greeted him and steadily coming closer to the side of the room where she stood. Then he was towering beside them, his few extra inches adding to the commanding aura.

'Cigarette?' He shook some partway out of the pack and offered one first to Marty.

'Thanks.' She took one while Mary Lynn refused.

The pack was offered to Cappy and she withdrew a cigarette. 'Have you been up flying today?' Mitch addressed the question generally as he took a pack of matches from his inside pocket.

'Not yet,' Marty answered while he lit her cigarette. 'It should be a good day for it, though.'

His hand cupped the match flame to Cappy's cigarette. She bent her head to it, her gaze straying over his long fingers, conscious of the strength in them. When Cappy straightened to blow the smoke to the side, her response was automatic. 'Thanks, Mitch.'

Silence seemed to thunder about her for a lightning-struck second while Marty and Mary Lynn stared at her. But Cappy had already felt the hard, accusing thrust of his look. She met it without outwardly flinching.

'It is Major Ryan to you, trainee.' The rough reprimand discouraged any further familiarity.

'My mistake, sir,' Cappy shot back at him, cold and angry. 'I thought I knew you.'

She dropped the cigarette and ground it into the floor

with her heel before she stalked onto the flight line, her visage frozen into an emotionless expression. She faced into the wind, letting the hot May air blow over her.

CHAPTER TEN

Minutes after Cappy had walked onto the flight line, Mitch came running out of the building accompanied by one of her classmates. As they crossed the apron to a waiting aircraft, it was clear Mitch intended to fly with the trainee to see for himself the type of training the women pilots were getting. He didn't so much as look Cappy's way.

She wished fervidly that he was flying with her instead. What a pleasure it would be to pop the stick and snap his Army neck. The propeller churned the air, blowing up the ever-present red dust. As the plane made its turn to taxi to the runway, the stinging dust cloud was kicked back at Cappy. She narrowed her eyes, blinking them to get rid of the smarting dust while she watched the plane leave the hangar area.

The lyrics to one of their marching songs, the one patterned after the Georgia Tech tune, kept flitting through her mind. It seemed to match this bitter and confused resentment she was feeling.

If I had a civilian check, I know just what I'd do;
I'd pop the stick and crack his neck, and probably get
* a U.*
But if I had an Army check, I'd taxi across the grass.
I'd flip the ship upon its nose, and throw him on his
* . . . Ooooo*
Oh, I'm a flying wreck, a-risking my neck and a
* helluva pilot too –*

The noise from the roaring engine of the BT-13 receded as it taxied away from the flight line. Marty and Mary Lynn emerged from the ready room and joined Cappy in the hangar's shade. Avid curiosity lurked behind Marty's close study of her baymate.

'It's obvious you know him, Cap. Aren't you going to tell us?' Marty prodded.

'I *knew* him.' All her attention seemed to be on the aircraft taxiing toward them. 'That's my plane coming in. See you later.' With a little skip, she broke into a slow jog to meet the basic trainer.

'Did you see that look in her eye when we first came out?' Marty said to Mary Lynn while she watched their departing baymate.

'What do you mean?'

'She was dirty-fighting mad.' Marty was willing to bet on it. 'It's kind of hard to believe, isn't it? Calm, competent Cappy was riled, but good.'

Mary Lynn didn't comment. The relationship between a man and a woman was a private thing, not to be aired in public. She respected Cappy's desire for silence on the matter. If she didn't want to talk about the major, then they had no right to ask.

After three hours of dual instruction, part of it hood time, Cappy landed the BT-13 and taxied to the hangar, where the rest of the planes sat scorching in the rays of the late afternoon sun. Fatigue from the strain of endless concentration left her feeling dull as she climbed out of the cockpit onto the wing-walk.

'Your mind wasn't on flying today.' The hard criticism came from her instructor, Jimmy Ray Price. He knew full well she could have done much better.

'I know.' Hot and tired, she pulled off the snood and ran ruffling fingers through her nut-brown hair.

'It's a cardinal rule for pilots – don't take your problems up in the air with you. Leave them on the ground. Up there, you need all your concentration on flying.' As always he was harsh with her, always demanding the best from the best.

Tears of exhaustion and self-pity threatened to spill over but she kept them at bay. Why was it the men she knew all seemed to be callous and demanding – her father, her instructors, everyone? She might try to deny it, but – damn, she did want their approval. Always she was expected to excel and even when she did, she received only faint praise for it.

Tired and miserable, Cappy walked toward the ready room with her head down. Her instructor kept pace with her, his silence merely weighting his previous tongue-lashing. Just let the day be over, she kept thinking. Before they reached the building, the base commander, his aide, and Mitch Ryan walked out the door and paused directly in their path. Cappy attempted to avoid Mitch's watching eyes as her glance skimmed the dark brown of his uniform jacket and, on its shoulders, the gold leaves signifying his rank. The hard bill of his officer's cap obscured his look, but the set of his mouth and jaw hadn't softened at all.

'Good flying today, Price?' The base commander directed his question at her instructor, his tone hearty. Then he turned to offer an aside to Mitch. 'This young woman is one of our best pilots.'

Obliged to stop, Cappy paused beside her instructor, stiffly tense. She forced a certain pleasantness into her expression for the benefit of the Army Commander of Avenger Field and kept her attention focused on him rather than Mitch.

'Very good, as usual,' Jimmy Ray Price lied. Cappy was convinced it was the kindest gesture he'd ever made, even if it hadn't been to spare her.

'I'm glad to hear it,' Mitch replied, and Cappy was equally certain that was a lie. So far, no one had addressed a comment directly to her. The omission wasn't corrected as Mitch turned to the commander. 'This trainee happens to be the daughter of a friend of mine.'

Surprised that he should choose this moment to acknowledge her, Cappy stared at him. He looked back, aloof and vaguely challenging. 'With your permission, Major,' Mitch continued, going through the motions of observing proper channels, 'I would like to take Miss Hayward to dinner tonight, off the post. I know the Lieutenant Colonel and his wife are anxious to learn how she's getting along.'

Lieutenant Colonel. The news of her father's promotion barely registered. Uppermost in her feelings was a raw resentment at his presumption that she would want to spend an evening with him. Cappy's response was tempered by the presence of the base commander.

'You'll have to excuse me this trip, Major Ryan. It has been a very long and exhausting day –'

His low voice cut across her polite refusal. 'I don't recall asking whether you wanted to come, Miss Hayward.'

She wanted to rail at him, to scream and stomp her feet in an uncontrolled protest, but it all lodged in her throat. She had been too well schooled against such outbursts. After a few seconds of hesitant uncertainty, the commander interpreted her ensuing silence to mean an acceptance of the invitation.

'If Miss Hayward is agreeable, naturally you have my permission,' he qualified his answer, giving Cappy an opportunity to protest. She didn't. Whatever their differences, she wasn't going to make them a public issue – and Mitch had known that.

'Good.' Satisfaction settled smoothly onto his features. 'I'll need the use of a vehicle from your motor pool.'

'Of course.'

'Can you be ready by eighteen hundred hours, Miss Hayward?' He leveled another glance at her, then swept her with it to indicate a change of attire was required.

'Yes, sir.' She had to agree, but her blue eyes glared at him.

Promptly at six o'clock, Mitch knocked on the bay door. Eden went to answer it while Cappy fastened the clasp on the scrimshaw necklace her father had brought her from Alaska. His presence in the room seemed to alter the atmosphere, sending an undercurrent of tension through it. Cappy listened to the brisk pitch of his voice as Eden made the introductions, but she didn't look around as she gathered up her purse.

When she finally turned, Mitch was standing just inside the door, his hat tucked under his arm. Without a cap, he looked more mature and masculine, less like a recruiting poster of a roguishly handsome officer.

'Ready?' The one word managed to convey the impression of a challenge.

Cappy simply nodded, and lowered her lashes to conceal the flaring surge of pride that wanted to defy him. Avoiding the glances of her baymates, she crossed to the door and brushed past him as he opened it for her. She caught the tangy scent of some aftershave lotion drifting from his smoothly shaven face before the hot, dusty air chased it away.

The impersonal pressure of his hand at her elbow guided her to the olive-drab jeep parked in front of the barracks and helped her into the seat. Mitch walked around the rear of the vehicle to the driver's side and hopped behind the wheel.

His hand paused on the ignition key while he sent her a sideways look. 'I've been told the Bluebonnet Hotel is the place to go in Sweetwater.'

'The dining facilities are probably the best in town,' she agreed stiffly.

'Then you have no objections if we go there?'

'None.' Cappy tied a scarf of sapphire blue silk around her head so her dark hair wouldn't be blown into total disarray in the open vehicle.

The jeep was not known for its smooth ride. Cappy gripped the side when they turned onto the main road and picked up speed. The roar of the engine made it impractical to talk and the rush of air would have swept the words away if they had tried. In silence, with their eyes to the front, they sped down the highway, traversing the short distance to Sweetwater, bouncing roughly over the bumps and ruts.

Within the town limits, they slowed and Cappy directed him to Sweetwater's lone hotel. The stiffness and awkwardness between them persisted as they parked in front of the six-story tan brick building. Mitch escorted her into the hotel lobby with its pink walls and art deco light fixtures. In addition to a small sitting area and writing desks in the lobby level, a set of three steps led to a separate sitting area for hotel guests.

'The dining room is this way.' Cappy indicated the direction and Mitch guided her to it.

The hotel dining room repeated the art deco theme and color scheme they'd seen in the lobby. The cloth-covered tables all were set with silverware and glasses, but few diners were seen.

'Not very busy,' Mitch remarked.

'It's relatively quiet during the week. You have to wait until the weekend for things to liven up.' Cappy was conscious of his body leaning over her as he pushed her chair up to the table.

'Do you come here often?' He placed his hat on the seat of a side chair and sat down opposite her, combing fingers through his hair to rumple its flatness.

'Yes, sometimes.' She opened the menu and pretended to study its familiar fare.

'What will you have?' After she told him, Mitch gave their order to the waitress. 'Do you have a good burgundy?'

The waitress gave him a blank look, and Cappy stepped in to inform him dryly, 'You aren't in Washington, Mitch. This is a dry county – no wine, no beer, nothing . . . except for some potent moonshine if you know the right people to ask.'

A curt nod of dismissal sent the waitress away from their table. Cappy felt the hard probe of his gaze. 'And do you?' he asked tersely.

'Let's say a friend of a friend does,' she countered, and

opened her purse to take out a cigarette. Ignoring his offer of a light, Cappy struck her own match, and dragged the smoke deeply into her lungs before exhaling it.

Finally, Mitch lit his own cigarette. For long minutes there was only silence at the table, broken intermittently by the tap of a cigarette on the shared ashtray.

'Aren't you going to ask me about your father's promotion?' Mitch inquired with a grim-lipped look. 'It only came through last week.'

'Did he ask you to mention it to me?' Cappy studied the lipstick – stained tip of her cigarette.

'No.'

'Then I don't have to bother to offer him any congratulations, do I?' she retorted, the hope dying that he might have sent her the message as a conciliatory gesture. 'How's Mother?'

'I think she's finding it awkward being caught in the middle between you and Colonel Hayward.'

'She isn't in the middle. She's on his side.' She shied away from further discussion on the subject of her father and their feud. 'Let's talk about something else.' Conversation, however stilted, was preferable to the strain of a continued silence.

But talking, instead of easing the tension, merely increased it. As the meal progressed, their exchanges became more staccatolike, as if each was trying to outdo the other's clipped sentences. When Mitch picked up the bill for their meal, Cappy nearly bolted for the door in her eagerness to have this wretched evening end.

Outside the sun had gone down, taking with it some of the searing heat. A handful of evening stars glittered in the purpling blue sky while a waning moon turned a sleepy eye on the occupants of the jeep speeding back to the airfield.

A guard at the entrance waved them through the gate. But Mitch didn't stop at the barracks. Instead he continued on to the criss-crossing air strips and followed an access road to the end of one of them. Flarepots had been set out on the adjacent active runway for that evening's group of night flyers.

The jeep bounced to a stop and Mitch switched the motor off. Frowning, Cappy turned to look at him. Both his hands grasped the wheel as he gazed out the front windscreen. In the deepening shadows of night, the muscles along his jaw stood out, catching the faint sheen from the moon and intensifying the grim and angry set of his features.

'Why did you bring me here?' Cappy demanded impatiently.

The blunt question seemed to prod him into action. A hard glance was thrown her way, as if he suddenly remembered she was there, then Mitch was swinging out of the jeep.

'Let's walk.'

Obedience to a command was almost a conditioned reflex. Cappy was out of the jeep and taking a step to follow the tall, uniformed figure whose hands were thrust into the side pockets of his creased trousers, before she realized what she was doing.

'No.' She came to a stop. 'I don't have to take orders from you.' Mitch halted and half turned to look at her, his face shadowed by the brim of his cap. 'You can go for a walk if you want, but I'm going back to the barracks.'

With her rebellion announced, Cappy swung away and aimed for the distant set of low buildings beyond the curved humps of the hangar roofs. As she started for the barracks, she heard the trotting thud of his footsteps break into a quick pursuit. When his hand caught the crook of her arm she tried to shrug it off, but his fingers tightened their grip and she was pulled around, held by her upper arms.

'You're not going anywhere, Cap, until I find out what's happening here. You've changed and I don't like it.' Mitch bit out the words, his teeth flashing whitely in the shadowed planes of his face.

'*I've* changed?' she repeated in stunned anger.

166

'You openly admitted tonight that you frequent the Bluebonnet Hotel. Do you think I don't know what's going on there? Do you think the talk hasn't gotten around?'

At first she frowned at him in puzzlement, then impatience swept it aside. 'You aren't making any sense.' Cap flattened her hands against his beribboned breast pockets to push him away.

His hands tightened their grip, giving her a hard shake. 'The word has spread to every air base in the area. At each stop before coming here, I was told by everyone from mechanic to lieutenant – if I wanted a good time, go to the Bluebonnet Hotel in Sweetwater where one of those "pretty little women trainees" would take care of me.'

'That's a lie,' Cap answered emphatically.

'From one source, maybe two, I would have questioned it.' His voice was tight and low. 'But it was all up and down the line, and several could personally vouch for the truth in it.'

'I don't believe it.' Her lips came firmly together in solid resistance to what she was hearing.

'Come on, Cap. Are you trying to tell me you don't know what's going on?' he taunted.

She pulled back to stare at him. 'What are you thinking, Mitch? That I'm one of these trainees supposedly bestowing her favors on any soldier that comes by?'

'I must have amused the hell out of you.' He ground out the words, his jaw tightly clenched. 'Always so damned proper and respectful – holding your hand and kissing you at the door when I really wanted . . .' Mitch hesitated a split second. '. . . to take you to my bed and make love to you till morning. Why aren't you laughing, Cap? It's very funny.'

'What's funny is how happy I was to see you when you walked into that classroom today –' Bitterness thickened her voice. '– and now, how I can hardly wait for you to leave.'

'Dammit, Cappy, tell me it isn't true.' He shook her

167

shoulders, whipping her head back, exposing the creamy arc of her throat.

'No.' Tears stung her eyes at his perfidy. 'You come here with a host of accusations and insinuations. It's up to you to prove them, not me.'

Cap felt the loosening of his hands, the withdrawing from her, and wrenched her shoulders slightly to twist out of his hold. She walked away, and this time no footsteps came after her. Anger and pain were all wrapped up in one another. The barracks looked so far away, long rectangular shapes a shade blacker than their dark back-drop. She wanted to break into a run, but pride and the impracticality of trying to run in high-heeled shoes kept her at a fast walk, her shoulders squared and her head high.

After she'd gone about a hundred yards, Cappy heard the motor of the jeep start up. Soon its headlight beams were sweeping the rough track in front of her and she moved to the side at its approach. When it pulled up alongside her and slowed to a crawl, she refused to look around.

'Get in the jeep, Cappy,' Mitch ordered, somewhat tiredly.

'I'll walk, thank you,' she retorted without slackening her pace or turning her head.

With a rough shifting of gears and a tromping on the foot-feed, the jeep lurched ahead of her and screeched to a stop. Mitch pushed out of his seat and vaulted over the low door to stand directly in her path.

'You're going to ride in the jeep, Cappy,' he said flatly.

'What's the matter, Mitch? Are you afraid someone might see me walking back to the barracks by myself?' she taunted. 'They just might figure that you got fresh with me – and what would they think of the major then? After all, he couldn't even make time with a so-called whore.'

'Shut up, Cap,' Mitch ordered through his teeth.

'I hope you don't expect me to believe for one minute that it's my reputation you're worried about.' She doubled her hands into rigid fists at her side. The jeep's engine idled in a steady growl while the headlamps cast twin trails of light piercing through the darkness beyond them.

'If you don't get in the jeep, Cappy, I'll pick you up and put you there. You'll fight me, but I'll win. Let's spare each other all that physical wrestling.' Again, he sounded tired.

His reasoning was inarguable. With a small dip of her head, Cappy conceded and walked to the passenger side, climbing in unaided. Behind the wheel again, Mitch shifted gears and the jeep lunged forward. They had nothing to say to each other, not then and not later when he dropped her off at the barracks.

In the bay, Cappy managed to elude most of the questions with a plea of fatigue. After morning reveille, too many other things crowded in to distract her baymates' attention from her outing the previous evening.

At noon mess, Marty was late in arriving so they saved her a place in line. When she joined them, Marty's gray-green eyes were bright with speculation.

'I just heard your major is going to be staying here a few days, Cap.'

'He isn't my major,' she said in an expressionless voice. 'He's a friend of my father's, not mine.'

Eyebrows were raised in skepticism, but no one pursued the topic. It was her coldness and closed-in look that told them the major was a touchy issue, so they didn't probe.

The following day, rumor raced through the base. Chicago carried it to her compatriots: 'I heard they're going to make the Bluebonnet off-limits.'

'What? Why?' Marty protested.

'There's been some complaints of some sort.' Chicago indicated her lack of more specific knowledge with a shrug of her shoulders. 'I think Cap's major has something to do with it.'

Marty turned, cocking her head to the side, wheat-colored strands of hair escaping from under the bandanna. 'Do you know anything about this, Cap?' She narrowly

169

eyed the brunette who had been so uncommunicative about the visiting officer.

'No.' Though it was a flat denial, Marty had difficulty believing it.

When Cappy arrived at the flight line on the third day of Mitch's extended tour, she saw the sleek, twin-engined AT-7 being given a preflight ground check – Mitch's plane. Good riddance, she thought, but with regret for the lost illusion of the warm, strong man she had believed him to be.

'Hayward.' Her instructor, Jimmy Ray Price, peremptorily summoned her with a wave of his hand.

'He sounds like his usual friendly self, doesn't he?' Eden murmured in dry mockery.

Her mouth briefly quirked in a smile of agreement before Cap split away from the group to jog over to her waiting instructor. She was ready to do some flying, hoping it would shake off some of this flatness she was feeling.

'You wanted me, Mr Price?' She crisply reported to him.

'Nope. But the major wants to see you before he leaves.' He jerked his head in the direction of the twin-engine.

Her glance skipped past the short bulldog of a man to the parked aircraft. Cappy wanted to refuse outright, but every instinct warned against it. Her credo of survival was not to let the other person know you'd been hurt.

It was a full minute before Cappy noticed the odd way the instructor was staring at her and realized how long she had been standing there. Self-consciously she let her glance fall away from his stare.

'Thanks,' she mumbled and headed across the hangar apron to the twin-engined transport.

As she walked in front of the airplane's nose, she spied Mitch in conversation with his pilot. She ducked under the wing tip, conscious of the little drum of her pulse. At almost the same instant, Mitch observed her approach and said something to the pilot, dismissing him. He came forward a few steps to meet her while the pilot climbed into the plane.

'I understand you wanted to see me, sir.' She kept her gaze level and her expression bland, but her teeth were gritted.

His gaze was narrowed and thoughtful while the corners of his mouth deepened in a line of regret. 'I was wrong, Cappy. I owe you an apology,' he said. 'I had the right place – the Bluebonnet – but I was mistaken about the women involved. It seems some . . . camp followers, shall we call them . . . set up business in the hotel. They have been telling the soldiers they're part of the contingent of female pilots training here at Avenger. I jumped to conclusions, Cappy, and I'm sorry.'

'Apology accepted. And it's Miss Hayward to you,' she countered with icy calm.

His look became impatient. 'I admit I made a mistake, and I'm sorry. Dammit, what more do you want?' Mitch demanded roughly.

'I could forgive a simple mistake, and even overlook the fact you were willing to take the word of other men. But I can't forgive that you wanted to believe it was true about me.' She observed the faint recoil, proving she'd hit the target dead-center.

With a smart pivot, Cappy turned to walk away. The air shimmered with heat, making the distant concrete look wet. That's the way her eyes felt, so hot and bright, yet they were painfully dry. She hadn't gone five steps when Mitch caught up with her, and swung her back around to face him. His expression was hard with anger.

'You're damned right I wanted to believe it,' he admitted. 'Ever since I've known you, you've never let me get close to you. I wanted to believe that behind your coolness there was some kind of passion. And I was jealous as hell that someone had tapped it before I could. Maybe that makes me a rotten bastard, but I don't care.'

Cappy was thrown by his totally unexpected admission. She stared at him in confusion as a propeller chopped the

171

air, caught, and revved into full power. They were blasted by the prop-wash, dust swirling around them in eye-stinging clouds. Mitch pulled his cap down tighter on his head and hooked an arm around Cappy to draw her out of the driven wind to the end of the wing.

'Nothing's changed, Cappy,' Mitch practically shouted to make himself heard above the engine noise. 'You're going to see me again.'

While she was scraping her wind-blown hair away from her mouth to deny it, Mitch took advantage of her momentary distraction and covered her lips with his own in a long, hard kiss. She tasted his hunger and frustration, the wanting to stay and having to go. Just for a minute, she leaned into him. The desire was strong to reach out to him, but she wouldn't give in to it, torn by the feelings he aroused and the bitter truths she knew. The Army was a rival that would always win. In the end, she pulled away from him, fighting the ache inside. His eyes were like dark velvet when he looked at her.

Above the roar of the engines, a cheering sound could be faintly heard. Both of them became aware of their audience of trainees, vocally offering their approval of the romantic scene they had just witnessed. Mitch smiled and winked at her, amused by it, but Cappy backed away from him, averting her gaze and striking out for an empty hangar.

From the coolness of its shade, Cappy watched the powerful twin-engined transport lift off the runway, its wheels retract into its belly, and its flap-setting change. She tensed at the sound of footsteps approaching her from behind. With a backward glance, she recognized the deep red-brown color of that pigtailed hair. Eden was the only one who sported that particular shade.

'Missing him already?' Those dark eyes were a little too keen in their inspection.

'Not hardly,' Cappy answered with a short laugh. 'No one in their right mind falls in love with an Army man.'

'But you fall in love with your heart – not your head,' Eden reminded her.

'Not if you're smart, you don't.' Cappy pushed herself away from the post she'd been leaning against. 'It's time to do some flying, isn't it?'

CHAPTER ELEVEN

Word came down from the control tower to the waiting press corps that the powerful AT-6s and the twin-engine AT-17s were entering the traffic pattern and would be landing shortly. Off to the side, dusty zoot-suited figures watched the scurry of activity. Unlike the reporters and photographers, they were interested in the planes themselves rather than the pilots.

'It won't be long before we'll be flying them.' Eden observed a sleek, single-engined advanced trainer zoom onto the runway. Beneath the certainty in her tone, there was also an eagerness.

Graduation ceremonies were scheduled on the following day for the 43-W-2 class of women pilots who had completed their training in Houston, staying behind when Rachel's group had transferred to Sweetwater. The long cross-country flight was the last one they'd be making as trainees. Tomorrow they would be full-fledged ferry pilots.

'Not all of us,' Chicago corrected her with a certain dullness. All of them went through the motions of denying her claim, but from one source or another, they'd all heard about her lack of proficiency in instrument flying. 'We all know it's true. I'll never pass my check ride.'

'You can't be sure of that,' Marty insisted, but she also had a hunch it would take a miracle.

The big planes came wheeling up to the hangars, the roaring engines churning clouds of dust. While newsreel cameras cranked the footage and photographers aimed their lenses at them, the pilots, one by one, bounded out of their planes and pulled off their nets to let the wind blow their hair. These female pilots were pictures of beauty and confidence with their bright eyes and shining faces.

'I wish that was us.' Marty expressed the envy all of them were feeling. Not because of the attention they were receiving, but for successfully completing the rigorous and demanding training program. 'I want it so bad I can taste it.' Her husky voice vibrated with the near ferocity of her desire.

No one replied or commented. It was a feeling that went too deep to articulate. Flying was an all-consuming passion for them. They wanted it so fiercely that, even in the beginning, they had gone against convention, defied the disapproval of parents or left behind families, and ignored the raised eyebrows of friends to have what they wanted. It was a bit like being horse-crazy. High flight had an addictive power and excitement to it that nothing else could match. They'd willingly go through the hotbox hell of the Link trainer and the brain-scrambling confusion of instrument flying for those moments of supreme exhilaration in the lofty solitudes of the sky.

Shortly after the last graduate landed, a stagger-winged Beechcraft came shooting down the runway. Eden recognized it and nudged the others. 'That's Jacqueline Cochran.'

After the women's director of flying climbed out of her aircraft, she headed toward the operations building. This time she was accompanied by another woman, her French-speaking maid, as the group later learned. Almost instantly she was engulfed in the wave of Houston graduates who gathered around her to pay homage. Eden shook her head in mild amusement at another spectacular entrance.

The 'cattle trucks' arrived to transport the Houston group into Sweetwater for a night's stay at the Bluebonnet Hotel. And the flurry of excitement passed.

The graduation ceremonies for the Houston class gave

174

all the Avenger trainees a chance to wear their new regulation dress uniforms and to show off the marching skills they had practiced for the generals who had never come. A flag-carrier and two flight lieutenants led the long, straight columns past the reviewing stand. Behind them, the Big Spring Bombardier School Band played with drum-pounding exuberance.

Since the graduates weren't officially Army, regulation wings couldn't be presented to them. A pilot without wings was unthinkable, so bombardier's 'sweetheart' wings were redesigned. A shield and ribbon, engraved with the squadron and class designation 43-W-2, were soldered to the middle of the 'sweetheart' wings.

Elated and high-spirited, the Inseparables swept into their bay, all of them talking at once, filling the room with their impressions of the ceremony. The graduation exercises had reaffirmed the sense of importance of their flight training, ennobling it with duty and honor and pride. Men were needed on the war fronts and they would be performing a vital service by relieving them of the home duties so they could go fight.

With continuing chatter back and forth, they began changing out of their uniforms of tan slacks and short-sleeved white shirts. Dawdling in various stages of undress, some in bra and slacks and some bottomless in shirts, they roamed the bay.

'You can bet there'll be an article in the *Sweetwater Reporter* tomorrow.'

'Do you suppose they'll have pictures, too? I know I was in one of them. The photographer was right there in front of me when he snapped it.'

'It depends on the background. They can't publish a photograph if there are more than two planes in the picture. The censors won't allow it. No mention can be made of the base, where it's located, or how many trainees are here.'

'I'm sure the enemy is anxious to learn all about us female flyers. We're such a threat.'

Laughing along with the others at the thought, Mary Lynn bent a bare knee to the floor in front of her footlocker and opened it to take out a change of clothes. Lying on top, Beau's smiling face looked back at her from the gilt-framed photograph. It jolted her. The smile, the laughter, died. Mary Lynn slowly reached to pick up the photo, then carried it to her cot, where she sat silently staring at it, indifferent to the continuing barrage of voices behind her.

'Has anybody looked inside Eden's locker?' Marty stopped beside the opened footlocker, and saw the rumpled clothes and underwear tumbling over the sides. 'It's worse than Fibber McGee's closet. Don't you ever fold your clothes before you toss them in there?'

'Butt out, Rogers.' Eden shouldered her out of the way and bent to dig through the mess for a change of clothes, further disheveling the contents.

'What's the matter, Miss van Valkenburg?' Marty razzed. 'Are you jealous 'cause Cochran gets to bring her maid along and you don't?' Laughing, she ambled back to her cot. 'God, Mary Lynn, you should take a look at her footlocker.' The lack of response, the absence of any sign her comment had been heard, drew Marty's full attention. She tipped her head to the side, trying to get a glimpse of the brunette's downcast face. 'Hey, Mary Lynn, is something wrong?' The more direct question seemed to pierce through Mary Lynn's absorption with the photograph of her husband.

Her expression was troubled and her eyes were dark with near panic. 'All this talk about Army censors and the enemy – we joke about it and none of it is funny. There's a war on. Men are fighting and dying.'

'Nobody meant anything by it,' Marty hastened to assure her, at a loss for the right words to comfort and reassure her friend. She sat beside her on the cot, awkwardly touching Mary Lynn's small-boned shoulder.

The others, including the tall, sleek Rachel Goldman, noticed the changed tenor of the conversation and glanced curiously at the huddled pair, discreetly listening in.

'Beau is over there.' Mary Lynn stared at the photograph. 'What if something happens to him? What if he's hurt or killed? What would I do without him? He's got to come back to me, Marty. I'll die without him.' She was scared for him and frightened by the thought of a future without him. The loneliness was awful now, but at least she could look forward to his letters and the distant tomorrow when he'd come home. 'I should be with him. I don't belong here.'

'That isn't true,' Rachel inserted. Usually there was minor resistance to any inclusion of her in their conversations. Marty stiffened at her unexpected participation, wary of Rachel yet willing to let her speak as long as she said the right things. 'We are at war, and your husband is over there fighting to protect all the things we believe in. At a time like this, we all have to make sacrifices – put aside our personal wants and do what is right.'

Mary Lynn raised her head, drawn by the forceful argument being put forth. The militance in Rachel's expression convinced her of the blonde's sincerity.

'Hitler and his Fascist armies have to be destroyed. We all have to fight in the ways that we can to protect our homes and the ones we love,' Rachel declared. 'You can do it by flying, by freeing a male pilot for combat and maybe to fly fighter escort for your husband's bomber. We are at war and this is where you belong – for his sake and everyone else's.'

For long seconds her words lingered, ringing in their minds. The rationalization, the justification was the assurance Mary Lynn needed.

'Thanks,' she murmured to Rachel, who was already self-conscious about her impassioned outburst.

Later, with the half-light of night coming through the barracks' windows, Mary Lynn lay on her cot, listening to the even breathing of her sleeping baymates. An awful, aching loneliness knifed through her as she strained to recall those nights of marital closeness with Beau.

Her lips could almost feel the pressure of his kiss. She closed her eyes, trying to make the ghostlike sensation more real. Months had passed since he had held her. She rubbed her arms, seeking to remember the feel of his muscles, flexed and hard. It had been so long. She caught her lower lip between her teeth, biting down on it while she tried to keep the wanting at bay.

She trembled with longing. Beau. She mouthed his name as her hand slid to the underside of her breast, feeling its rounded firmness. The sensation stimulated a driving ache. She turned her face into the pillow to smother any sound she might inadvertently make. Doubled into a fist, her hand pushed its way between her legs where her thighs clamped themselves on her wrist to hold it there.

Long-ago childhood memories came rushing back. She could hear her mother's voice again, so strident and condemning. 'Mary Lynn, what are you doing? You get your hand out of your panties this instant!' The censure and the stinging slaps for a wrong she didn't understand. 'Nice little girls don't do such things. Don't ever let me catch you doing that again.' Words that drove her to secrecy – in the darkness of night and the hiding cover of blankets – and the ultimate easing of that terrible tension.

'Beau,' she whispered in near apology as her body sagged in relief against the thin mattressed cot.

Check-ride time came around for the basic training stage of their flying program. Those who passed civilian rides with their instructors went for their Army check rides. When it was over, the ranks of the trainee class were thinned considerably. Chicago was among the group who washed out.

The mattress of her empty cot was rolled up, and all her personal belongings had been removed from the premises.

'Do you suppose she's gone already?' Mary Lynn wondered.

'Yes,' Cappy replied.

'I bet she was out of here within a couple of hours. They

'don't let them hang around long once they're out of the program.' By the ubiquitous *they*, Marty meant the command staff at Avenger.

'I suppose she failed the instrument flying.' Eden sank onto her cot and drew a knee up to her chest.

'I suppose.' Cappy shrugged an agreement, aware they would never know for sure.

Some of the military inspectors had been known to wash out a student for no more cause than the check pilot's decision that the trainee wasn't strong enough to handle a plane in difficulty. Even being female was reason enough for some.

'Remember when they caught those two girls in bed together?' Marty recalled. 'They were packed up and off the base within an hour.'

There was a nod from Eden, but no one said anything. The Inseparables were no more. The empty cot was a mute testimony of that.

The hot Texas summer found the combined Houston and Sweetwater class of 43-W-3 just entering the advanced phase of training, cut almost in half. This was the final stage.

No more BT-13s; instead they were flying the AT-6, known as the 'Texan,' built by North American Aviation. The advanced trainer had 150 more horses in its engine than the 450-horsepower BT-13. For the first time, the girls had to deal with retractable landing gear, which not only gave the single-engined plane, with its pushed-in nose, a very sleek look on takeoffs but also gave the aircraft a cruising speed of 145 miles an hour.

The training concentrated on long-distance navigation, cross-country trips that would be invaluable experience for future ferry pilots. Many lessons were learned the hard way, as attested by red-faced pilots who knocked at the doors of ranch houses after running out of gas and making forced landings in someone's pasture or cotton field.

A triangle that went from Sweetwater to Odessa to Big Spring and back to Sweetwater was flown countless times by the trainees, both solo and with their instructors. After a while, most of them swore they could fly it blindfolded.

With the summer sun sending temperatures soaring into the hundreds regularly, any chance to crawl into a Texan AT-6 and climb into the sky was welcomed. For every thousand feet of altitude, the temperature dropped three and a half degrees. The air blowing through the plane's ventilators was about as refreshing as a fan blowing across a block of ice.

Rachel leveled her advanced trainer off at eight thousand feet and adjusted the trim tab for straight and level flight. The rush of cool air was directed squarely at her, ruffling the map she tried to study. In a break from the usual routine, she had elected to fly a different cross-country route, going to San Angelo, then to Abilene and back to Sweetwater.

The flight leg from Sweetwater to San Angelo had been fairly routine. After Rachel had turned north to Abilene, she'd had trouble locating her first few checkpoints. Taking out her little round-wheeled flight calculator, she refigured her airspeed and flying time to approximate the distance, then plotted it on the map. The wind velocity would affect her groundspeed, but, even allowing for that variance, Abilene should have been in sight.

Craning her neck, Rachel strained to see out the front of the mullioned canopy. There was no sign of a town on the hazy horizon. She tipped the plane on its wing to look below and behind, in case she'd overflown it. Nothing.

Without a radio frequency to turn to, she couldn't cross-check her position. Her uneasiness grew as she considered the possibility she was off course. It was too soon to panic. The winds aloft might be stronger than she'd been told. It would be silly to turn back, especially if her destination was just ahead. Rachel decided to fly her heading a while longer.

Another twenty minutes in the air and she knew something had gone wrong. Somehow she had missed Abilene and she was lost. Below her, there was nothing but mesquite brush covering the dark red earth. Then she spied the iron tracks of a railroad leading into a small town. Immediately, Rachel angled the AT-6 into a steep descent and buzzed the train depot. FREDERICK, the sign on it read.

Not knowing the frequency, she was unable to call the control tower as she entered the traffic pattern on the downwind leg. A combination of nervousness over her situation and limited experience with this faster and more powerful ship caused her to land the AT-6 about twenty miles an hour faster than the recommended speed. It was a 'hot' landing, the kind usually made by highly experienced fighter pilots.

Her confidence was being chipped away – first, because she strayed off course, second because this airfield wasn't shown on her maps, and third because the power-on landing made her question her mechanical flying skills. Men in uniforms were hurrying out of the operations building to meet her as Rachel taxied her plane to the flight line.

The searing heat of the afternoon hit her as she crawled out of the cockpit and stepped onto the wing. The looks on the faces of waiting soldiers weren't too friendly. Rachel took a deep, silent breath and walked down the edge of the wing, shaking her long pale blond hair loose.

Their expressions took on a stunned look when she hopped onto the ground in front of them. The officer, a captain, stepped forward to eye her with wary and angry suspicion. 'Just who the hell are you? And what are you doing with that plane?'

Rachel retaliated in self-protection. 'Since I'm the pilot, I guess I'm flying it.'

Just about then, a jeepload of MPs came charging onto the scene. It suddenly hit her that they really had no idea who she was. They were probably ready to believe she was some kind of saboteur, a possibility that was reinforced when the MPs crowded around her and the plane with their rifles at the ready.

'That's an Army plane you've got,' the captain pointed out.

There she was, standing beside the AT-6, her six feet making her the tallest one present, a striking blonde with sloe eyes, and surrounded by armed men. This was no time to react in kind.

'Yes, sir.' Rachel schooled her voice to answer with terse calm. 'I'm Rachel Goldman, a trainee with the 319th Army Air Force Flight Training Detachment at Avenger Field in Sweetwater.'

'You surely don't expect me to believe that?' He challenged her harshly. 'The Army doesn't have any women flying planes.'

'Excuse me, but you are wrong, sir. As a matter of fact, there are a couple hundred of us at Avenger Field – and we all fly Army planes.

'If you would just tell me where I am . . .' Rachel struggled to hold her temper. 'I'm a little confused because my map doesn't show an air base outside of Frederick, Texas –'

'That's because you're in Frederick, Oklahoma.'

It was all she could do to keep her mouth from falling open. More than off course, she had been lost. She didn't even have maps that went this far.

'Now you know why the Army doesn't have any women flying its planes,' the captain jeered. 'A woman has no business behind the wheel of a car, let alone at the controls of a plane.' He waved a hand at the military police. 'Check out the plane.' Then he turned to the young officer next to him. 'Get a hold of the CO, Crawford, and let him know about this. And you' – he faced Rachel and reached for her arm – 'are coming with me.'

She yanked her arm out of his hold. 'Listen, Captain.' She managed to put a wealth of sarcasm in the reference to his rank and resisted the urge to call him a sawed-off little punk. 'All you have to do is call Avenger Field in Sweetwater and they can verify who I am.

'I'll call them,' he promised her, certain he was calling her bluff as well.

'Don't you think we ought to see if she's armed?' one

of the MPs suggested. 'There's no telling what she might be concealing in the baggy suit she's wearing.'

'You're right.' The captain nodded.

Protest screamed through her nerves, but Rachel gritted her teeth and said nothing. Unmoving as a statue, she stood there submitting herself to the indignity of a physical search. All the while the hands were unzipping her flight suit, sliding under her arms, down her waist and hips, and brushing her tautly held breasts, she glared at the captain.

'Nothing, sir,' the MP concluded.

'This will be reported, Captain,' Rachel assured him with icy stiffness. Yet she knew that in the face of his belief that she was some kind of enemy agent, he was probably following the proper military procedure.

She was escorted to his office in the operations building, where she was again questioned and her story challenged. Her repeated efforts to have him call Avenger were brushed aside. Everything was being checked, he told her.

Half an hour had passed since she'd taxied her plane up to the building. Rachel was beginning to think they'd lock her in the guardhouse next when the phone on the captain's desk rang. Evidently, the call was from his commanding officer, judging by his almost subservient manner. Rachel caught a glimmer of displeasure in his expression when the conversation ended.

'It seems there *is* some sort of training program for female pilots at Avenger Field,' he acknowledged reluctantly as he pushed himself out of his chair. 'You are free to go, trainee Goldman. May I suggest the next time you keep your mind on flying instead of daydreaming and you'll be less likely to get lost.'

There were no apologies, and no attempt to hide his contempt for her sex in the cockpit of a plane. It required all her self-control not to tell the captain precisely what her opinion of him was.

'Yes, sir.'

With considerable satisfaction, Rachel straightened up to tower over the shorter man, then walked out of his office, aware that he was following. An MP was standing guard by her AT-6 when she emerged from the operations building. He started to block her access to the plane, until he caught the signal from the captain to let her pass.

Rachel was in the cockpit with her belt fastened before she realized she had been given neither a map nor a heading back to Sweetwater. She was determined she'd fly the plane into the ground before she'd ask that captain for anything.

'Clear!' she shouted out the side of the opened canopy, then turned the switch that brought the propeller blades churning to life.

After taking off from the Oklahoma airfield, Rachel picked up the railroad tracks that had guided her to this strip and followed the reliable iron beams south. The encroaching darkness of night was about to obscure the landmarks on the edge of Sweetwater. Seconds later, she spied the runway at Avenger Field, outlined with flare pots.

Her instructor, Joe Gibbs, was waiting for her on the flight line when she landed. He chewed her out, but not too roughly, sensing that she'd suffered enough for her mistake. Rachel didn't tell him all that had happened. It was enough that she'd gotten herself lost.

After he'd left her, Rachel's friend Helen Shaw came out of the ready room to meet her. The ex-Hollywood actress eyed her curiously. 'What happened?'

Before she was through, Rachel ended up telling her fellow Woofted about the entire incident, her treatment in the hands of the insolent captain, and the blind-luck flight back to Sweetwater.

'Men,' Helen said, commiserating with Rachel's sentiments.

'To paraphrase an old quotation – "Men are bastards ever,"' she replied, and meant it.

At the barracks, Rachel and Helen parted company to go to their separate bays. There was the usual confusion, everyone trying to shower and change before evening mess, when Rachel entered. Her late arrival didn't escape Cappy's notice.

'Where've you been, Goldman?' she inquired with idle curiosity. 'Did you have plane trouble or something?'

After a second's hesitation, Rachel told them the whole story, chastened by the experience but still seething over the way she'd been treated.

Marty's initial reaction had been to scoff, 'Oklahoma?! How could you have made a mistake like that?' By the time Rachel had finished, she was saying, 'Officer or not, I think I'd have punched him in the nose.'

CHAPTER TWELVE

There was no relief from the hundred-degree July heat. The rows of barracks were lined up in a north/south direction, the same as the prevailing summer wind, allowing for no cross-ventilation in the bays.

In the suffocating stillness of the night, Marty lay on her cot, hot and sweating. Her legs were spread apart to keep her thighs from sticking together with the prickly dampness of perspiration, and her arms were flung over her head to avoid touching her sides. Nothing seemed to offer any relief from the miserable, oppressive heat, not even the wet towel she had draped over herself.

From outside the barracks came the tantalizing whisper of a breeze. It danced by the opened windows and the screened door. Not once did it come inside. Marty listened to it, feeling so sweaty and irritable.

'Oh, hell.' She sat up. 'How can anybody sleep in this hot hole?'

'Shut up, Rogers.' Eden's voice was half muffled by the mattress on which she was lying face down, motionless with her arms away from her body as Marty's had been.

'You can stay here if you want, but I'm moving.' Marty piled out of her bed and grabbed the end of her cot. The legs made an awful scraping sound as she started dragging it across the floor. 'Somebody want to give me a hand with the door?'

'What the Sam Hill are you doing?' Cappy rose on an elbow to glare at her.

'I'm going to sleep outside where at least there's a breeze,' she declared.

Within minutes, they were all dragging their cots outdoors and setting them up between the barracks. As other bays heard the commotion, they joined them until cots were strung out the full length of the buildings. It wasn't much of a breeze, but it moved the air and revived them.

'Would you look at all those stars?' Marty lay on her back and gazed at the millions of rhinestone lights in the black velvet sky, each one so individually brilliant. She glanced at Mary Lynn with a wry look. 'Now where's that cowboy who wanted to show me the Big Dipper?' She chuckled in her throat at the memory of the amorous cowhand she'd met at the rodeo-barbecue given the girls by a local rancher on the Fourth of July.

'It is a beautiful night,' Mary Lynn sighed and pillowed her head in her hands.

On the other side of them Cappy mused, 'It won't be long until they start checking us out in the AT-17s.' Flying the twin-engined aircraft would be the last stage of their advanced training, giving them a multiengine rating before graduation the first week of August.

'The good ole "Bamboo Bomber,"' Eden joked dryly, referring to the plywood construction of the airplane, dubbed the 'Bobcat' by its Cessna manufacturer.

Marty overheard their talk. 'You mean the "Bunson Burner"?' she mocked. 'The damned thing looks as if it would go up like a matchstick.'

Lying silently on her cot, Rachel listened to the low discussion about the twin-engined plane. She remembered hearing Woofteds in classes ahead of hers talking about the AT-17. The plane had a seat behind the pilot and copilot that was low and seemed to be sunken in a well. Even those who weren't prone to airsickness had grabbed for paper bags when they'd sat in that seat.

Somewhere down the line of cots came a shriek. 'A snake! A rattlesnake!' The cry went up. 'Somebody kill it!!'

In a wild scramble of bodies, some girls sought the safety of the barracks while others perched atop their cots to peer over the edges, and more searched for a weapon. The rattler, which had so foolishly crawled onto the walkway, was subsequently clubbed to death.

'Poor snake,' Marty said in absent pity.

'It was a rattlesnake,' Eden protested.

'I've heard they always travel in pairs,' a trainee down the way offered.

A moment of silence followed. Then a clamor began anew as a search was started for the mate of the dead snake. Some of the trainees gave up and hauled their cots back into the bays, but Marty yawned and stretched out more fully on her cot. A second snake was never found, but most of the trainees spent a restless night, listening for the slightest rustle of grass that might betray the presence of a snake beneath their cots.

Before graduation, each trainee was required to make a long, solo cross-country flight to a destination prescribed by her instructor. It was sheer chance that Mary Lynn was assigned to fly to her own home town of Mobile on Alabama's Gulf Coast. Midway, she stopped to refuel her AT-6 and wire her estimated time of arrival so she could squeeze an hour or longer visit with her family.

On the last leg, favoring winds added another hour to her allotted ground time in Mobile. Upon landing, she called to say she was on her way and disregarded her mother's veiled complaints over having her sleep interrupted. Working the graveyard shift meant that her mother slept during the day while her father had the coveted day shift at the shipyards. Unfortunately, she wouldn't get to see him on this trip.

Outside the air base, she caught a bus into town. The giant cranes of the shipyards ranged across the skyline, by their presence transforming the sleepy Gulf seaport of Mobile, Alabama, into a boom town. Coal smoke drifted in layers, held aloft by the sea winds, its smell tainting the salty air. The city sidewalks were crowded to overflowing.

Mary Lynn got off the bus to connect with the line that went to her neighborhood and waited impatiently at its stop. At first, she didn't notice the trio of young girls dawdling outside the corner drug store. Dressed somewhat alike in blouses and skirts, bobby socks and saddle shoes, they wore heavy makeup, garish paint on young faces, slashing lips an unkind scarlet red. They eyed Mary Lynn, in her tan gabardines, white short-sleeved shirt, and perky general's cap on her midnight-dark hair, with the mistrust of the young toward the older, and of the female toward another of her own gender. Mary Lynn seriously doubted if any of the three had celebrated her sixteenth birthday.

Looking away, she glanced down the street to see if the bus was coming and debated whether it would be faster to find a cab. After nearly six months in Texas, she was unused to the hot, humid climate of the Deep South – a sticky heat that not even the breeze coming off the Mexican Gulf could alleviate. She felt its oppressive weight as she looked down the busy thoroughfare. No bus was in sight. Mary Lynn turned back to the trio of bobby-soxers.

'When's the next bus due?'

Her inquiry was met with shrugs and one politely drawled, 'I don't know, ma'am. Soon, I expect.'

Mary Lynn smiled briefly in response and suppressed a deep sigh, resigned to waiting for the bus to make its appearance. A sailor came strolling up the street, setting the young girls to tittering and giggling behind their hands while they eyed him with flirtatious interest. Mary Lynn was absently amused by their adolescent silliness over a young serviceman, until she saw the brazen way they approached him.

'Where are you from, sailor?'

'Gee, you're cute. I'd be proud to keep you company if you're lonely.'

'Wanta buy me a soda?'

The three girls practically threw themselves at the sailor, pressing close with the straining urgency of their young bodies. Such behavior from seemingly well-brought-up young ladies was scandalous to Mary Lynn. The sailor was being virtually offered his pick of them. Each seemed to melt when he looked her over to make his choice.

'What's your name, honey?' He familiarly slid a hand around the waist of the chosen one and let it ride down low, resting suggestively near the curve of her bottom.

'Donna May.' Adoration dominated her expression, not even a hint of objection showing at the near-intimate contact.

The sailor bent down and whispered something in Donna May's ear, then straightened to say, 'I'll take you to a movie. How's that?'

'I'd love it just fine.' She was atremble with some kind of wild excitement, triumphant while the other two girls started to drift away, disappointed yet already looking down the street in anticipation of another chance.

When the young girl started to move off in the company of the sailor, it was more than Mary Lynn could tolerate. 'Does your mother know you're doing this?' she demanded. 'How old are you?'

The girl turned, angry and defensive, clutching the sailor's arm as if she was afraid she might lose him. 'It's none of your business, lady.'

Mary Lynn glared at the sailor, finding him equally to blame. 'She's hardly more than a child.' The sailor was unmoved by her protest.

'I'm old enough,' the girl, Donna May, insisted, and jerked her head in the direction of the oncoming bus. 'Why don't you get on your bus and leave us alone. No one asked you to butt in.'

Brake shoes screeched against the drums as the bus rattled to a halt at the curb stop. Mary Lynn hesitated a second longer, staring at the sailor and the child-woman, then swung aboard. The crowded bus reeked of sweaty, unwashed bodies and stale tobacco smoke, odors made all the more objectionable by the hot and humid July air. A small space was available on a front seat and Mary Lynn wedged her hips into the narrow section between two seated passengers as the bus lurched forward.

Through a dust-filmed window, Mary Lynn watched the sailor and the girl stroll along the sidewalk, acting more like lovers than the strangers they were. Mary Lynn's apple-cheeked features wore an unusual expression of stern disapproval. The woman passenger on her right, dressed in the garb of a factory worker, noticed it and the object of its censure.

'Disgusting, isn't it?' she agreed.

'She's too young to know what she's doing.' It was a frustrated protest.

'Khaki-wacky, they call it,' came the dryly cynical response. 'Some of these young kids go crazy over anyone in uniform. I've seen them in drug stores trying to buy . . . you know . . . protection. This war, it's doing things to all of us.' She lit a cigarette, something manly about the way she exhaled the smoke and pinched out the match. 'I don't know. Maybe they're right and we should grab everything we can today.'

Mary Lynn fell silent rather than continue the depressing conversation. As long as the bus moved, a wind swept through the opened windows and offered the passengers some relief. But it was short-lived, dying down at every block corner while the bus let passengers out and took more in, letting the stifling close air fill the interior. Old, mansard-roofed homes with vine-choked iron grillwork and tall colonnades lent a shabby elegance to the city gone wild with the war boom, which crowded its streets with

190

people and littered its gutters with fly-attracting trash.

Outside a movie house, jammed around the ticket booth, were children of all ages, from a sleeping toddler held in the aching arms of a seven-year-old to a cigarette-smoking nine-year-old dictator keeping his brood of siblings close by. Few adults were in sight.

'Lock-outs, most of them,' the woman said.

'What?'

'They're locked out of their houses. Their mothers are working somewhere and don't want their kids alone in the house so they lock them out and send them to the movies – a cheap babysitter,' the woman announced. 'Doorkey children are the other kind. They wear the key to the front door around their necks so they don't lose it. It's sad. It's really sad.'

They moved past the theater and the wind was once again blowing through the windows. The bus turned onto a tree-shaded street and Mary Lynn strained to see the white frame house with its long front porch.

Her mother's welcome was less than warm when Mary Lynn reached the house. A more pinched and worn-out look marked her mother's features, but her eyes remained dark, burning coals of light – angry and hungry for something, Mary Lynn knew not what. She was taking in boarders now, renting out the spare rooms.

'You're working too hard, Mama.' Pity rose at the driven weariness she sensed in her mother. There were four boarders, she'd learned, occupying the spare beds in shifts. 'Holding down a night job plus keeping up this house and renting out rooms . . .'

'Sleeping space is at a premium in this town,' her mother declared. 'If this war will just last a few more years, your papa and I will be able to pay off the mortgage on this house and have some money set aside for our old age as well.'

The greed she heard in her mother's voice twisted her insides. To wish for the war to continue because of the money that could be made from it struck Mary Lynn as selfish and callous. Beau was fighting in this war. If it was prolonged, his exposure to danger would be that much longer.

But while she bitterly resented her mother's greed, Mary Lynn could understand it. Her parents had lost a lot during the Depression, barely managing to keep the family home. Her mother had hated being poor and doing without. It had soured her and made money an obsession.

Without thinking, Mary Lynn took a cigarette from the pack in her small purse. She tapped it on the table to pack the loose tobacco. With a jaundiced eye, her mother observed the action.

'What other dreadful habits have you picked up in Texas besides smoking and wearing men's pants?' she asked reproachfully.

'Mama, it's difficult to climb in and out of planes in a skirt.' Mary Lynn defended the practicality of her attire, but made no attempt to justify the cigarette in her hand.

'It's certainly not ladylike.'

She lit the cigarette and took a drag from it. Trails of smoke were released as she responded to the remark. 'Maybe it's time you looked at yourself in the mirror, Mama.'

The visit with her mother wasn't a pleasant one. It was almost a relief when it was time to return to the airfield and make the long flight back to Sweetwater. The next time she came home, her stay would be longer and a pair of silver wings would be pinned to her uniform.

The incessant hot wind flung dust at Rachel's face, making her eyes smart with the fine particles, but it provided some relief from the blistering temperatures on that early afternoon in late July. She stood outside the ready room with Helen Shaw and two other Woofteds, waiting for their instructors to arrive. The twin-engined Cessna Bobcats were parked on the flight line, all serviced for an afternoon of radio navigation practice. Graduation was so close all of them could taste it.

'My parents are catching the train from Oklahoma to be here when I get those silver wings pinned on me,' Helen said, adding wryly, 'presuming, of course, that I pass the check rides.'

'You will,' Rachel replied confidently.

A shirt-sleeved instructor stepped out of the building behind them. 'All right, let's cut the gabbing and get the plane checked out.' The order was directed at Helen and her flightmate that day, Carla Ellers.

'It looks like we'll be the first off the ground. You can follow us in your Bunson Burner. That way you won't get lost on your way to Big Spring,' Helen gibed at Rachel, and winked as she headed for the planes with the boxy fuselage, constructed of plywood.

Despite the five-minute head start Helen had, Rachel had her AT-17 in sight shortly after taking off from Avenger Field. Both had successfully bracketed the radio beam to Big Spring and had the unbroken hum of its signal droning in their ears. Helen's twin-engined aircraft kept the lead. It was always within Rachel's range of vision as she flew the beam with her instructor in the copilot's seat and Barbara Frye, a fellow trainee, sitting in the unenviable position of the rear seat.

That low, irregularly shaped hill, the landmark she always associated with Big Spring, jutted onto the horizon. Their destination was just ahead. Rachel reached to turn down the volume of the radio signal so her hearing would be attuned for that brief cone of silence when they passed over the beacon.

Out of the corner of her eye, she caught the flash of something in the sky just ahead of her. Rachel looked up as the AT-17, the notorious 'Bunson Burner' flying the lead, exploded into a yellow ball of flowering flame that turned quickly into smoke and fiery chunks of debris.

'My God.' The whispered words came from Joe Gibbs, her instructor.

Rachel's throat was paralyzed; nothing could come out. In silent horror, she watched bits and pieces of burning, smoking debris scatter through the sky while the main core spiraled to the ground – a slow, tortuous death spiral. There was no need to look for parachutes; there hadn't been time for anyone to bail out.

Mesmerized by the nightmarish sight of the burning wreckage falling to earth, Rachel stared at it, turning to watch as they flew over it. It had been consumed by flames within seconds. Death had come swiftly to the occupants, maybe right after they heard the explosion or saw the first flames. One charged second of fear, surrounded by fire, and it had been over.

Sweat ran from her pores, drenching her skin. She was afraid to close her eyes; already she could see engulfing flames leap around her in yellow glee. Rachel started shaking with fear as the first sob rose in her throat.

'All right, snap out of it, Goldman,' Joe Gibbs ordered harshly. 'Pay attention to what you're doing. You're way off the beam. What kind of a pilot are you? No wonder you're always getting lost.'

His harsh criticisms forced her attention away from the smoke trailing from the crash site. The *da-dit, da-dit* in her earphones confirmed she had strayed to the left of the beam, but she couldn't have cared less. She turned an embittered look on her instructor, tears blurring her eyes.

'That was my friend in that plane.' Her teeth were clenched together in a combination of intense pain and anger.

'Are you piloting this plane or not?' he challenged coldly.

'Yes!' Rachel flashed, and grimly turned the plane back on course, locating the beam, while he radioed a report of the accident to the base at Big Spring.

It wasn't until later that evening that Rachel remembered Helen's instructor, Frank Lawson, had been a close friend of Gibbs's. Likely as not, he'd been yelling at himself as much as at her, but she couldn't forgive his callousness at that moment, any more than she could forget the fire in the sky.

Avenger Field was stunned and shaken by the deaths of the two trainees and their instructor. The tragedy transcended the petty feud between the Houston half of the class and the Avenger pioneers. Flying had always been an exciting challenge to them, something of a thrill. On this eve of graduation, they were forced to face the reality that it was also dangerous. Flying might seem a glamorous duty to be performed for the war effort, but they were also risking their lives in doing it.

That night in the bay, Cappy urged Rachel to tell them what had happened. Rumor had already circulated the base that she had been a witness to the midair explosion.

When she had finished, Rachel lowered her head and bitterly recalled, 'On the flight line, Helen jokingly referred to it as the "Bunson Burner." We all called it that, I guess.' The cockiness had been knocked out of them.

On graduation day, the class of 43-W-3 marched by the single-engined Texan toward the reviewing stand where Jacqueline Cochran waited to pin on their wings, while four more classes undergoing staggered training looked on. All women pilots, those in the Army Air Force, in training, or in the ferry division of the Air Transport Command, were now under the sole jurisdiction of the Director of Women Pilots, Jacqueline Cochran, whose offices were located in the newly built Pentagon. Nancy Harkness Love would continue as the Director of the WAFs in the Air Transport Command.

On August 5, 1943, the women pilots and trainees were finally given an official designation: the Women Airforce Service Pilots. From that day forward, they would be known by their acronym, the WASPs.

CHAPTER THIRTEEN

Proudly sporting her hard-earned silver wings on the collar of her white shirt, Marty hefted her suitcase and walked away from the taxicab backing out of her parents' driveway. Detroit had changed. The numerous war plants had attracted thousands of workers to the city, a large number of them 'po' whites' from the South. On the drive from the train station, Marty had noticed the increased number of tents and tarpaper shacks, and the dank basements of houses that would never be built, called 'foxhole homes.'

She climbed the porch steps of the rambling two-story house, conscious of the sweltering August heat. A service flag hung in the window, white with a red border and one blue star which signified the occupant had one child in the service. The front screen door opened under the turn of her hand and Marty walked in, the heavy suitcase banging against her leg.

'Hello! Anybody home?'

'Who is it?' a woman's voice answered in imperious demand.

'Surprise! It's me. I'm home,' she called in a rasping and happy voice.

'You aren't supposed to be here until tonight.' Her mother appeared in the molded archway to the entry hall.

'I caught an earlier train. Remember that rich girl I told you who lived in my bay? Her family chauffeur was driving her car back to New York and I hitched a ride with him as far as Dallas and managed to catch a different train.' She set her suitcase down by the newel post of the staircase and stood proudly at attention, her chest out and the boat-shaped general's cap perched atop her short, sand-colored curls. 'Well, what do you think of them?'

Althea Rogers checked the embrace she had been about to give her daughter and frowned. 'What?'

'My wings!' Marty said in exasperation and grasped the collar of her shirt to show them to her mother. 'See.'

'They are very nice,' the small and slender woman said with some enthusiasm, but Marty detected the perfunctory note in it. Age had lightened her mother's dark hair to an iron shade of gray and she wore it in a matronly bun, long sweeping waves softly framing her face before being drawn back to the nape of her neck. Dark eyes critically surveyed Marty's attire. 'Martha Jane, you didn't travel in that outfit, did you? Slacks in public?'

'You know how I hate that name. I wish you wouldn't call me that,' Marty protested, her elated spirits flattening. 'And, yes, I wore this on the train. It's our uniform, until we get an official one.'

'Is that right?' Her physician father came into the foyer, tall and ramrod straight, a stern-faced man accustomed to withholding his emotions and not allowing himself to become too personally involved with others.

'Dad.' Marty hugged him and received a kiss on the forehead. 'We've been officially named the WASPs by the government,' she went on to explain, '– which is short for Women Airforce Service Pilots. So now you have two children in the service and you can put another star on that flag in the window.'

'I'm afraid we can't do that,' he replied with a distantly kind look. 'Those stars are supposed to represent those in service in one of the armed services. You're in a civilian organization attached to the Army but not a part of it.'

'We will be,' Marty insisted. 'Right now we have officer status and all the privileges of rank. If David was home, he'd have to salute me because he's just an enlisted man.'

'I wish you could have been here when he was home on leave the last of June. He looked so handsome in his uniform,' her mother declared and took her arm. 'Come. I want to show you the pictures we took while he was here. He had so many ribbons and little badges he wore on his uniform – sharpshooting medals and things.' She led Marty into the living room. 'The heat was terrible while David was here. Here he was, home on leave, and wanting to go out and have a good time, and Detroit was under martial law with curfews and federal troops patrolling the streets. It ruined his furlough.'

'I heard about it.' Resentment swelled in her; the conversation was already centering on David and she'd barely been home five minutes.

'Did your mother write that David shipped out?' Her father lowered his long, lanky frame into an armchair while her mother sat down on the matching sofa and opened a leather-bound photo album. 'The entire Hundred-and-first Airborne Division has been sent to a staging area in England.'

'I'm supposed to report to Jacqueline Cochran in the Pentagon. A bunch of us got the same orders, so we don't know what we'll be doing. It's kind of mysterious.'

'I expect David will be going into action soon,' her father said.

'Look at this photo of David. It was taken the very day he came home.' Her mother lifted the photo album onto Marty's lap and pointed out the picture. 'You can't see it very well, but we had a big Welcome Home sign strung across the front porch.'

The pages of the photo album were filled with pictures and her brother David was in the center of every one of them. Bitterly deflated, Marty realized that while Detroit might have changed, nothing was any different at home.

Surrounded by thick, white carpeting, the black marble tub sat in the middle of the room, filled with hot, scented water and mounded with bubbles. Reclining along the full length of it, Eden let her body go limp. Her hair was piled on top of her head in a mass of sorrel curls, its length sleeked away from her neck to avoid the dampness of the perfumed bubbles.

Through slitted eyes, she saw the maid enter, an older

woman with muddy gray hair who didn't appear entirely comfortable in the starched, black uniform. She approached the marble bath, raised by two steps onto a platform.

'Your drink, miss.'

With a motion marked by languor, Eden removed the glass of iced Scotch from the proffered tray. 'Thank you.' She couldn't recall the maid's name. In her absence there had been almost a complete turnover of servants in her parents' Manhattan apartment. She took a sip of the aged liquor and felt the velvet fire burn her throat.

'Miss?' The maid continued to hover by the tub, and Eden unwillingly opened an eye to acknowledge her. 'There's a gentleman to see you. What should I tell him?'

'Tell him I'm indisposed and to call later. No, wait!' Eden lifted the glass of Scotch in a detaining gesture. 'Who is it?'

'A Mr Steele, miss.'

'Ham?! Show him in,' she insisted, instantly delighted at the thought of seeing her faithful suitor again.

There wasn't much about Hamilton Steele to make her heart beat faster, but he was a dear friend. She ignored the maid's stiffnecked disapproval as the woman withdrew from the spacious bath. Eden took another drink of Scotch and savored its smoothness going down.

Scant minutes had passed before the maid returned with the scion of a New York banking family in tow. Conservative to the core, Hamilton Steele was dressed in the requisite dark pin-striped suit and silk tie. Wire-rimmed glasses snugly hugged his head, their thick lenses magnifying his shrewd but kindly eyes. Short of stature, he was trimly built despite his staid life style and forty-plus years, revealed by his fast-thinning hairline. Eden laughed at his briefly disconcerted expression when he saw her lounging in the tub full of bubbles.

'Ham, darling, come in.' The hand holding her drink gestured toward the dainty brass chair in the corner of the bathroom, its cushioned seat covered in white velvet. His hesitation was momentary before he turned to give his hat to the maid. 'When the masseuse comes, have her wait,' Eden informed the maid, then cast an amused glance at Hamilton. 'Would you like something to drink, Ham?'

'No. I think not.' He watched the servant leave the bathroom, then with a hitch of his trousers he sat on the delicate chair to face the marble bath. Recovering his aplomb, he managed a touch of wry humor. 'My grasp of history may be faulty, but I don't believe ladies have entertained gentlemen callers in their boudoirs – let alone their baths – since before the Victorian era.'

Eden laughed in her throat and sank a little deeper into the tub, luxuriating in the sensation of bathing in scented bubbles and nearly two feet of hot water. 'If you only knew how I have fantasized about this moment after six months of lukewarm showers,' she murmured. Then, in the middle of a sip, 'I nearly forgot to thank you for the flowers. They were waiting for me when I arrived yesterday. It was especially nice since neither Mother nor Father was on hand to welcome me home.'

'I'm sorry. If I had known, I would have picked you up at the station.'

She gazed at him across the frothy clouds of bubbles, aware he meant it. It was funny how time had a way of altering the memory of a person. His dark hair was thinner than she remembered, although it was artfully combed to conceal the encroaching baldness. At the same time, she'd thought of him as being shorter, when he was actually the same height that she was. The gold-wire glasses gave him a very studious look, but she had forgotten the way his eyes could sometimes twinkle. For all his staid character, he was a good man. She could certainly do worse than marrying him. Eden almost laughed out loud when she realized what she was thinking.

'If you had really wanted to be thoughtful, Ham, you would have had a case of the best Scotch in New York waiting for me,' she declared. 'You can't know how I've missed all this. I've already warned Father that I intend to make the most of my leave. I've earned myself some time on the town and I'm going to have it. The theater, the best restaurants, the fanciest clothes – and dancing until dawn.' On the last, she lifted her glass in a salute to her plans. 'No more jukebox music, Texas bootleg, or stew!'

Her avowal eased the concerns that had been bothering him while she'd been away. The glamor and excitement associated with flying had not supplanted her love of life's creature comforts. What he lacked in virility and charm, he made up for in patience. He had weathered her affair with the chauffeur and that dalliance with the impoverished Italian count, and other would-be lovers who didn't have his staying power. Always, she'd come back to him. Hamilton Steele was confident that she would ultimately marry him.

If basically she was selfish and spoiled, she was also a caring woman. Hamilton understood that, just as he understood that her dream of a *grande passion* still lingered, whether she acknowledged it or not. He could have told her that was all so much romantic nonsense. He was older, by some eighteen years, and wiser, so he knew.

A sound, lasting marriage was founded by two people of similar backgrounds and tastes, such as they shared, with differing personalities to spice their joint existence. Her outgoing, uninhibited nature kept him from becoming too dull and unadventurous, while his stability prompted her to be more circumspect about her behavior. They were a good match – his maturity and experience, and her vitality and youth.

'I am so glad to hear you say that, my dear Eden.' Hamilton reached inside the jacket of his suit to remove the small envelope from the inner breast pocket. 'Because I happen to have two tickets for this evening's performance of *Oklahoma*! The critics have been giving it rave notices, and I was hoping to persuade you to accompany me tonight.'

'Ham, you darling! Of course I will. And afterwards we can have dinner at Twenty-One or maybe the Stork Club, then to the Copacabana, the Latin Quarter . . . Who's at the Wedgwood Room? We could go there. I want to visit them all!' Eden finished with a rush of enthusiasm.

His gaze slipped from her face, distracted by the tantalizing glimpses of her milk-white body. A patient man he might be, but a saint he wasn't. It was impossible to sit calmly and view her growing nakedness without being stirred by it, nor could he affect nonchalance.

'I hate to inform you on this point, Eden, but your . . . cover of bubbles is dissolving,' he murmured discreetly.

'Poor Ham.' She laughed at his demand for modesty, but acquiesced to it. 'Fetch me another drink while I climb out of the tub.'

Nearly every night of her leave, Hamilton Steele escorted Eden somewhere – to the blacked-out district of Broadway or the garishly plush nightclubs with their elaborate floor shows. He ignored the crowds of shirt-sleeved war workers, flush with their big paychecks, sitting in front-row seats, and the multitude of servicemen crowding the dance floors at the clubs, fully aware they cut a more dashing figure than he did.

As long as he was willing to pay scalpers' prices, he could obtain tickets to any show in town, and a hundred-dollar bill would get him the best table at any nightspot. They were sitting at one such table, surrounded by two-inch-thick pile carpeting, velvet-covered walls – the ones not studded with mirrors – and satin drapes, all the extravagance and waste an escape-hungry public could want.

'It stank.' Eden sipped at her twelve-year-old Scotch while she offered her opinion of Moss Hart's *Winged Victory*. 'God help us if our combat pilots are as brainless as the ones in that play.'

'I could sympathize with the wives,' Hamilton ventured. 'Especially when one of them complained that all her husband talked about was flying.'

'Are you implying that I do that?' she asked innocently.

'My dear, you have talked of little else. I probably know as much about the idiosyncrasies of an AT-6 as you do,' he replied dryly. 'For someone who has complained as vociferously as you have about the hardships you endured, you show a remarkable affection for it. If you hated it as much as you pretend, you would have quit.'

'I loved it,' Eden admitted. 'Sand, sun, and all.' With a rare bit of honesty she added, 'Of course, I knew it was only temporary, too, which added to the feeling of adventure.'

'That's true.' Hamilton relaxed.

'You don't like to fly, do you?' She studied him with a sideways glance.

'If man were meant to fly . . .' He didn't bother to finish the obvious thought. 'Let's find another subject to discuss tonight.'

'Such as?' Nothing interested her as much, so she looked away, seeking a diversion. Her eye was caught by a tall, willowy blonde just emerging from the backstage area by a side curtain. Without the familiar flight togs, it was a full minute before Eden recognized the glamorous woman. 'Rachel!' She blurted out the name, their sometimes less-than-cordial relationship momentarily forgotten in the surprise of seeing a fellow flyer.

Hearing her name called, Rachel turned to glance around the luxurious club. When she spied Eden, she appeared to hesitate before she finally approached their table. Hamilton politely stood up, self-conscious as Rachel towered over him with her six-foot height.

Eden glossed over the introductions, then cloaked her curiosity with an idle remark. 'I never expected to run into you. I guess it proves New York is just a small town after all.'

'I was visiting some friends backstage.' Rachel was aloof and defensive under Eden's prying look. 'I used to dance in the floor show here.'

'Would you care to join us for a drink?' Hamilton gestured toward the empty chair.

'I'm with someone.' As if on cue, a man wound his way through the crowd of tables to Rachel's side. He had jet-black hair and piercing blue eyes; though he was shorter than Rachel by two inches, his stature was oddly not diminished by her.

'More friends of yours?' he said, prompting Rachel to introduce them.

She did so with reluctance. 'Eden, Zach Jordan, a friend of mine.' She seemed none too certain of that.

'Eden van Valkenburg. Rachel and I flew together at Sweetwater,' Eden informed him while she appreciatively eyed the darkly handsome man in the Army uniform, a little surprised by his enlisted status since theoretically WASPs weren't supposed to fraternize with enlisted men. 'This is Hamilton Steele.'

'A pleasure.' With a certain arrogance in his style, Zach Jordan shook hands with Hamilton, bowing slightly.

Hamilton began to repeat his earlier invitation. 'I was just suggesting we all have drinks –'

'I explained we were leaving,' Rachel pointedly interrupted him, while Zach Jordan appeared amused by the assertion.

'Another time, perhaps,' he suggested to temper the curtness of Rachel's refusal.

Thoughtfully, Eden watched them work their way through the packed house to the club's exit. When they disappeared from her sight, she took an absent sip of her drink and noticed the way Hamilton was eyeing her.

'Is something wrong?' she wondered.

He lifted a shoulder in a dismissive shrug, then commented, 'He is a handsome soldier.'

A smile spread slowly across her scarlet lips. 'Ham, I do believe you're jealous.'

'Jealous.' He seemed to consider the possibility. 'Perhaps. But I know the day will come when you'll discover you can love me.'

For a long minute, she simply looked at him, at a loss for a reply that wouldn't hurt his feelings. She was fond of him, but it was the kind of attachment one had for a pet. The kind thing would have been to end their relationship years ago, but she selfishly wanted his friendship.

Behind a diaphanous curtain a big band struck the opening note of a song, signaling the start of the flashy costumed floor show, and the need for a response was eliminated.

Outside, it was a warm, summer's night in Manhattan. An occasional breeze found its way amid the canyons of tall concrete structures. With the lithe stride of a dancer, Rachel walked along the sidewalk, ignoring the soldier who effortlessly kept pace with her. People were sitting on building stoops, young and old alike, enjoying the night air.

With a turn of his head, Zach Jordan inspected the rare beauty of her profile. 'Why are you ignoring me?'

Rachel stopped and swung around to challenge him. 'Look, I didn't ask you to come along with me tonight. You invited yourself. All you do is talk about Palestine. And all my father does is pray.'

She had an immediate image of her father with his black-and white prayer shawl about his shoulders while he rocked and talked with his God. As more stories about Hitler's persecution of fellow Jews filtered through to the United States, her father seemed to become that much more religious. For Rachel, the little knot of fear in her heart for her grandmother's safety grew tighter.

'No lectures.' A smile etched itself into the corners of his mouth, deepening them. 'You and I are alike, Rachel. The things that drive your father to prayer fill us with the need to fight.'

The man bothered her, irritating her with his arrogance, that glitter in his eyes stirring up a restlessness which contradicted all her dislike. She'd met Zach Jordan two days after she'd returned. Homeless, he was spending his leave with a Jewish family whose son was a friend of his in the Army.

They lived in the same neighborhood as Rachel's parents. In that first accidental meeting, their chemistries had mixed with instant results.

'I don't fight. I fly planes.' She seized on the small detail to deny any common calling. 'The Army doesn't believe a woman can fight.'

'They have never heard of Deborah,' he replied smoothly.

'What does it matter?' Impatiently, she would have turned away and resumed walking, but his hands caught her shoulders. His touch was warm against her skin, firm without being hard. That crazy ambivalence kept her motionless, struggling between two conflicting emotional responses.

'It matters,' Zach said. 'After the war is over, you and I are going to marry.'

'No!' The shocked denial rushed from her at the preposterous suggestion she would marry a virtual stranger.

But he continued as if she had said nothing. 'We will go to Palestine. No more will we be wandering Jews without a homeland.' His hand cupped the side of her face, his thumb stroking the point of her chin in an idle caress while his gaze roamed her features and came to a stop on her lips. 'Our children will be born there, true sabras.'

With fingertip pressure, he urged her to him. Before their lips met, Rachel caught the warmth of his breath and the male scent that drifted from his lean cheeks. Then her senses were engrossed in the persuasion of his mouth as it moved against her. She liked the taste and feel of the kiss, the confident ardor that solicited her response.

When he drew away, his gaze ran over her face to gauge her reaction. A small smile of satisfaction appeared on his mouth, that intense light in his blue eyes darkening a little. Zach Jordan was so damned sure of himself Rachel wished she hadn't found so much pleasure in his kiss.

The hard shell snapped back in place to cover up her vulnerability as she turned away and began walking down the street again, looking straight ahead. 'You presume an awful lot, Zach Jordan,' she said mockingly. 'What makes you think I care about any of those things?'

He matched pace with her, eyes to the front as well, with that smile still etched in the corners of his mouth.

'Because we are alike, you and I. We want the same things – including the freedom to be a Jew, and we are willing to fight for it.'

'Such idealism.' But her tone of voice scorned him. 'Am I supposed to believe all this nonsense?'

'I mean every word of it,' he insisted smoothly.

'In other words' – Rachel threw him a sidelong glance – 'you are asking me to marry you?'

Blandly he met her skeptical gaze, taking note of its challenge, and answered simply, 'Yes.'

Startled by his easy reply when she had expected to catch him out, Rachel stared wildly straight ahead once again. 'Do you feel safe in saying that because you know I'll refuse?' Her voice accused him.

'Partly. But believe this, we will marry and you will have my sons,' Zach said with calm assurance.

Rachel was shaken by how much she wanted to believe him. A door opened as they passed, momentarily throwing light onto the sidewalk. Her side vision caught the tan color of his Army uniform.

'You're a soldier going off to war,' she tersely reminded him.

He caught her hand as his smile deepened. 'I promise you I'm not going to die.'

It irritated her that he should treat the possibility with amusement. 'You joke,' Rachel accused.

'You care,' Zach replied, that arrogantly pleased look spreading across his darkly good-looking features. His claim was suddenly impossible to deny. 'Rachel, Rachel.' He murmured her name with such longing and tested patience. 'My leave will be up soon, and I'll have to be reporting back to my company. Let's spend what time I have left together.'

The windows of the darkened hotel room stood open, letting in any vagrant breeze that happened by. Bedsheets rustled as their bodies moved, their heads turning on pillows to gaze at one another through the dimness of night. The sounds of the city street below – the blare of a horn or the shout of a reveler – intruded not at all.

Studying his face, its thick black brows and unbelievably blue eyes, Rachel felt all warm and loose, blissfully spent. The moment had an intimacy to it that exceeded the sexual closeness they had enjoyed only moments ago.

'Didn't I tell you it would be good?' Zach boasted. He leaned over to kiss the rounded point of her shoulder, then stayed close, his hand sliding around to rub the smooth ridges of her lower spine.

'Do you know I don't remember agreeing to any of this?' she countered, the bemused smile of satisfaction never once leaving her mouth.

'That's because I didn't ask.'

In this present whipped-cream mood, it was impossible for Rachel to take offense at that very male remark. Especially when Zach followed it with a nibble of her sensitive shoulder ridge, a sensual foray that eventually lowered to nuzzle a small breast. Her fingers curled through his black hair and dug into his scalp as she arched her body forward. That darting tongue encircling her erect nipple was arousing her again.

The weight of his hard, muscled body pressed her backwards while his hair-roughened legs entwined with her long limbs. Talk was unnecessary, but they murmured to each other, meaningless love words, as hands roamed and caressed all the intimate places. Soon the spiral of desire had them straining for an even tighter embrace, bodies moist, tongues tangling and mating.

The looming shadows of the war lent an urgency to everything. Each moment of happiness had to be snatched and savored. If she was letting herself in for a big hurt, Rachel didn't care. For all his promises, Zach couldn't guarantee he would survive the war. It was only a matter of days before he would be leaving – possibly never to return. This time together had no right or wrong to it. Its very impermanence made it all the more cherished.

As dawn's first light was tinting a gray sky, Zach walked

Rachel to the front steps of her parents' home. 'I'll speak to your father about us.'

'No.' Rachel wasn't going to pretend there was a future for them. 'Do you think the Army will send you to the Pacific?'

'The Seventh is fighting in Sicily,' he replied after a small pause, then went on. 'The beachheads of the Pacific belong to the Navy and the Marines. Artillery fighting is a war of nerves. The big stuff will be sent to Europe.' He angled his body closer to her, his hand gliding down her arm in an absent caress that seemed to say he couldn't get enough of her. 'We only have two days left.'

So little time, Rachel wanted to cry, but there was a war on. In her heart of hearts, she wished only that she could go with Zach and fight at his side. She looked at the door of her parents' house, then suggested, 'Let's go eat somewhere.'

Everything was crowded in Washington, DC. The plush Mayflower Hotel on Connecticut Avenue was no different. The patrons in the dining room were elbow to elbow; tables and chairs were jammed to fill every available inch of space, leaving little room for walking. Military uniforms of every style and branch colored a room otherwise populated with dark-suited men, an assorted collection of government officials, 'dollar-a-year' men, and 'five percenters.' The latter were so called because that was their cut of the government contracts they negotiated for a business. The dollar-a-year men received that amount as their government salary, supplemented by their own companies while they held down government jobs and used their influence on behalf of their company whenever they could. Spicing the dining-room atmosphere were the foreign accents of visiting dignitaries and their resident diplomatic corps.

Exhaling the last drag of smoke, Cappy crushed the cigarette in the ashtray and glanced across the table at her mother. 'I can be as stubborn as he is,' she said, regretting that her mother was caught in this tug of war between her father and herself. 'I'm not coming home until he invites me.'

'He's a proud man.' She pleaded with Cappy to be reasonable. 'He doesn't own a monopoly on pride,' she countered stiffly. Then she signed the check, charging it to her room. With the restaurant check and her purse in hand, Cappy pushed away from the table. 'Shall we leave?'

Without waiting for her mother's nod of agreement, she rose to wend her way through the labyrinth of tables and chairs to the cashier. After she'd shown her room key to the cashier and left the check, Cappy continued into the richly appointed hotel lobby, typically packed with people. Once there, she paused to let her mother join her.

'I don't see how you can afford to stay here.' Sue Hayward looked about her surroundings with a dubious expression.

Actually she couldn't, but Cappy didn't admit that to her mother. She had been lucky the first two weeks of her leave, staying at the apartment of a friend who was between roommates. But no one in Washington could afford the rent being charged. Cappy had contributed her share during her stay at Annie's, but when her friend had a chance for a permanent roommate, she had to take it. And Cappy had checked into the Mayflower.

'It's only temporary,' she reminded her mother. 'I have to report to my new assignment in two days.'

Her stay at the hotel was more temporary than her mother knew, since hotel policy limited an individual's stay to three days. Cappy had just used the last night. If she couldn't persuade the management to bend the rules a little, she'd have to find a room at another hotel.

'I'm so glad you're going to be stationed close by,' her mother said. 'I was afraid they'd send you to California or some other place far away.'

'I know.' Despite an earlier denial by her mother, Cappy suspected that her father had pulled some strings to arrange this assignment for her, stationed at an air base just outside of Washington. It sounded like something he'd do to keep an eye on her.

A minor stir was created in the lobby as a tall, gorgeous redhead swept into the hotel, followed by a small entourage consisting of a well-dressed but self-effacing man, a maid carrying hatboxes, and three porters with an equal number of trunks. A smile of recognition flashed into Cappy's expression.

'Eden!' She hailed her friend and dragged her mother across the lobby to meet the woman chicly suited in blue linen. 'Talk about making an entrance,' Cappy chided after they had clasped arms in a laughing embrace of surprise. She glanced at the steamer trunks. 'You didn't learn a thing at Sweetwater, did you?'

'Oh, no, I'm not about to make that mistake again,' Eden assured her. 'Two of these trunks will be shipped right back to New York *before* I report. Ham and I decided to come down a couple of days early, and I wanted to be sure I had plenty of clothes to wear,' she explained with a sly smile at her extravagance. 'Who knows when I'll get another chance to wear all of them again.'

A moment was taken for introductions. After Cappy presented her mother, she was introduced to the older man accompanying Eden. She recognized Hamilton Steele's name and curiously eyed the man who, Eden had said, wanted to marry her. Cappy wondered if there was any significance to their traveling together – if perhaps absence had made the heart beat faster. But Eden seemed to treat her companion very casually.

'Excuse me while I make certain our reservations are in order.' Hamilton Steele smiled politely to Cappy and her mother, then withdrew.

'He seems nice.' But Cappy's glance at Eden was quietly speculating.

One shoulder lifted in an elegant shrug. 'They're either too young or too old,' she said wryly. 'I decided old was better.'

'That's not very kind.' She was surprised by Eden's apparently callous attitude.

'No,' she agreed. 'But then I'm not very kind to Ham.'

The significance of these remarks seemed to escape Mrs Hayward, whose interest was focused on her daughter. 'Are you going to be assigned to the same base with Cappy, Miss van Valkenburg? After flying together at Sweetwater, it would be wonderful if you could continue together.'

'I don't know anything about my assignment,' Eden replied. 'It's all very secret and mysterious. My orders simply said to report to Jacqueline Cochran, room 4D957, the Pentagon. As a matter of fact, everyone in our bay – except Cappy – received the same instructions.'

'How strange,' Mrs Hayward murmured.

'Yes. Have you had lunch?' Eden inquired, changing the subject.

'Yes, we have,' Cappy replied as her mother glanced at her watch.

'It's time I was catching the bus home if I want to avoid being caught in the late afternoon crush. It was a pleasure meeting you, Miss van Valkenburg. Cappy.' She kissed her daughter's cheek.

As she left them, Eden surmised, 'You still haven't patched things up with your father?'

'No,' Cappy admitted without remorse.

'Where are you staying?'

'I had a room here.' Cappy explained her predicament, the hotel's policy, and the uncertainty about where to-night's lodging might be.

Despite considerable persuasion on Eden's part, and that of her friend Hamilton Steele, the management wouldn't budge, insisting they didn't dare make exceptions. In the end, Cappy packed her suitcases and had the bellboy carry them down to the lobby for her.

'I know some of the staff at the Carleton,' Hamilton Steele volunteered when Cappy rejoined them. 'If you would like, I –'

'Cappy!' The anger and exasperation in the male voice

calling her name was evident in its explosive quality. Cappy turned to see Mitch Ryan in his major's uniform pushing through the lobby crowd to get to her. Along the way he was forced to pause now and then to perfunctorily salute a superior officer. The irritated snap stayed in his voice when he reached her. 'I've been trying to get hold of you for the last three days. What are you doing here? You were supposed to be staying at Annie Kramer's apartment. I finally went over to where she works and she tells me you're staying here.'

Cappy briefly explained her situation, then belatedly introduced Eden and Hamilton. Mitch acknowledged them and attempted to stifle some of his impatience.

'I've been on an inspection tour these last two weeks,' he began. His glance strayed beyond Cappy as he paused, coming to military attention, and threw a salute at a set of general's stars on an Army brown uniform. Then he relaxed. 'I've been trying to reach you ever since I got back.'

'I didn't know,' she said a shade defensively.

'Is this your luggage?' He indicated the set stacked next to Eden, and began grabbing it up when Cappy nodded in the affirmative. 'I've got a jeep out front,' Mitch said, tucking a hand under her arm and excusing them from Eden and Hamilton's company. As he guided her toward the door, another officer, this time a colonel, passed him, requiring another salute from Mitch. 'Let's get out of here,' he muttered near her ear. 'I've never seen so many caps with scrambled eggs on them in one place before.'

Outside, Mitch helped her into the open jeep and stowed her luggage in the rear. 'I haven't had time to make a reservation at another hotel,' Cappy warned him.

'Never mind. I know where you can stay.' He vaulted into the jeep and slipped behind the wheel, his hat pulled low on his forehead.

The heavy traffic on the capital's streets demanded Mitch's undivided attention. Cappy didn't distract him with questions about their destination as he drove through the snarled jams of cars and assorted motor vehicles. With the Lincoln and Washington Memorials behind them, they crossed the Potomac and approached the National Cemetery at Arlington.

Nodding his head, Mitch directed her attention to it. Burial services were being held on a hill slope, a dark rectangle of exposed earth cut into the summer-yellow grass.

'There will be more of those before it's over,' he said flatly. Cappy knew it was true, but the remark didn't warrant a comment. Shortly, they passed the huge Pentagon building, and Mitch turned the jeep off the main road onto a residential side street. When he stopped they were parked in front of an apartment building.

'Who lives here?' Cappy asked, studying the well-built complex as she climbed out the jeep.

'I do.' Hefting her luggage under his arm, Mitch started for the entrance.

'I'm not staying here.' She followed him to the apartment door, stunned and not altogether sure of his intentions.

'It beats a high-priced hotel room,' he said and unlocked the door, knocking it open with her suitcase.

'Where are you staying?' Cappy demanded as she entered the compact two-room apartment. It was hot and stuffy from being shut up all day, but the accommodations did appear to be very comfortable, especially the big sofa with its thick seat cushions.

Having deposited her luggage on the floor, Mitch began unbuttoning the dark brown military jacket and shrugging out of it. 'Why don't you open those windows so we can get some circulation going through here?' He was already heading for another set, stretching his neck to unfasten the shirt button at the throat and strip off his tie.

Within minutes, a fan was blowing, Cappy had a cold beer in her hand and Mitch was lighting her cigarette. As she breathed out the smoke, he settled back against the sofa cushions and propped his feet onto the long, low table in front of it. In all the times she'd seen him, he'd never been out of uniform. Her glance strayed to the tanned

214

hollow at the base of his throat, and those springy chest hairs poking out from the edges of his white undershirt. She found such details vaguely unsettling.

'Are you still angry with me over that mixup in Sweetwater?' Mitch wanted to know, quiet and intense in the way he studied her.

'No.' She stared into the amber liquid in her perspiring glass.

'Have I gone about this all wrong, Cap?' Mitch mused, continuing to regard her from his lounging position. 'Have I courted you when I should have been making passes?'

His questions were too close to her own thinking. She straightened from the couch and wandered over to a screened window. 'What's this transport assignment I've been given going to entail, do you know?'

Behind her, Cappy could hear him set his feet on the floor, then he was rising and walking over to where she was standing. Her fingers tightened their grip on the slippery sides of the beer glass.

'You'll be flying generals, colonels . . . and some majors . . .' His hands settled onto her shoulders and absently rubbed them. '. . . to various bases in the area. It'll be real rough duty – staying in the best hotels, eating at the Officers' Club.'

'Was my father responsible for getting me this assignment?'

'What makes you think that?' Mitch bent his head and began nuzzling at the lobe of her ear.

Her breath seemed to get caught in her throat, and Cappy jerked away from the stimulating nibble of his teeth to face him. 'Did he?' She kept to the subject, trying to ignore the suddenly erratic beat of her pulse. All his attention seemed to focus on her lips. She quickly lowered her chin and turned back to the window to take a puff on her cigarette.

'I think I would have heard if he had,' Mitch said. 'Only the best pilots draw this kind of duty, Cap, and you rated the highest among all the graduates at Avenger Field.'

'How do you know that?' She was conscious of his breath stirring the ends of her hair.

'I made it my business to know.' A long sigh came from him. 'Cappy, what's it going to take for you to look at me? I was ready to tear this town upside down to find you. I ended up dragging Annie out of a meeting and I had to throw some Army-weight around to do that.'

Upset, Cappy swung around to face him. 'Mitch, stop it.'

'No.' He wouldn't hear any more of her denials. He covered her lips with his mouth, rocking over them with hungry force.

He took the cigarette and beer glass from her hands and shoved them somewhere so he could gather her into his arms. Cappy didn't attempt to deny the pleasure she found in his driving kiss, but she didn't want him taking control of her emotions. When he untangled his lips from hers and drew a mere inch away, she felt the hot, sweet rush of his breath on her face.

'Cappy, I want you.' His voice was husky and rough with need.

Wrapped in the hard, lean force of his body, she understood that and the hands that moved restlessly over her waist and hips, pressing and urging their message on her. She pulled away from him.

'I just remembered –' Cappy had her back to him, her head angled partly in his direction. An awareness licked through her nerves, creating a thready tension. '– you never did answer my question when I asked where you were staying.'

Mitch studied the tenseness, the wall of reserve she erected against the world. Behind it, she was fire and striking passion. He struggled with his heavy urges, bringing them into check.

'I'll find a bed somewhere.'

'There's no need. I can get a hotel room –' she began.

'No.' Mitch swung her around, but he was careful to keep the circle loose. The smile that pulled in the corners of his mouth had a trace of tautness about it, an ease that was forced. 'Stay here. I want to know where you are.'

'All right.' She seemed to relent, but cautiously.

'Since your father's booted you out of the nest, the least I can do is take you under my wing these last two days before you have to report for duty.' There was something jesting in his comment, an attempt to make light of the arrangement, and disguise the personal, selfish motives behind it.

The deep blueness of a glacier colored her look. 'In case you haven't noticed, I have my own set of wings.'

Again, there was that assertion of independence, that hinted denial of any need for another person.

'You're doing it again.' He closely studied her expression. 'You're always flying away before I get too close. Why, Cap?'

'There's no great mystery to it.' She attacked his question head-on. 'I'm not interested in becoming romantically involved with you. There's a war on, and we each have a job to do.' Her tone was very matter-of-fact.

'We also have off-duty hours,' Mitch reminded her. 'What's the harm in spending them together?'

'None, I suppose – as long as you realize I'm not one of those Washington typists caught up in the glamor of the uniform and the glory of the war, living for today and leaving the regrets for tomorrow.' She seemed all cold and angry with him.

'All of us are sorry about something in our lives. The saddest is not living it.' Mitch struck closer to the target than he knew. He moved away from her to light a cigarette and missed the flicker of longing that briefly broke through her closed expression.

'How about dinner? Where would you like to go?'

They dined at a quiet, out-of-the-way Italian restaurant, one of the few uncrowded places in the capital. Afterward, they strolled under the cherry trees and sat on the steps of the Lincoln Memorial, talking and sharing a rare moment of peace. It was a companionable evening, without contact.

Mitch doubted that he could maintain this platonic posture for long. And while Cappy enjoyed his undemanding company, she wondered how long she'd be content with it before she wanted more.

Part Two

Oh, I'm a flying wreck, a-risking my neck,
*   and a helluva pilot too –*
A helluva, helluva, helluva, helluva,
*   helluva pilot too.*
Like all the jolly good pilots, the
*   gremlins treat me mean;*
I'm a flying wreck, a-risking my neck,
*   for the good ole three-eighteen.*

CHAPTER FOURTEEN

When they entered the new Pentagon, billed as the world's largest office building, the two dozen graduates from Avenger Field still had no idea of the future roles they were to play for the war effort. The last two days had been spent sightseeing around Washington, except for the bus trip to Bolling Field in Virginia, where they were tested in a high-altitude chamber and certified to fly up to 38,000 feet.

Upon entering, they were given clearance badges to pin to their shirts, after which a guide led them into the corridor maze. The Pentagon was deserving of its reputation, since it held the population of a small city within its walls, thirty-five thousand workers. Carved into niches the length of the hallways were offices, creating a multitude of doors and openings.

'It's worse than a rabbit warren,' Marty said in a husky undertone. She peered at a painting of a general who was completely unknown to her and mildly shook her head. Mary Lynn's absent glance was the only response to her remark.

Their curiosity had escalated to almost uncontrollable excitement, and brought with it the certainty that all this was leading up to something important. Over the last two days, they had considered and discarded so many possibilities that no assignment seemed too far-fetched now.

There was a slowing toward the front, which indicated that either their guide was lost or they were nearing their destination, Eden decided wryly. A door opened just

221

ahead of their group and an officer appeared. He waited, with a hint of impatience, for the young women to pass.

After coming this far through the military complex, Eden was just about convinced that all men in uniform looked alike. But there was something familiar about this tall, hatless Army officer with his dark, gleaming hair.

'Major Ryan. I didn't expect to see you.' Eden paused to speak to him, her dark eyes alight with interest as she looked at him, all the while making sure the group didn't get too far ahead of her.

The shutters were closed on his expression, his lean, square-jawed face revealing none of his feelings. 'Miss van Valkenburg.' He inclined his head in greeting, polite but aloof.

'I never heard from Cappy. I was hoping she'd call so we could all get together for dinner. Did she find a room at another hotel?'

'She found suitable accommodations.' One side of his mouth twitched in a bland facsimile of a smile. 'I believe your group is going into the conference room. Perhaps you should join them.'

'Thanks.' She started to take a step to rejoin them, then paused. 'Do you know what all this is about, Major?'

Behind those smooth looks and the cool Army discipline, she sensed a keen intelligence – and a power that operates behind the scenes. She had been around her father too much not to recognize that. Perhaps he worked at a war desk, but he did more than push papers. She was almost sorry he belonged to Cappy, but then the strictures of an Army life weren't really for her anyway.

To her question, he merely replied, 'You'll be briefed.'

A typically military response. Hurrying, Eden caught up with the last of the group. They were ushered into a conference room, dominated by a large, long table around which they were seated by their director, Jacqueline Cochran. The padding of wine-red leather seemed a definite break with the usual Army drab of olives, khakis and browns.

The slightly awed silence was broken when the general arrived and chairs were pushed quickly back from the table while they automatically stood to attention. Tall with a rocklike solidness, General 'Hap' Arnold had an infectious smile that seemed to reach out from his strong face to all of them. His eyes had a glint to them, close to both humor and battle fire, and his hair was a distinguished white.

After greeting them, the general congratulated them. Only the top pilots in their graduating class had been selected to participate in this program, he informed them, without actually telling them what this special program was. Eden couldn't help wondering why Cappy had been excluded from their number, but there wasn't time to dwell on it as General Arnold introduced Jacqueline Cochran, who now held the title of Director of Women pilots.

When she stood, she leaned her hands on the table as if to impress each and every one of them with the importance of this moment. Then she began talking, stressing first that this was a top-secret mission which would entail flying planes bigger and faster than women had ever piloted.

They would not be ferrying airplanes, which they had trained for the last six months to do. Their new duty was one of the most crucial assignments of home-based pilots in the Army Air Force. How well they performed would determine whether female pilots would be able to venture into other flying fields and free up more men for combat roles.

Mitch was in the outer chamber with a sheaf of new directives in his hand when the general returned to his office at the conclusion of the meeting. As he stopped at the desk to look them over, Mitch's glance strayed to the open door and the young, attractive women filing past outside. General Arnold followed the direction of his look.

'You did tell me they could fly, Major,' the general remarked in a mocking vein, as if belatedly seeking confirmation of that fact.

'Yes, sir.' A faint smile edged his mouth, but Mitch

remained vaguely distracted, his thoughts not fully focused on the moment.

'This isn't going to be the most popular decision I've ever made,' the general sighed grimly. 'Towing targets for green air gunners and ground artillery to practice on is not the safest flying job around, but it's one of the most war-essential domestic duties we've got.' He released a short, harsh laugh. 'These combat-hungry male pilots with their dreams of achieving ace status will resent the hell out of me even more when they learn I've demeaned their job by assigning women pilots to do it.'

'Yes, sir. It's rough either way, sir,' Mitch agreed blandly.

'I need those pilots for combat missions. If this experiment works, I'll have more men to fill the ranks.' He paused to eye his young staff officer. 'You don't have much faith in the program, do you, Major?'

'I think it's a fine program, sir,' Mitch assured him after the smallest start of surprise.

'I noticed you pulled that Hayward woman from the group and had her orders changed. She was one of the top-rated pilots in that class. It's obvious you didn't want her up there while a bunch of raw recruits shot up the sky trying to hit the muslin target she would be towing.'

'Transport needed a well-qualified pilot. As you said, sir, WASP Hayward is one of the best in her class,' Mitch responded and steadily met his general's probing glance.

'Of course,' the general remarked finally, a knowing light in his eyes as he gave the directive back to Mitch and turned his attention to more pressing matters.

The view of the sunset from the windows of the DC-3, the passenger version of the Army's C-47 cargo transport, was spectacular, the green, rolling grasslands of Virginia's Piedmont Range awash with the reds and golds of a dying sun. Rachel wondered about their destination as the plane flew south with its two dozen WASPs aboard, heading toward their new assignment as pilots of tow-target planes. All their faces showed the same hopeful enthusiasm for the challenge and adventure this new duty might afford.

Always the loner, Rachel sat aloof from the others, not drawn in by their speculating conversations. Out of the twenty-five WASPs who had been picked for this assignment, three were her former baymates – Marty Rogers, Eden van Valkenburg, and Mary Lynn Palmer. But they had never really become close friends, and Rachel was just as glad Eden hadn't tried to follow up that chance encounter in New York.

During the long flight Rachel absently listened to the excited chatter around her and gazed out the window. As dusk spread, darkening the skies, she noticed the glistening waters of the Atlantic. Below were the barrier islands of North Carolina's Outer Banks, treacherous shoals that had claimed hundreds of ships and lives over the centuries. The long stretch of beach along the coast was a pale finger against the gleaming black ocean. The watery graveyard of ships had taken more vessels to its bosom in recent months, as cargo ships were torpedoed by German U-boats and sunk within sight of the American coast. Rachel searched for the silhouette of a darkened ship following the route that hugged the eastern seaboard, but saw none.

Somewhere down there was Kitty Hawk, the site of man's first powered flight. Rachel looked, wondering which island hill had been the takeoff point for the Wright brothers' flying machine.

The plane veered inland, flying over blacked-out settlements, and began a descent. 'Camp Davis, just ahead,' one of the pilots in the cockpit shouted back to his passengers.

No runway lights were allowed on this coastal base, located near Cape Fear. Rachel could barely make out the airstrip. The big twin-engine flew in low, skimming over the cypress thickets of a swamp before dipping onto the runway.

'I guess this is it,' someone said.

*   *   *

225

Camp Davis was one of the oldest and largest training bases for antiaircraft artillery. Inland from Wrightsville Beach to the north of Cape Fear, it was almost surrounded by swamps; Holly Shelter and Angola Swamp to the north and east, Green Swamp to the west and southwest. Farther up the coast was Wolf Swamp.

Quartered in the nurses' barracks, Marty awakened the next morning and sat on the edge of her cot, flying to shake the grogginess out of her head. Outside, the vibrating roar of an airplane engine came closer and closer until it was rattling the windows of the barracks. Marty charged out of the small private cubicle, certain the plane was going to crash into the building. It roared over the roof. A nurse looked at her wide-eyed expression and smiled in sympathetic understanding.

'You'll get used to it,' she assured Marty.

'It sounded like it was taking off right over the barracks.'

'It was.' The nurse confirmed her suspicion. 'We sit at the end of a runway.'

With their new quasi-officer status, the WASPs breakfasted in the officers' mess, then reported to the flight line for duty. The male pilots in the ready room greeted them with looks of scorn and skepticism. Marty bristled at the barely veiled contempt they were shown.

The commander of the tow-target squadron to which they were assigned was a short, balding man with a thick-set body. Major Stevenson spoke with a heavy southern accent and his attitude revealed much of the southern view of women and their traditional roles. Mary Lynn doubted that his opinion of them as pilots was any better than what their male counterparts had shown them.

As they followed the commander down the flight line in the sunshine of a bright Carolina morning, he walked them past dive bombers, twin-engined bombers, and transports. When he reached the row of small piper Cubs, he stopped and informed them that, after they had checked out in the L-4s and 5s, he might let them fly some administrative missions.

'He's kidding,' Marty said in disbelief.

'I don't think so,' Mary Lynn murmured.

'My God, doesn't he know we've been flying AT-6s and twin-engined 17s?' Eden protested. 'These are kiddie planes.'

'I think someone forgot to tell him the program,' Marty declared grimly and headed for the nearest Cub. Griping wouldn't accomplish anything. It appeared they would have to prove all over again to another set of Army personnel that they could fly virtually anything with wings.

She felt a tug of nostalgia as she climbed into the cockpit of the piper Cub. She hadn't flown one since she'd gotten her license in the L-4 her brother David had owned. Aware that other WASPs were following suit, Marty taxied to the active runway and took off. After the fast, sleek Army trainers, the little plane seemed like a putt-putt. She stayed in the traffic pattern to circle the field and practice touch-and-gos.

When she came in for her first landing, Marty set her feet on the rudder pedals. A little warning bell rang in her mind, but the reason for it was vague. The instant the wheels touched the runway and Marty attempted to steer the plane with the rudder pedals, she remembered the unusual characteristics of this plane. The brakes, instead of being at the tops of the pedal shoes, as had been the case in all the Army trainers she'd flown for the last two hundred hours, were located at the base of them.

With the first screech, she corrected the mistake, steering with her toes and avoiding the heel brakes. Applying power, Marty liked the plane off the runway again and went around. From the air, she watched her friends land their Cubs, unaware of this major difference. The planes jerked, bounced, and came close several times to nosing over. They unquestionably looked like the worst bunch of pilots ever given wings. Marty watched them and groaned, wishing she had remembered about the brakes in time to warn the others.

It was a subdued and chagrined collection of women

who regrouped at the flight line. The male pilots were standing around, openly laughing at them. Most of the other WASPs were merely exasperated at their inability to show themselves well, but Marty was bitter, feeling they'd been tricked. Her teeth were clenched together and her fists were jammed into the pockets of her flight suit. The look in her gray-green eyes was as turbulent as the stormy Atlantic Ocean they resembled as she strode into the ready room with Mary Lynn and Eden.

'It looks llke those Cubs turned out to be more than you girls could handle,' a freckle-faced pilot spoke up, a mere boy by Marty's standards.

She stopped and leaned toward him, topping him by a good inch, to belligerently challenge him. 'I can take any plane out there on that flight line and fly circles around you any day of the week.'

But he simply drew back in mock respect and laughed with his buddies. 'We've got ourselves a hot pilot here.'

Struggling with that awful feeling of impotence, Marty turned away and muttered bitterly to Mary Lynn, 'I wish I could haul off and hit him.'

Outside on the flight line, they saw more of their number buck-jumping the Piper Cubs on landing and struggling with the ignominy of not being able to master the little airplane. They had been expected to fail as pilots, and they had, but they were determined to conquer the plane and show the male pilots they were every bit as qualified. In the meantime, they had a peculiar gauntlet to run, a combination of wolf whistles and male jeers.

By the third day, Eden was just about ready to throw in the towel. This was not the reason she'd joined the WASPs, and she didn't like being the object of ridicule. Another L-5 was taxiing toward the flight line, so Eden waited on the hot and muggy flight line, rather than enter the ready room alone and endure patronizing remarks from her male counterparts.

After the Cub had stopped neatly in line with the others, she watched the long-legged blonde emerging from the

228

cockpit. 'Nice job,' she complimented Rachel Goldman on her handling of the heel-braking airplane.

Rachel gave her a brief look of surprise before she lowered her head to shake a hand through her long hair, freed of its bandanna turban, and continued walking in the direction of the ready room, showing indifference when Eden fell in step with her.

'You should have seen me,' Eden said with a short exasperated sigh. 'I did just fine, perfect in fact, right up to taxiing to the flight line until I had to stop the Cub. And I tried to brake with my damned toes. I had to circle the plane around and bring it back into line with the others.'

'That's tough,' Rachel offered in vague sympathy.

Far off in the distance, they could hear the low rumble of artillery fire shooting at the muslin-sleeved targets towed by planes. It was a bitter reminder of the job they'd come to Camp Davis to do, before they had been relegated to flying Piper Cubs, just about the lowest rung on the ladder.

The roar of a powerful engine attracted their attention to the Beechcraft taxiing to the flight line. Eden thought she recognized the stagger-winged aircraft with its huge, churning propeller nearly grazing the ground, and paused. Catching her lower lip between her teeth, she chewed thoughtfully on it, and watched for the pilot to climb out of the cockpit.

'If that's who I think it is,' she murmured to Rachel, whose curiosity was more idle, 'maybe they'll make some changes around here.'

Sure enough, Jacqueline Cochran stepped from the plane. When she saw the two waiting female pilots, she walked over to greet them, her large brown eyes studying them with interest. Her expression was aloof, but pleasant, warming slightly as she recognized Eden.

'Hello. How are you getting along down here?' She plainly wasn't prepared for Eden's frank answer.

'We're not.' The hardships of their previous training, the spartan living conditions of the Sweetwater barracks, and the lack of creature comforts there still had held a degree of glamour and adventure. But this situation had none. Eden found it humiliating and degrading, and she refused to be stripped of her pride.

'What do you mean?' the Director of Women Pilots demanded.

'Major Stevenson has us checking out in Piper Cubs.' At that moment an L-5 landed with a screech of grabbing brakes and jerked down the runway. 'Here comes one of our group now,' Eden said dryly and observed the sharply interrogatory look from her superior. 'None of the Army trainers have heel brakes.'

Their director's lips came together in a grim line. 'I'll speak to him,' was all Jacqueline Cochran said before she turned away from them to stride toward the operations building.

'I think we'll see some changes,' Eden mused.

A military transport truck came roaring and rattling by them. Its back end was loaded with GIs in uniform and full gear. When it skidded to a stop in front of the ready room, an officer hopped out of the cab and went inside. As Eden and Rachel approached, the whistling GIs hung out the open sides of the truck to ogle them with good-natured, if lascivious, interest.

None of the girls had quite gotten used to receiving so much attention from the tens of thousands of men on the base. The best course was to ignore it. Eden would have done the same this time, except one of the soldiers sparked a glimmer of recognition. She stared for a full second, then turned an amazed glance on Rachel.

'That guy in the truck looks just like the Army private you were with that night at the club. I'd almost swear it's him,' she declared. 'His name was Zach . . . something or other.'

'Zach Jordan. It can't be him, because he was shipping out ov –' Rachel broke off her denial in midword. Zach was in the back of the truck.

Through the hiya-honeys and what-are-ya-doin'-

tonight-babes, his voice pierced the jumble of remarks and whistles. 'Rachel, what are you doing here?'

She wouldn't – she couldn't – answer him. At first, she simply felt betrayed. Then she realized she'd fallen for the oldest line in the Army. He had let her think he was going overseas, that she might never see him again. How could she have been so gullible?

As they passed the rear of the transport truck, Zach called to her again. 'Hey, Rachel. Wait up.'

Rachel ignored him as best she could, conscious of the speculating look she was receiving from Eden. Inwardly, she kept berating herself for being so stupid. As they headed for the door to the ready room, there was a clatter of boots scrambling out of the truck and a thud as they landed on concrete.

'Rachel, I can explain.' Zach came running after her, catching her by the arm and making her stop to face him.

'Let go of my arm, soldier,' Rachel warned.

'Jordan!' An officer stepped out of the ready room, barking Zach's name in sharp reprimand. 'Get back in that truck.'

'In a minute, sir.' His dark gaze continued to probe Rachel's face.

'Now, soldier.'

'Look, Lieutenant. She's a friend from back home. Just give me a few minutes to explain something to her.'

'Not on the Army's time, Private. Back on the truck before I put you on report.'

Rachel said nothing as Zach reluctantly backed away and moved toward the truck. Bitterly, she called herself a fool again. It was a hot August day, sticky and miserable. The burning humiliation and hurt only made the rest seem worse.

CHAPTER FIFTEEN

Cochran's visit to Camp Davis achieved its objective. No more Piper Cubs. The WASPs were checked out in the Douglas Dauntless dive-bomber, the A-24. Eden's ride had been less than instructive. The rear cockpit, which was actually the gunner's seat, had no working instruments, so she could only guess at what the pilot was doing and when.

Her head was still sore where she'd hit it on the gunsight when the plane had been pulled up so abruptly an instant before landing. It throbbed as she sat in the cockpit, familiarizing herself with the position of the gauges and going over the operations manual for the Dauntless. The instructor had walked off and left her, without bothering to see if she had any questions.

Irritated, Eden looked around, but the only person passing by her aircraft was an Army mechanic in a pair of greasy fatigues. 'Hey!' She whistled shrilly. 'Come here a minute!'

He stopped, and looked uncertainly in her direction. 'You talkin' to me?' His voice was thick with a Texas twang, as he pointed to himself with a slightly skeptical expression.

'Yes, you,' Eden confirmed, her patience thinning. But it was difficult to be irritated with the tall, lanky Army sergeant who hopped onto the wing of her plane and walked up to the cockpit. Everything about him was wide – as wide as Texas – his jaw, his mouth, and his smile. Smile lines ran up his face to his eyes, like spreading ripples in a pond. And when he smiled, he put his whole heart into it. The result was decidedly likable.

'What can I do for ya, ma'am?' That warm politeness and respect was ingrained by his western upbringing. It had nothing to do with Army training.

'Can you tell me something about this plane?' She looked again at the panel of instruments, the corners of her mouth deepening in a kind of grim exasperation.

The lanky mechanic tried not to show his surprise that the question would be asked of him, but his nut-brown eyes looked at her askance while he explained. 'The dive flaps act as a kind of brake. Ya see, the Dauntless was designed mainly for Navy use – to land quick and short on the flattops. When you're comin' in, ya aim that nose right at the runway, then pull up jest before the wheels touch.'

He showed her how the hydraulic flaps operated, extending from the trailing edge of the wings, and informed her about takeoff, landing and stalling airspeeds, and other pertinent information. His cooperative attitude prompted Eden to ask more questions about the idiosyncrasies of the Douglas Dauntless.

'Have you checked Form One on this plane?' the mechanic asked after Eden ran out questions.

'Form One?' At Avenger Field, the instructors had taught them to always check the form in the cockpit to verify the plane's airworthiness and note any repairs recommended by the previous pilot and the subsequent work done. It was such a perfunctory thing Eden hadn't given it a thought. It was hardly more than routine procedure, but for the mechanic's benefit, she got it out.

'You're in luck,' he drawled in mild amazement.

'Why?' Eden sensed something was wrong.

'This plane's in pretty good condition. A lot of them here are red-lined.' When a plane was determined to be unfit to fly, a red X was marked on the airworthy form. But half an X, or diagonal red line, indicated the plane could have something wrong with it yet could still be flown. 'Sometimes if the wings and tail are attached and the engine runs, that's all it takes.' The mechanic grinned with his ear-to-ear smile.

'That's just great.' Eden wasn't sure whether she should believe him or not. It could be just an attempt to scare her a little. The men around here didn't seem to be very receptive to the idea of women in cockpits.

'Is that it, ma'am?' He straightened, wiping his big hands on a greasy rag that had been sticking out of the pocket of his fatigues.

'Yes, I think so.' Then she remembered one other thing, and removed a plastic packet she'd found stowed in a side flap in the cockpit. 'What is this for?'

'You don't need that, ma'am.' He took it from her and stuffed it back in the pocket, so flustered he was actually blushing underneath his tan.

'But what is it?' Eden persisted.

'It's a . . . it's a pressure release valve,' the mechanic mumbled, scowling and uncomfortable, and hopped off the wing before she could come up with any more questions. As he backed away from her plane, he called to her. 'Land as easy as you can, ma'am. Those tires are gettin' kinda worn.'

'Can't you put on new ones?'

'Ma'am, there's a war on,' he reminded her patiently. 'Practically every rubber tire is bein' shipped overseas to combat zones. We jest don't have a surplus of them sittin' around. It's best ya be cautious with the tires on these planes.'

That night in the barracks, they sat around the common room and exchanged experiences, some of them harrowing. Eden had been lucky. Except for a rough-running engine, her flying had been without incident. Others had not been so lucky.

'My engine failed. It just coughed and quit. I barely had enough altitude to glide back to the runway and land.'

'I had just landed. There I was whipping down the runway when all of a sudden, it was as if somebody yanked the plane to the right. I braced myself away from the panel and jammed on the rudder pedal, but it just wouldn't answer. There I went, tearing off the runway into the grass. I thought, This is it, I've had it now. But the plane finally stopped. When I crawled out, I saw I'd blown a tire. You wanta talk about somebody being scared shitless, that was me.'

'These planes aren't safe,' Marty protested, sitting astraddle a chair facing the back. 'I'm beginning to understand what the CO meant when he said the planes were dispensable – and so are we. Hell, he didn't want us here to begin with – and now he's found a way to get rid of us.'

'The men have to fly these planes, too.' That was small consolation.

'There's a shortage of spare parts and tires. The combat planes have the top priority on all that.' No one was impressed with that justification either.

'Speaking of parts,' Eden inserted, 'did any of you figure out how that pressure release valve works?' None of them knew what she was talking about so Eden described the plastic packet.

Marty let out a hoot of laughter. 'Don't you know what that is? It's a pressure release valve all right. It's a urinal tube for men.'

'No wonder that poor mechanic was so embarrassed when I asked him about it.' Eden remembered his expression and broke into laughter.

An Army nurse stuck her head into the room. 'Hey, is there a pilot here named Rachel Goldman?'

From her listening post on the edge of the jagged circle, Rachel lifted a hand. 'What is it?' She sat on the floor, her long legs folded in a half-lotus position.

'A soldier waylaid me outside and asked me to give you a message,' the nurse said, and Rachel came to her feet in a gracefully fluid motion, ignoring the interested looks the announcement attracted.

The soldier had to be Zach. She had been half hoping he'd attempt to contact her. She thought it would prove he had some feelings for her and it hadn't all been a ruse to get her in bed. At the same time, she was still hurt and angry, unwilling to forgive him for his trickery. The last thing she wanted was to have any of her peers learn the way she'd been taken in by this Jewish Romeo, especially her former baymates at Sweetwater. So she had no intention of allowing Zach's message to be relayed in their presence.

In the relative privacy of the outer hall, Rachel confronted the young nurse. 'What did he want?'

'He's waiting outside to talk to you.' The nurse eyed her with a mildly disapproving look. 'Both of you could get into a lot of trouble if an officer catches you together. You're not supposed to fraternize with enlisted personnel.'

'I'm still a civilian,' Rachel asserted, although she knew it was a moot point.

The nurse shrugged, 'It's nothing to me if you want to meet this guy, but there's others who won't see it that way. I'm just giving you a friendly bit of advice – don't get caught.' With the officers' privileges the WASPs had acquired, there also came restrictions.

'Thanks.'

Blackout curtains darkened the barracks windows. Nowhere on the coastal base were lights allowed to be seen. Rachel stepped out into the August night, its warm humidity tempered by a sea breeze. She scanned the black shadows beyond the walkway. The swamps, the tall sea pines and moss-draped cypress, came right up to the edge of the field, filling the air with the songs of their night creatures. A dark shape loomed in front of her, and Rachel was barely able to conceal her start of surprise.

'Rachel.' His voice reached out to her in pleasure, and she had to remember to harden herself against him. 'I wasn't sure whether you'd come.'

'Weren't you?' she countered; she'd caught the satisfaction and confidence that had entered his tone.

'I decided there were three possibilities – you wouldn't come, you'd have me arrested for making improper advances to an officer, or . . . you'd meet me.' Zach moved to take her into his arms, but Rachel turned out of them, his arrogance riling her.

'You didn't know where they'd be sending your outfit,'

she mocked him bitterly. 'But you were almost sure it would be Sicily. It's funny, but this doesn't look like Sicily.'

'I never said I was going overseas right away,' Zach reminded her with unabashed ease.

'Not in so many words, maybe,' Rachel conceded angrily. 'But you implied it. You were going off to war, and we might never see each other again.'

'I promised you I'd survive,' he reminded in an almost teasing fashion, amused instead of chastened by her icy temper.

'But you knew that's the way I would think,' she accused.

'I hoped you would,' Zach admitted. 'I wanted you, Rachel. I still do.'

'I'm sure you'd like to pick up where we left off.' She wouldn't look at him, too aware of how persuasive his charm could be. 'What kind of fool do you think I am?'

'I stretched the truth a little bit, but as soon as we finish our gunnery training here, we will be shipping out.'

'Zach, I'm not going to fall for that line a second time,' Rachel warned him.

'I was going to write and tell you I'd been sent here for more training,' he insisted.

'I'll just bet you were.' Her doubt was impregnable.

'How can I convince you it's true?' A beguiling smile played with the corners of his mouth as Zach urged her to believe him. The night's shadows brought out the strong planes of his handsome features.

From her left came the low murmur of voices, men's voices, and the sound of footsteps. When Rachel turned, she could barely make out the dark shapes of two figures. As they came closer, the silhouette of their caps warned they were officers.

'Someone's coming,' she whispered and pushed Zach toward the deep shadows off the walkway, following on his heels.

The large trunk of a tree offered them some conceal-ment, but its narrowness forced them closer together, shoulder against shoulder. As she strained to catch the sound of the officers passing, all her senses were heightened. She was conscious of the muscled feel of his body and the spicy scent of some shaving cream lingering on his skin. His handsome face, his dark brows and jet black hair, were very near. What was more, Zach was leaning into her, pressing the advantage of this forced closeness.

'You aren't as mad at me as you pretend,' he murmured into her ear.

'Shh, they'll hear you,' Rachel whispered.

His arms circled her body while Rachel tried to stand rigid within them, but Zach wasn't deterred. His hand wandered over her arm and shoulder, traveling up to her neck and tracing the line of her throat. She had no doubt that he was enjoying the situation.

The minute the officers were out of hearing, Rachel demanded, 'Will you let me go?' She refused to struggle with Zach and give him an excuse to be more aggressive.

'You really do care about me, don't you?' he said.

'I'm sure you're conceited enough to believe that,' Rachel retorted.

'It's true. If you really wanted to get rid of me, you'd have let those officers find us together. And maybe,' he challenged her lazily, 'you'd like to explain why you hid with me?'

'I'm not going to let you use me again.' It was the only defense she had against him, but it was a weak one.

'You silly fool, Rachel.' Zach laughed softly at her and moved in closer until his dark features filled her vision. 'Don't you know I love you? My daughter of Deborah.'

His mouth sought the outline of her lips. The deep, thoroughly satisfying kiss assuaged her hurt pride. She felt all atingle inside, warm and glowing with life. There was no trickery involved in the love she felt for him. It was genuine and fierce.

Ensconced in the cockpit of the Dauntless, Eden made a last survey of the panel, conscious of a little flutter of nerves. She switched the radio to the intercom position and pressed her fingers to the throat mike.

'Are you strapped in back there? What's your name? Frank?' Eden frowned with the effort to recall the name of the extremely apprehensive enlisted man who was acting as her tow-target operator.

'Yes, sir – ma'am.' He stammered out the correction.

Eden supposed the affirmative reply was to both her questions but she didn't bother to obtain a clarification. The private was in the rear cockpit under obvious duress. She'd heard all about the mass demand for transfers by the cable operators the minute they learned they would be flying in planes piloted by females.

'We'll be rolling in a minute, Frank,' she said and took her hand away from her throat.

After an all-clear check, Eden started the powerful Curtiss-Wright engine. A ground crewman removed the wheel chocks and scampered away from the plane. Eden applied the throttle to initiate the roll. The engine rumbled with deafening noise and vibrated roughly until the whole plane seemed to be shaking. Eden didn't like the sound of it.

With the radio switch on intercom, she depressed her throat mike again. 'Something's wrong with this plane. I'm taking it back to the hangar, Frank.'

'Yes, ma'am!' The voice coming through her earphones was unmistakably relieved by the decision which seemed tantamount to granting him a stay of execution.

She taxied back to the flight line and ordered her tow-target operator to fetch a mechanic. She kept the engine running to see if it wouldn't smooth out, but it continued its ominous rumble. Frank came back with a young gum-chewing mechanic, barely in his twenties.

'What's the problem?' He sauntered up to the plane, and walked the wing to the front cockpit. Eden slid the canopy open and he leaned on the edge, giving her the eye.

'Listen to that engine.' It was vibrating the stationary plane so noticeably that she didn't see how the mechanic could ask such a stupid question.

'It's running a little rough,' he acknowledged with gum-cracking indifference. 'They all do.'

As he turned away, Eden couldn't believe he would summarily dismiss her complaint. 'Aren't you going to check it out?' she protested.

'Look, lady, I got better things to do with my time. If you're too scared to fly it like that, mark the problem on the form and find yourself another plane.' He hopped to the ground.

Furious at his attitude and his insubordination, Eden shut the plane down with lightning precision and piled out of the cockpit before the propeller blade stopped turning. The mechanic had stopped to make some comment to her cable operator. When he saw Eden charging toward him, he looked more amused by her anger than anything else.

'Okay, lady –' he began.

'That is not the way you address an officer.' And she was entitled to that status of respect.

'Yes, sir . . . ma'am,' he snidely corrected himself.

'I want that engine checked, and I want it checked now.' She jabbed a stiff finger at the parked Dauntless, her feet planted apart in a challenging stance and her arms akimbo.

'And I told you there was nothing to worry about. The engine's just running a little rough, that's all. I know my job.'

'A little rough, huh? Would you stake your life on it? Why don't you climb into that plane and fly with me a couple times around the field?' Eden challenged.

The invitation was plainly not to his liking, as he took a step backward, eyeing this red-haired female who was easily his height if not taller. 'I can't do that, ma'am,' he protested vigorously.

Their raised voices had attracted the attention of other members of the ground crew. Some ignored them after first locating the source, but most watched with ill-disguised amusement. One mechanic left a plane undergoing repairs in the hangar and came out to investigate the cause of the disagreement.

'What seems to be the trouble, ma'am?' That drawllng, respectful voice had a familiar ring.

As Eden swung around, she recognized the strong, wide face, sobered now with a frown, but capable of a Texas-size smile. He was grease-smudged from his overalls to his face, even to the billed cap on his head, but he was unmistakably the mechanic who had helped her become familiar with the Dauntless dive-bomber.

'I want the engine of this plane checked. And this so-called mechanic won't look at it. He claims there's nothing wrong with it.'

'It's just running rough –' the accused mechanic attempted to defend his position.

'Why don't you finish puttin' that plane back together in the hangar, Simpson, while I check out this lady's engine?' It was less a suggestion than an order.

'Yes, sir.' Disgruntled by the outcome, the mechanic moved off in the direction of the hangar.

This time the Texas mechanic was smiling when Eden glanced at him. 'I jest can't get it through that boy's head that the customer is always right.' The conciliatory remark brought a grudging smile to Eden's mouth. 'I'll look at your plane.'

'Thanks.' Eden intended to be there when he did. It wasn't that she didn't trust him; she simply didn't want someone going through the motions with the idea of pacifying her fears. Before she followed him to the plane, she instructed her cable man, 'You might as well wait in the ready room and have some coffee. Let them know we have a mechanical delay.'

He showed his disappointment at the word 'delay,' implying that he would have preferred an aborted mission. 'Yes, ma'am.'

The experienced sergeant quickly located the problem, and drained more than a cup of water from the carburetor. 'I figured that was the trouble,' he said. 'Somebody on the ground crew might have forgotten to top the fuel tanks last night and the water vapor condensed. Or they might

241

have filled it from an almost empty fuel drum that could have had some condensed water in it,' he suggested.

'That sounds awfully careless to me.' But she'd seen more than one example of that kind of indifference from the overworked ground crew. 'None of these planes are safe to fly.' It was an angry protest at the appalling conditions of the aircraft they were expected to fly. 'The instruments don't work half the time, so you don't dare rely on them. The seats are broken. The radios are usually so full of static you can't hear most of the time.' The list was endless.

'I can't argue with anything you say, ma'am,' the mechanic admitted. 'Even if we could get all the spare parts we need, we don't have the manpower to keep the planes in top shape. All we can do is keep the engines running so these tow-target missions can be flown. The base doesn't even get enough fuel. Sometimes we have to put in a lower octane than the manufacturer requires for proper engine maintenance.'

Eden realized just how dangerous this assignment was. No wonder the men pilots balked at taking this kind of non-combat risk – towing targets for artillery practice in marginally safe airplanes.

'What's your name?' she demanded suddenly.

He gave her a briefly startled glance. 'Sergeant William Jackson, but my friends call me Bubba.' His eyes narrowed. 'Why?'

'Bubba, I'm Eden van Valkenburg.' She shook hands with him, then scrubbed at the grease that came off on them, using an embroidered handkerchief from her pocket. 'Before I climb into the cockpit of one of these planes, I want you to check it out, so at least I can know the kind of trouble to expect and make a judgment on whether I want to fly that particular plane or not.' When he showed signs of hesitating, Eden hastened to add, 'I'll make it worth your while, Bubba.'

'I'll be happy to look 'em over for you, ma'am. And you don't have to give me any money for doin' it either. I don't reckon your pay is much better than mine.'

'Believe me, I can afford it, Bubba.' She laughed at the suggestion that she had to watch her pennies. She had never worried about the price of anything in her life.

Her reply seemed to trouble him. 'I don't know as I'd feel right takin' money from you, ma'am.'

'We'll worry about that another time,' she said. 'And the name is Eden.'

'Yes, ma'am,' he drawled in his ever-respectful way.

It was an idyllic August morning with the sun glistening diamond-bright off the waters of the Atlantic and the surf rolling onto the beaches of the outer bank of islands on the Carolina coast. But the scene was marred by the presence of the antiaircraft batteries that occupied more than a mile-long stretch of sandy beach.

Still some distance from the artillery range, Rachel activated the throat mike with her fingers. 'It's just ahead of us,' she told her cable operator. 'I'm going to see if they're ready for us.'

'Okay,' came the nervous response.

With a grim smile, Rachel recalled the way the private had gawked at her six-foot-tall frame. No doubt he believed he had been assigned to fly with some Amazon. He had acted afraid of her, the plane, and probably his own shadow.

She turned the radio key and contacted the gunnery officer, reporting her position and eight-hundred-foot altitude. As they approached the artillery range, she could begin to see little clusters of men moving about the big guns. She wondered if Zach was down there. The officer responded to her call with an order to reel out the target and bring it on.

'Roger,' she replied and flipped the switch to intercom. 'Did you monitor that?'

'Target going out,' her operator confirmed.

The target was a long muslin sleeve attached to a cable which the operator cranked out by means of a winch. As he let the target out, the A-24 began to slow. Rachel advanced the throttle to maintain her airspeed, conscious of the little frissons of tension she was feeling on her first mission.

Luckily, today the wind conditions were ideal. She would have to make few corrections for crosswind drift. She tried to shut out her thoughts and concentrate on the long line of anti-aircraft guns on the beach. The big three-inch guns were first in line, followed by the .40- and .35-millimeter artillery, and lastly the small-arms range, which would require her to fly at a lower altitude for the rifle fire to hit her target.

The huge barrels of the heavy guns lacked maneuverability. The gunners were unable to track their target while the barrels swiveled clumsily in their casings, their snouts fifteen to twenty feet in the air. They were being taught how to lead their target and shoot at a spot ahead of it.

With the white target trailing behind her Dauntless, Rachel made her run down the beach. She watched the burps of white smoke from the guns and heard the thudding explosions. Her glance darted to the altimeter to make certain she was holding her pattern altitude. The prop of her plane sliced the air with a roar, and its powerful vibrations seemed to travel up the stick through her hand and into her body.

The plane began bumping through some turbulence. It seemed the noise of the guns was getting louder. Then Rachel noticed the black puffs of smoke punctuating the air in advance of her plane. That was flak! The realization hit her with sobering force. She felt that first shiver of alarm as she discovered what it was like to fly in combat. Along with the taste of fear came the rush of adrenaline and that crazy sense of excitement.

With fingers to her throat mike, she called the ground command. 'That flak is bouncing us around the sky,' she warned.

A few seconds later, the air around her plane cleared of the telltale black puffs and the explanation came back,

'Sorry. Some of the gunners thought they were supposed to take a lead on the plane instead of the target. We've got them straightened out.'

'Roger.'

The small-arms range was coming up and Rachel swooped the plane to a lower altitude for their rifle fire, leaving the explosions of the big guns behind her. The soldiers were lined up like little stick-men on the sand, the supervising officers stationed to the rear of their positions, some of them pacing. Beyond were the dunes, hairy with waving stalks of sea oats, and below, the ocean colors ranged from the aqua blue of the shallows to the turquoise green of the deep. To Rachel, the wild beauty of the coastline seemed an incongruous setting for artillery practice.

At the end of the gunnery range, she executed a slow, banking turn and made another pass. Upon completion of the pass, ground command ordered her to drop the target in the designated zone. Her tow-target mission was over.

Flying low over the drop area, she told her quiet operator to release the target. The cone-shaped sleeve was unfastened by a lever near the gunner's seat, which the tow-target operator occupied. There was a sudden lurch of the plane as it was released from the drag of the target.

As she banked the plane into a climbing turn, Rachel saw a jeep speeding across the beach to the drop zone to recover the target and check the accuracy of the gunners. In the briefing, she had learned that each gun was loaded with bullets marked with a different dye, so the color as well as the number of hits would be checked by the officers.

'What's your name again?' the artillery officer radioed.

'Goldman, WASP Goldman.' She experienced a moment of apprehension that somehow she had fouled up her first mission.

'Well . . . good job, Goldman.' The praise was grudgingly given, tainted with a bit of surprise.

'Thank you, sir.'

CHAPTER SIXTEEN

In that first week, it only took a few missions for the WASPs to realize what they had let themselves in for. These missions at Camp Davis bore little resemblance to the idealized image they'd had of their roles in this war upon graduation at Sweetwater. They weren't ferrying spanking new planes cross-country for the Army. They were flying the dregs of the Army Air Force, and in exercises that practically put their life on the line every time they went up.

After morning flight, a handful of subdued women pilots clustered on the flight line, lingering in the shade of a hangar building on the summer-hot August day. The low morale was evident in lowered chins and drooping heads.

'You should see my plane.' One of the WASPs, a former Olympic diver from California named Betty Cole, dragged nervously on her cigarette, trying to hide the tremor in her hands. 'There's a half-dozen holes in the fuselage, less than a foot from the fuel tanks. Do you realize how close I came to going up in flames?'

'I think I've got it all figured out,' Marty declared, the only one among them not unnerved by the situation. 'This is a trapshoot and we're the clay pigeons.'

'Brother, is that ever the truth!' another agreed.

'Half of those fools on the beach don't know how to aim the guns and the other half don't know where.'

As Marty crushed a cigarette beneath the heel of her shoe, she glanced sideways at Eden, crouched beside her, her weight balanced on the balls of her feet. 'Your Jacqueline told us this assignment was an experiment.'

'And we're regular guinea pigs,' Betty Cole complained grimly.

'It's funny.' Mary Lynn studied the sky overhead, watching the planes in the pattern. 'I always wondered what it was like . . . for Beau to fly through flak. Now I know.'

The noise, the violent shudders and hard rocking of the plane, the smell of brimstone, all were fresh impressions on her senses. She chain-smoked, nervously puffing on a cigarette and twisting it in her fingers. The experience had left her badly shaken. It was small consolation that she wasn't alone.

'I don't know about the rest of you' – another of their number spoke up – 'but the thought of going up again in another red-lined plane so a bunch of green soldiers can use me for target practice – I get all sick inside just thinking about it.' Her declaration was followed by a forced laugh, a brittle attempt to make light of her feelings. 'Maybe I'm losing my nerve,' she joked very weakly.

Others faked smiles to go along with her pretense of humor. The area was aptly named Cape Fear. The smell of it was in the air, enveloping them in a chilly dread that made their skin clammy and set their blood to pounding.

'Let's get a Coke,' someone suggested.

There were a lot of dry mouths, but the sweltering afternoon heat was not to blame. No one was comfortable with the subject of conversation. In a loose group, they drifted toward the ready room.

A poker game was – perpetually it seemed – in progress in a shadowed corner of the room. The whirring blades of a rotating fanhead moved the hot, smoke-stale air to offer some relief. The players at the table, all young male pilots, looked up when the sober bunch of flight-clad women wandered in. Their collective unease was almost tangible. The freckle-faced pilot spied Marty in their midst and rocked his chair onto its back legs.

'Look who made it back, fellas – it's our hot pilot,' he taunted.

Marty didn't miss a beat. 'I haven't seen you on the flight line lately, Freckles. Don't tell me a big, brave boy like you has been ducking his missions and letting a female take them?'

'I had a mechanical problem,' he retorted stiffly.

'Called what? No guts?' she derided.

Mary Lynn pressed a squatty Coke bottle into Marty's hand, protesting in an undertone, 'That isn't fair.'

'You notice he isn't denying it,' Marty declared with cutting scorn.

'If you're stupid enough to crawl in the cockpit of one of those planes and be a sitting duck for a bunch of artillery gunners, I'm not going to stop you,' Freckles said. 'You survive in this man's Army by letting the other guy – or gal – get his head blown off. You wanted a man's job. Now you've got it, so what's your complaint?'

'You're brave as hell, aren't you?' she sneered.

'I'm alive.'

'That's really something to brag about, isn't it?'

A pilot burst into the ready room. 'Dusty went down! We're all ordered up in the air!'

Cards were discarded and chair legs scraped the floor in an instant reaction to the summons. Pilots, male and female alike, ran out of the ready room onto the flight line, fanning out to seek out their aircraft.

An air search for a downed pilot was fairly routine for the men in the squadron, but it was still new to the WASPs. Each pilot was assigned a certain quadrant to fly, criss-crossing a given area and watching for the glitter of metal wreckage in the tangle of cypress and swamp grass that surrounded the camp. The proper procedure in the event of a forced landing was to pancake the plane in the swamp so it would leave a wide path that could be spotted from the air. If possible, a parachute was to be spread on the ground to aid in the spotting. Above all, a pilot was to stay at the crash site.

After better than an hour's search, Mary Lynn felt the eyestrain and the tension that ridged her neck muscles. She hadn't seen anything but the white dots of herons in her section of swamp. Subconsciously, she was always listening to the sound of her plane's engine in case it started giving her trouble.

Finally, the downed plane was located in another quadrant. The message was radioed to the search planes that the pilot and his cableman had been found and all aircraft were ordered back to the field. Mary Lynn turned her plane onto a heading for the strip, relieved yet conscious of the jangled tearing on her nerves.

That evening, all of them were slightly strung out. At mess, lack of appetite was blamed on the heat. The August weather was held responsible for a lot of the frayed tempers and irritable moods. Marty was the only one who seemed to have some immunity to the common condition. It didn't take much urging on her part to persuade Eden and Mary Lynn to have a drink at the Officers' Club and unwind a bit.

Male officers at Camp Davis outnumbered the women a hundred to one. The three of them walked in. The base band was playing a Glen Miller tune while another major pushed his chair into the circle that surrounded their table.

After an hour of being plied with drinks and urged onto the dance floor at every song, they escaped to the powder room for a breather. Eden sat at the mirrored vanity to freshen her lipstick. 'Two weeks ago, I was complaining at the lack of eligible men. Out there, a girl can have her pick.'

'Ah, but why settle for one when you can have a whole squadron,' Marty countered as she fluffed the short curls of her honey-light hair.

'They all seem so lonely.' Mary Lynn supposed Beau felt the same. 'You get the feeling they're happy just to have a woman to talk to.'

'It's more than talk they want.' Marty shook her head at Mary Lynn's innocent interpretation of a man's needs. 'Ready to go back among the wolves?'

'Yes.' Eden stood up, joining them as they moved toward the door. 'They drink a lot, have you noticed?' Her observation drew little comment beyond affirmative nods.

Later, Eden discreetly covered her mouth to hide the yawn she couldn't suppress. She tried to appear interested in the ramblings of the officer with the silver oak leaves on his uniform, so confident of his ability to impress her that he couldn't see her boredom.

Her glance strayed to the dance floor where Marty was tightly entwined in the arms of her partner, a devastating lieutenant with sun-gold hair. For a fleeting instant, she wished for Marty's sense of freedom with men, then changed her mind. Its very impermanence lacked style. She turned back to her lieutenant-colonel and faked an attentive smile.

In an Army camp capable of housing ten thousand soldiers, innumerable hiding places existed for those who had reason to need them. It was in such a forgotten corner of the base that Rachel and Zach lay on a scratchy Army blanket, mostly clothed even though few of the buttons were fastened.

Rachel rested her head on the pillow of Zach's muscled shoulder while he stroked the silken strands of her hair. She was turned toward him, her hand lying on his chest where it could feel the heady thud of his heart. There was a languor about the warm night air that soothed and put distance between Rachel and the half-known fears of her assignment.

'You and your artlllery buddies almost got me today,' she informed Zach from the secure comfort of his embrace. 'You shot the cable in two just three feet from the tail of my plane.'

'We're a trigger-happy bunch.' A smile was in his voice.

'This is ridiculous, you know that,' Rachel murmured, casting an eye at their surroundings. 'We'll probably be carried off by the mosquitoes.'

'The facilities are on the primitive side,' he conceded, his voice rumbling deep in his chest and vibrating against her ear. 'But it's the best I can offer right now. Marry me, Rachel.'

For a little second, she let the fanciful words turn around her before she faced the reality. 'You can't marry without the Army's permission. They'd never give their consent to a marriage between an officer and an enlisted man. Even though we aren't officially a branch of the Army, we do have officer status.'

'Who said anything about asking? We don't need them,' he countered evenly. 'We'll marry the ancient way. Find two witnesses and vow before them, "Behold, thou art consecrated unto me according to the law of Israel."'

'Zach, you talk such nonsense.' But for all her denial, it filled her with a warm glow to hear him speak like that, simplifying everything.

His fingers fitted themselves to the point of her chin and lifted it so he could see her face, glowing in the pale light. 'Why is it nonsense to love you, Rachel?' His handsome looks were so dark and devastating they took her breath away, that ebony-black hair, those azure-blue eyes, and those nobly chiseled features.

'Maybe because there's so much uncertainty around.' She curved her fingers along the back of his neck. 'I love you, Zach. Sometimes . . . I just don't know what I'd do if anything happened to you.' There was an underlying fierceness in her low voice.

A frown flickered across his expression. 'I keep telling you,' he insisted, 'nothing is going to happen to me.' He rocked a hard kiss across her mouth in a sealing promise, then rolled her out of his arms and sat her up so he could light a cigarette. 'Want one?' He offered her a Camel from the squashed pack in his breast pocket.

'Thanks.'

When the match flared suddenly in front of her, the brilliant yellow flame coming toward her, Rachel recoiled in a terror that seemed instinctive. It shook her, and she turned from it.

'What's wrong?' Zach looked at her, puzzled by her reaction. 'It was too bright. It hurt my eyes.' She came up with this plausible explanation and pushed the unlit cigarette at him. 'Light it for me, will you?'

The match went out and he had to strike another. Zach saw her turn her head rather than look at the fire. It puzzled him as he passed her the burning cigarette and bent his head to light his own. She circled her knees with her arms and drew them up to her chest, hunching over them in a tight ball.

'What is it, Rachel?' he asked gently, sensing the fear in her that she didn't want him to see. 'You seemed afraid of the match flame.'

'I wasn't.' She sounded impatient with him. 'It hurt my eyes. I told you that.'

For a long minute, Zach stayed silent and studied the white spiral of smoke rising from his cigarette. 'In the barracks, some of the guys talk a lot about what it's like in the fighting . . . some of the things they've heard . . . what happens to guys on the front. It's as if they have to talk their fears out – in case they're the one who gets hit by an artillery shell and blown into so many bits they can't even find his dogtags.' His glance flickered to her, measuring and keen. 'I've heard pilots are afraid of fire.'

A tension seemed to electrify her. For an instant, Zach expected to hear an explosive denial. Then a sudden sigh loosened her, although a twisting agitation remained.

'It doesn't have anything to do with flying, not really.' Her mouth was grim-lipped and tight, a frustration seething somewhere inside. 'A girlfriend of mine – she was an actress in Hollywood for a while – just before graduation, she was flying an AT-17 to Big Spring. I was following her in another plane. All of a sudden, there was a big, blinding ball of flame where her plane should have been.'

'Rachel –'

'But I had this . . . aversion before that.' Impatiently, she broke in to reject any possible sympathy. 'When Helen was killed, I thought it was a premonition of her death, but it hasn't gone away.' Finally, she looked at him in the darkness, her face all white and rigid with tension. 'I'm afraid to look into the flame – afraid I might see you . . . or maybe my grandmother.'

The haunted depth of her strangely violet eyes was more than Zach could stand. He looked away. Words seemed inadequate comfort. The burning tip of his cigarette glowed in the dark, the red heart growing hotter and pulsating with an eerie life. He ground it into the dirt, then reached for the tight ball Rachel had made of herself and gathered her into his arms.

'What are you doing?' Rachel protested when he took the freshly lit cigarette from her fingers and threw it into the night.

'No cigarette. No fire. No flames to see faces in. For now, there is only love.' A smile was on his mouth as he lowered it onto her lips. His body followed it down, its weight gently driving her backwards onto the blanket.

The hot, drugging kiss lasted long seconds before Zach lifted his head to study her face and see if he'd driven the fear aside. The heady sweetness of her was on his tongue, adding to the high run of pleasure he felt.

Rachel fingered the black silk of his hair, absently combing through its sleek thickness. 'You are crazy.' Her lips lay softly together, all the previous tension eased.

'I must be to love you,' he agreed smoothly. Their embrace had pushed her blouse apart where the lower buttons were unfastened, exposing the pale flesh of her stomach. Zach bent to kiss it, feeling her skin quiver under the caress of his mouth. 'I'm waiting for the day our baby will grow inside you.' When he lifted his head to look at her, his hand lovingly rubbed her flat stomach. 'Why don't we start making one now?'

'Zach, no. What am I supposed to do with a baby while you go off to fight?' Her words resisted his suggestion, but her face appeared warm.

'What's the matter? Can't you fly a plane with a baby on your hip?' he mocked and began nibbling on the sensitive cord along her neck.

'Zach.' Her hands tightened around him to press him closer. 'Love me.'

CHAPTER SEVENTEEN

OUTSIDE THE pilots' ready room, all was black. After sundown, no lights were permitted; the field was under blackout orders and even the runways were darkened.

Yet in the battle zones the war was fought by night as well as by day. Radar trackers and searchlight operators had to be trained in the skills they would need in their combat roles, skills which required night practice . . . and pilots were needed to fly the planes for them to track on their screens or with their lights.

'Cigarette?' Eden shook a Lucky Strike from the green pack and offered it to Rachel.

The tall blonde refused with a shake of her head and turned away as Eden snapped a flame from her lighter and held it to the end of her cigarette. She pulled the smoke deeply within her lungs, then exhaled in a nervous rush. The hastily crushed butt of her previous cigarette still smoldered in the ashtray.

There was little Eden could do to rid herself of the tension that honed all her senses to a razor-fine edge of animal keenness. Danger lurked out there – stalking around the darkened field.

There was no mission to fly. Tonight was merely a check ride to test their night-flying proficiencies. In a way, it was a compliment to the female pilots that they'd done so well on the tow-target missions they were now being considered for other assignments, but Eden was too conscious of the added risks to feel flattered by the commanding officer's show of faith.

'I'd feel better if we were going up in multiengine planes.

At least if an engine failed, we'd have a back-up.' It was the closest Eden could come to admitting the trepidation she felt. Accustomed all her life to the best, she still had trouble accepting the junky craft she flew.

At night, the land was shrouded in darkness, making it difficult – if not impossible – for a pilot to determine wind direction and select a safe landing site in an emergency. The airfield was surrounded by swamp, and the thought of going down in its snake-infested marsh was even more harrowing.

Rachel was never very communicative. If she shared any of Eden's apprehensions, she kept them to herself. Taking a drag of smoke deep into her lungs, Eden guessed at a great many of Rachel's secrets. She'd already figured out that Rachel slipped away in the evening to meet her handsome, enlisted lover. With a twinge of envy, she'd identified the look of love she had sometimes glimpsed in Rachel's expression. Naturally, she didn't let on that she knew about the trysts, and Rachel was hardly likely to confide in her about them.

The instructors arrived to give check rides to the group of WASPs ordered to report to the flight line. The inaction and the inability to talk about the misgivings they all shared were finally put behind them as they went about the business of checking out the individual aircraft they'd be flying. But they kept reminding themselves that male pilots had been flying these night missions all along, and they were here to replace them.

In the warm, languid air of late summer, Eden read the Form One sheet of her aircraft's log. The only defect listed on the form was a broken seat, a very minor item in Eden's opinion. Other than that, her plane was in good flying condition. Still, when she saw Bubba Jackson going over her A-24, it gave her added reassurance.

The lanky mechanic waited by the wing to give her a hand up while her instructor spent a last few minutes conferring with one of his colleagues. 'You're working awfully late, aren't you?' Eden observed, smiling and aware of the strength in the hand that assisted her onto the wing. Usually, only the ground crew was around the flight line for the night missions, the mechanics long gone.

'Had to check the planes out for you ladies; make sure they were safe for you,' Bubba replied with a warm, wide smile. There was about him a generous, loving nature, sparked with an easy humor, steadied by a solid will, and tempered by an iron strength.

'No major problems?' Eden climbed into the front cockpit. Bubba followed her onto the wing and helped her get settled in the seat.

'None, not in any of them,' Bubba stated, then qualified his words. 'It's all fairly minor – broken seats like yours, static problems with radios, a sticky canopy latch, but no trouble with the engines on any of the planes.'

'Thanks,' she said and meant it. Just knowing that Bubba had checked out her plane eased her fears. She tried to tell herself that tonight would be no different from the many times they'd practiced night-flying in Sweetwater.

With a wink, Bubba slapped the metal skin of the plane in a kind of farewell pat and hopped off the wing. Her instructor took his place in the gunner's seat. Down the shadowed row of aircraft, Eden saw the shimmer of something white, then the small silhouette of Mary Lynn crawling into the cockpit of an A-24 with the pillows which enabled her to reach the foot controls.

Engines sputtered and coughed, then revved into a steady roar. When they taxied away from the ramp, Eden followed the plane Rachel was piloting down the darkened taxi strips to the unlighted runway. She closed her canopy and made her run-ups while she awaited her turn. As soon as Rachel's Dauntless cleared the runway, Eden started her roll, hurtling her plane down the blacked-out airstrip. It was like flying blind, relying solely on her instruments to direct her liftoff.

Airborne, they were to stay in the pattern and practice takeoffs and landings from the darkened field. In order to see the dimensions of the strip, they were forced to fly low, always keeping in mind the swamp pines that loomed so close to the foot of the runway.

On her first circuit, Rachel wasted a lot of runway before setting her plane down by coming in too high, an error her instructor pointed out as she went around to try again. It was difficult to distinguish the long, black shapes of the camp buildings below, but one of them was the barracks that housed Zach. The thought of him stabbed into her concentration, bringing a momentary break in focus – and a smile to her lips.

'Bring it in low this time, Goldman,' her instructor advised from the rear gunner's seat. 'You can't see where the runway starts if you come in like a cautious old woman.'

'Yes, sir.' She bridled at the slur of female timidity and aggressively attacked the pattern, swooping down to make her approach.

In the changing colors of darkness, the runway lay before her, a wide swath of gray-black. With all her concentration focused on setting up the A-24 for a turn down the center of the strip, Rachel failed to see the trees rushing up to meet her. Suddenly the plane was jolted, the wheels snagged by the treetops.

Rachel heard a cry, but didn't recognize it as her own. There was barely time to brace herself as the Dauntless tumbled forward, nosing for the ground. On impact, there was a wrenching tear of metal, a violent jarring that bounced her from side to side. When the crashing, crunching noise stopped, it was a dazed instant before Rachel realized she was still alive.

Then she saw it – the leap of yellow flame from the engine, a searching serpent's tongue, flicking and darting and disappearing, only to show itself again. Terror sucked at her throat. Her fingers tugged frantically at the buckle to free herself from the seat, then turned their efforts on the canopy.

GET OUT!

She jerked at it, but the latch was stuck. Panic flashed through her mind as she remembered the Form One sheet had warned the canopy could only be opened from the outside. The fire blossomed into a roar, sweeping back from the engine while Rachel screamed and beat on the mullioned canopy.

GET OUT!!

She clawed at the latch in a frenzied attempt to escape as the yellow flames swirled through the cockpit. The fire trapped her inside its searing net, and rolled her up inside its life-snatching heat.

On her downwind leg, Eden saw Rachel's plane shudder to a stop in midair, hang there for interminable seconds, then topple into the swamp at the edge of the field. The impact snapped it in two, separating the front cockpit from the gunner's seat. She saw the yellow tongues of flame lick over the engine as it caught fire.

The landing pattern took her directly over the burning wreckage. In horror, she looked at the scene below her. Time and space seemed to stand still, hovering, while she heard Rachel's screams and watched the figure in the blazing cockpit make a last desperate attempt to push open the canopy before the fire consumed her.

Then she'd flown past, the screams ringing in her ears and the sight of a fiery figure, arms, legs, and body all aflame, emblazoned in her mind. Afterwards, Eden didn't remember landing the plane or taxiing it to the flight line.

One of the first things she did upon landing was to open the canopy of her A-24 and drink in great globs of air. Distantly she heard the wail of sirens as rescue trucks and fire engines raced to the crash site. She was sweating, but she felt cold and shivery.

Vaguely she became aware that someone was calling her name. Still encapsulated in a kind of dazed shock, she became aware of someone standing on the wing outside her cockpit. He reached in to switch off the engine and shut down the systems.

'Eden.' Bubba's strong, wide face was close to hers, examining it in the night's darkness. 'Are you all right?'

In the strain of the moment, Bubba had dropped the formality of 'ma'am.'

The deep caring and concern she saw in his anxious expression broke the paralysis of shock. 'I saw it, Bubba. I saw it all.' Her gaze clung to his big-jawed face. 'She hit the trees.'

'I know.' He was very matter-of-fact as he urged her out of the cockpit. 'Come on.'

Mechanically, she climbed from the plane. Her instructor was on the ground, but she paid little mind to him. It was Bubba she turned to as she tried to shake off the dazed terror that gripped her. The instructor hovered uncertainly until Bubba indicated he should leave.

'I'll look after her. They'll probably want you in operations,' he said quietly and kept a hand on Eden. In an absent gesture, she took off her scarf and let her shiny auburn hair tumble free, as if releasing it would rid her of the dreadful images.

'I could hear her screaming,' she told Bubba in a flat voice as the instructor moved away. 'The engine caught fire. She couldn't get the canopy open and –' She couldn't get the rest of it out, the horror of it too much for speech.

'My God,' Bubba said, softly at first, then in a clearer, flatter voice. 'My God.' He remembered the canopy with the faulty latch that could only be opened from the outside.

'Bubba, it was awful,' she said with a sob.

When his arm circled her shoulders, she gratefully turned into his body and buried her face in the hollow of his shoulder. He held her tightly against his lanky frame, absorbing the violent shudders that racked her body. His low, softly drawled voice murmured near her ear, dulling the memory of those terrifying shrieks while he suffered pangs of remorse and guilt. 'If only I had . . .' but he hadn't.

The night was a din of noise – the strident wail of an ambulance, the shrill sirens of fire trucks, and the roaring engines of other planes landing and taxiing back to the flight line. The check rides had come to an abrupt end; the planes landed on the air strip one after another. Eden stayed hidden in the shadows of her plane and isolated in the island of Bubba's arms.

'I didn't even like her,' she said in an odd mixture of guilt and regret.

'Shh.' He cupped his hand to the back of her head and pressed it more tightly to his shoulder while he gently rocked her.

By the time the fire trucks could put out the fire, Rachel's body was charred beyond recognition. In fate's strange way of working, her instructor had been thrown clear of the fire-engulfed front section. The ambulance whisked him away.

Within minutes of the crash and the first shriek of sirens, word of the accident swept through the Army barracks. Zach joined the cluster of soldiers outside his bay and stared at the odd light reflected in the sky.

Nearly all party invitations in Washington, DC, included instructions on which bus to take. Mitch Ryan, however, had a military vehicle at his disposal, a mark of his status regardless of his rank.

When they reached the exclusive Washington suburb of Chevy Chase, Mitch had no difficulty locating the manor-sized home. Lights blazed from virtually every window of the two-and-a-half-story structure, throwing long, rectangular streamers into the night, sometimes spotlighting glimpses of the partying crowd beyond the sheer drapes. Cappy couldn't help regarding it as an extravagant display.

'Will they let me in like this?' she asked when he left the vehicle parked in the drive. Mitch ran a quick glance over her uniform of tan slacks and white shirt, a tan boat-shaped cap sitting atop her midnight-dark hair. Women in slacks were still frowned on in a great many circles.

'We're at war. It would be unpatriotic to turn away an officer in uniform,' he returned glibly. Then he assured her, 'We won't be staying long – whatever time it takes to make my presence known – then we'll go off by ourselves.'

'Okay.' Even though she was stationed close by, flying out of a base on the outskirts of Washington, she'd only been out with Mitch on two occasions since starting her new assignment almost two weeks before. Each time she found herself looking forward to seeing him more and more.

The hectic pace of wartime Washington made it socially acceptable for guests to arrive in street clothes or office garb. But Cappy's uniform slacks did succeed in raising a few blasé eyebrows. However, the plethora of military uniforms, especially field grades, took much of the strangeness out of her appearance.

Caterers circled the rooms with trays of drinks balanced on their hands. Cappy was holding a glass within minutes of entering the house. Either there weren't any shortages in Chevy Chase or the black market was the popular shopping place, she decided, upon seeing the silver platters of canapés and hors d'oeuvres, which were not only plentiful but also stuffed with an array of meats rarely obtainable.

While Mitch squired her through the noisy, laughing clusters of guests, Cappy quietly observed the avidly gossiping crowd, spreading the latest rumors. This scene was all too familiar to Cappy, the currying of favor and the back-stabbing She'd seen all these games played; she'd seen the advancements and promotions that had nothing to do with merit.

She had become so inured to the sight of Army uniforms that she almost didn't notice the gold stars adorning the shoulders of the officer now receiving Mitch's respectful attention. Then she heard Mitch introduce her and the broadly smiling general turned an interested glance on her.

'WASP Hayward, at last I have the pleasure of meeting you.' He warmly clasped her hand, the gleam in his eye hinting at the many things he'd heard about her. The glance he sent Mitch revealed the source.

'You're very kind, General Arnold.' She inclined her

head to him, respectful of his rank but unawed by it. Protocol and pettiness too often walked hand in hand. She was well schooled in the ways of paying lip service to rank. 'Please forgive my less-than-feminine appearance,' she said, drawing attention to the gabardine pants tailored to her slim hips and long legs. 'But I'm afraid I came straight from the flight line.'

'I wouldn't worry about it,' he replied easily. 'I'd wager half the women at this party wished they looked as attractive as you do in slacks.'

'Now you are being gallant, General,' Cappy demurred with practiced ease.

His chuckle held approval as he glanced at Mitch. 'No wonder you're so taken with this young lady. She'd be an asset to any man.'

'That's always supposing I would want to be,' she murmured. Pride straightened her shoulders and lifted her head as she gave him the full strike of her gaze. She refused to exist in a man's shadow the way her mother did.

On an amused intake of breath, the general glanced again at Mitch. 'The trouble with letting women wear pants is getting them to take them off.' His attention returned to Cappy. 'You're Lieutenant Colonel Hayward's daughter, aren't you? He's a crack polo player, I've heard.'

'Yes, sir.'

'He must be very proud of you,' General 'Hap' Arnold remarked.

'I wouldn't know, sir.' Her smile was reserved as she turned military on him, clipped and opinionless.

An aide approached and discreetly called the commanding general of the Army Air Forces aside. The content of the whispered message caused a frown to furrow the general's wide forehead. He looked soberly from Cappy to Mitch, lingering on the latter as if he had half a mind to call him away, too.

'Excuse me, I . . . have a phone call. You'll be around for a while yet, won't you, Major?' The polite inquiry was an indirect order to remain.

'Yes, sir.' Mitch confirmed with a small nod of his head. 'We'll be here.'

'Good.'

After the general had gone off to some private room to take the phone call, Cappy sipped at her drink and surveyed the gaggle of guests over the rim of her glass. 'I thought you said we wouldn't be staying long,' she mockingly reminded Mitch.

'I'd like to think you're complaining because you want to be alone with me.'

'Maybe I do.' When she turned to look at him fully, her eyes were big and blue, demanding in their keen brilliance.

'What do you want from me, Cappy?' There were many meanings to his question, but Mitch knew she'd pick the one that suited her, as usual.

This time she surprised him. 'I don't know. I've been asking myself that lately, too.'

It was a subject he would have preferred to pursue, but the party made it impossible. Someone came up to speak to him and the conversation was sidetracked. They became caught up in the social chatter of the war, the endless talk and speculation and the hinted-at secrets.

Twenty minutes later, Cappy observed the general's return. He was an imposing figure, solidly packed and vigorous as he moved through the room, always in their direction. The congenial smile that came so readily to his lips seemed distant and preoccupied, an automatic response while more serious matters dominated his mind. He stopped when he reached them and looked at Mitch, a serious light in his hazel-colored eyes.

'Would you excuse us for a moment?' The perfunctory request was addressed to Cappy as General Arnold drew Mitch aside.

No response was expected from her beyond an agreeing nod while she pretended to focus her attention elsewhere and not listen to the words spoken in undertones. But when Cappy heard 'WASP' and 'crash' mentioned, followed by the location, 'Camp Davis,' she did the unforgivable – she intruded.

'Whose plane crashed?' she demanded and watched the general's thin lips come together to hold back the information. Impatience and agitation swept across her features, writing an unbearable tension and strain all over her expression. 'I heard you say a WASP crashed at Camp Davis in North Carolina. please, I have friends there.'

'Sorry, sir,' Mitch muttered and tried to silence Cappy with a look as he reached for her arm to lead her away.

'No.' She refused to be removed, aware that her actions were attracting the unwanted attention of those around them. A false calm steadied her. 'General, you did say a WASP crashed. Who? Was she . . . hurt?'

For a long span of seconds, he merely looked at her, then a gently sad quality suffused his hard visage. 'Positive identification has not been made. There was a fire,' he explained, and had to say no more. Cappy's jaw was tightly clenched as a kind of paralysis gripped her throat. 'At this time, it's believed the victim was a young woman named Goldman – Rachel Goldman.'

The shock of recognition broke the superficial barrier of calm. Tears sprang into her eyes and Cappy quickly lowered her head to hide them.

'Did you know her?' the general probed.

'We were baymates at Sweetwater.' She lifted her head, stunned and shaken. 'I never thought it might be her.' Her fears had been for Eden, Mary Lynn or Marty.

'Come with me.'

This time Cappy didn't protest against being led away, letting the hand at her elbow guide her across the room. A set of pocket doors was slid open and closed after they walked through. The chattering noise of the party didn't intrude inside the paneled den. General Arnold motioned his aide toward a liquor cabinet while he paused to inspect the titles of the books lining the wall shelves.

'I love books,' he remarked in a deliberate change of subject. He looked around to be sure he had an audience.

'Have you seen those new, small-sized books with paper covers? A publishing company named Pocket Books is putting them out. Handy for the soldier to carry with him. But when it comes to reading, I like the solidness of a hard-bound book.'

A wave of vertigo made Cappy sway and she felt Mitch's hands steady her. She leaned into the support he offered, finding a warmth and a strength that she needed. The general's aide brought her a snifter of brandy, but she didn't really want it.

'Drink up,' General Arnold urged.

'Yes, sir.' Perforce, she was obliged to take a sip.

'It was an unfortunate loss,' he said, referring to the crash. He didn't inquire as to the closeness of her relationship with Rachel, nor did he invite her to confide.

'Yes, sir.'

To Mitch he said, 'There'll be a board of inquiry looking into the crash. I'd like you to be there . . . in an unofficial capacity.' In other words, as his eyes and ears, with the findings to be reported directly back to him. 'Perhaps' – he seemed to consider the suggestion he was about to make, before actually saying it – 'Miss Hayward could fly to Camp Davis with you . . . as your pilot.'

'Thank you, sir.' Cappy was grateful for the favor granted, a cynical part of her aware that it was given out of an Army loyalty to one of their own, daughter of a respected Army officer and girlfriend to one of the general's prized staff members.

'I must be getting back to the party,' the general said, taking his leave of them.

Alone in the den, Mitch asked, 'Were you close to this Rachel Goldman?'

'No,' Cappy admitted. 'Is it all right if we leave the party now?'

'Of course.' An instant later, a guiding hand rested on her waist to direct her through the maze of people and rooms.

The night air was summer-warm and still. Cappy rode

in the passenger seat without talking. Her fears about the fate of her friends had been eased, but there lingered an unsettling feeling that gnawed at her. She turned her gaze from the traffic on the capital's streets and the lighted windows of its houses and buildings to look at Mitch. The present route would take them to Bolling Field, where she was stationed.

'Please, I'd rather not go back to the barracks right away.' Cappy felt him looking at her, wary and curious while he searched her expression. 'Could we go to your place for a drink?'

'If that's what you want,' Mitch consented.

An odd silence lay between them for the rest of the ride as Mitch changed directions, crossing the Potomac to the Virginia side, where his apartment was located. Once they had entered the apartment, the long silence was interrupted by short questions and one-word responses, all very correct and polite, as Mitch fixed them each a drink.

A restlessness moved Cappy about the room, finally drawing her to a window where she looked out into the starry night, but she could see little beyond her own reflection in the windowpane. When she turned back to the room, Mitch was standing the width of it away from her, watching her.

'Why are you standing clear over there?' Cappy tried to make light of her question, needing to alleviate the heavy mood.

'If I come any closer, you might bite,' Mitch replied with a vague shrug of his shoulders.

'That's ridiculous.' She was suddenly impatient with his answer.

'It's the truth,' he insisted, with no glint in his eye. 'Whenever anybody gets too close to you, you start snapping until you drive them away.'

'Is that what you think?' A small, hurt frown entered her expression.

'It's what I know. Do you want to see my scars?' Behind

his half-smile was a hard deep hurt. 'You remember the old saying, Once bitten, twice shy? I'd hate to count the number of times I've reached out to you and received the cutting edge of your tongue instead.'

She shook her head, trying to dismiss a subject she was reluctant to discuss. Tears were stinging the back of her eyes, and she opened them wide to try to dry them out. He spoke too quietly, his jest was too piercing.

'How could you room with someone for nearly six months without being close to her?' Mitch wondered at the way she could hold people away from her. 'Why are you afraid to let anyone get near you, Cap?'

'None of us got along with Rachel. I don't know why.' She looked at her drink, not really seeing it. 'The Army takes. Haven't you noticed that, Mitch? The Army is always taking things. I'm tired of it. I want it to be my turn.'

Cappy was aware of the selfishness in her needs. But the crash that had taken Rachel's life had brought her face to face with her own mortality, and she wanted to grab at the things she wanted and hold them for as long as she could.

Mitch stood, silent and unmoving. It was difficult for her to cross the room – she, who had always contained her feelings and kept them bottled inside where no one could see or know how vulnerable she was. But the fear that maybe there wouldn't be a tomorrow pushed her. She'd been alone and lonely for so long. This time she was going to do the taking.

Halfway across the room, she deposited her drink on top of a table so her hands would be free when she reached Mitch. His stance was unchanged, a stone-statue stillness about him, his lidded gaze veillng his thoughts. With a downcast head, Cappy took the drink from his unresisting fingers and set it aside. A rigid pulse hammered along her throat.

His expression remained unchanged, silence his only response while she lifted her hands and curved them to the rigid muscles standing out tensely along the back of his neck. Slowly his muscles gave in to the pressure she exerted to bring his head down the few inches so her lips could reach his mouth. Her contact with the unyielding line of his lips was tentative, warming gradually from the heady taste of him and the stimulating male scent that clung to his skin.

For long seconds, he was immobile and it was Cappy doing the kissing. When the lines of restraint broke, it was a violent break. His arms pressed her closer to him while his mouth ground down upon her lips with punishing ardor. Cappy didn't complain.

When he pulled back from the kiss, her hands tightened around his neck. 'Hold me, Mitch,' she urged in that tight voice, afraid to let go of her emotions. 'I don't want to be alone tonight.'

The inviting push of her hips, the hot urgings of her lips, and the stirring roundness of her breasts all made their impressions on him, but it was the pooling blue of her eyes that pulled him down.

'Where you're concerned, I swear I'll always be the fool,' he muttered thickly. With a scoop of his arms, he picked her up and carried her into the bedroom. 'I won't let you go tonight.'

In the faint light that spilled into the room from the hallway, they watched each other undress. Their uniforms were cast aside, until they were stripped bare of clothes, facing each other as only man and woman.

On the bed, the closeness was savored. The hungry deepening of kisses and stroking of bodies was slow but eager as their needs pushed them, and they tried not to rush the wonder of it. Their play – the erotic sucking of nipples and fondling of bodies – was drawn out as long as possible.

When the moment could no longer be prolonged, he mounted her and penetrated the last barrier. Still, Mitch murmured to her, 'Let me in.'

Later in the night, while Cappy slept curled up like a

kitten in his arms, Mitch reflected on the shared ecstasy. A keen disappointment knotted the pit of his stomach. She had given him her body and her willingness, but she had kept her feelings apart and not allowed him to get too deeply under the surface of them. Yet they were there; he could sense their wanting.

She confused him – her silence, her fear, her lack of trust.

His hands knew her body, roaming over every crest and crevice of it; his lips knew the taste and texture of her flesh; and his body had rocked with the rhythm of hers, matching and mating. He had gotten into her, and known her physically. But she had not allowed words, had silenced anything he tried to say. She had wanted him and he had satisfied her. But he wanted more than that.

CHAPTER EIGHTEEN

Eden prowled the room like a cage-crazy tigress. A tense, restless energy permeated the air, the strain and tension showing on both Mary Lynn's and Marty's faces. None of them looked as though she had slept a wink since last night's crash. Cappy had difficulty assimilating the changes that had been wrought in her friends within such a short space of time. She had expected shock and a certain amount of grief over Rachel's death, but not this bitter anger. Her glance strayed to Mitch as she wished she hadn't asked him to stay. She doubted that Eden understood the gravity of the charges of dereliction she was throwing about.

'Eden's upset,' she said to him, calmly coming to the defense of her friend.

'You're damned right I am,' she snapped.

'Maybe I should leave,' Mitch suggested, aware that his uniform was a less-than-welcome presence in the room.

269

Tempers had been whipped raw, resentment ran high.

'No. Stay,' Marty insisted with belligerence. 'Somebody from the top brass oughta hear what we think. No one else is interested enough to listen, so why not you, Major Ryan.'

'Mitch isn't here in an official capacity.' Cappy held back the knowledge that he was at Camp Davis to observe and report his findings to General Arnold. But she didn't want him carrying tales back about her friends either.

'Official or not, he's Army, and somebody in command needs to know the kind of rotten business that's going on down here.' Eden joined with Marty to insist that Mitch stay. The flash of her dark eyes was hard and her lips were thinly compressed. 'You don't see our leader anywhere around, do you? The great Jacqueline Cochran is conferring with that red-necked commanding officer – as if he's going to tell her what's been going on around here.' Her sarcasm and bitterness was thick. 'Of course, she has agreed to speak to us – tonight at seven. I beg your pardon – at nineteen hundred hours,' she corrected in mock deference to Mitch.

To hear Eden make such snide comments about their director when she'd always expressed such an admiration for Jacqueline Cochran added to Cappy's surprise. Beside her, Mitch seemed to settle back, those dark eyes and that quick mind not missing anything.

Cappy thought Eden would have learned from the Sweetwater experience that the Army's attitude toward complaints was 'Tough.' Whatever their gripes about conditions here, it would do them no good to tell Mitch. It would merely put them in a bad light.

'Rachel's death was a tragic accident.' Cappy had seen the preliminary report, identifying the faulty canopy latch as a contributing factor to her death, although pilot error had been the obvious cause of the crash.

'The tragedy is it could have happened to any of us.' Eden paused, plainly agitated. 'You don't know the deplorable conditions of the planes we're expected to fly.'

'Eden –' Cappy began, but never got any further.

'She's right.' Marty sided with the New Yorker, one of the rare times in Cappy's memory. 'Yesterday, two engines failed and the pilots had to make a forced landing. Since we've been here, we've flown air search for eleven planes that went down in the swamps. And the tires on these planes are so worn, there were five blowouts in one day. Those are just the major things; this has nothing to do with the radios that don't work, the flap levers that won't stay locked in position – or canopies that won't open from the inside.' Stormy-eyed, she ran a hand through her touseled, light brown curls. 'Some experiment, huh?'

'Are you serious?' Cappy was appalled by the charges.

'It isn't just the planes.' Mary Lynn appeared more subdued, less inclined to critical outbursts, but the strain was evident in her pale cheeks and worn expression. Her eyes were very dark, without their usual inner light. 'Most of the instructors here know less about the planes than we do, yet they're giving us check rides.'

'They're rejects – all of them.' Marty was more sweeping in her condemnation. 'You can almost bet that they were assigned to this tow-target squadron because they washed out of some other program. If they were such hot pilots, they'd be flying missions overseas in the combat zones.'

'Do you realize the seriousness of the charges you are making?' Cappy believed them, yet she was stunned by what they were telling her too.

'Don't take our word for it.' Eden stopped her pacing to challenge both Cappy and Mitch Ryan. 'Just ask any of the mechanics.'

'Yeah,' Marty agreed. 'They've told us more than once that all they try to do is keep the engines running. It's a waste of time to write anything on the Form One sheets. They don't make the repairs.'

'They can't get the parts,' Eden inserted. 'That flight line out there is filled with junk aircraft and we're expected to fly them.'

'Or kill ourselves trying, the way Rachel did,' Mary Lynn offered quietly.

271

A long silence followed, which no one tried to fill. Eden took another cigarette from her pack and tamped the tobacco in it, hitting it on the side of the pack with short, incisive taps that bespoke her impatience. She carried it to her lips, letting it dangle there while she struck a match to light it.

Her glance sliced to Mitch. 'What's your recommendation, Major?'

'Go through channels,' he replied easily, not rising to her challenging tone. 'Tell your story to Cochran when you meet with her at nineteen hundred hours tonight.'

'Will you be there, Major?' Mary Lynn asked, accustomed to her southern world where men played the dominant roles.

'No.' The answer was simple and direct, emphasizing his detached observer status.

When the conversation became a rehash of complaints already covered, Mitch excused himself. Cappy hesitated before she accompanied him to the door, wanting a private word with him. Outside the building, an August sun broiled the Army grounds. The air was still and heavy; disciplined columns of men marched through it with sweaty backs and perspiring lips, constantly drilling until they could act without thinking. In the Army, a soldier didn't think – he obeyed. Someone else did his thinking for him.

Cappy knew this, yet she turned to Mitch, troubled by all she'd heard. 'What do you think, Mitch?'

His handsome face, chiseled in such strong, clean lines, was devoid of expression. 'I think there's a war on and there isn't always time to do things the right way.'

'I don't want an Army answer!' she flared.

'Maybe not,' Mitch conceded with a smooth, dismissing shrug. 'But it's likely that's all you'll get.'

She knew better than to argue the point, and asked instead, 'Where are you going?'

'Between you and me?' An eyebrow lifted to extract her promise of silence, and received her affirmative nod. 'To

272

ask a few questions on my own. Then, I'd better sit in on the inquiry.'

At precisely nineteen hundred hours, the women pilots met with their director in the operations building. It had been nearly twenty-four hours since Rachel's plane crashed near the end of the runway; time for the seething anger to come to a rolling boil. Every incident was recapped, every rumor retold, and every fact related. Agreement was unanimous among them.

After the meeting, when the trio of Mary Lynn, Eden, and Marty arrived at the Officers' Club, Cappy was relieved to see they had calmed down considerably. But the tension hung about them, the waiting air of expectancy.

'What did she say when you told her?' Cappy asked after drinks were ordered round.

'She promised she'd check out the planes herself.' Mary Lynn answered the question about Jacqueline Cochran.

In the early cool of the following morning, a short memorial service was held for Rachel Goldman. Mitch escorted Cappy to the small chapel on the base. Mary Lynn had saved a space for them on the wooden pew where she sat with Marty and Eden.

They felt a closeness to her in death that they'd never known in life. Rachel, tall and feline-sleek with a cat's grace, passionately giving back whatever she got – friendship or hostility. Rachel, the proud and the wary. Rachel, the stranger.

For Mary Lynn, there was regret that she hadn't been kinder. Eden couldn't shake the horrifying image of yellow flames swirling around Rachel while she flew by overhead. A sense of obligation and duty brought Cappy to the chapel, and Marty was there to pay her respects to a fellow flier, a lover of the sky.

As they were filing quietly out of the chapel at the conclusion of the service, Eden noticed the man sitting in the back row, wearing an enlisted man's uniform. His head was bowed, a crown of thick, black hair absorbing the shine of the sunlight streaming through a stained glass window. His hands were folded in his lap, tightly clutching his soldier's cap. Although she couldn't see his face, Eden was sure she knew him.

'Excuse me.' She sent the others out of the chapel while she stayed behind to move quietly into the pew. After a second's hesitation, she sat on the smooth-worn seat, angling her body toward him.

'You're Zach Jordan, aren't you?' she guessed in a low voice, and watched him stiffen. 'Rachel introduced us in New York. I'm Eden van Valkenburg.'

With a small turn of his head, he cast an identifying glance in her direction. 'I remember.' The deep, haunting blue of his eyes glistened with a contained wetness while his patrician, proud features had the pinched-in look of grief to them, feelings sucked in tight.

'I can't tell you how sorry I am . . . about Rachel.' Some of Eden's bitterness came through – the resentment at the jeopardy all their lives were in because of slipshod maintenance and a poorly equipped staff of mechanics.

'I stood outside my barracks last night and watched the light the fire made in the sky.' His tightly clenched hands could not disguise the tremors that vibrated through him, but his expression remained stony. 'A plane had crashed and burned, they told me. And I hoped Rachel hadn't seen it. She was afraid of fire – afraid of seeing faces in the flames.'

His words made the image she carried in her mind even more horrifying. 'She shouldn't have died,' Eden insisted in a trembling, emotion-riddled voice, her anger resurfacing.

'After the war, we were going to have children . . . lots of children. We were going to go to Palestine – to Jerusalem. After the war.' His voice faded into the blankness the future held out for him.

His throat worked convulsively, then Zach turned from her and stood. He walked out of the chapel, still clutching the folded length of his cap.

The morning inspection of the aircraft was conducted by Jacqueline Cochran, her executive assistant, the squadron commander, Major Stevenson, a representative from the Air Safety Board, and the chief maintenance officer. From the sidelines, Mitch watched the group going over the engine logs for all of the A-24s.

Pragmatically, Mitch decided on another course to obtain the information and wandered into a hangar. A soldier slogging through the mud had a better knowledge of road conditions than a general flying over it at a thousand feet. A tall, rangy mechanic was bellied over the engine of an A-24. Perspiration made a wet stain on his greasy fatigues, ringing his underams and making a dark patch between his shoulder blades. It took Mitch a minute to discern the chevrons amidst all the dirt and grime.

'Hello, Sergeant.'

The mechanic glanced backward in his direction. 'Sorry, sir,' the mechanic drawled. 'It's kinda hard to salute when you got a wrench in your hands and a bolt half loosened. Be through here in a minute.'

'No hurry.' Mitch waited, observing the man's clean, decisive actions.

'I suppose you'll be wantin' your plane rolled out.' The sergeant talked as he worked, occasionally punctuating his words with grunts of energy exerted.

Judging by the man's apparent competence and rank, Mitch wasn't surprised that the sergeant knew generally who he was. 'No. Just some information.' Something clicked in his memory. 'By any chance you wouldn't be Sergeant Jackson?'

'Yes, sir.' He looked again at Mitch, silently questioning how he had known.

'Eden mentioned you.'

'Miss van Valkenburg? Yes, I know her, sir.' There was a small pause, almost deliberate as if considering the next words. 'How is she? She was tore up the other night . . . saw the crash and . . . everything.'

'Fine.' Mitch couldn't really comment on Eden's emotional state, so he glossed over his answer. 'The investigation going on now – what do you think they're going to find?'

The sergeant stopped to wipe his hands, his wide, strong-boned face serious with concern. 'It's likely that they'll find most of the planes are overdue for an engine overhaul – according to combat standards.'

'What do you know about the plane that went down?'

'It had five hundred hours on the engine – maybe two hundred tow-target missions flown,' he admitted.

'And?' Mitch prompted.

Bubba gave a telling shrug, and avoided stating an opinion. 'Our orders are to keep 'em flying. Most of the time we accomplish that, even when we don't have the spare parts, or the gas allotment gets shorted.' His head dipped for an instant, his glance darting away. 'That canopy latch, it was such a small thing. Hell.'

'Right.' Mitch agreed with the mechanic's assessment.

That afternoon, another meeting was convened by Jacqueline Cochran to relay the findings to her pilots. But it wasn't to be the informal gathering of the previous night. She was accompanied by some of the top brass from the base. Eden had the feeling their director had chosen sides, and it wasn't theirs she was on.

Brisk and businesslike, the dark-eyed, blond director of the women's flying program read the engine time logged on the A-24s her girls were flying. The implication was clear that the aircraft were not as poorly maintained as they had believed. While it was true many of them were past due for overhauls, that criterion was mainly applied to combat planes. It wasn't practical to expect that degree of maintenance on the planes flown at home.

As Eden realized they were being given the official explanation, she looked down the row of seated women pilots. Few liked what they were hearing but they seemed perforce to accept it. The Army officers were very plainly supporting their director, so there was no place to appeal the decision.

But Eden was in no mood to be bought off by a

bunch of officers, no matter how much brass they carried. 'That's a whitewash, and you know it,' she called out, in open criticism of the aviatrix she had once admired.

Marty was quick to take up the cry. 'The mechanics don't pay attention to those engine logs. I doubt if they're even up to date.'

But their protests were ignored. No one acted as if they'd even heard them as the commander of the base got up to speak, expressing his delight at having the women at his camp. After he had given his little spiel, it was the chief surgeon's turn, then the public relations officers', who promised them publicity.

When they filed outside after it was over, Cappy was waiting to hear the results. Their sullen faces told her almost as much as their words as they recounted what Eden regarded as a betrayal by their leader.

'The chief surgeon gets up there and says we have his permission to use the nurses' quarters. It's obvious the old fart doesn't know that we're already living there,' Marty muttered in her whiskey-rough voice.

'It was another one of the Army's famous snafus,' Mary Lynn concluded, less bitter than the others.

'Do you know what snafu stands for?' Marty asked her in wry mockery. 'Situation Normal – All Fucked Up.'

No one spoke of resigning as a protest to the Army's response. They had been warned the assignment would be tough and dangerous, and long ago had learned they had to be better than the average male pilot. They couldn't quit; it was a matter of pride.

Late that day, the UC-78 Cappy was piloting lifted off the ground, following in the wake of the AT-17 flown by Jacqueline Cochran. Mitch occupied the right seat, letting her silence run its course. They had barely exchanged five words beyond the requisite communication prior to takeoff.

His sideways glance studied the mutinous set of her jaw and the hard sparkle in her blue eyes. Her ire was aroused, and Mitch was fascinated by the animation it gave her face. She so rarely allowed her feelings to show.

'Why, Mitch? Why?' Cappy demanded once the aircraft was trimmed to its angle of climb. Flying over Cape Fear, they banked to the north. Far out to sea, ships steamed in a convoy, hugging the coastline. 'Eden wasn't lying about the shoddy condition of those planes.'

'No, I don't think she was lying,' he agreed.

'Then surely something can be done.' It was a protest, and an expression of frustration. 'You've been here. You've seen what's going on. Surely you –'

'Why?' Mitch interrupted, reacting to the disparaging emphasis she placed on him, as if he was some tin god she despised. 'Because I have the general's ear? What would you have me suggest? That he detour a shipment of spare parts and reassign mechanics from the battlefront? Maybe I could just have him call off the war while I'm at it.'

For an instant she didn't respond. 'Are you saying it can't be helped?' There was a steely quiet to her voice.

'Yes, that's what I'm saying.' He sighed heavily. 'I'm not telling any tales out of school when I admit our planes are getting shot out of the sky faster than we can replace them. Maybe we have managed to drive Rommel out of Africa, but we're still fighting a defensive war in the Pacific.'

'Why didn't Cochran say that?' Cappy answered, subdued but still angry. 'Why did she try to whitewash the whole situation?'

'It's simple, really,' Mitch said, his gaze automatically searching the sky for air traffic. 'She wants "her girls" to obtain a lot of flying assignments besides ferrying aircraft around the country. You have no idea what she went through to persuade command to let those girls into the tow-target flying. Now she can't admit it might be too dangerous, any more than she can admit that "her girls" might not have the guts to take such risks. If this experiment fails – for whatever reason – her whole plan to broaden the women's flying program will be set way back.'

'I see,' Cappy murmured, understanding yet not liking the situation any better.

'Satisfied?' A dark brow was quirked in her direction.

'Yes.'

'Well, I'm not.' He reached across the space between their seats and turned her head toward him. He saw the protest beginning to form as he leaned across to kiss her. His vision narrowed, like a camera lens closing in its focus on one object, until all he could see clearly was the unbroken line of her lips. His mouth moved onto them, meeting initial stiffness that soon gave, and the warm pressure was returned. Mitch suspected it was not so much a giving in to his wants as it was a giving in to her own.

When he pulled away, he saw her lashes lower to conceal the look in her eyes. But he welcomed such a concealment from Cappy, since it meant he had aroused some feeling she didn't want him to see.

'I was beginning to wonder if you weren't tired of me already,' Mitch said complacently. 'I wondered whether you were regretting the other night.'

'I never do anything I'll regret later,' Cappy stated emphatically.

His narrowed glance skimmed her, but he kept his response light. 'Then you're obviously a better man than I am.'

'Obviously,' she agreed and leveled the wings of the twin-engined craft as they attained the desired altitude.

CHAPTER NINETEEN

Leaving her car parked on the firm shoulder of the beach road, Eden wandered across the dunes to the outer shoreline. The chauffeur had arrived with her car about two weeks before, two days after Rachel died in the crash.

Overhead, the morning sky was a sharp blue. Not even the brightly burning sun could warm the cool air that blew in from the sea. Her high-necked sweater of biscuit-colored wool held in her body warmth. The loose sand sifted over the tops of her shoes and collected inside them. On the hard-packed beach, Eden stopped and emptied them, standing cranelike, first on one foot, then on the other.

The tide had left windrows of seaweed, driftwood, and broken shells tangled together. Interspersed in the wrack were fragile treasures: the jewel-colored wing of a butterfly, a chip of emerald-green glass, and the pure white of a gull's feather. The wet sand of the beach was crossstitched with the prints of birds' feet, the patterns running every which way on the spume-speckled shore. The restless ocean matched her mood and she turned her face to the salty breeze, letting it muss her red hair. Swooping, soaring gulls seemed to be everywhere, their strange cries punctuating the rhythmic rush of the waves onto the beach.

Two weeks had passed since the fatal crash. For the first part of the time, the women pilots had been grounded. Then it was back in the air for all of them, the same as before, checking out in the little L-4 and L-5 Cubs and graduating to the A-24s and tow-target missions. A new group of WASPs from the class behind them had arrived fresh from Sweetwater, ignorantly eager. Nothing had changed. They were flying under the same perilous conditions. Rachel's death had served no purpose.

The solitude of the beach reached to her as she walked along the waterline, pensive and silent. The churning sea threw its waves at the shore, pounding the sand into hardness, then retreating to gather strength and come again. As the waters ran away, leaving their spume behind to melt into the sand, a few of the plovers, sanderlings and funny boat-tailed grackles gave chase.

Lifting her head, Eden looked far out to sea where a smoky haze obscured the horizon. Fear gripped her, made her ache and put a haunted look in her deeply brown eyes. Never in her life had she been confronted by this kind of mortal fear. So she walked, waiting for the quietude and the wild beauty of the coast to ease the rawness of her nerves.

Birds flew up, startled into the air by her leisurely approach. She watched them wheel and turn and land farther down the beach, lowering their landing-gear legs and back-flapping their wings. She dragged the windblown strands of hair from her face and continued plodding up the beach, mindless of the sea spray that dampened the legs of her fine wool slacks.

Twenty yards ahead of her a surf fisherman was casting his line into the foamy waves. Eden hesitated, nearly changing course to avoid contact with another human, but she continued on. Almost idly she observed his actions, the narrowing distance still giving her enough room to watch without appearing rude. With the line out, the rod was set butt-end on the sand and propped at an angle by a forked branch, relieving the fisherman of the burden of holding it.

He was wearing a pair of tough denim Levi's, boots, and a water-resistant jacket, half unzipped. Nothing covered his head, and the wind was making free with a shaggy crop of dark hair. As the tall, lanky man lowered himself onto the sand behind his pole, something seemed familiar about him. The rumble of the surf onto the shore and the screech of the herring gulls overhead masked the sound of her approach. Eden was still trying to decide whether she knew him when he saw her and promptly came to his feet.

'Hello, ma'am.' He drawled the greeting, a keenness in his look.

'Hello, Bubba.' She smiled. 'I almost didn't recognize you without those greasy coveralls.'

'I know what you mean, ma'am.'

Eden avoided his gaze and looked out to the building waves, scraping the wind-twisted strands of hair from her cheek. 'How come you aren't in town with the rest of your buddies? I thought all you soldiers made a beeline there the minute you were given a pass.'

'After spendin' nearly every wakin' hour breathin' in exhaust fumes and smellin' oil, I get to needin' some fresh air. And when you live on top of one another like you do in a barracks, there isn't much allowance made for privacy. So it's kinda nice just to come out here and be alone with your thoughts for a while.'

'I know what you mean,' she agreed with a wry, fleeting smile. Her hands were shoved into the side pockets of her jacket while she idly watched the tremor at the tip of his fishing rod. 'Are you catching anything?'

'Naw, but I'm not really tryin' yet. I only want to catch what I can eat, and if I do that too soon, I won't have any more reason to stay here,' Bubba replied, a smile twinkling his eyes at such logic.

'That sounds reasonable to me.' Humor laced her answer, the shared kind that was so enjoyable. 'What about you, Bubba? Where's your home in Texas?'

For a moment, he appeared surprised by her show of personal interest. But his skepticism disappeared as he searched her friendly, open face.

'I come from a little town along the Gulf. It's not likely you ever heard of it – a place called Refugio.' At his questioning look, Eden shook her head, admitting her ignorance of his home town. 'There's more cows than people there. But I was always fascinated by motors. I grew up tinkerin' with cars – anybody's. My momma swore I was born with grease under my fingernails. I been diggin' it out ever since.'

She laughed, but her eyes were noticing how different he looked from his usual workaday appearance. Without its usual grime, his sun-leathered face had a healthy vigor. And his thick, rumpled hair had a sheen to it now, instead of looking dull and flattened by his cap. Without the bulk of his fatigues to conceal it, his long body was flatly muscled, all sinew, tough and hard. There was an earthy aura to him that seemed to do away with all pretense and hone things down to the basics. He was so straightforward – and intelligent. Eden eyed him with close curiosity.

282

'Where did you get a name like Bubba?' she wondered, because it seemed to fit some hulking, dumb brute – not this man.

'Now, I tell you. I picked it myself,' he admitted with his head tipped back and one leg bent, putting all his weight on one foot.

'Why?' Eden laughed her surprise.

'Well, where I come from, a fella just never gets called by his right name. I was christened William Robert Jackson. Now, when I was growin' up, I figured I had a choice of bein' called either Billy Bob or after the General Jackson. I didn't much like either one, but my daddy had a friend named Bubba who always used to let me mess around with his car. I liked him, so I took his name.'

'Is that true?' She eyed him skeptically.

He drew back in pretended dismay. 'Would I pull your leg, ma'am?'

She studied him with wondering interest. 'I don't know.'

His expression became serious; a second later his glance was falling away from her. 'Hell, ma'am, you know you can always trust me,' he insisted. But he seemed uncomfortable with her, nearly angry, and tried to conceal it by reaching inside his jacket for a cigarette. Bubba hesitated, then offered the pack to her. 'Want one, ma'am?'

'Thanks.' She carried it to her mouth and waited for a light. 'And, Bubba, please stop calling me ma'am all the time.'

'It's a habit. I've ma'amed and sirred everybody all my life.' He cupped his hands around the match flame to protect it from the blowing wind and offered the welled light to Eden.

As she bent her head, she noticed the scoured cleanness of his callused hands, the undersides of his blunted nails completely free of grime. Lifting her head, she expelled the smoke she'd dragged into her lungs and the wind whipped it away.

'Sometimes, Bubba' – she watched him light his cigarette – 'I think you put on an act with me. All that talk about dirt under your nails and just look at your hands.'

'It's no act, ma'am. I'm just a poor ole Texas boy,' he insisted with a faint grin.

'See what I mean,' Eden accused.

His hand was curled around the cigarette as he took a drag from it and idly shrugged. 'It could be, ma'am, that I'm just a sergeant, and a poor one from the country at that, whereas you're an officer and a rich city lady.' Behind his smiling study of her, there was a sober light in his eye. 'It would be foolish for a man in my position to get ideas. It could spoil a good friendship.'

Eden stared at him for a long second, realizing just how much she trusted this strong, rangy man on whose judgment she relied. The sudden nodding of the fishing pole caught her eye at the same moment that Bubba noticed it.

'Looks like I've hooked one.' He grabbed up the rod to begin playing the fish.

It was impossible to remain detached while Bubba struggled to land his catch. She found herself searching the waves, trying to get the first glimpse of the hooked fish. But neither saw what was on the line until he had reeled it in. Eden started laughing when she saw the small-sized fish that had put up such a large-sized fight.

'I'd like to see how you'll make a meal of that,' she teased.

'Watch,' Bubba replied, and gently removed the hook from the fish's mouth, then gave the small fry a toss beyond the oncoming wave. 'Swim out and tell your big brother how I saved you,' Bubba called to the fish. 'Then send him back to bite on my hook.'

'You should have kept it.' Eden chuckled to herself. 'It's liable to be all you'll catch.'

'Not a chance. That fish is going to send his big brother back. Wait and see,' Bubba assured her with a deadpan expression.

'I think I will,' she declared. She crossed her feet to sink down onto the sand.

'Hey, you can't sit down there.' He caught her by an elbow and pulled her upright before she could sit. 'You'll ruin those good slacks you're wearing.' He unzipped his jacket to shrug out of it. 'Just a minute. You can sit on this.'

The sincere and chivalrous gesture was so typical of him. 'I'm certainly not going to ruin your jacket to save my slacks,' Eden retorted, and she sat firmly down on the sand before he could stop her. 'Besides, I have a whole closet full of slacks at home even if I do ruin these.'

'Yes, ma'am.' Subdued by her remark, Bubba sank down onto the beach beside her and made a show out of checking his fishing rod to be sure it was securely positioned. She wondered why it bothered him that she was so careless about her clothes.

Twenty minutes later, there was another strike on his line. This time, when he reeled the sea bass in, it was a big one. 'See? What did I tell you? It's the big brother.' He ran a stringer through its gills.

'Why don't you throw it back and tell him to send a whale?' Eden suggested.

''Cause I figure that little fish has a bunch of big brothers and they're all gonna show up here sooner or later. So settle back and relax.' He winked broadly. 'We're gonna have us a fish fry tonight. Better start gatherin' up some driftwood for a fire.'

The sea wind scuttled the smoke from the low-burning fire. The unburned portion of a stick fell onto the hot coals when its support crumbled and the flames briefly leaped anew. The broken trunk of a huge tree cast ashore by the ocean during a fall-cleaning purge acted as a partial windbreak, both for the fire and for the couple leaning against it.

'This sea air sure does give you an appetite, doesn't it?' Bubba declared on a full sigh as he set the lid of the cooking pot, his improvised plate, onto the sand. Only fish bones were left on it. Then he noticed the way Eden was picking at the succulent flesh of the baked fish. 'Is something wrong with my cookin'? I know it's not like those fancy restaurants where they poach 'em in wine.'

'It's very good,' she assured him, then she shrugged. 'I'm just not very hungry.' Eden set her plate on the sand and rubbed her hands against each other. 'Sorry, I just can't eat any more.'

'You peck at your food like a bird. No wonder you're so thin for as tall as you are.' When he saw the troubled moodiness settle over her again, his eyes narrowed to study her thoughtfully. Several times she'd gone silent on him and brooded. 'Still thinking about the crash, ma'am?'

'No.' The denial was too quick, like the forced smile that flashed across her expression. 'I was just thinking – Water, water everywhere, and not a drop to drink,' she quoted, looking at the rush of waves onto the beach, the tide thrusting them higher and higher as the afternoon sun lowered the angle of its light.

Bubba wasn't fooled. Daydreaming she might have been, but not about anything pleasant. But since she didn't choose to confide in him, it wasn't his place to press the issue. Hell, he was just a mechanic with sergeant's stripes and she was a refined lady with the prettiest copper-red hair he'd ever seen. Why, she had more class in one little finger than he had in his whole body.

'That's not quite true, ma'am,' Bubba corrected her. 'I did bring along a drop to drink. I've just been waitin' for it to get good and cold.'

Her curiosity was aroused, deliberately, Eden suspected. Despite her initial intentions, she had never resumed her walk along the beach. She had spent practically the whole day in Bubba's company while he had entertained her with stories about his childhood and pulled her leg with a few Texas tall tales.

His skill in aircraft maintenance she'd always known, and the friendliness of his broad smile. His leadership capabilities had been indicated by the stripes on his uniform. This afternoon, he'd even let it slip that his CO had recommended him for Officer Candidate School. Naturally, he'd refused; at least, it had been natural in Bubba's way of thinking, because he enjoyed working with engines and people, and didn't see the need to give either one of them up to be some clean-nailed lieutenant. His command of logic and common sense amazed her, delivered as it was in drawled phrases. There was no doubt in her mind that Bubba was a rough diamond – completely unpolished but a genuine gem just the same.

In sand made wet by the incoming surf, Bubba pulled an anchor pin, buried deep with only its curved ring showing above the surface. Eden watched as he began coiling in the attached rope cord that was strung into the ocean. At the end of it was a fisherman's net, holding a half-dozen loose bottles. He brought his dripping catch back to the fire and knelt on the sand near the drift log.

Eden eyed the long-necked containers of brown glass. 'What is it? Beer?'

'I'll bet you haven't drunk too much of it,' Bubba surmised as he removed two bottles from the mesh trap and produced a metal opener from his pocket.

'Scotch is usually my choice,' she admitted.

'Well, let me initiate you into the fine art of beer drinking,' he said, and he settled himself back against the dead trunk so they sat side by side. 'You gotta know how to appreciate the good stuff.' He pried the top off one of the bottles. 'Now you see this cork inside the cap –' Bubba held it out for her inspection while he explained in mock-serious tones, 'Ya gotta check to see that it's in good shape and the edges haven't started to rot, 'cause that'll mean you'll have little bits of cork in your beer and you'll have to strain it through your teeth when you drink. Then you sniff the cork, too.' He lifted it to her nose so Eden could smell it while she tried to hold back the laughter bubbling inside. 'Smell good?'

'Wonderful,' she assured him, amused by the entire farce.

'Next comes the bottle.' The wet sides of the glass

287

container were still slippery, and Bubba waited until she had a secure hold of it before he let go. 'Carefully run your fingers around the lip to make sure it hasn't chipped. It ain't healthy to drink beer with glass chips in it.'

'No, I wouldn't think so either,' Eden agreed, her mouth twitching with the effort to hold it in a straight line.

'Now the last thing is to run the bottle past your nose so you get a little whiff of the beer,' Bubba instructed. 'What you're lookin' for is that good, malty smell you get when the grains are fermented just right.'

'How do you tell if it's aged properly?' she asked, joining in with his joke.

'When it comes out of the brewery, it's old enough to drink,' he said. 'Now give the bottle a little shake, sorta swirl it around and see if it makes a good head.' As she followed his instructions, a white foam began building inside the brown glass. 'Now, *that's* a good beer,' he promised her. 'And you got that straight from a real beer connasewer.' He clinked his bottle against hers. 'Drink up. It's only good when it's at just the right temperature.'

She took a swig of the beer and gurgled with laughter. It was such a funny parody of the wine snobbery displayed by some of her New York friends. She drank his beer, not finding it as tasty as her Scotch, but it had its place.

They talked and laughed, with Bubba doing most of the talking and Eden doing most of the laughing, until the sun lingered above the sand dunes. Its golden, glowing fire spread out to encompass sand and sea in its burnished light.

Her hand held the last bottle of beer by its brown neck while she gazed at the golden-hued waters. The fear that she had successfully blocked from her mind for a while came back, and Eden restlessly pushed herself to her feet and walked a few steps away from the fire toward the tumbling waves, all but forgetting Bubba until he appeared beside her, taller by a couple inches, his dark eyes discreetly questioning.

'You know something funny?' she began, again turning

seaward. 'The Civil Air patrol won't let women fly coastal patrols because it's too dangerous, but when we're out on a tow-target mission, sometimes we're fifty miles out over the Atlantic. And we're getting shot at, too, by our own Army. It doesn't make sense, does it?'

'The Army doesn't have to make sense. It just has to win the war,' Bubba reasoned, sensing the comment was close to the cause of her restless moods.

She fell silent once again. Bubba noticed the way her fingers flexed and tightened their grip on the bottle neck, nervously worrying it. Her glance sliced sideways to his face, apprehension widening her dark eyes.

'I think I'm losing my nerve, Bubba. Every time that plane lifts off the ground, I wonder if I'll make it back.' Although she tried to keep it steady, there was a vibration in her low voice. 'I know you check the planes over thoroughly, but . . . how many accidents do we have here a day? How many tires are blown? How many engines quit? How many planes wind up taking hits in the fuselage? I just have the feeling my number's going to come up. One of these times it's going to be me. I'm scared, Bubba.'

She tried to laugh, but the sound became choked by a sob. Looking away, she widened her eyes and blinked furiously to keep back the tears. She felt the comforting touch of Bubba's hand on her shoulder. Blindly, Eden turned into it while his arms went around her to gather her in, as he had done the night of Rachel's crash.

'Nothing's going to happen to you. I won't let it.' His rough hands made an attempt to smooth her tangled, rusty hair while the warm feel of her body filled his senses.

The instinct to live is a primitive one, potent and compelling. The physical contact made Eden subtly aware of the hard, male vigor in Bubba's lean muscled frame. It was the combination of vitality and comfort that first attracted Eden, then compelled her to seek the sustaining pressure of his mouth. As her lips grazed his cheek, she was met with an instant of stillness and hesitation. Then Bubba was turning to hasten the contact.

There was so much rawness inside her, so much built-up pressure, that it all seemed to explode as Eden strained against him, kissing him with a kind of fierce, yet desperate anger. She didn't let him be gentle, but he consumed all the force she threw at him and gave her back ease.

Once the high tension had burned itself out, she could enjoy the slow moving pressure of his mouth across her lips. It touched some needy core of her, so simple and basic in its expression of clean desire.

Bubba slowly pulled away from her lips and studied their swollen softness with heavy-lidded eyes. Eden gazed at his strong, broad features with an odd wondering. He was without guile or pretension. She was drawn by this honest, direct man with his natural intelligence and warm, wonderful sense of humor.

When she felt the pressure of his hands on her, Eden expected to be pulled back into his kiss. It was a surprise when Bubba gently set her away from him instead.

'We'd best get the fire out before the sun goes down and the beach patrol comes along to warn us about it.' After he'd made his explanation, Eden had a moment to wonder which fire he was talking about while Bubba walked to the smoldering campfire in the sand.

Mounding sand on the coals with a shoveling action of his foot, he buried the fire and Eden came over to watch him. The rumble of a motor grew into a roar as a jeep came rolling over the wave-pounded firmness of the sand, making one of its regular patrols of the beach. The sun was sinking behind a sand dune when they stopped, the motor idling, to remind the pair that no one was allowed on the beach after dark.

After the noise of the jeep's engine had faded, Bubba looked across the short expanse of sand to the hump showing where the fire had been, and held Eden's glance. 'Maybe it was a good thing they came along when they did,' he suggested.

'Maybe it was,' she conceded.

'Guess we'd better get movin'.' He seemed to push

himself into action against a feeling of reluctance, as he gathered up his tackle box and the case with his fishing rod, and hooked his arm through a strap of his knapsack.

'Do you need a ride? My car's parked down the road a ways,' Eden said, indicating its general direction with a wave of her hand.

'Thanks, but I left my bicycle just over the dunes.'

'I've got a convertible. You can throw it in the back end,' Eden persisted.

After a long minute of consideration, Bubba nodded an acceptance of her invitation, but there was a reluctance here, too, that indicated it went against his better judgment.

They reached his bicycle before they reached her car, and Bubba pushed it through the heavy sand to the road's shoulder. He took one look at the canary-yellow roadster and its white leather interior, then issued a low whistle of appreciation. He walked around it, exclaiming over every feature and asking endless questions about the engine's performance.

'I don't believe it,' Eden declared on a faintly disgusted note.

'Don't believe what?' Bubba looked up, a frown creasing his forehead.

'How many times does a girl offer you a lift and you fall in love with her car?' she challenged.

A rueful grin split his face as he scratched the back of his neck. 'Reckon I did get a bit carried away,' he agreed. 'But it is a beauty.'

'Want to drive?' Eden tossed him the keys.

'Sure.' He clambered behind the wheel with a beguiling boyish enthusiasm.

The wind tunneled through her red hair, roping it into tangled curls as Bubba put the car through its paces on the lonely beach road. The light faded and the blue shadows deepened with the coming of nightfall. The car's head-lamps were hooded to keep its beams cast downward in this blackout area along the coastline.

A mile from the entrance to the Army camp, Bubba turned into a small lay-by and switched off the engine. After the roaring engine and rushing wind, the silence was vibrant.

Bubba ran his hand carelessly over the arc of the steering wheel, rubbing it with unconscious ardor. 'This car is really something.'

Amused and vaguely disgruntled, Eden sat sideways in the white leather seat and rested her back against the door. 'What about its owner?'

Bubba looked sideways at her and smiled, a deep line breaking from the corner of each eye. 'She's really somethin', too.' He paused, his look turning serious and compelling as his dark eyes took her apart. The scrutiny made Eden self-conscious about her appearance after the sun and the wind had stung color into her pale skin and the salt spray had dried it. Her clothes were gritty with sand.

'The owner's a classy number, too,' Bubba said quietly. 'Highly sensitive and temperamental, like a finely tuned racing engine. Not something you can manhandle. She needs . . . an easy touch to get the best out of her.'

'Is that right?' Eden murmured and began moving toward him, his words striking a chord deep within and drawing her to him.

'Yes –'

She pressed the ends of her fingers against his mouth. 'So help me, Bubba, if you call me ma'am I'll –' But she didn't have to finish her threat. He gathered her into his arms and murmured her name many times over.

CHAPTER TWENTY

In full uniform, Major Mitch Ryan stood at his desk in the small Pentagon office and flipped through file folders, selecting certain ones to go in his case. Behind him the door opened, and Mitch glanced idly over his shoulder, then stiffened to come to attention.

'At ease.' General Arnold waved off any salute as he briskly swept into the small room. He eyed the coffee thermos sitting atop a file cabinet. 'Is that the strongest you've got?'

'No, sir.' With the smallest of smiles, Mitch went behind his desk and opened the bottom drawer. He reached to the back and brought out a fifth of whiskey, the seal broken and a third of the contents gone. After he'd poured a shot into a coffee cup, the only available drinking vessel in his office, he handed it to the general. 'How was the fashion show?'

'You wouldn't believe it, Ryan.' There was a definite gleam in his eye as he lifted the cup to his mouth and took a quick swallow. 'It was supposed to be either the uniform the nurses rejected or else a new design out of that surplus Army green material we had left over from the WAAC uniforms.'

'That's not the way it was?' Mitch asked the question being fed to him.

'Here are these two nondescript typists from the pool wearing the uniform choices – and in walks a professional model in a blue jacket and skirt. I took one look at Cochran and knew damned well whose idea it was and which one I was supposed to choose.' He chuckled and took another sip of the whiskey. 'Those WASPs of hers are finally going to have their own uniforms – blue, like the sky they fly in. It was a pretty color.' His forehead creased with a thoughtful frown. 'Santiago blue, or something like that. After all, when you're a woman you just can't call it blue,' he joked.

'No, sir. I guess not.'

'Well, anyway, you can tell your Hayward girl that Neiman-Marcus will be sending a tailor around to get her measurements.' His look became almost fatherly as he studied Mitch's closed expression. 'Have you had a chance to see her lately?'

'As a matter of fact –' Mitch removed the bottom folder from the stack he'd been going through and inserted it in his attaché case. It snapped shut with a resounding click. '– I have.'

'She has accumulated a considerable amount of multiengine time.' The general showed an inordinate amount of interest in the liquor covering the bottom of his cup. 'I half expected her name to be on the list of candidates for this B-17 training. Wouldn't you say she's qualified?'

'Yes, sir.' Mitch set his case on the floor and picked up the remaining folders to return them to the metal cabinet.

'It isn't too late to add her name to the list,' the general remarked as Mitch opened a drawer and began stuffing the folders one at a time into it. 'Do you want me to do it?'

'*No* –' The file drawer was slammed shut, emphasizing the force of his denial as Mitch swung around to face his commanding officer. Belatedly, and in considerably modified tone, he added, 'sir.'

'Cochran is convinced her girls can handle any plane, even a Flying Fortress. Hell, I know Cochran and Love can fly anything with wings. 'Course, you know what's coming next if we get a bunch of WASPs with B-17 experience,' he said with a laughing snort. 'She's going to start agitating to let her girls fly them across the Atlantic to England. Love damned near did. I still don't know what was going through Tunner's mind when he authorized that flight.'

The general had been in England conferring with the Allied forces when he had learned of the proposed flight. Immediate orders were issued to ground the plane with its two women pilots, stopping it in Goose Bay, Labrador, before it made its oceanic hop.

'It would have been a hell of a precedent to set without any forethought as to the potential consequences. Can you imagine the uproar in Congress if the damned Jerries shot down a B-17 being ferried to England by a female crew? Talk about political hot water – they would have had my head.' He stopped, and a long, weary sigh came from him. 'They're pounding the hell out of us, Ryan.' Standing, he pushed the coffee cup onto the desk top with a prowling kind of agitation. 'I just got the losses on that last raid over Germany.'

'Not good, sir?' Mitch finally understood the purpose of the general's visit.

'We lost thirty percent; another hundred planes are grounded for repairs.' The familiar smile was nowhere in sight as 'Hap' Arnold stopped in front of his young major. 'They're sitting ducks up there. We've got to give them some damned protection . . . extend the range of our fighters.'

'Yes, sir.'

Statistics. The war was fought with numbers – casualty lists versus the percentages of expected losses. The many times Mitch had seen the war rooms in England, where uniformed British women moved markers across a map with sticks to show the progress of a raid and indicate enemy movements to counterattack, reminded him of a chess game. And the bombers, with their ten-men crews, were the pawns. In the pentagon, the war was logistics and strategy. In Europe and the Pacific, it was fighting – and killing or dying.

New orders came through, informing Martha Jane Rogers to report to Lockbourne Army Air Base, Columbus, Ohio. They weren't accompanied by an explanation of the transfer nor a description of her new duty. No leave time was given; she was to report immediately. That was the Army way.

The unknown had always sparked Marty's interest, although this time, the glitter of excitement that lighted her olive-gray eyes was tinged with regret when she looked at Mary Lynn. Marty was all packed, ready to leave. The time had come to say goodbye.

'I wish you were coming, too.' Marty hugged Mary Lynn and stepped back. The parting was awkward for her.

Almost from the time they'd met, Marty had felt like a big sister to Mary Lynn, always looking out both for and after her, cheering her up when she was down, and offering a shoulder when she needed to cry at the loneliness of being separated from her husband. Marty hated leaving her alone. She worried that Mary Lynn wouldn't be all right on her own.

'I'll be fine,' Mary Lynn assured her, but she had tears in her eyes.

'Look out for her,' Marty said to Eden, who was hovering in the background.

'Sure.'

It wasn't an idle request. Another one of their number had been killed when her plane crashed under questionable circumstances. The verdict had come back, laying the blame on a sticky throttle.

Unable to deal with the poignant feelings that tugged at her, Marty didn't prolong her goodbyes. Her wide mouth quirked with a near smile as she picked up her bags and headed out the door. Together Mary Lynn and Eden watched her go.

'She's lucky to be leaving here,' Eden remarked in a flatly serious tone while tears ran down Mary Lynn's cheeks. 'If we were smart, we'd request a transfer.'

Upon arrival at the Lockbourne Army Air Base outside Columbus, Ohio, Marty met up with five other WASPs, newly graduated from Sweetwater and members of the 43-W-6 class, whose orders read the same as hers – to report immediately to the flight operations building. The spectacle awaiting them at the flight line was awesome – a seemingly endless row of the huge B-17 four-engine bombers. Their three-bladed propellers were almost twelve feet across, in proportion with the hundred-foot wingspan. Marty longed for the chance to sit in the cockpit of one of those Flying Fortresses.

Inside the operations office, a young flight lieutenant greeted them. 'I'm your instructor, Lieutenant Winthrop.'

296

He was a tall, strapping man in his middle twenties, red lights burnishing the brown hair under his cap. 'I'm going to teach you ladies how to fly those Big Friends out there.'

In all, seventeen WASPs had been chosen for training in the B-17s. Looking around, Marty decided it was easy to see the reason they'd been picked. All of them were tall, an inch or two under six feet, with a couple reaching that mark.

When it was her turn to sit in the pilot's seat of the mammoth bomber, excitement thudded through her veins. The rubber earphones curved over her head like earmuffs while she went through the checklist, finally coming to that moment of power when her fingers rested on the button to start the number-one engine. She pressed it and watched the first shudder of the big prop. Four massive 1,325-horsepower engines powered the bomber. Soon, the roar of all four was vibrating the plane.

From the right seat, her instructor taxied the B-17 to the end of the runway, maneuvering the big plane with the outer engines, while Marty felt through his movements of the controls. The plane lumbered like a huge elephant and it seemed to stand about as much chance of getting off the ground.

With the instructor's voice guiding her through each procedure, Marty pushed the four throttles slowly forward and the Flying Fortress began its takeoff roll down the runway. When the airspeed indicator showed 110 miles an hour, Marty pulled back on the wheel. Smooth as silk, the giant flying machine lifted off the ground. The gear came up with a hum and folded into the plane's belly, and the airspeed increased by twenty-five miles an hour.

The sensation of raw power couldn't be matched, the engines thundering with their deafening throb until they became part of her own heartbeat. Marty became drunk with the feeling. It filled her up until she wanted to shout with the excitement of it. Wait until her brother, David, heard about this. He was still sitting out the war somewhere near Wiltshire, England, with the rest of his division.

When she wrote to Mary Lynn, which was regularly and often, she raved about the Flying Fortress, undaunted by its upwards of fifteen tons and the prospect of maneuvering a plane of that bulk and power. The required three months of intensive schooling in the operations of the complex bomber, including 130 hours of air time learning to fly it proficiently, didn't bother her either. As she told Mary Lynn, it wasn't any more grueling than it had been at Sweetwater.

Formation flying had that combination of danger and excitement that was exhilarating. Midair collisions always seemed seconds away as she learned to edge her wing tip closer and closer to another bomber, riding out the bumpy air of its prop-wash until she finally reached the smooth currents where the wings broke the air together.

Marty loved every minute she spent in the cockpit of the B-17, with its myriad gauges and dials, learning to stall and spin the monstrous plane. She was learning to fly one of the biggest and most famous bombers in the war. The thrill of it was something she knew Mary Lynn would understand. She missed having her there, missed the long talks, and missed hearing the odd fragments of the war in Beau's letters to Mary Lynn. Marty wasn't the kind to admit to being lonely – not when there were plenty of male pilots in the same B-17 training class who were more than willing to show her a good time. But none of that could make up for the closeness she'd had with Mary Lynn. So the letters came and went.

At Camp Davis, the merits of the tow-target squadron's female members – beyond the admitted decoration of pretty faces on the flight line – were finally being recognized. Artillery officers on the beachhead were asking for the women pilots to fly the tedious patterns on the gunnery range. Too many of the male pilots became bored with the constant figure-eight precision work, and either took off to practice aerobatics or else pleaded excuses not to fly the missions at all, aware some.eager females would volunteer to take their places.

Sometimes, to fill the hours, Mary Lynn flew on afternoon as well as morning missions. There were only so many letters she could write to Beau or her parents – and now Marty too. Flying gave Mary Lynn many things she needed. Riding out the flak from misguided artillery fire, for those moments, made the war seem very real to her – made her feel part of it, seeing, hearing, and feeling some of what Beau went through. Temporarily she was elated by the sense of it. Flying provided an escape from the pressures of loneliness and the slow trickling time. The strain and tension of hours in the air made for an exhaustion that allowed her to fall asleep, too tired to think about the achings inside.

With a Coke and a cigarette in her hand, Mary Lynn sat on a chair in the ready room, still dressed in her droopy flying togs and bent over her legs, her forearms resting on her thighs. She noticed the operations officer glance at his watch for the third or fourth time, an irritation starting to seep into his expression.

'Something wrong?' she asked.

'Carlson was supposed to be here ten minutes ago to fly a diving mission. All the gunners are in position on the beach, just waiting for him. If I have to cancel, I'll really catch it.' The disgust in his voice was edged out by the exasperation of being caught in the middle, between the officers who had to fill their quota of gunners and the pilots who loathed missions in the 'coffin,' as they called the A-25 Curtiss Helldiver.

Two weeks ago, Mary Lynn knew who would have leaped up to volunteer – Marty – who was always ready to dare something new. It suddenly hit her that she was out from under everyone's wing – her parents, Beau, and Marty. She was truly on her own, free to do what she pleased.

'I'll take the mission.' She stood up, all five foot two and five-eighths inches of her.

Skeptically, he looked at this pipsqueak of a woman with the dark, lively eyes and rounded cheeks, a dark-haired, cherub angel. 'Have you ever flown a diving mission before?'

'No,' Mary Lynn admitted. 'But you need a pilot and here I am.'

The operations officer appeared to remember the gunners in place on the beach, and perhaps the wrath he'd incur if he failed to send a plane out to them. 'Go ahead,' he said with a gesture that seemed to say the outcome was out of his hands.

The A-25 Curtiss Helldiver was a more powerful Navy dive-bomber than the A-24 Dauntless Mary Lynn flew on tow-target missions. She managed to find a Helldiver on the flight line that wasn't red-lined, which, in itself, was unusual. Although she'd never actually flown a diving mission, she'd seen A-25s dive at the gun emplacements along the beach. Cameras were located in the gun barrels, and recorded how well the gunner followed the diving plane.

After takeoff, Mary Lynn set a course for the artillery range. As she approached the beach, she adjusted the collar with her throat microphone and contacted the gunnery officer. He instructed her to climb to 8,000 feet, then dive at the artillery positions and level off at 200 feet to simulate a strafing run.

When she had achieved altitude, she nosed the A-25 at the beach. The roaring whine of the engine seemed to be building to a crescendo. Seven tons of airplane were screaming toward the ground, and Mary Lynn had a strange, disembodied sensation of watching it all.

Out of the corner of her eye, she caught sight of the altimeter needle spinning away the feet. She pulled back on the stick to level out of the dive, and felt the resistance. Bracing herself, she pulled with all her might. The plane, bent on its headlong course, was slow to respond. The force of gravity pressed its weight on her, flattening her and blackening the edges of her consciousness. Then the plane was swooping out of the dive, so close to the breakers that she could see the frothy spume.

'That was great! Sensational!' The artillery officer's excited voice chattered in her earphones. 'Do it again!!'

'Yes, sir!' Exhilarated by the diving run, she went back up to altitude and attacked the beachhead again.

When Mary Lynn returned to base, she learned Jacqueline Cochran's experiment was soon to be put on parade. Generals from the Pentagon as well as the First and Third Air Force Headquarters, accompanied by the national press, were flying in to review the female tow-target squadron. The public relations officer's promise to generate publicity for them was about to come true.

The day before the generals' expected arrival, Mary Lynn completed an afternoon mission and landed at the field. Leaving her plane on the flight line to be serviced by the ground crew, she headed for the ready room, flight strain tearing her muscles.

'Mary Lynn, come here!' Eden called to her from the door and waved her to hurry. 'You've got to see this.'

She picked up her pace and jogged the last few yards to the building, her interest only mildly aroused. 'What is it?'

'Come on.' Eden led her up the stairs to the door of a storeroom located above the pilots' ready room.

The door stood open, and the room had been cleaned out. In place of the crates and boxes were card tables and chairs. The storeroom had become a small, private lounge. Eden pointed to the sign on the door. It used the acronym for the Women Airforce Service pilots, and made its own cute play of it to read: 'WASP Nest – Drones Keep Out or Suffer the Wrath of the Queen.'

'You're kidding,' Mary Lynn declared upon seeing it. 'Whose idea was this?'

'I have the feeling the PR officer put the idea in Major Stevenson's ear – a real catchy publicity stunt for the newspaper photographers tomorrow. It's bound to make an impression on them.' A certain grimness was in the curve of Eden's lips.

'What difference does it make?' Mary Lynn reasoned with a trace of irony. 'Let's enjoy it.'

With an agreeing shrug, Eden followed her into the new lounge where they sat at a table and smoked the cigarettes that had become almost a constant preoccupation with them. As the 'Nest' was discovered more joined them, and the talk turned to the cause of all this – the impending visit of the generals.

'I wish we had our new uniforms,' one of them griped.

'Have you been measured for yours?'

'What did you think of that tailor from Neiman-Marcus? He rattled on so . . . trying to describe what color Santiago blue is, that it took him forever to get my measurements,' a buxom pilot complained.

'I'll just bet that's what took him so long,' another said with a laugh.

'That man loves his work,' a brunette declared.

Until the new uniforms were issued, they were forced to wear their old improvised uniforms – tan gabardine slacks, white shirts, and battle jackets. The next day, they paraded past the beribboned generals and their director, Jacqueline Cochran, then came to a halt and stood at attention in their spit-shined military shoes, their columns lining up in front of two huge bombers.

The generals and their entourage approached to review the squad of women. Eden scanned the ranks of gold braid, wondering if Cappy's major was among them, but he wasn't in evidence. After the generals and Jacqueline Cochran came Major Stevenson, the commander of the tow-target squadron, and his staff.

The front row were nodded to and smiled upon by the starred Army officers while they murmured questions to the women's director of flying with her honey-gold hair and soft, southern voice. As they walked between the rows of women, the generals dawdled. Eden had the distinct impression they would have liked to get their chest decorations caught on a busty battle jacket or two.

With the review of the WASPs completed, the short,

squatty Major Stevenson slapped the last girl in line on her bottom and whispered, in good male fun, 'Get!' And they were dismissed.

As they broke ranks to be descended on by the reporters and photographers in attendance, Eden muttered to Mary Lynn, 'If he'd done that to me, I'd have punched him in the face.'

Articles about these 'brave' women pilots ran in newspapers across the country for weeks afterward. But the next morning when Mary Lynn and Eden reported to the flight line for their first mission, the WASP Nest no longer existed. The sign had been removed, as well as the tables and chairs.

Feeling used and bitter, Eden walked to her plane and with a barely controlled fury made her groundcheck of the craft. The parachute pack, strapped to her back, and her coveralls made a shapeless figure of her tall body.

The pudgy enlisted man who acted as her tow-target operator hadn't arrived to take his position in the gunner's seat. Eden wished she had a cigarette, but smoking was forbidden on the flight line, with all the high-octane gasoline around. She felt brittle and angry. Not even the sight of Bubba's long, familiar shape approaching made her feel better.

'Good morning. You look to be in fine fettle this morning.' He grinned at the snap of temper in her dark eyes.

But Eden wouldn't be cajoled out of her mood. 'What did you find when you checked out this plane?'

'The usual,' Bubba answered, watching her closely. 'The radio keeps breaking up and the engine's using oil so you might want to keep an eye on the pressure gauge. The flap handle's broken, but it's operational.'

'Wonderful,' she offered caustically.

'You're as cranky as a cow with a twisted tail,' he observed, unamused. 'What is it?'

Her hesitation didn't last long, as her complaint exploded. 'It's Stevenson and his cheap publicity stunt. I'm sick of being treated like this. I'm sick of flying worn-out planes.' Unconsciously she dug her fingers into the flesh of her arms, trembling with the force of her anger. 'I don't have to take this kind of abuse and I'm not! I'm putting in for a transfer.'

His broad features took on a closed-in look, all emotion pulled deep inside. 'If that's the way you feel, I reckon it's what you ought to do.'

She was struck by the realization that a transfer would take her away from Bubba. It drained the anger from her. After that day on the beach, they no longer met accidentally, although his noncommissioned status forced them to be circumspect in their choice of meeting places. While Eden might concede that the touch of the forbidden added some spice to their affair, it was nothing at all like the silly fling she'd had with her chauffeur. Her desire to be with Bubba wasn't based on any rebellion against money or class. And while the passion might match what she'd experienced with that impoverished count, Bubba was not shallow and selfish. He was strong and wonderful; more than that, he loved her – the person that she was – and her money and social position meant nothing to him.

'It won't change anything.' She was stiff in her attempt to convince him of that. She didn't want to lose him, not when they'd just found each other.

'If you say so, ma'am.'

'Stop it, Bubba.' Eden was irritated with his formality when they'd gone so far beyond it.

His hazel eyes bored into her, letting some raw, exposed feeling be seen in his expression. 'I don't think you know what you mean to me.' There was a wealth of emotion in the simple words. His feelings couldn't have been expressed more clearly.

'Half of all the couples in this country have been separated by the war. Why should you and I be any different?' The flight line was much too public a place for their feelings to be declared, with ground crew all around, engines revving, and pilots in their cockpits, yet their eyes locked. Their bodies strained toward one another as their emotions found a third level of communication. 'You make me feel alive, Bubba.' Stripped of all its flowery description, what she felt for him was love, passion-deep and basic.

A sexually charged tension electrified the air as Eden gazed at him, standing so close to her. She wanted to touch him, to be inside the circle of his arms, to taste the earthy flavor of his kiss.

'I wish we were somewhere else.' All his attention was on her lips.

'Can't you get a weekend pass?' Eden urged. 'We'll go somewhere – far from the Army's frowning eyes. A friend of mine has a mountain cabin. I know he'll let us use it.'

He hesitated. 'I don't know.'

'We can meet in town and take my car.' She was already making plans.

'In town.' He drew back, caution flaring in his eyes. 'There'd be hell to pay if we were seen together.'

'To hell with the Army and what they think,' Eden retorted impatiently.

'That's easy for you to say. You aren't the one who'd be facing a possible court-martial.'

Eden doubted if he'd receive any more than a stern reprimand if they should be seen, which wasn't likely. 'It's a chance to spend an entire weekend together. Don't you want that?'

'You know I do.' A muscle jumped along his wide jaw.

'Should I arrange to use the cabin?' she challenged, hurt that he hadn't jumped at the opportunity. 'Or are you going to let the Army tell you whom you are permitted to see and what you can do?'

'I'll get the pass and you get the cabin,' Bubba agreed.

Her pudgy tow-target operator came trotting up to the plane, ready for the morning's mission. His curiosity was aroused by the silence that suddenly fell between the sergeant and the red-haired pilot. He was used to hearing a free-flowing banter, a warmth and friendliness that knew no rank. But he didn't ask any questions, and simply climbed into the rear cockpit.

The sergeant helped the pilot get snugged into the front cockpit, then waited on the ground while the engine warmed. He was still standing there, watching them as the A-24 taxied to the runway.

CHAPTER TWENTY-ONE

Hamilton Steele leaned closer to the telephone, unable to subdue his pleasure at the sound of the voice coming through the receiver. 'I'm delighted to hear from you. How are you?'

'Fine.' The long-distance connection crackled into Eden's voice. 'Ham, darling. I have a favor to ask you.'

'I didn't think you called just because you missed me,' he said with a dry smile, some of the eager light fading from his eyes as his well-schooled patience came into play again. 'You have only to ask, Eden. You know that.'

'It's your mountain hideaway. You said I could use it any time I wanted. How about next weekend?' The ring of her voice brought her image vividly to his mind. Eden was a woman of passions and spirit. Her temperament, well reined through practice, was always present, its aliveness radiating from her being. 'We thought we'd slip away from the war for a couple days.'

'I'll wire the groundskeeper in the morning so he can have it stocked and ready for you,' he assured her, and settled back in his chair. 'As a matter of fact, I just may join you.'

There was a small silence on the other end of the line, followed by a throaty laugh. 'Please don't, Ham. It might prove awkward.'

Beneath that playful mockery, Hamilton recognized a trace of protectiveness. 'Ah.' He concealed a heavy sigh, having been through all this before. 'I thought perhaps you and a few of your female flying friends were planning this getaway. Obviously, your companion is a male. May I inquire as to your friend? Is he a pilot too?'

'Bubba is an aircraft mechanic.'

'Bubba,' he repeated with mild disbelief.

'Ham, darling, you are sounding like a snob,' she chided. She didn't want to hear him make fun of her lover.

But Hamilton had heard more than she realized. Her voice had contained a small, possessive inflection when she said Bubba's name. It was all too familiar to him, and he breathed out a weary sound that resembled a laugh.

'What is it?' she demanded.

'I'm half tempted to gamble away all my money on the stock market and buy myself a little farm in Pennsylvania with the few pennies I'd keep back,' he declared.

'You? A farmer?' Eden laughed at the ludicrous picture of her conservative dark-suit-and-vested Hamilton Steele in a pair of bibbed overalls. 'Why on earth would you ever wish such a thing?'

'It seems . . . that you invariably fall for the impoverished or the plebeian.' His mildly mocking voice was gentle, but a sadness – which she wasn't able to see – was in his eyes.

'It's a fatal flaw in my character, I'm afraid,' she admitted and juggled the phone while she shook a cigarette from her pack of Lucky Strike Greens. 'And stop making it sound as if I always pick losers. Bubba is different.' But it seemed kinder not to discuss it with him. 'How's New York?'

'It's turning colder.'

'I had a letter from Cappy. She flew some colonel to New England last week. She said the autumn colors were spectacular this year.'

'Indeed.'

The conversation sparkled for another minute in that same false vein. Finally, Eden reaffirmed that she would use his mountain lodge the following weekend and Hamilton gave her instructions on where to obtain the key.

*   *   *

A November chill frosted the early morning air with its cool breath. Dressed in what had become regulation clothes for Cappy, the improvised uniform of khaki gabardine slacks, white shirt, and a flight jacket, she inched the zipper closure up a little higher and stepped out of the operations building at Bolling Field to proceed to the DC-3 parked on the ramp, the passenger version of the Army cargo C-47.

'How many passengers will we have this morning?' she asked her copilot, a brash man in his early twenties who couldn't quite conceal his resentment at flying second seat to a female.

'Ten.' He looked at the flight sheet. 'A light colonel's heading the group. His name's Hayward, the same as yours.' A wondering inflection entered his voice as he gave her a speculative look.

'Really.' She was struggling to conceal her dismay while wishing she'd looked at the flight orders first. It simply hadn't occurred to her that her father would be among the passengers on this flight to Republic Aviation's modification plant in Evansville, Indiana.

'I'll make the ground check,' her copilot, Lieutenant Franklin, volunteered.

The insistence that she would handle her own preflight of the aircraft died on her lips. She could hear the little triphammer beat of her pulse thudding in her ear as she watched Lieutenant Colonel Robert Hayward climb out of the Army vehicle stopped on the flight line. She hadn't seen him since that wintry day ten months earlier when she'd walked out of his Georgetown house.

'Go ahead.' She nodded permission to the copilot to make the ground preflight check.

One thing she had learned since being assigned here and repeatedly given check rides in multiengine planes was that any slacking of duty was duly noted, regardless of the reason. Every time she went up, it seemed she had to prove herself all over again to some new officer who didn't think a female was capable of piloting him anywhere.

Cappy doubted that she'd have a stiffer test than the one she'd get today from her father. She watched him approach in his Army brown jacket and tan pants, the officer's cap sitting squarely on his head, militarily precise. As he came closer, that familiar rigid-backed bearing, that face she'd known all her life, prompted a smile to start across her lips. But Cappy noticed too his coldly aloof demeanor, and her smile never got past its first beginnings.

'I've learned you are to be our pilot.' No greeting, no personal recognition.

'Yes, sir.' Cappy followed his lead, swinging around to escort him and his group to the transport. 'Lieutenant Franklin is finishing the ground check now. If you have any baggage you want stowed, the lieutenant will see to it.' She became all business, slipping into the role with ease, yet conscious of his still physically trim figure marching beside her. 'The latest forecasts indicate we should have good weather all the way.'

'Good.'

The ground time was eaten up with the usual delays involved in getting everything and everyone on board. Cappy was strapped into the pilot's seat and ready to begin the checklist when her father entered the cockpit.

'Sir?' She waited for him to explain his presence, a faint glitter of irritation showing in her china-blue eyes.

He tapped her copilot on the shoulder and motioned for him to move. 'I'll fly the right seat. You can ride in back and have yourself a nap.'

No lieutenant in his right mind argued with a lieutenant colonel. Franklin was disgruntled by the loss of logging flight time, but he complied. On the way out, he gave Cappy a look which seemed to blame her for the change.

No doubt she was the cause of it. She wished her father was joining her in the cockpit for the sake of old times and all the hours they'd flown together in the past, but she suspected it was a lack of faith in her ability to handle the big twin-engined plane.

After Lieutenant Colonel Hayward was all buckled into the right seat, Cappy made sure she had her maps and charts in order, then gave him the checklist to read off. The steady sound of his voice and the teamwork involved in the plane's start-up gave Cappy a renewed sense of nostalgia.

Unconsciously she asked, 'Ready, Dad?' before advancing the throttle to initiate a taxi roll.

'Let's keep it formal, WASP Hayward,' he replied curtly.

'Very well, sir.' Rebuffed, she silently vowed not to let her tongue slip again.

After takeoff, Cappy executed a climbing turn to put the plane on course to Wright Field in Dayton, where they'd refuel. When they had achieved the desired altitude, she trimmed the DC-3 for straight and level flight. The clouds were few and widely scattered. Below, the thinning fall colors painted the spiny ridges and slopes of the Appalachian Mountains with rusty shades of gold and orange.

Gazing out her window, she admired the burnished hills and the irregular patchwork of farm fields cut out of their elongated valleys, interspersed with small coal towns and the black taluses of mines. She didn't venture a comment on the beauty below them. With any passenger other than her father, Cappy would have drawn attention to it, but his grim-lipped silence didn't invite idle pleasantries. She had the feeling this was going to turn into a long flight.

'Aren't you going to ask how your mother is?' he inquired challengingly.

'How is she?' Cappy obliged. 'I imagine she's quite active in the Gray Ladies now.'

'Maybe if you'd call once in a while, you'd know for yourself.'

'I do call,' she retorted with a touch of anger. 'She probably just doesn't tell you.'

'I've heard you've attended some parties on the Hill with Mitch Ryan. Is it serious between you?'

'No.'

Conversation disintegrated totally after that brief combative attempt. The next hours were taken up solely with the business of flying.

In preparation for entering the traffic pattern at Wright Field, Cappy called the tower operator for landing instructions. When she received no response, she tried again – with the same results. After verifying the frequency and fiddling with the radio, she called again. In the back of her mind, she was becoming concerned that her radio was malfunctioning.

On her fourth try, a disgruntled tower operator came back, 'Will you please stay off the air, lady? This base is restricted to military personnel, and we've got some brass due to arrive any time.'

'This is a military flight, Wright tower,' she replied. 'Lieutenant Colonel Hayward and his staff are passengers. I would like landing instructions, please.' Her clipped voice demanded a response. She knew all about throwing military weight around.

'Sure, and I've got Ike's staff up here in the tower with me,' came the scoffing reply. 'Listen, missy –'

Her father broke into the talk. 'Wright tower, this is Lieutenant Colonel Hayward. I suggest you comply with my pilot's request.'

'Yes, sir!' The surprise in the man's voice was evident.

After he had related the pertinent data to Cappy – the wind's direction and velocity, the active runway number, the barometer setting, and her landing sequence – she acknowledged the information. All her attention was devoted to locating her traffic and setting up for a landing. Once on the ground, she taxied to the flight line. Her father's stern directive kept running through her mind, the words 'my pilot' echoing with an increasingly proud sound. It softened her.

'Thanks,' she said to him.

'For what?' He started reading through the shut-down list.

As he called them off to her, Cappy switched off systems

and double-checked others. In between, she managed to say, 'For straightening out the tower.'

'What do you expect? Women don't belong in military planes.' It was a flat statement of opinion, one that hadn't changed in nearly a year.

Cappy clamped her teeth shut and said no more, biting down hard on the waves of disappointment. Her father was Army-mule stubborn. It had been foolish to think his opinion might have changed, that a little gray might have entered the blackness of his opinion.

As soon as the aircraft was fueled, they took off again. This time Lieutenant Franklin occupied the copilot's seat and her father re joined his group in the rear passenger seats, evidently assured of her competence at the controls. Franklin kept up a steady run of patter. Oddly, Cappy found herself wishing for her father's silence.

Upon arrival at the aircraft plant at Evansville, Cappy and her copilot were taken to the cafeteria for lunch by one of the plant managers. Her father and his group of staff officers went off with one of the company heads.

That afternoon, they were given a tour of the facilities. A large percentage of the workers, Cappy noticed, were women. They were doing everything from welding to assembling parts. Cappy watched them with a sense of affinity. They all were performing jobs that had been previously regarded as a strictly male domain – and doing them well. The war was lowering many barriers that had always been raised against them. When the afternoon break signal sounded, a young woman about Cappy's age finished her weld before she turned off her torch and removed the protective goggles she wore. Cappy said something to her about the job she was doing. The woman looked at her and shrugged.

'I need the money. I can't live on the allocation I get from Ernie. He's just a private in the Army,' she explained, then sighed tiredly. 'I'll be glad when he comes home and I won't have to work anymore.'

'Yes.' Maybe if she wasn't doing something she loved

so much, she'd feel that way too, Cappy decided.

The subject didn't interest her copilot in the least, as he looked around with obvious boredom. Suddenly, he lighted up. 'Hey! Look!' His burst of excitement caught her attention.

A big, ugly plane with a large, four-bladed propeller attached to a blunt engine cowling was being rolled inside a hangar. It was the powerful P-47 Thunderbolt, a fighter plane that was earning the name 'Little Friend' to the Flying Fortresses.

'What I wouldn't give to be crawling into the cockpit of that,' Lieutenant Franklin declared.

'Me, too,' she agreed.

His look was scoffing. 'That plane's a powerhouse. They'll never let a woman at the controls of it.'

Cappy didn't argue the point, but she wondered what the young lieutenant would say if he knew the Army was teaching women to fly the B-17 bomber. It was certainly more airplane than the P-47 pursuit.

Late in the day, they were taken to the hotel where they'd be spending the night. In the short time she'd been on the job, Cappy had learned that piloting Army officers around the country also meant staying in the best accommodations available and dining at the best restaurants. The trip to Evansville was no exception. But dinner that evening proved to be an uncomfortable affair with her father glaring at her from another table the minute any male even walked close to her chair.

'Afterwards I wished I had eaten in my room,' she complained to Mitch, recounting the experience two days later. 'I know he expected me to be accosted at any minute – a woman alone in a public place. Obviously I was supposed to be fast.'

'It's a common misconception.'

A piano player was providing soft background music to the ever-louder talk in the bar. The pianist was no better than average, but with her platinum hair and a well-

endowed figure, more than mediocre talent wasn't necessary. Cappy brought her attention back to the table and
tapped out a cigarette from the half-empty pack. Mitch
immediately offered her a light and she bent toward the
match flame.

'I thought –' She stopped to exhale the smoke, then
shook her head. 'Never mind.'

'You thought what?' The warm and steady regard of his
dark eyes was interested and admiring. Cappy experienced
that rush of pleasure his handsomely rugged looks so often
evoked in her, and looked away before it became too
strong.

'I thought that once my father saw what a competent
pilot I was, he'd give up his stupid prejudices about a
woman's place. When he got on that radio to the tower,
he wasn't demanding respect for me or the job I was doing;
he wanted it for his daughter. That flight proved nothing
to him. If he had his way, I'd be out of the skies tomorrow.'
She was impatient and resentful as bitter thoughts tangled
darkly behind the blue surfaces of her eyes. 'He's impossible.'

'He loves you,' Mitch stated.

'Well, he has a fine way of showing it.' To her, love
was not something that possessed and confined. It was
supposed to be an acceptance and appreciation of a person's individuality, not an attempt to stifle it.

'Just the same, he does,' Mitch repeated with calm
insistence. 'Whenever I see him, he always asks about
you.'

It moved her, but Cappy answered, 'He still doesn't
approve of what I'm doing, so don't try to convince me
otherwise.'

'I won't. But you still love him.'

'He's my father.' This was an explanation rather than
an answer.

'Let's dance.' Mitch slid his hand underneath her fingers
and rubbed the top of them with his thumb.

Dancing was better than talking. She stubbed out her

314

cigarette before standing to be guided onto the crowded floor. The piano player began singing a throaty accompaniment and Cappy recognized the Frank Sinatra hit of a couple years before, 'I'll Never Smile Again.'

Other couples were making slow circles of the area as she turned in his embrace. With one arm curved around her back and lower rib cage, he held her loosely against him. Her eyes were level with his mouth, and she caught the heady scent of bay rum lotion clinging to his shaved jaw. She felt the pressure of his thighs against hers as they moved in shuffling rhythm to the slow ballad.

'Your father is a proud man, Cappy.' Mitch picked up the conversation where they'd left it at the table. 'All he has is the Army and his family –'

'In that order,' she interrupted.

A small smile touched his mouth, but he went on as if she hadn't spoken. 'I think it's normal for every man to want a son, someone to carry on the family name and tradition. I have the feeling your father regrets not having a son, although it's not something he'll admit, because he doesn't want to hurt your mother. But because he does regret it so much, it's probably the reason he doesn't want you doing the things he would have wanted his son to do. Consciously or unconsciously, he doesn't want to expect things from you that he would have expected from a son. His standards for you are very rigid because a man wants his daughter to be a certain kind of woman.'

His logic was sound, but she had her father's stubbornness. 'He wants the same blind obedience from his family that he gives to the Amy,' Cappy replied dryly. 'He isn't the least bit interested in what I want.'

'What do you want, Cap?' His head was inclined toward her, interest deepening in his expression as he tried to fathom her desires.

'I want a home of my own – and friends that I choose. I want to fly.' She heard the building pitch of her voice and stopped before the desperate longing broke through.

'Those are relatively simple things to obtain.' Mitch

drew back to study her, not quite sure what he had thought she would say, but not expecting such a basic reply.

'Are they?' she countered, a trace of mocking irony in her glance. 'Look around you and what do you see? Soldiers, traveling businessmen, secretaries from the Midwest. Impermanence. Nothing is sure. Nothing is certain.'

For a moment, he didn't say anything as he gathered her more closely to him, until his cheek was resting against her silken-dark hair, and he was breathing in its sweet smell. At last he was beginning to understand some of what kept her from caring for anyone or anything too deeply.

'It's the war,' he murmured.

And Cappy didn't contradict him.

The yellow convertible curved up the mountain heavily timbered with pine and leaf-bare hardwood. Drifts of leaves filled the ditches and carpeted the forest floor, making hiding places where the squirrels could store their winter caches. As the car breezed by, its wind whisked up the dried leaves, spinning them in a devil's whirl and leaving them to spiral slowly back to earth – in a scurry and a rush, and finally a whisper.

A blue jay took a shortcut through the trees to wait for the flashy car at the tall log chalet, nestled amongst the trees. Stained a dark brown color, the huge logs lay two-and-a-half stories tall, ringed by a galleried porch with a view of the Carolina mountains, smoky in the November afternoon.

The road came to a dead end at the lodge. Bubba slowed the car to a stop in front of it, and stared at the massive structure with a frown. Eden was busy gathering up her purse and loosening the silk scarf that had protected her hair from the tearing wind.

'I thought you said we were staying in a cabin,' Bubba stated, retreating into a thick drawl. 'Now I've never seen a cabin this size – not even in Texas, where everything's big.'

Eden just laughed at him and climbed out of the car. 'Come on.'

'You're really serious? This is it?' Bubba followed her skeptically, pausing by the trunk to unload the luggage.

'Leave that. Haines will bring it in.' She tucked a hand through the crook of his arm and walked him to split-log steps.

'Haines? Is that your friend?' Bubba looked down at her.

'He's the groundskeeper.' The door opened before they reached it and they were welcomed inside by a plump, matronly woman with gray hair drawn back in a bun and a chubby-cheeked smile. 'Hello, Ida Mae,' Eden greeted the woman familiarly, then breezed on by her, not bothering to introduce Bubba.

The interior walls were exposed logs, the same dark brown color as outside, but the spaciousness of the living room – with its massive stone chimney and hardwood floors spattered with bright area rugs and animal skins – eliminated any sense of darkness. The high ceilings were ribbed with wooden beams, rustic chandeliers of hurricane-style lamps suspended to light the areas below.

The kindly-faced woman had prepared the liquor trolley for Eden and discreetly withdrawn. Bubba wandered over to stand next to Eden while she fixed them each a drink.

'Who was she?' Bubba asked in an undertone.

'Ida Mae? She's the cook.' Eden handed him a drink, then touched her glass to his in an unspoken toast, the delicate ring of fine crystal making a bell-like sound.

He glanced at her face, that gleaming devil-light lurking beneath the surfaces of his hazel eyes, exciting her. Maintaining the eye contact, Eden sipped the iced Scotch in her glass, then raised herself on tiptoes to nuzzle his lips and taste the whiskey on them.

With fingers linked, she drew him with her to the Chesterfield, positioned in front of the mammoth stone fireplace. She pulled him onto the smooth cushions and sat with her legs curled beneath her. Like an orange-haired tabby cat she arched against his side. The hem of her skirt had inched up to show her silk-stockinged knees.

'Something tells me' – Bubba looked at her askance and hooked an arm around her shoulders to bring her comfortably closer – 'this weekend isn't going to be quite what I thought.'

Her smile teased him. 'I hope you weren't expecting me to do the cooking.'

'I didn't think too much about food,' he admitted.

'Oh?' She playfully walked her fingers over the ribbed white wool sweater covering his chest, up to the jutting angle of his wide jaw. 'What did you think about?'

'You and me walking through the woods, or sitting in front of a cozy fire,' Bubba replied with a kind of shrug.

'The woods are just outside and the logs in the fireplace are simply waiting for a match.' She was more interested in his mouth and the delights it could hold.

The door opened and a spare-built man entered, toting their suitcases. Not a single glance was sent in their direction as he walked through to the rustic log-railed stairs, as if he were unaware of the couple sitting so closely on the davenport.

'It's not exactly you and me.' The groundskeeper illustrated the difference between Bubba's imagined weekend and the reality. 'And this isn't exactly a little ole cabin in the woods.'

'But we're together . . . with all the comforts of home,' Eden reminded him.

'Maybe your home . . . but not mine,' he corrected her drolly. 'I'm used to doin' for myself.'

'And just what is it that you "do" so well?' she asked with her face uplifted in provocative invitation.

A half-muffled groan came from his throat as he roughly gathered her in and reached around to rid himself of the impediment of the whiskey glass, shoving it onto an end table. His mouth rolled onto her lips, heavy with the weight of his needs. She threaded her fingers into the shaggy thickness of his hair, nails digging in like a purring cat flexing its claws. The driving pressure of his kiss was too demanding, yet he couldn't check it, and she seemed to revel in it. A fine sweat broke across his upper lip with the rising heat that flared between them.

'You are Eden to me.' He held himself a breath away from her softly swollen lips, a fevered huskiness in his low, trembling voice. 'All the things of paradise on earth. You are my sun, heating me with your fire – and the blackness of night, taking me into your endless reaches. God, how I love you.' His lips settled onto hers again.

A tap of footsteps on the hardwood floor brought Bubba's head up sharply. The carpet runner on the stairs had muffled the sounds of the groundskeeper's descent until he crossed the open foyer to the door. Bubba flushed darkly under his tan and pulled away from her to run a self-conscious hand through his hair. Eden couldn't completely conceal her amusement over his embarrassment.

'You'll get used to them. Eventually you won't even know they're in the room.'

But Bubba never did get accustomed to their silent comings and goings in the lodge. When Ida Mae brought them breakfast trays the next morning, she didn't bat an eye at the sight of him in the bed, stark naked under the satin sheets. Eden teased him about it until he found a mutually satisfactory way to silence her.

Against his better judgment, he let her drive him all the way back to the base, dropping him off inside the gates instead of leaving him in town to catch a ride on an Army transport. But Eden was completely unconcerned about any problems that might arise from being seen with a noncom, confident she could handle it. She had her chance when she was ordered to report to Major Stevenson.

'It's come to my attention that you were seen with an enlisted man,' the squadron commander announced accusingly, keeping the width of his desk between them so it wouldn't be so obvious that she was taller than he was. 'I want the name of this sergeant who was with you.'

'Sir, in a manner of speaking, I wasn't "with" anyone.'

In this situation, Eden was very sure of herself, drawing on the cool hauteur that could stop any man, coldly daring him to deny her word. 'I was driving back to base and saw Sergeant Jackson waiting for a ride, so I gave him a lift back to camp.'

'Sergeant Jackson?' His arched eyebrow prompted a fuller description of the man.

'He's the mechanic who's worked on some of the planes I've flown.'

'Then you admit you were with him?'

'I was *with* him,' she agreed in an implied denial. 'Sometimes I ride in the front seat with our family chauffeur. I've never regarded that as being *with* him, but I suppose you could say that.'

'I see,' he murmured.

Afterwards, Eden laughed about it to Mary Lynn. 'When I reminded him that I was a pilot and Sergeant Jackson was merely a mechanic, he was so incensed I thought he was going to burst a blood vessel. You could tell how disappointed he was that our meeting had been so innocent.' But Mary Lynn didn't laugh, causing Eden to add, 'I thought it was amusing. The major is such a pompous snob himself.'

'Yes.' Mary Lynn's attempted smile fell short of its mark. 'I was just remembering Rachel. Everybody knew she was sneaking out to meet that private.' She reached inside her jacket and took out an envelope, overseas V-mail. 'This came for you. It's from Rachel's private.'

After a small hesitation, Eden tore it open and read through the short missive from Zach Jordan. It was a reaching out, expressing his gratefulness for the words of sympathy she had tried to offer him after the chapel service for Rachel.

'He's in Italy,' she said.

320

Part Three

I just called up to tell you that
  I'm rugged but right!
A rambling woman, a gambling woman,
  drunk every night.
A porterhouse steak three times
  a day for my board,
That's more than any decent gal
  can afford!
I've got a big electric fan to
  keep me cool while I eat,
A tall, handsome man to keep me
  warm while I sleep.
I'm a rambling woman, a gambling woman,
  and BOY am I tight!
I just called up to tell you that
I'm rugged but right!
HO-HO-HO – rugged but right!

CHAPTER TWENTY-TWO

'I have denied your request for transfer.' The papers were pushed across the desk to the two women seated in front of it.

'We'll resubmit them,' Eden stated, not backing down an inch. 'It won't do you any good.' Jacqueline Cochran rose from her chair and came around to the front of the desk in the borrowed office, facing her two rebellious pilots. She did not tolerate opposition well. 'I'll simply turn them down again.'

'Then you'll have my resignation,' Eden countered.

'I won't accept it.' The director's dark eyes hardened. 'Don't you realize that your actions could jeopardize future programs for women pilots?' she argued firmly. 'Any failure to endure by any woman will be a detriment to all of us. I cannot allow the two of you to knock down what the rest of us have achieved. Conditions are perhaps not the best, but we are at war. The pilots here are performing a vital function –'

'I'm not interested in a lecture,' Eden cut in, not giving Mary Lynn a chance to talk. 'And conditions here have not improved that much. We are still flying red-lined aircraft daily. There haven't been any more fatalities because we finally got smart and started looking out for ourselves instead of depending on those in command.'

At the interruption, Jacqueline Cochran turned coldly angry. 'As your superior –'

'You are in charge, Miss Cochran, but you are not my superior,' Eden corrected her.

Mary Lynn was a silent participant in the exchange,

watching the clash of two strong wills. Her nature was quieter, but no less resilient.

Wisely, Jacqueline Cochran did not pursue her earlier remark. 'My position is unchanged; your requests for transfers are denied. If, in a month, you still feel strongly about this, we will discuss it at that time.'

'No, Miss Cochran.' Eden wasn't impressed by that ambiguous offer. 'We won't discuss it. I either have my transfer or I resign. It doesn't matter whether you accept it or not. If I walk off this base, what will you do? Have me arrested? That might make for some unpleasant publicity – and believe me, I'll make a scene.'

'That sounds distinctly like a threat.'

Mary Lynn spoke up, 'Our leaving is not going to affect the experiment here. We have proven we can fly tow-target missions. Our record is excellent. No army expects a soldier to remain on the front line for the entire war, Miss Cochran. Our request for a transfer is not unreasonable under the circumstances.'

'That is a valid argument,' the Director of Women pilots conceded.

'Does that mean you'll grant our requests for transfer?' Eden wanted a more definite response.

'I'll take them under advisement and see what can be arranged. You'll hear from me.' She retreated behind the desk, in effect dismissing them.

Eden stood, but didn't leave the office. 'When?'

With a trace of impatience and grudging admiration, Jacqueline Cochran replied, 'Within the week.'

They filed out of the office, not pausing until they were outside the operations building. The Carolina air on that December day was cold and damp, the sky overhead gray and leaden. They halted to zip their jackets against the seeping chill.

'What do you think?' Mary Lynn asked.

'She doesn't have a choice,' Eden replied complacently. 'We'll get our transfers to the ferrying division.'

A dismal, drenching downpour saturated the Carolina ground. Eden picked her way across the winter grass, taking a shortcut to the barracks, her boots squishing through the mud. She darted inside, dripping water in a trail that followed her down the narrow corridor to Mary Lynn's private cubicle.

'Mail call!' Out of breath and barely able to contain her excitement, she whipped several envelopes from beneath her rain slicker and shoved them at Mary Lynn, who was curled on her cot in the midst of her Christmas writing. 'Open this one first.' Eden indicated an official-looking envelope and watched with bright, shining eyes as Mary Lynn tore at the flap with her finger. 'New orders, right?' she guessed.

At first glance, Mary Lynn nodded affirmatively while she read a little farther. 'Yes.'

'Mine came, too.' Solid triumph put a steady gleam into her dark brown eyes. 'Can you think of a better Christmas present than getting transferred out of this place?' She didn't wait for an answer. 'Where are they sending you?'

'To the Sixth Ferrying Group in Long Beach, California.'

'Same here,' Eden said with some surprise, and sank onto the cot in front of Mary Lynn. Satisfaction radiated across her features. 'I can hardly wait to enjoy some of that California sunshine. This constant gray gloom is depressing.'

Mary Lynn's glance fell on another envelope and recognized Beau's familiar scrawl. 'It's from Beau,' she said, offering an unnecessary explanation as she eagerly ripped it open and skimmed the first few paragraphs. His letters were always read many times. 'Listen to this.' In a quick recap of the letter's opening paragraphs she explained, 'Beau was on a raid and lost two engines. He was forced to land at an RAF base. But listen to this part. "They told me luck had run out for the old girl and she was destined to be scrapped for spare B-17 parts,"' she read. '"I went to have a last look at her. Some fighter pilots were standing around. One came over and started talking to me. It turns out that he knows you."' Mary Lynn stopped reading to tell Eden the astounding news. 'It was Colin Fletcher! Can you imagine? He and Beau are having dinner over the Christmas holidays, he said. At least he won't be alone at Christmas.' She released an excited sigh. 'Won't Marty be surprised when I write and tell her about Colin!'

An agreeing sound came from Eden, but she looked absent and preoccupied. The wet hood of her rain slicker had fallen to the back of her head. Wispy tendrils of damp, dark copper hair curled along her temples. Her dark eyes were troubled.

'Is something wrong, Eden?' Mary Lynn inquired even though the redhead hadn't shown an inclination to confide in her in the past.

A heavy sigh broke from her lips. 'Finally we have transfers that will take us out of these awful planes and away from this miserable weather – something I've wanted for months – and now I don't want to go.' Eden pushed herself to her feet on that impatient declaration, half angry. 'I don't want to leave Bubba.' She hung her head for a dejected instant, then darted a proudly assertive look at Mary Lynn. 'I'm crazy about that man.'

Hooded and coated once again to keep out the cold, dripping the rain that misted the field from low-hanging clouds, Eden splashed through the puddled water collecting on the concrete apron around the hangars. She ran with her head down and her shoulders hunched against the bone-damp chill. The massive hangar doors were shut against the inclement weather and Eden ran to a small side door, quickly rushing in out of the drizzling rain.

Pausing inside, she pushed the slicker hood to the back of her head and scanned the cavernous interior. The light patter of rain drummed a thousand finger-tappings on the corrugated metal of the hangar's roof. All sound echoed in the empty hollow of the building – the clank of metal tools, the idle call of male voices, and the thud of walking feet on the concrete floor. The humid, heavy air smelled strongly of gasoline fumes, motor oils, and grease from the disemboweled planes parked inside.

In her second sweep of the hangar, Eden spied Bubba's long, lanky figure in loose-fitting overalls, standing by a workbench along the near wall. She walked immediately toward him, her step quickening. The soft-wrapped package stowed under her raincoat for protection from the elements made a rustling sound as she moved, but it was mostly drowned by the wet swish of her slicker.

With his concentration centered on the valve lifter in his hand, Bubba failed to hear her approach. At the last minute, the sound of her footsteps reached him and his keen hazel eyes looked her way. His wide, intelligent features immediately glowed with pleasure.

'Hello.' The drawled greeting managed to convey a host of caresses. They had learned to do this – to touch and feel each other with words and looks, to mentally make love while abstaining from contact.

There was an excited quiver in the pit of her stomach. 'Hello.' Her dark gaze searched his face for an anxious second. 'My transfer came through.'

The soft expression on his face suddenly hardened. His oil-grimed fingers fiddled with the lifter. 'Are you going?' His tone was an attempt to sound offhand, yet under it was deep, painful alarm.

'It's what I've wanted,' Eden reminded him and watched him for some sign that he would insist that she stay.

'Yep,' Bubba agreed to that.

'They're sending me to Long Beach . . . in California.' Another mechanic paused at the workbench to pick up a tool, and Eden waited until he was out of earshot before continuing. 'There isn't any reason why you can't ask for a transfer.'

Bubba breathed out a sound that dismissed the thought. 'My CO has made it real plain that he isn't going to approve any such thing. I'm needed here.' His pause was short. 'Besides, I've been told if I leave this camp, it's likely to be for the Pacific. That's where they're usin' so many of these dive-bombers.'

'Not the Pacific.' That suggestion brought a cold chill down her spine. 'The Japanese scare me.' In a diversionary gesture, she brought forth the package that had been protectively hidden inside her coat, and offered it to Bubba. She wanted to remind him of the continuing patterns of life that war couldn't change. 'It's your Christmas present. I didn't know when I might have another chance to give it to you before I left.'

Self-consciously, Bubba wiped at the grime on his hands before he took the tissue-wrapped package from her, glancing around to see who might be watching.

'What is it?' he asked with a vague, boyish smile lifting his lip corners. He was trying to respond to Eden's gift-giving spirit, but not too successfully.

'Silk pajamas . . . from Saks.' She'd guessed at the size, then had Ham pick them out for her in New York and send them to her. It had all required considerable time, effort, and expense. Her dark eyes glowed with anticipation, awaiting his look of surprise and pleasure.

His brows arched high, taken aback. As always when he was in an awkward situation, Bubba retreated into a thick drawl and a country-boy pose. 'I haven't worn pajamas since I was a pup,' he joked. 'What do you aim for me to do with these?'

'You were so embarrassed about having nothing on when Ida Mae brought the breakfast tray in, I thought you should have something to wear the next time a maid brought you breakfast in bed,' Eden replied easily, warmed by the memory of that weekend.

His wide, raw-boned features grew grimly smooth and serious. 'But there aren't any maids in my house, Eden,' he pointed out with quiet pride.

Laughing, she didn't hear that underlying note. 'But there are in mine.'

*   *   *

On the day they left Camp Davis, Eden wangled a driver and jeep from the motor pool to take her and Mary Lynn to the train station. When the Army private picked them up at the nurses' barracks, she ordered him to stop at the flight line. No explanation was offered to the driver and Mary Lynn needed none. She sympathized with Eden's desire to see Bubba one last time.

As the jeep rolled up to the hangar area, Bubba spotted them and came trotting over to meet them. His work cap was reversed, the bill pointing down the back of his head, and he wore a wide smile at the sight of Eden. In between wipes of his greasy hands on a rag, he gave the two of them a careless salute.

'What can I do for you?' he asked, conscious of the eavesdropping private behind the wheel.

'We just came by for one last look before we left,' Eden replied, smiling too.

'The boys on the ground are gonna miss you. The place won't be the same with you gone,' Bubba said.

'We'll miss you.'

The weight of parting lay heavily between them as their smiles faded. They looked at each other with undisguised longing, memorizing details for the lonely times ahead. Mary Lynn ached for them, understanding the conflict between the love and the sense of duty they each felt.

Bubba finally broke the contact, lowering his chin and turning his head aside, and resumed the wiping of his hands. 'I guess you'd better be on your way before you miss that train.' He stepped away from the side of the jeep and stood well clear of its path. 'Good flying.'

'Take care of yourself, Sergeant,' Mary Lynn offered, aware that Eden was too choked up to say anything.

Her attempt at a salute became a tearful wave, but only Mary Lynn noticed. Except for the wetness in her eyes, Eden's poise was otherwise intact. As she ordered the private to drive on, someone in the hangar yelled for Bubba. Her last glimpse of him came as he walked away in that long, rolling gait. They'd be together again, Eden never doubted that, but she still regretted the separation.

Because of the Christmas holidays, the trains were more crowded than usual. There was always a crush of servicemen and passengers in the dining and club cars. It didn't matter how discouraging the war news was in Italy and the Pacific, a holiday spirit prevailed on the train. Like Mary Lynn, Eden joined in with the caroling in the club car, each of them drawn a little bit closer to the other because of the men they missed.

As the train slowed its clacking wheels to pass through a small town, Eden absently glanced out the club-car window. A yellow convertible was stopped at a highway crossing, a street lamp shining down on it. She poked at Mary Lynn.

'Do you think that's my car?' They were past it before Eden could tell for sure. 'It looked like it, didn't it? The chauffeur is somewhere en route to California with it.'

'Wouldn't it be something if we just passed it on the way?' Mary Lynn declared.

'Many more of these cross-country jaunts and I'm going to need a new car before this war is over,' Eden joked, then she turned faintly serious.

'When we start ferrying planes, we're going to cover a lot more country than your car has.' Mary Lynn sipped at her soda-pop rickey, an innocent concoction of soda, lime juice and sugar.

'That's true,' Eden agreed.

When they arrived in California, they reported to Air Transport Command's Sixth Ferrying Group in Long Beach. New orders awaited their arrival, sending them to Palm Springs to attend the ATC pursuit school, where they would learn to fly the Army's fighters, the hottest ships around.

The first three weeks of training were spent in the rear cockpit of the AT-6 Texan, the plane they'd flown so often during their advanced flying phase in Sweetwater. The Texan's rear cockpit allowed them to simulate conditions in the nose-high 'Jug,' the pilots' nickname for the P-47 Thunderbolt because of its thick, blunt-nosed cowling. The training was intensive but it had to be. There wasn't any room in the Thunderbolt for a second pilot, so the first time up in the fighter plane had to be a solo ride.

The cockpit of the P-47 was just Mary Lynn's size, measuring roughly three feet by three feet. In that small space a mass of levers, gauges, and navigational and communication equipment was crammed, not leaving much room for the pilot. But Mary Lynn didn't take up much room.

She ran through the cockpit check, seat belt and shoulder straps fastened tight – and her heart somewhere in her throat. Thirteen separate buttons and switches had to be in position for flight preparation and Mary Lynn mentally counted them off. With the stick back and the brakes locked and the primer feeding juice to the engine, she pushed the starter switch.

A rumbling groan came from deep inside the plane, and the four – bladed propeller cranked, slowly rotating and picking up speed. So did her pulse. The rumble grew louder as the Pratt and Whitney engine took power and vibrated the aircraft with its bass-deep roar.

On the ground, her instructor gave her a thumbs-up sign, wishing Mary Lynn good luck on her first ride in the powerful plane. She scanned the dials once more – temperature and pressure gauges all reading right – and eased the throttle forward to start her taxi roll, a scared feeling in the pit of her stomach.

At the end of the runway, Mary Lynn reached up and grasped the canopy bar, located just behind her shoulder. With a squeeze of the lever, she pushed the canopy forward to close the cockpit, then locked it.

'Okay, Army Three forty-seven,' the tower operator's voice sounded in the ear sets. 'Clear for takeoff when ready.'

'Roger.' Mary Lynn depressed the button on the stick to activate her throat mike and acknowledge the clearance. She was in position, but the Thunderbolt's high nose kept her from seeing down the length of the runway.

For all her apprehensions, she was mentally committed to a take-off. Her hand slowly pushed the black throttle knob forward while the powerful engine changed from a rumbling pitch to a deepening thunder. She took her feet off the brake pedals and kept pushing the throttle forward. The Thunderbolt seemed to catapult itself down the runway, its high acceleration pressing Mary Lynn against the seat and the tremendous roar of the engine filling the cockpit. She let the stick come forward, lowering the nose and lifting the tail wheel. Applying more and more right rudder to compensate for the powerful engine torque, she kept the fighter plane pointed down the center of the runway.

She was unconsciously holding her breath as she glanced at the airspeed indicator. The needle swung past 85, then past 90, still moving. The plane wasn't fighting the controls so much now. Another glance at the airspeed and Mary Lynn gently pulled back on the stick at 110 miles an hour. The ground fell away as the pursuit surged into the air, not using even half of the runway, and the sensation turned her nervous qualms into soaring excitement.

With the gear folding away inside the fighter's belly, she trimmed the craft for a climb and the Thunderbolt streaked for the clouds like a homesick angel. Palm Springs was behind her and the blue of the Salton Sea reflected the desert sky. She put the plane through its paces, exulting in its power and high maneuverability. She was sorry when she had to return to the base.

That night her letters to Beau and Marty were filled with the thrilling experience of that first solo flight. It seemed fitting somehow that, while two of the most important people in her life were flying B-17 bombers, nicknamed the 'Big Friend,' she was now flying P-47 Thunderbolt pursuit aircraft, called by some the 'Little Friend.'

When their month of training was finished, Eden and Mary Lynn joined the Sixth Ferrying Group in Long Beach and began delivering the fast pursuits all over the country.

CHAPTER TWENTY-THREE

Jeweled turquoise waters surround the chain of islands that trail off the southern tip of Florida like stepping stones into the Gulf of Mexico. The clear barrier of the B-17's plexiglas nose was all that separated Marty Rogers from the white-capped blue waters and the sun-drenched Keys below. The February skies were clear and limitless, stretching to the end of the sea and beyond. Through them, the Army-drab B-17, painted olive green, headed to its home field at Buckingham Army Air Base outside of Fort Myers, its training mission for turret gunnery operators complete for this trip.

Belly down in the glass nose of the Flying Fortress, Marty let the panoramic view ease the tension from the previous concentrated patterns she'd flown. Her copilot took the controls for the homebound flight while she enjoyed a break. From here to the airfield, it was all fairly routine.

'It's hard to believe that a month ago I was zipped to the throat in a fleece-lined flight suit, with long underwear, a leather jacket, and wool-lined boots, trying to keep warm twenty-four thousand feet above frigid Ohio.' Her chin rested on the cup of her hand and her voice rumbled deep from her chest as she flashed a wry glance at the uniformed officer sharing the close quarters of the B-17 nose with her.

Graduation from the four-engine school at Lockbourne Amy Air Base had also signaled the end of the grueling, strength-building exercises. Marty had gladly abandoned the Bernarr Macfadden wrist developers and now picked up a newspaper only to read it, not to crumple it into a ball in her fist.

'I know what you mean,' the chestnut-haired lieutenant agreed. He was one of the many transient pilots temporarily stationed at Buckingham awaiting overseas assignments or more training in heavier bombers. Scott Daniels was a bomber pilot, but on today's flight he'd come along to observe the patterns and procedures.

The constant coming and going of pilots suited Marty. She wasn't interested in establishing any permanent relationships. Besides, it wasn't wise with so many of the pilots bound for combat overseas. Airmen had a notoriously higher mortality rate than the regular soldier. She'd had fun with all the flyboys but she'd restricted intimacies to a very few.

From the corner of her eye, she studied Lieutenant Scott Daniels, strongly attracted to his fair skin and burnished brown hair. More than once he'd looked at her with a flirting, questing gaze, making his interest in her obvious. Marty wasn't particularly bothered by the gold wedding band on his ring finger as long as he wasn't. He turned, caught her eyeing him, and smiled with a slow, knowing warmth. A second later, his glance shifted past her, locking onto something in the blue sea below them.

'Look.' He leaned closer and pointed out a small white dot in the aquamarine waters. 'Isn't that a boat? What do you suppose it is? A fishing trawler, maybe?'

'Probably.' Marty watched the bobbing speck, so small from the bomber's great height.

But her senses were picking up other messages – the slight pressure of his body making contact against her length, the warmth of his breath stirring the touseled, tawny curls of her short hair, and the spicy scent drifting from his smoothly shaven cheeks. He was very close. She turned her head slightly, feeling the little run of her pulse as her gaze darted to the full line of his mouth so near to hers.

'I wangled myself a weekend pass,' he murmured. 'A buddy of mine is lending me his car. I thought I'd drive over to Miami. Would you like to ride along?'

'Sure,' Marty agreed in her whiskey-thick voice. 'Why not?'

'Why not,' the lieutenant repeated, then he closed the space that separated their lips.

The kiss was both seeking and satisfying, a controlled exploration that invited and promised something more. Marty responded to the simple demand that didn't press. Intense passion usually required some kind of commitment. She usually backed off from that, preferring something freer, less confining.

Slowly they drew apart. Her breathing was faintly uneven, warmly aroused. Marty held his gaze while she turned onto her side and shifted so she was slightly under him.

'Tell me, Lieutenant,' she murmured, gravelly mischief lacing her voice, 'have you ever made love in an airplane before?'

A dark gleam entered his brown eyes. 'Are you a member of that famed Mile-High Club I've heard about?' he taunted, referring to the supposedly select group of female fliers who had made love at an altitude over 5,000 feet.

'Not yet,' Marty replied, then chuckled in her throat as her hand curved itself to the back of his neck and urged him down.

Miami Beach with its palm trees and endless stretches of sand was a hive of tourists, workers whose pockets were stuffed with dollars from high-paying war jobs, uniformed servicemen, and wives, stubborn in their insistence to be close to their soldier husbands for as long as they could. The beaches were a strange blend of cadets drilling in columns, sun-worshipping factory employees wading in the surf in the civilian version of a furlough, and Coast Guardsmen patrolling the shores on horseback.

Nearly all the hotels were taken over by the Army as rest and recuperation centers for the war's victims, prominent among them the Air Force pilots returning from overseas with their bodies intact and their nerves shattered. Vestiges of the war were everywhere, creeping into the idyllic world of sand, surf, and sun, like a widening shadow in paradise. The shadow lurked in the corners of people's lives; their backs might be turned to it, but they were unable to banish it completely.

A bright sickle moon silvered the beach Marty strolled with Lieutenant Scott Daniels, the loose sand weighting her steps, making them slow and meandering. The salty breeze had a tangy taste, invigorating and clean. The small breakers rolled in slowly.

'I've heard ships have been torpedoed just a few miles off shore,' she remarked.

Her boat-shaped cap sat jauntily atop her short, honey-dark hair. In the moonlight, her silver wings gleamed on her semi-regulation shirt. She wore her uniform-tan pants and unbecoming but serviceable shoes. The night was warm, making a jacket unnecessary.

'Yeah, that's what I've heard, too,' Scott agreed and tipped the beer bottle to his mouth. No more than a swallow was left, and he frowned at the bottle. Hotels loomed in tall, irregular boxes close to the sand, darkened into black silhouettes. 'Want another beer?' he asked. 'There's bound to be a bar in one of these places.'

Marty shrugged, not really caring. 'Sure.' Altering their direction, they headed for the nearest blacked-out building. Where the hotel's sundeck jutted into the beach sand, Marty checked her pace. 'I'll wait for you out here.' For once, she wasn't in the mood for the noisy, smoky scene of a bar.

The pilot didn't protest. 'I'll be right out.'

While he disappeared toward the hotel's beach entrance, Marty wandered over to claim one of the lounge chairs, angular shapes in the shadows cast by the palm fronds. She stumbled over a pair of feet thrust into the walkway and nearly fell into a chair before she recovered her balance.

'Sorry,' she said to the unknown person, his outline

barely discernible in the deep shadows. 'I didn't see you sitting there in the dark.'

'The hotels are under blackout orders again.' The figure shifted, catching some of the moonlight. An officer's cap sat sideways on his head, the bill dipping over one eye and shadowing most of his features except for the smile that seemed to lurk permanently around his mouth, infected with a hard, cruel bitterness.

'I noticed the cars had the top half of their headlamps hooded' – Marty strained to see more of this stranger, wary and conscious of the hair rising on the back of her neck – 'and the blackout curtains at the windows.'

'Only on the ocean side, though,' he pointed out with dry cynicism, in case she hadn't noted how limited the precaution was.

There was something about this man Marty instinctively disliked. She couldn't name it, but she felt on edge, ready to snap. Even though she couldn't see him clearly, she could feel the slow rake of his eyes. She wished she hadn't sat down next to him, but she wasn't about to get up and leave now.

'What are those wings you're wearing?' He lifted his hand to gesture in the direction of the specially designed wings on her shirt collar, ice cubes clinking against the glass he held. The potent smell of rum came to her. 'Did your flyboy lover give them to you?'

'No. I earned them,' Marty stated in a flat, decisive voice.

He seemed to straighten with interest, and she caught the reflection of moonlight off the captain's bars on his shoulders. 'The hell you say.' Some kind of scornful amusement mocked her accomplishment. 'And just what is it you fly? Cubs?'

'A B-17 Flying Fortress,' she retorted. A long silence followed, broken by the sound of ice cubes rattling as a drink was thrown back, then the glass lowered. 'Surprised?' Marty couldn't resist taunting him.

'I guess the Army doesn't give a damn who they stick into their planes,' he mused, uncaring.

His head was lowered; moonlight splashed across more of his face, revealing rugged, once handsome features that were lined and pitted. Silver wings, too, were on his uniform. The Army had few pilots over thirty, but this captain looked to be every bit of that and more. Despite his lazy, slouched posture, he seemed a coil of restless, brittle energy.

'What do you fly?' Marty asked.

'Nothing. Not any more.' Something akin to hatred was in his voice as it turned mocking and bitter. 'You see, I fooled the Army. I survived my fifty missions. When they extended it another ten, I survived that, too. They tried, but they couldn't kill me off. Now they gotta figure out what to do with me.'

'Did you lose your nerve, Captain?' Marty said with disgust.

'Maybe. I don't know.' He lapsed into silence and looked away, seaward.

'What *did* you fly?'

'Why, that great armada ship, the B-17 Flying Fortress.' The declaration was laced with a biting irony. 'They sent waves of them over Axis targets just to see how many of them would come back. We went again and again.'

'Where were you stationed? England?' Mary Lynn's husband was there . . . and Colin. Fate had thrown them together – fate and war. Wouldn't it be something if –

'North Africa in the beginning, flying Liberators, then England.'

'You wouldn't happen to know a B-17 pilot named Beau Palmer –' she began.

'No. Everybody I knew is dead,' he interrupted flatly and coldly. 'And I made it a point not to meet anybody else. It's better if you don't know the name of the pilot flying on your wing.'

His bitter self-pity irked Marty. 'I guess no one knows your name. If you'd died, no one would have missed you.'

'How true,' he agreed, unscathed by her attempt to

wound. 'Here comes your friend. I'm sure he's missed your cheerful company.'

'I'm sure you won't mind if I leave you to yours. You seem to love it so much.' She swept out of the lounge chair to rejoin Lieutenant Daniels emerging from the hotel with a pair of beer bottles in his hand.

When she joined him, he noticed the man in the shadows and asked, 'Who's he?'

'Some pilot' – the scorn was in her voice – 'who has lost his nerve.'

'I heard of a bomber pilot back from England who couldn't stand the sound of a car riding over the joints in the highway.' The lieutenant passed her a bottle of beer. 'The thumping reminded him of flak.'

Weary and nerve-torn, Cappy Hayward mounted the steps to the nurses' barracks. She'd flown for hours over cloud hills, guided solely by her instruments, not seeing the ground until she'd broken through the solid murk upon entering the traffic pattern for Bolling Field. To make matters worse, she had a nervous passenger aboard who constantly questioned her ability to find the field.

The strain of gritting her teeth and smiling thinly at his implied insults had knotted the muscles in her shoulders and neck. Not once had she said anything that smacked of insubordination, although she had been tempted on countless occasions to inform the oft-decorated colonel what he could do with the airplane and precisely where.

As Cappy entered the barracks, she was hailed by one of the nurses. 'Hayward.' She waited for Cappy to turn in acknowledgment. 'There's someone waiting for you in your room. She said she knew you. The two of you had trained together or something. I thought it would be all right if she waited for you there.'

'Thanks.' Puzzled and wondering if it could be Eden en route on some ferrying assignment, Cappy shook off some of her tiredness to walk quickly to her room.

As she opened the door, she spied the long-legged girl in the improvised WASP uniform with a mop of mussed, sandy curls in their typically shorn and carefree style. It was funny, but Marty Rogers was the last one of their group she had expected to see. Marty was sitting on her cot, her legs outstretched and her back propped on the pillows Cappy had stacked against the wall to give the room a homey touch. Smoke spiraled from the cigarette Marty held between her fingers.

'Surprised?' Marty mocked Cappy's slightly wide-eyed expression.

No demonstration of affection was expected. After a small hesitation, Cappy walked the rest of the way into the room and shut the door to shrug out of her battle jacket.

'Yes,' she admitted as she gave the leather jacket a toss and reached for her own pack of cigarettes. 'What brings you here? I thought you were basking in the Florida sunshine and flying all over those blue Gulf waters in a Fortress.'

'I was.'

The use of the past tense seemed significant. Cappy picked up the altering of pitch, the faint emphasis on the verb.

'Was?' she repeated in a prompting fashion.

'I've just been raked over the proverbial coals,' Marty replied on a scornful breath. 'They've pulled me out of the heavy bombers. I was lucky, though.' She shrugged. 'They damned near threw me out of the WASPs.'

'For what?'

'The Army pilot I was seeing happened to be married.' She swung her legs off the bed and turned to sit on the edge, her hands on the side of the cot.

'How'd they find out?'

'Scott was a fool. He wrote his wife a Dear Jane letter.' Her mouth curved wryly. 'She, of course, fired off a nasty note to the commander about this bitch who's stolen her husband.'

'That's tough.' Cappy was distantly sympathetic. 'So where to now?'

'I've been demoted to the ferrying division. Every cloud has a silver lining, though. I'm being sent to Long Beach, so I'll probably hook up with Mary Lynn and Eden. It'll be almost like old times.'

'Be sure to say hi for me, will you?' Cappy said, reaching for the ashtray that held the lipstick-stained butt of Marty's cigarette.

'I didn't come just to chat,' Marty stated, and met Cappy's questioning glance. 'I need a favor. You were always the one who knew everything. I figured you could help me.'

'With what?'

'You know a lot of people in town. Maybe you can give me the name of someone to contact to arrange an abortion. On top of everything else, I'm pregnant.'

After the first shock had receded, Cappy breathed out a troubled sigh and frowned. 'Are you sure that's what you want?'

'I want to fly. I've always wanted to fly,' Marty retorted grimly. 'What would I do with a kid? Hell, the father is already married. And even if he was free, I wouldn't want to marry him. So what's the alternative? If they find out I'm pregnant, I'm washed out.'

The olive-gray eyes remained steady, not a glimmer of doubt on their calm surface. Still, Cappy hesitated, not liking any of this, yet feeling a loyalty to her former baymate.

'How soon? How much time before you have to report to California?' she asked finally.

'Counting travel time, I've got three days.'

Cappy pulled in a breath and held it before letting it out slowly. 'That isn't much.' She cast another look at Marty. 'You are sure this is what you want?'

'I'm sure.'

Cappy nodded. 'Okay. There's an empty room down the hall. I'll arrange for you to stay here while I see what

341

I can do.' She paused. 'Just about anything is available in Washington, legal or not – moral or not.'

Being brought up in the Army included lessons in rumor. Cappy had learned well how to piece them together. Someone hinted this; another whispered that; this one suspected another thing; and that one heard something else. Things that weren't discussed and things that were – they were part of knowing what went on and pretending otherwise.

Between the confidences of a few discreet Army nurses and contacts in the ocean of Washington typists, Cappy got the name and address of a reputable abortionist – in her opinion, almost a contradiction in terms. Marty made her own contact.

When the time came to keep the appointment, Cappy couldn't let her go alone. Whether she liked it or not, she had become involved in this and she had to see it through to its conclusion. Marty didn't argue; with or without Cappy, she was going through with it.

Expecting the worst, Cappy was surprised when the address didn't take them into the slums which covered nearly half of the city, occupied mainly by Negroes. There, it was said, among the dreadful 'alley houses' where several families sometimes lived in a single room, gangs of seven- and eight-year-old boys roamed the streets armed with knives, and girls barely into their puberty were prostitutes on the corners.

The address was in an old neighborhood of the city, the back office atop a two-story building housing a pharmacy at the street level. Paint and plaster were peeling off the walls of the narrow, steep stairwell. Marty paused at the bottom of the steps and looked up.

'This is melodramatic as hell,' she muttered dryly and resolutely started up the stairs. Cappy followed, her lips pressed firmly together.

The frosted glass door on the right of the second-floor hallway was identified only by a number. Marty tried the knob and it turned under her hand. The air had a musty, closed-in smell, faintly tainted by an antiseptic odor. The small anteroom was devoid of furniture except for a standing ashtray by the inner door, but it was clean.

A soft scuffle of sound came from the adjoining room. The door was opened by a chocolate-dark Negro in a white starched jacket. There was a scrubbed look about him. His neatly trimmed hair was gray, and wire glasses sat smartly on his nose. Almost absently, Cappy noticed his shoes squeaked when he walked, a disconcerting sound.

'May I help you?' he said.

'I'm Miss Smith.' Marty calmly stepped forward.

'Of course.' The name mattered not – to either of them. He moved out of the doorway. 'Would you like to come in?'

'I'd like to go with her,' Cappy asserted, stepping to Marty's side.

The black gentleman hesitated, then politely inclined his head, granting permission. 'It isn't necessary, but you may observe if you wish.' His inflection betrayed an education, although a trace of southern accent remained.

The inner room was larger. At first, it appeared to be a storeroom for pharmaceutical supplies. However, behind the shelves and bins was a long table, standing beneath a bright ceiling light. The strong medicinal smells in the air were almost overpowering. A lighter-skinned Negro woman in a long white smock was standing by the table, of an age to be the man's wife or sister, her face unlined but her hair salty gray.

Modesty and dignity had little chance in this room. Outwardly, Marty appeared very casual, disrobing and climbing onto the table without a trace of awkwardness. Cappy couldn't tell what she was really feeling – remorse, fear, loneliness – and she did not want to know.

The black abortionist allowed Cappy to stand by the table and hold Marty's hand, more for her own moral support, since Marty didn't seem to need any. She kept her gaze fixed on Marty's face. She didn't want to know what those pink-palmed hands were doing between Marty's legs.

343

The minutes trickled by like slow-running grains of sand. She shut out the sound of half-muffled voices speaking in the shorthand of a close-working team. She felt hot.

When the white-smocked woman moved away from the table, Cappy glanced after her. Her gaze fell on the bloody placenta-covered embryo in the basin the woman carried, unrecognizable as anything human. She was shaken by the sight of it, and tried not to let it show.

The whole experience took on the hazy quality of a dream, something that really wasn't happening to her. When Marty came around, weakened more by the effects of the anesthesia than the operation, Cappy helped her out of the barren rooms and down the steep, narrow-walled staircase to the capital streets.

Back at the nurses' quarters, Marty lay down to rest and sleep off the drugs lingering in her system. Rid of her unwanted burden, she was almost back to her old, brassy self. 'You didn't really approve of all this, did you, Cappy?' she asked as she settled back onto the cot. 'I don't have any regrets. Why should you?'

Cappy left her without answering and went to sit in the large living room she shared with the nurses. She shouldn't have let it touch her, but it had gotten through the barriers. Somewhere there was someone to blame. Marty. The married officer who had impregnated her. The Army for its damned discriminatory system. Little unborn babies. At the disjointed connection, Cappy pressed her hands against her eyes.

Although oddly detached from her surroundings, Cappy vaguely knew others were around, moving, talking. Someone approached, invading that invisible sensory circle that enveloped her body. As she started to lower her hands, someone touched her shoulder. She looked around with a start, wanting to be alone and not welcoming company.

With a hitch of his trousers, Mitch folded his length onto the chair next to hers and leaned toward her. His look was warm, yet probing.

'Hi. Are you all right?'

Something close to anger or impatience flashed in the blue glitter of her eyes. She pushed to her feet before he could see more.

'I'm fine,' she insisted.

Mitch came slowly to his feet to stand next to her, studying her with closer interest and observing the unconscious toss of her head as she turned to look at him. Her temper was set against him, resisting him and wanting no part of him to intrude.

'What do you want? What are you doing here?' The words were a challenge.

But Mitch didn't respond to it. He had learned that that wasn't the way to handle her. 'Have you forgotten? We were to have dinner together tonight.'

Cappy dropped her gaze. 'I'm sorry. I did forget.' But there was more impatience than regret in her voice.

It stung him. 'Thanks,' he said, mocking her absence of artifice, then switched. As hard to fathom as she could be at times, this was not like her. 'What's wrong, Cap?' Before she could deny anything, he went on. 'Before I came out here, I called to make sure you were back from your flight. I was told you had switched with another pilot who was off duty. What's going on?'

'Nothing. A friend of mine – Marty Rogers, a girl I roomed with in Sweetwater – she had a couple days' leave and came by to visit.'

'In that case, I'll take you both out to dinner tonight,' Mitch offered.

'I don't think so.' She avoided his eyes. 'Marty's lying down. She wasn't feeling well.'

Something told Mitch he was close to the source of concern that preoccupied Cappy. He watched her, wondering what it was she held from him.

Someone swung into his side vision, drawing his glance. One look at the long, slim woman striding toward them and it clicked with a memory in his head. The name Marty Rogers hadn't meant anything to him until he saw the fair-haired woman with the lively face and those glittering gray-green eyes. No man could forget that earthy zest, that lusty sexuality that was refreshingly honest – and therefore somehow right.

'Hello. Major Ryan, this is a treat,' Marty declared in her throaty voice. 'Remember me? Marty Rogers from Sweetwater.'

'Of course.' Mitch clasped her hand and let his glance slide once again to Cappy. 'I had understood you weren't feeling well.'

There was a quick meeting of glances between the two young women, then Marty was declaring, hardly missing a beat, 'Whatever it was, I got rid of it. Now I need something to eat to get my strength back. Why don't we all have dinner together – and celebrate the occasion?'

'That's just what I suggested earlier.' He turned to Cappy, curious to see her reaction.

Her lips were red and full at the center, pressed firmly together in an expression of grim displeasure. Mitch was surprised to see a half-veiled dislike shimmering in the look she gave her friend. His own gaze narrowed, but when Cappy saw him watching her, she quickly wiped all expression from her face.

'If you feel up to it, we'll go,' she said to Marty, but something ran under the surface of her words, something pointed and hard.

'I never let little things bother me very much,' Marty answered. 'It's better than going through life like you do, always on guard against the slightest hurt and never living at all.'

Mitch was amused by the little flashing of claws between them, the little bitchiness. He glanced over at Cappy, and saw her consider the observation Marty had made, wondering at its accuracy.

'It'll take me a few minutes to get ready, then we can go,' Cappy said.

As she walked away from them, Cappy came close to hating Marty. It was one thing, she felt, to accept the abortion as the only recourse open to her, but it was entirely another to be jubilant about the outcome. Cappy was disgusted by Marty's desire to celebrate. She couldn't understand that kind of callous indifference.

But Cappy was too caught up in the pullings and tuggings of her own ambivalent attitude to see the brittleness underlying Marty's ostensibly high spirits. The deed was done and though Marty was never one to look back with regret, she couldn't wipe away her sense of loss. Yet it was not so much grief Marty felt as failure. Marty had looked at herself and seen that she could never live up to her image of an ideal woman, the faithful wife, the adoring mother, and the happy homemaker. She had been born without the nesting instinct.

But she recognized it in others, just as she recognized all the moves of the mating ritual, the life coupling between male and female. During dinner, Marty saw the signs of it between Mitch and Cappy, the courting passes he made, the attempts to attract her interest, and the blind eye Cappy turned to all of them, the elusive way she kept slipping from him.

Something went wrong with the evening; Marty could feel it even while she laughed too loudly, drank too much, and flirted too often with the handsome major. In a way, she did it to rile Cappy – out of jealousy maybe, because she had what Marty didn't. But Cappy simply turned moody and quiet, withdrawing behind that self-sufficient pose of hers. And Mitch – Marty could almost feel sorry for him. He appeared to be losing ground with Cappy instead of making headway.

'Thanks for the evening, Major,' Marty said when he escorted the two of them back to the barracks. 'My train ticket's taking me out of here in the morning so I won't see you again before I leave. I'll say goodbye now and leave you alone with Cappy to . . . have your good nights.'

His brown eyes were faintly gleaming, thanking her for the moments he'd have with the silent brunette. The night air was briskly cool, but Marty didn't think he'd notice.

She'd known too many men not to recognize those urges, disciplined though they were for the time being. The major was a strong, handsome man, potently combining an easy charm with a shrewd intelligence. If she didn't owe Cappy something, she might have thrown up some competition for him.

'I'm glad you felt well enough to join us,' Mitch said graciously, then sent a puzzled glance at Cappy when she visibly stiffened.

'Old "button-lip" will never tell you, Major, but I think you should know the reason I was feeling "indisposed" earlier. I had an abortion,' Marty announced carelessly. 'A man and a woman shouldn't have secrets between them. And there's no need for you to wonder whether Cappy was lying to you earlier when she said I was sick and how I happened to have such a miraculous recovery.' There was a certain wryness, a self-mockery almost, in her voice. The confession was a way of repaying the debt she owed Cappy by eliminating any possible mistrust. 'Goodbye, Major.' With her good deed done, Marty left them and entered the barracks building.

At Marty's announcement, Mitch had gone rigid. When the door shut, his words exploded in a low rush.

'My God, you let her?' he said accusingly.

'I arranged it!' Cappy snapped, his fire striking her flint. Somehow she had known how he would react. 'She came to me. What was I supposed to do?'

'You could have refused,' Mitch replied stiffly.

'And have her wind up in the hands of some butcher?' she challenged in a taut, hurt voice. 'She was my friend. She didn't want the baby. What was I supposed to suggest? Using knitting needles or inhaling paint fumes?' Impatient, she looked away from him. 'What do men know about it? It isn't your life and it isn't your body. Most of the time, you don't even want to claim it's your responsibility. You take the Army's attitude – if the girl gets pregnant, tough. You know what would have happened if they had found out she was going to have a baby. They would have grounded her, or washed her out altogether because she wasn't married.'

'Does flying mean more than the life of an unborn baby?'

'To some it does,' Cappy flared.

His hands caught her shoulders and swung her around to face him squarely. 'To you?' His dark gaze burrowed into her.

Her glance fell, ever so slightly. 'No.' She couldn't do what Marty had done; that wouldn't have been her choice.

'I knew it.' The low, exultant words rushed out of him, vibrant with satisfaction.

The press of his hands brought her into his circling arms while his mouth came down to cover hers. The hot, fierce urgency of his kiss was consuming, firing her skin with its heat and pressuring a response that would match the fever of his needs.

When he drew back, his breath spilled in a moist, hot wave over her face and his restless, needing gaze went over every feature. 'I love you, Cap.' His voice vibrated in his throat. 'I've always loved you.' He stroked her hair with a trembling hand, smoothing the dark silk strands and touching its softness. 'I want to marry you, Cap. I want you to be my wife.'

The words ran coldly through her system, and a rejection of all he offered erased the inroads he had made on her will. Her hands pushed at his chest.

'No.' It was a choked refusal, too much pain lodging in her throat.

Mitch didn't believe her protestations after tasting her willingness and her answering passion. Instead, he read another reason into her denial and attempted to assuage it.

'I'm not saying we should get married right away,' he murmured, not letting her go, and continuing to let his hands roam while he held her. 'I know how you feel about the war and the future uncertainty. We'll wait until it's over to have the wedding. In the meantime, though, I want you to be wearing my ring. I –'

'No!' Her hands hit at his chest, surprising him with her violence, and his arms loosened around her. Cappy pushed free, twisting angrily out of his hold. 'I won't marry you – not now and certainly not later! I wouldn't marry you if you were the only man on earth!!'

Stunned, Mitch stared at her, his brows pulling together in a frown. 'What are you talking about? You don't mean that.'

'I do,' she insisted, breathing hard from the great pain in her chest. 'I won't ever marry you, Mitch.'

'Why?' Beneath the growl of his voice was an anguished demand.

'If I marry you, it means I marry the Army – and I'll die before I do that.' The words were wrenched from her, as tortured in their anger as his. 'I was an Army brat – never having a home or friends – and I swore I'd never be an Army wife. And I won't! If you want me . . . if you love me . . . you'll quit the Army.'

'There's a war –' Mitch began angrily.

'After the war!' she hurled back at him.

Silence pressed on them, the late winter chill finally touching them. His lips came together in a long, firm line as Mitch grimly eyed her. Cappy had known the answer to her ultimatum the minute she made it. Looking at him now, she didn't even need his words to confirm it.

'You can't ask a man to give up his career and think you'll be happy together.'

'You can't ask a woman to live a life she despises,' she countered in a rasping tone.

'Dammit, Cappy,' Mitch swore, his head turning away to hide the stinging in his eyes. 'I love you.'

'Not as much as you love the Army.'

'You've gone all right by the Army,' he flared. 'It's been good to you.'

'The Army has never given me anything. I've earned everything I've got.' The cool temperature turned her moist breath into puffs of smoky vapor, trailing exclamation marks that punctuated her words.

'You're wrong,' Mitch stated flatly. 'This job – this plum of flying assignments – you never earned it.'

'But . . . you told me that my father had nothing to do with it,' Cappy reminded him with a narrowed, suspicious look.

'He didn't. I did the string-pulling.' His strong, lean jaw didn't let the words out. He pushed them through his teeth, his lip curling back as Mitch roughly spoke them. 'I wanted you close at hand . . . where I could see you.'

'That was your mistake, Mitch,' she said. 'But I'll see if I can't correct it for you.'

CHAPTER TWENTY-FOUR

The southern California air shimmered with the silken distortions of a heat wave. Fresh from a flight in a fast and powerful P-47 pursuit, Mary Lynn was still trapped in the exhilarating spell of the hottest plane around. When she recognized Marty standing on the sun-warmed concrete of the flight apron, she thought it was a mirage.

A second later, she knew better, and broke into a running walk. 'I don't believe it! What are you doing here?' she cried in delight.

Between the hugs and laughter, the how-are-yous and I'm-fines, Marty gave her a rough synopsis of how she came to leave the four-engines, toning it down some and making it more of a lark and a misunderstanding so she wouldn't be placed in such a bad light. 'So I got my hands slapped and sent out here.'

'He was married?' That part troubled Mary Lynn, although she was loath to be critical of Marty.

'Hey, Scott and I were friends,' Marty insisted, deliberately implying her innocence. 'They made a big deal out of it.' By mutual accord, they left the flight line to seek the shady interior of the operations building. 'I saw Cappy while I was in DC,' Marty volunteered, but she left out any mention of the abortion.

'How was she?'

'Fine. She hasn't changed much.' Marty shrugged. 'She still walks around life rather than reaching out to embrace it. I guess that's why she flies – to soar above all of life's problems into an aesthetically pure sky.' Marty the astute.

'Don't we all,' Mary Lynn murmured.

'Not me.' Marty dropped a coin into the Coke machine and listened to the tumbling jangle as it tripped the lever and fell into the money box. 'You can bet I wouldn't let that major of hers walk around hungry if he were mine.'

Mary Lynn shied away from any speculation about Cappy's personal relationships. There was too big a hole in her own life. It had been too long since she'd had a man's company. Some nights, she felt the lonely ache for it, a need shared by thousands of other wives across the country whose husbands had gone to war – the simple yearning to feel a man's touch and once more to have the warmth of his body in the bed. With a faint shake of her head, she tried to dismiss such thoughts.

'Is Eden around?' Marty passed her a Coke bottle and turned back to the machine to get another for herself.

'No. She left a couple days ago to deliver a P-38 to Newark. It's anybody's guess when she'll be back. You don't always get orders to ferry another plane back. Usually it's some round-robin jaunt, dropping off planes in Farmington, Indiana, or Great Falls, or Dallas, and picking up new ones. If you're really unlucky,' Mary Lynn added, 'you catch a train back.'

'The glamorous life of a ferry pilot,' Marty remarked wryly, and she lifted the Coke bottle to her lips.

They drifted away from the machine, paying little attention to the other pilots and base personnel in the ready room. Some pored over tech manuals or cross-country maps, and others were simply winding down from the final leg of a return flight. The place was busy; it was a major

352

clearing house for one of the largest domestic ferrying divisions and soon to be home for the largest contingent of women pilots in the country.

'I won't be staying long this trip myself,' Marty said. A wry gleam was in her gray-green eyes as she met the questioning look Mary Lynn gave her. 'It's one of the Army's usual boners. They've got me – a multiengine-rated pilot with heavy bomber experience – and they're sending me to Palm Springs for pursuit training.'

'P-47 Thunderbolts and P-51 Mustangs are going out of here like crazy.' The demand for qualified pilots to fly the hot pursuits was a sufficient explanation for Mary Lynn. 'Wait until you fly one of them. There's only room for one pilot in the Thunderbolt – so your first flight is solo. But you'll love it.' She beamed with the fierce joy that came from sitting at the controls. 'In most of the planes we've flown, a hundred, a hundred ten miles an hour was a good speed. The P-47 *stalls* at a hundred and five.'

'Yeah, they say bomber pilots need a lot of guts, stamina, and leadership ability, and the fighter pilots are lone wolves – daredevils. I've heard that when they check a pilot out in a pursuit, they fail him if he can count to ten because he thinks too hard.' Smiling at her own joke, Marty glanced at a dark-haired woman walking by, dressed in gray-green slacks and a light gray shirt. She nudged Mary Lynn with her elbow and nodded in the direction of the female pilot in the unusual uniform. 'Who is she?'

'A WAF, part of Nancy Love's group before we were all brought under the umbrella of the Women Airforce Service Pilots.' The WAFs were an elite group of experienced female pilots, former aircraft instructors, racing pilots, or barnstormers, who were incorporated almost directly into the Air Transport Command as a separate ferrying squadron at the outset. 'They have their own uniforms.'

'I wonder when we're ever going to get ours,' Marty sighed. Mary Lynn tipped her head to the side and rubbed at the knotted muscles in her neck. Her glance skipped past the nearest group of pilots, hangar-flying around a table, and fell haphazardly on a man lazing in a corner of the ready room. One leg was stretched across the width of a chair seat while his other foot hooked the side rung to act as a ballast as he rocked his own chair onto its back legs. He was a study of indolence, with his officer's cap sitting sideways on his head, the bill dipping over one eye.

Something about him – that lazy attitude or the rake of the hat on his head – for a split second reminded Mary Lynn of Beau. But the resemblance ended there. He looked every bit of thirty or older; his face was lined, and his skin was pitted and unnaturally scarred. That hint of a smile on his mouth seemed infected with a hard, cruel humor, and insinuating interest glittered in his dark eyes.

His gaze was boldly traveling the full length of her body and taking note of every curve along the way. She looked away, her heart striking quick, small beats. Amidst all the talking voices and walking footsteps, she heard the sound of the chair coming down on all four legs.

Soon, a drawling male voice said, 'What's a little thing like you doing here?' Mary Lynn didn't turn when Marty looked around, but she was aware of the slow-moving man drifting toward them. 'Don't tell me you're flying those big, bad planes out there.'

It was a deliberately condescending remark, designed to elicit a response. 'Are you talking to me?' Mary Lynn gave him a falsely blank look.

'No one else,' he said lazily.

Marty's gaze narrowed on him, conscious that Mary Lynn was the focus of his attention. She took note of the captain's bars on his uniform. She was almost certain she'd seen him somewhere before.

'Don't I know you?' Marty frowned.

His dark glance skimmed her once and dismissed her. 'No.' His interest centered again on Mary Lynn as he pushed the officer's cap to the back of his head. Thick, unruly hair, the color of Army coffee, strayed onto his forehead. 'What do you say, Little One?'

From the first, something had told Marty this man was trouble in capital letters, and the obvious play he was making for Mary Lynn merely confirmed it. Her dislike of the man was instinctive as Marty observed the stiff and agitated way Mary Lynn avoided the man's look. Marrying young, and to her childhood sweetheart, it wasn't likely Mary Lynn had come across many wolves like this one.

'You're a little off base, Captain,' Marty informed him.

'Walker. Captain Samuel Jamieson Walker.' He introduced himself with a mock bow to Mary Lynn. 'But you can just call me Walker.'

'She's married.' Marty bridled.

'Is that right?' He seemed amused by the discovery rather than put off by it. 'I promise I won't hold that against you over dinner tonight.'

'Dinner?' The word broke from Mary Lynn in surprise.

'I told you she wasn't interested, Captain,' Marty interposed in a cold and naturally husky voice.

'Does she always do your talking, Little One?' he mocked. 'Or don't you have a tongue? Now, that would be a pity.'

'Please.' Mary Lynn felt hot all over, an anger flashing at his continued impudence. 'I am married so I'm not interested.'

'A pretty little wife,' he marveled. Lifting her chin with the tip of his finger, he continued, 'Would you just look at all that goodness shining out of her?'

His eyes admired what his tongue mocked. But there was something bitter behind his taunting humor, and Mary Lynn jerked away from his touch, hurt and bewildered by his behavior. Marty was instantly at her side, aggressively shielding her.

'Why don't you pick on somebody your own size, Captain,' she challenged.

Those hard, laughing eyes skimmed Marty, testing, probing, measuring; then he was shrugging. 'It isn't as much fun,' he said, backing away while Marty glared at him. She had the feeling he was just biding his time until he saw another opening.

'Come on. Let's get out of here,' she said under her breath to Mary Lynn and both of them headed out of the ready room.

Still dressed in his full military regalia, medals and ribbons pinned to his jacket breast, the AAF Commanding General 'Hap' Arnold sat behind his big wooden desk, pushed back in his large chair. The meeting with the House Committee on Military Affairs on Capitol Hill had not gone as smoothly as he had expected.

March was on its way out, but it was an irritated lion who was rumbling over the opposition he'd encountered from the congressional committee over the proposed bill to militarize the WASPs, as had been done with the WACs, and the WAVES the year before. The bill had been presented to Congress in February. In the past, anything the Commanding General had wanted for the war effort had been routinely approved.

'They didn't ask me a half-dozen questions about the WASPs,' the general snorted. 'Typical Congress, there were only two things they were concerned about – whether the women were paid and if they flew in combat situations. I explained again that they were not being used in war zones – that they were replacing men in domestic operations to free them for combat roles. That was all they needed to hear, they said. Then they started asking me questions about the shutdown of all the primary cadet flying schools we closed in January.'

In quick, sharp taps, Mitch Ryan hit his cigarette on the hard surface of the chair arm, tamping the tobacco and releasing some of his held-in anger at the subject matter under discussion. Women pilots were a sore topic with him, heart-sensitive as he was to anything that reminded him of Cappy.

Two weeks ago, one of the staff personnel from that department had called him aside and advised him that Cappy had put in a request for a transfer. It would have been a simple matter to block it, as he had maneuvered other things in the past. This time he hadn't stepped in, leaving it to be granted or turned down by someone else. With a certain fatalism, he felt whichever way the cards fell would be a sign, an indication of whether things could ever be worked out between them or not.

When Mitch had learned the request had gone through, he had gritted his teeth so no one would know how much it mattered. But it ground at him, turning him bitter and angry.

'We all knew there'd be some heat from those civilian pilots,' he replied in response to the general's previous statement. Roughly fourteen thousand men, instructors and trainees, had lost their jobs and their draft-deferred status. They were being called to active duty and assigned ground jobs.

'Yes. And those that qualify are being signed up as pilots. But I'll be damned if I'll lower the physical and intellectual standards of our pilots for them. It seems strange to me that now that these pilots have lost their safe, noncombat instructor's jobs, they are suddenly clamoring for the more dangerous assignments the WASPs have undertaken – like towing targets and testing planes coming out of the repair depots.' The general did not think much of these grousing Johnny-come-latelies, and it showed. 'Look at the morale problems we had with the male pilots over the B-26. They were half scared to fly the damned "Flying prostitute" until the women climbed into the cockpits and showed them how it was done. Hell, my own son's unit would never have qualified for an overseas assignment if a WASP hadn't willingly towed targets for the rough-terrain practice. The male pilots at Camp Irwin refused to do it.'

'Yes, sir. I know,' Mitch responded dutifully.

Rough-terrain maneuvers required armored vehicles, called half-tracks, to tear across open country at forty miles an hour while the gunners operating the fifty-caliber guns mounted on its back shot at an aerial target. With all the bumps, dips and gulleys it was invariably a wild ride, and the shooting was often equally wild until the gunners got the hang of it.

'Dammit, those girls are entitled to the same privileges and benefits the Army pilots receive,' General Arnold insisted impatiently. 'The committee says it's going to recommend passage, but we haven't heard the last of those pilots, I'm afraid.'

'I doubt that we have.' He rolled the burning tip of the cigarette around the inside rim of an ashtray, watching the paper-thin flakes of gray ash fall off.

'The whole complexion of the war is changing.' The chair creaked under the movement of his solid weight as General Arnold shifted to sit with shoulders squared. 'We're on the move. Those boys are off the Anzio beachhead and pounding their way to Rome. Our air raids have crippled their aircraft industry and we can start concentrating on the Germans' transportation and oil refineries. And the airfields in France. Britain is bulging with troops for Ike's Overlord operation. We not only have to soften the bastards up, but we've got to give air cover for our guys when they go in.'

'I've been wanting to talk to you about that, sir.' Mitch crushed out his cigarette and grimly faced his general. 'With the big push on . . . I want to be part of it. I want to be there when it happens, not . . . tucked away in some damned office. I want a transfer, sir.'

'The hell you do.' The challenging response was flattened by a kind of offhandedness. 'I doubt if you're alone in that.'

'You're going to need good pilots, qualified men to make these strikes. I've seen some of the estimates of losses for these planned raids on the oil refineries in Rumania, Hamburg, and the Ruhr,' Mitch argued.

'A soldier serves his country best where he's needed. And you are needed here. Transfer denied,' the general snapped impatiently. 'You surprise me, Mitch. I never expected you to stoop to such unprofessional heroics. You know damned well you've got a job to do here – a damned important one. I'll be the first to admit there isn't much glory in pushing papers around, but it has to be done.'

'Yes, sir.' Mitch grudgingly gave in, not liking it and not trying to hide it.

'I don't want to hear any more talk about transfers.' The general picked up a sheaf of papers on his desk and began glancing through them, muttering his displeasure under his breath. 'Grandstand play. Anybody'd think some gal singed your feelings.' He stopped to peer at Mitch. 'Haven't seen that Hayward girl with you in a while.'

'No, sir,' he admitted. 'It seems she doesn't like the Army.'

'It's probably just as well.' 'Hap' Arnold looked back at the papers. 'After today, I'm afraid it's going to be a fight to get her . . . and the rest of the women pilots . . . into the Army Air Force.'

Mary Lynn's orders instructed her to deliver the spanking new P-47 Thunderbolt to the Embarkation Center in Newark, but such flights in planes fresh off the assembly lines were seldom routine. There always seemed to be a few bugs in them somewhere and Mary Lynn found a problem in the flaps' hydraulic system which forced her to land in Tulsa.

While the Thunderbolt went to the hangar for repairs, Mary Lynn was given a new set of orders to deliver a P-39 Aircobra to Great Falls, Montana, a staging base for planes bound for Alaska, Russian lend-lease fighters. From Great Falls it was a PT-19 to Nevada, and a hop over the Sierra Mountains in a P-51 Mustang. In all, her two-day trip turned into four, ferrying four planes and covering approximately three thousand miles.

She had barely set foot inside the WASPs' barracks at Long Beach when Eden grabbed her. 'Come on. I've got something to show you.'

'What did you buy this time?' Mary Lynn assumed she had indulged in another one of her wild shopping sprees, almost a regular event since they'd been stationed in Los Angeles.

But Eden merely laughed and pushed Mary Lynn into her room, where she told her to sit on the cot. Then Eden darted to the door of her own room, an impishly gleeful light in her dark eyes. A tired smile lifted the corners of her mouth as Mary Lynn shook her head and leaned against the wall to wait for the expected fashion parade.

The door opened and Eden's voice began intoning, 'And here is Cappy Hayward.' Mary Lynn's heavy-lidded glance went to the doorway as Cappy came into view. Her eyes immediately widened in stunned surprise. 'You will notice she is wearing a belted jacket of wool serge and a matching skirt in fashion's latest color, Santiago blue. The outfit is completed with the deep blue color repeated in the tam she wears. The snowy white blouse provides a contrast to the suit, adorned with silver wings and a gold WASP insignia.'

'What are you doing here? And in our new uniform?' Mary Lynn released a bewildered breath at the sight of Cappy modeling the uniform suit, slowly turning with arms shifting and posing in mock stances.

'Miss van Valkenburg, you will see, is wearing' – Eden continued her mock recital as she swirled into the room, crowding the small floor space – 'slacks and the Eisenhower jacket, a sure choice for high fashion, in Santiago blue.'

The pseudo fashion show fell apart as Mary Lynn scooted off the cot. 'You look gorgeous, Cappy. When did you get here? Did you fly someone here?'

Eden jumped in with the explanation. 'She's been transferred here. Isn't that wonderful? She's been assigned to the Sixth Ferrying Group, too.'

'You're kidding.'

'It's true,' Cappy assured the disbelieving Mary Lynn. 'I'm going to be flying the C-47 Skytrains from the McDonnell Douglas factory to various bases around the country.'

'We're all going to be flying together again,' she marveled. 'Marty said she saw you in Washington so you know

360

she's going to be joining us. She's in Palm Springs right now, finishing the last two weeks of the pursuit course.'

'Yes, I know.' Cappy nodded, but carefully said nothing more.

'I can't believe it.' Mary Lynn shook her head again. 'You're here . . . and our uniforms.'

'Wait until you see the flying suits,' Eden declared and dragged out her regulation jumpsuit, in that same deep blue color that was to become their trademark.

'Did I get mine, too?' Mary Lynn wondered belatedly.

'We picked it up for you,' Eden assured her, then cautioned, 'Don't get too excited though. In case you haven't noticed, we've been issued winter uniforms. Wool . . . in sunny, southern California.' The absurdity of it was obvious. 'Supposedly the summer uniforms are on their way.'

But winter uniforms were better than none at all. For Mary Lynn, just the thought of wearing an outfit measured to fit her small frame was a special bonus. All three of them piled into Mary Lynn's room while she tried on the Army issue of two jackets, a skirt, slacks and flight suits. She had saved one of her shoe ration stamps just for the new uniforms when they came.

Standing in front of the mirror, Mary Lynn studied her reflection, the cut of the deeply blue uniform on her petite frame and the set of the English-style tam on her raven hair. She reached up to touch the silver wings on her lapel, smaller than the regulation pilot wings, and traced the satin-finished silver lozenge in the center that had replaced the shield in the new regulation wings.

'I think I'm going to miss my old wings. They were special,' she said, not really needing to explain to Eden and Cappy. 'They're the ones we started with.'

'I know,' Cappy said with an agreeing look of regret. 'I heard the lozenge is supposed to represent the shield of the Amazons.'

'What does that make us?' Eden retorted. 'Mythical female warriors?'

'I suppose.' Cappy smiled faintly.

Mary Lynn swung away from the mirror. 'Why don't we go celebrate tonight?'

At the Officers' Club that evening they made an occasion of it, dining on the best steaks and ordering wine. No French brands were available so Eden decided they would sample a burgundy from one of the California wineries. Three unescorted females in the male-dominated club created a stir of interest and countless invitations to provide them with male company. But they kept the dinner strictly among the three of them.

'When I was in Great Falls –' Mary Lynn paused to sip cautiously at the after-dinner drink Eden had ordered for her. '– a WASP from the Romulus Base in Michigan was telling me why we aren't allowed to fly the ferry route from Great Falls to Fairbanks, Alaska, and only men can.'

'I always thought they were worried one of us might go down in those frozen wastes and maybe die from exposure.' A perplexed frown drew lines in Cappy's forehead as she eyed Mary Lynn, suddenly suspecting that wasn't the reason.

'So did I,' Mary Lynn agreed. 'But it seems some of the men have been stationed in Alaska for almost two years. They aren't afraid we might get killed flying there. They are worried about what might happen to us . . . on a base with all those men who haven't seen a woman in months.'

Eden laughed. 'It certainly doesn't speak very well of the men stationed there.'

'When I was flying out of Washington,' Cappy inserted, 'I landed at some bases that didn't have nurses' quarters and I stayed in the BOQ with men sleeping in the next bed and only a screen between us.' She shook her head in faint disgust. 'Half the time the Army doesn't make any sense.'

'I'll drink to that,' Eden agreed, and she lifted her glass.

After dinner, they took their celebration into the lounge side of the club. Few tables were empty. When they appeared, officers eager for their company scrambled to pull out chairs. In a laughing eeny-meeny-miney-mo atti-tude, they picked a table. Once they were seated, the men fell all over themselves to crowd around it.

Except one, Mary Lynn realized, as she recognized that hardened captain sitting on the edge of the circle and watching the other officers with a detached amusement. Then his lazy, half-lidded glance swung to her.

'Celebrating?' The small slur in his voice led Mary Lynn to suspect the drink in his hand was not the first of the evening.

'Is that why you're here, Captain?' she returned instead.

'I'm always here – from the time they open to the time they close.' He looked at Mary Lynn. 'Whatever possessed your husband to let you out of his sight, Little One? If you were mine, I'd keep you under lock and key.'

Few were so boldly disrespectful of her marital status. Mary Lynn avoided more than fleeting contact with his glance, unsure whether she should be offended or flattered by the attention he gave her.

'That would be difficult, since he flies B-17s in the Eighth Air Force.' She took a cigarette from the pack on the table.

Before she could strike a match to light it, a flame was in front of her, the match held between Walker's fingers. It wavered slightly, and Mary Lynn steadied his hand with her own. The rough texture of a man's hand was a sensation she'd almost forgotten.

'Your husband's a pilot with the Eighth? Where?' He watched the release of smoke from her lips.

'In England.'

'Whereabouts? I was stationed over there, too. Maybe I know him.' He leaned back in his chair, a complacent smile tugging at the corners of his mouth, fully aware of the carrot he dangled.

'In the Cotswold area – somewhere near Gloucester-shire, I think.' Beau had never been able to give her too much specific information as to the location or the censors wouldn't pass the letter. Mary Lynn eyed Walker, hardly daring hope he might know Beau.

'Well, isn't that a coincidence,' he murmured.

'You were there?'

'For a while.' His half-smile became more pronounced, containing considerably less humor and warmth. 'But I fooled the Army and survived all those missions over Germany.'

That hard, embittered statement explained some things Mary Lynn hadn't understood. Those lines in his face and the cynicism in his eyes were products of that combat experience. It had given him those silver strands in his dark hair and made him old – and hard – beyond his years.

As she gazed at him, she wondered if Beau would come home to her like this. She felt a cold chill raise her flesh and absently rubbed a hand over her upper arm to rid herself of the sensation. She shook away the unpleasant thought and leaned forward, going for the long shot.

'Did you know him? My husband – Beau Palmer.' The cigarette was left to burn itself out in the ashtray as her earnest gaze watched him.

'The first time I saw you, you looked familiar to me.' Walker let his gaze wander over her face, lingering on each feature. 'I'll bet I've seen a picture of you. He probably has one, doesn't he?'

'Yes. It was taken on the beach. He has it in the cockpit.'

'That's it,' Walker said with a snap of his fingers. The music playing in the background changed tempo as the band, consisting of soldier-musicians from the base, began a slow tune. Taking her by the hand, he urged Mary Lynn to her feet. 'Let's dance.'

His hand at the small of her back guided Mary Lynn through the maze of tables to the dance floor. A thousand questions about Beau raced through her mind as she turned into Walker's arms.

'How long has it been since you've seen him? How did he look?' She paused at the amused expression on his face and realized she was starting to rattle like an excited child.

364

'I suppose I sound silly to you, Captain. But you don't know how happy it makes me to meet someone who's talked to Beau.'

'Let's drop the Captain and call me Walker,' he suggested while his arm curved around her lower back, molding her hip to thigh. 'And you don't know how happy this makes me.' That small smile on his mouth suggested many things, none of them related to her husband.

Mary Lynn had a moment of unease as he bent his head and carried the sensitive ends of her fingers to his lips. 'How was he?' She raised the subject of Beau again.

'Fine, as far as I know.' His knowing eyes watched the growing disturbance in her expression with a certain satisfaction. He continued his absent nibbling of her fingertips. 'That photograph didn't do you justice, Little One.'

Beyond a token shifting of feet, he was barely moving to the music. The smell of rum was strong on his breath. Mary Lynn blamed his behavior on the considerable quantity of alcohol he had consumed.

'About Beau –' she tried again.

'What about him?' Walker turned her hand palm upward and investigated the center with a nuzzling mouth.

The sensuous action prompted a little quiver of pleasure to run down her nerve ends. At the traitorous reaction, Mary Lynn strained to draw her hand down. Walker lifted his head at her show of resistance.

'Sorry.' But he didn't sound sorry. 'I got carried away. It's easy with a little thing like you in my arms.'

She chose to ignore his remarks. 'Tell me about Beau.'

His attention drifted from her in a bored fashion. 'What do you want to hear?'

'Anything. Everything.' It was difficult to be specific when any detail would suffice, any piece of Beau's life held importance, anything that would make where he was and what he was doing seem real to her. 'What's it like over there?' Mary Lynn meant England, the air base, the barracks – the place where he lived.

But Walker put another construction on the question

and his expression turned cold and forbidding. 'What's any war like?' he challenged harshly. 'It's about killing and dying. It's faceless enemies shooting at you, and bombs dropping on faceless victims. It's a living hell.'

Up close, she could see the graveled marks that scarred his face, recent wounds in a random pattern, like splintering glass or metal. She tried not to think how it might have happened, but a kind of terror clutched her throat. Her mind recoiled from the kind of war-horror Walker's words depicted in favor of the glory of a Hollywood war. She wanted to believe Beau was taking part in the latter.

'I'm sorry.' She felt so cold.

Then her skin was warmed by the moist heat of his rum-tainted breath along the side of her cheek. 'You are beautiful enough to make me forget all the ugliness.' His arm tightened around her while his mouth buried itself in the silken curls of her black hair.

Just for an instant Mary Lynn failed to protest, letting her flesh recall the feel of a man's body pressed against it – and letting his embrace melt that icy shaft of fear that Beau might never hold her like this again.

'You were saying about Beau.' She pushed firmly at his chest and lowered her head to draw a few inches away from him.

'Ah yes, Beau.' His low voice mocked her choice of subject. 'Let's see – what do I remember about him?' He lifted a shoulder in a careless shrug, then bent his head, angling toward her lips.

'Please,' Mary Lynn protested under her breath, and turned her head aside.

'Please what?' Walker challenged in faint amusement, not raising his head. It was only inches from her averted face.

'You shouldn't be making these advances to a married woman,' she said stiffly, a very prim tone in her soft, southern voice.

'I can't help thinking that if Beau had known I'd be seeing you he would have asked me to give you this.' As his mouth neared the corner of her lips, Mary Lynn turned, ever so slightly, to let him find them.

But it wasn't the shattering sweet recall of Beau's kiss that Mary Lynn experienced. The pressure of Walker's lips obliterated any memory of her husband's gentleness, imprinting his own rougher brand of masculinity that cared nothing about tenderness and the sweet sentiment of love. In confusion, Mary Lynn broke off the kiss, never guessing she could respond to one man's kiss when she loved another.

'It's been a long time, hasn't it?' Those lazy knowing eyes studied her.

'I don't know what you're talking about.' She lied rather than admit there were physical needs, longings to be touched that had no basis in emotions.

The song ended, but his hand kept her from turning completely away from him.

'Yes, you do,' Walker asserted. 'Your Beau is going through the same thing, only it's worse for him because of the need to reaffirm life before he goes to – maybe – meet death. For him, there's always that kind of woman around to satisfy his urge. Wives usually aren't that lucky.'

'Are you trying to tell me Beau has been unfaithful?' It seemed a cheap trick to play on her fears and jealousies.

'Do you honestly believe he's been celibate all this time you've been apart?' Walker jeered.

'It's none of your business what I believe.'

He was slow to respond as his cynical gaze thoughtfully studied her defiant expression. 'Maybe not,' he conceded. 'But I have my own beliefs. What's good for the gander should be good for the goose. Why should you go to sleep all tied up in knots when he doesn't?'

'Stop it.' She couldn't stand any more of his cruel insinuations about Beau's infidelity. She pulled her arm free of his hold and walked blindly toward the table.

Pausing, Walker watched her run away without a glimmer of remorse. Such a beautiful little creature with raven hair and eyes. She was running . . . straight into his arms, eventually. He knew.

CHAPTER TWENTY-FIVE

An ominous squall line of dark clouds loomed in the path of the racing, sleek P-51 Mustang. Eden pulled her gaze away from them to look at charts on her lap. At her last stop, they had warned her about the summer storm front along her route from Fort Myers to New Castle, but she had decided to fly as far as she could until the weather forced her to land. Her worry faded when she saw the Army base located near her present position. It wasn't the closest, but she could make it to Camp Davis, North Carolina, before the storm reached it.

In the swift-running Mustang, Eden made her approach to the swamp-surrounded field. She didn't look at that fire-scorched spot where Rachel's plane had crashed and burned. She landed the hot pursuit and taxied to the flight line. Pilots were streaming from the ready room to stare at the fighter plane all of them ached to fly. After cutting the engine, she pushed back the canopy and climbed out of the cockpit onto the wing.

A strong breeze ran ahead of the black storm clouds and swept thick strands of her titian hair across her face. She heard the male pilots' murmurs of shock that it had been a female at the controls of the powerhouse fighter, but she missed the stunned look on Bubba's face, the unbridled ache in his eyes at the sight of her, posed on the Mustang's wing.

Pilots from the tow-target squadron, male and female alike, crowded around Eden and the plane, asking endless questions. She didn't have a chance to speak to Bubba at all. The first fat raindrops sent everyone scurrying for cover before the storm broke. Eden retrieved her briefcase from the cockpit and ran between the drops to the operations office.

No improvement in the weather, she was told, was expected. Overcast skies and thundershowers were forecast for the next three days – through the weekend. She filed a RON, which meant Remain Over Night, one of the Army's endless acronyms, adding the code for weather as the cause. All movement of aircraft was considered top secret and the ferry pilots used a code to keep their home base informed where the plane was and why it was grounded.

After the first warning splatter of rain, it had stopped. The sky had turned prematurely dark and threatening. Eden ran across to the hangar area, scanning the ground crew working hurriedly to secure the aircraft on the flight line. Bubba was standing inside the towering doors, talking to one of the other mechanics. When he observed Eden's approach, he said something to the young corporal and the man left.

Conscious of the blood heating her veins, Eden stopped in front of Bubba, her brown eyes radiant at the familiar sight of his wonderful, broad-featured face. His hazel eyes smiled at her, crinkling at the corners.

'Long time, no see,' she murmured inadequately.

'Yeah.'

The place was too public, too open; too many eyes witnessed their meeting. Frustrated, Eden let it show.

'It looks like I'll be grounded for the weekend,' she told him. After looking around to see if anyone was close enough to listen, she lowered the pitch of her voice. 'Can you get a pass?'

'Hell, I'll kill to get it if I have to.' His extravagant assertion relieved some of the tension and brought a hint of a smile to both faces.

'I'll meet you in Wilmington at ten o'clock on Saturday. Where?' she asked.

'Greenfield Lake,' Bubba suggested.

'Okay.' Out of the corner of her eye, Eden was aware of two members of the ground crew coming their way. She backed away before they aroused too much interest and speculation. 'See you then.'

The rain-washed air was heavy with humidity. Low clouds carrying the threat of more moisture turned the sky a dark translucent oyster gray, pearlized and thick. Eden stood on the bank of Greenfield Lake, moss-draped cypress trees rising out of the water before her on their long, sinewy roots. Diamond beads of rainwater weighted the scarlet-pink azalea blooms and they drooped on the bushes, the spring profusion of blossoms waning with the advent of summer and spreading a red-pink carpet of petals on the wet ground.

Voices that had been a low murmur in the background suddenly broke into shrill, female laughter. Eden half turned to look their way. A trio of soldiers had obviously said something funny to two teenaged girls sauntering by them, hips waggling invitations while their red, red lips signaled encouragement over their shoulders. Finally, the girls stopped to let the soldiers catch up to them.

As she watched the byplay, Eden heard the whooshing run of bicycle tires over the water-laden ground. When she turned, Bubba was rolling his bike to a stop near her. Again, they were restrained by the potential onlookers, and the kiss they shared was achingly brief.

They started walking, side by side, bodies deliberately brushing while Bubba wheeled his bike alongside. They talked about nothing that mattered. The things they were saying to each other with their eyes were more important.

Eden released a heady sigh and looked around, expecting to see sunshine and a world bursting with the same life force she felt. Instead, clouds backed the dripping silver-green moss in the trees and a kind of stillness lay over everything. She looked at the two teen-aged girls flirting with the soldiers in the park.

'Those girls –' she began, nodding in their direction, and Bubba turned to look.

'You mean those V-girls?' he asked.

'V-girls?' She frowned at the strange term. 'What does that mean?'

'V for Victory,' he said, then made a motion with his head. 'Never mind.'

'Why do you call them that?' Eden persisted, all the more intrigued by Bubba's obvious discomfort with the subject.

'Forget I said it,' he insisted in his heavy drawl.

'Why?'

'Because it's an unseemly thing to discuss with a lady.'

Eden laughed at the thought that she needed to be protected from talk about something evidently wicked. 'What is a V-girl?' Her sidelong glance teased him. 'I'm not one of your southern belles who's liable to blush at indelicate talk.'

'You're Yankee-bold-as-brass, that's for sure,' Bubba agreed, but his look was lazy with deep affection. 'I guess the kindest thing to call 'em is camp followers. Wherever there's a bunch of soldiers, you're apt to find them.'

'Are you serious?' Eden took another look at the girls, trying to match what he was saying with the relative youth of these sixteen-and seventeen-year-old girls.

'They're crazy over anything in uniforms. Maybe they're attracted to the glamor of it,' he suggested with a shrug. 'Take 'em to a dance . . . hell, buy 'em a Coke and you can have what you want from them. They're amateur whores . . . better than the professionals 'cause at least they aren't indifferent, but . . . the bad thing is . . . a soldier's more likely to catch something from them.'

'How . . . sad,' Eden concluded finally.

'Yeah.' In a change of mood and subject, Bubba began, 'Now I know my chariot isn't as fancy or fast as yours' – indicating the bicycle he pushed along to the side of them – 'but it's the only transportation we got. If you'd like to hop on these horns' – he patted the curved handlebars – 'I'll give you a ride to town.'

While Bubba held the bicycle steady, Eden climbed onto the precarious perch and gingerly rested her feet on the fender. Not feeling very secure, she gripped the handlebars

371

at a point slightly behind her and balanced her briefcase on her lap. She yelped a laughing alarm at Bubba's wobbly push-off.

'Hold on,' he warned.

'I am!'

He leaned forward, pumping the pedals hard with the added weight. 'You make a helluva nice-lookin' hood ornament,' he told her.

'Thanks.' Eden was dubious.

'Better hope it doesn't rain. This convertible doesn't have a top.'

It was a wild ride into the town situated on the Cape Fear River. Hanging on for dear life, Eden always seemed to be gasping halfway between a shriek and a laugh. When they reached the business streets and traffic buzzed around them, she demanded a halt, shaky-legged and out of breath from the madcap ride.

Bubba went back to walking his bike as they wandered down the sidewalk, past the window displays of merchandise in the various stores along the way. Eden glanced idly at them, only mildly interested until she saw a man's tweed sports jacket hanging in a window.

She caught Bubba's arm and directed his attention to the jacket. 'That would look great on you.'

'Do you think so?' He sounded interested, her comment appealing to his ego.

'Let's go inside,' she urged, her eyes bright on him.

After a scant second's hesitation, Bubba leaned the bike against the side of the building and walked with Eden into the store. A clerk brought out the same jacket in his size and let Bubba try it on.

The tailored wool tweed jacket gave breadth to his wide shoulders, erasing that lanky, country-boy look, and hinted at a muscularly trim physique. The camel-soft brown in the tweed highlighted the streaks of dark gold in his hair and deepened the brown. Bubba flexed his shoulders, testing the freedom of movement, while he studied his reflection in the mirror.

'What do you think?' he asked as Eden looked on with gleaming, satisfied eyes.

'We'll take it,' she told the sales clerk.

'Wait a minute. How much does it cost?' Bubba flipped over the sales tag tied to the sleeve button.

'It doesn't matter.' Price was not an object as far as Eden was concerned. 'It's my present . . . from me to you.' She opened her shoulder bag to pay for it.

'No.' It was a flat refusal. A second later, Bubba was shrugging out of the jacket and handing it to the clerk. 'I changed my mind. I don't like it.' He looked at Eden, an anger lurking beneath his expression. 'Come on. Let's go.'

This show of temper surprised Eden into silence. Bubba had always seemed so easygoing; nothing ever riled him. She didn't protest as he steered her out of the store and back onto the sidewalk.

'What's wrong?' She eyed him cautiously. 'Surely you didn't –'

'Forget it.' He cut harshly across her words, then paused, regret flashing across his expression as he lowered his head. 'Just forget it,' he said in a quieter tone.

Eden started to speak, then let her lips come together. Maybe it was better to let it alone for now, she decided. Bubba stood his bicycle up and they started walking down the street again.

After they'd gone a block, she asked, 'Where are we going?'

He seemed to hesitate, then looked at her directly. 'There's a hotel I know about, not far from here.' He paused, as if to await an objection from her, but she had none to make. 'It sits kinda outa the way. Best of all, I guess, it doesn't ask any questions.'

'Let's go there, then.' She slipped her hand into the grasp of his roughly callused, work-worn hand. Her touch seemed to tame him and bring the warm glint back to his eyes.

Twenty minutes later, Bubba unlocked the door to their hotel room and carried her briefcase and his small duffle bag inside. The room was small and furnished with only the necessary bed and dresser. The fringed area rug was threadbare, its pattern and colors fading. He laid their things on the bed, and turned, a trifle self-consciously, to face Eden.

'It isn't much.'

'It definitely isn't the Waldorf,' Eden agreed, a smile in her voice as she stepped forward to link her hands behind his neck. 'I missed you.'

His gaze became fixed on her lips while he seemed to hold himself on a tight rein. He rested his hands on the points of her hipbones, covered by slacks of Santiago blue. 'I missed you one helluva lot.'

Pent-up hungers were released as he took her lips, driving into them with a fevered need. She answered the pressure of crushing arms, her own winding around him in an ever-tightening circle. The strain was raw and wildly sweet. It was some moments before they broke apart under the weight of it, to catch their breath.

Eden moved away, turning her back to him while she took the blue tam from atop her red hair. She was disturbed by him, more deeply than she had been by any man. She was used to having control of things, but now she had none.

The tam was left to sit on the dresser while she unbuttoned her Eisenhower jacket. Wire hangers hung in the small closet in the room. She took one down and slipped her jacket onto it. When she turned, Eden caught Bubba watching her.

'If you want to look halfway decent on these ferry trips, you have to look after your clothes.' No maids came along to do it for her. 'You never know how long you'll be away . . . or how long you might have to wear your uniform before you can have it cleaned. There's only room in the cockpits of these pursuits for the briefcase. By the time you put your tech manuals, your orders, toothbrush and makeup in that, you're lucky if there's room for a clean blouse.'

She smiled at him, because it was really quite humorous. Her reputation as a clotheshorse was notorious. She laid her briefcase flat and unfastened the catches to open it and unpack.

'You'd be surprised at the tricks we've learned to stay looking neat,' Eden told him. 'We wash our underwear out at night and drape it over the radiator or the bedstead to dry. If you can't count on getting an iron, then you just rub the collar of your shirt clean and set it under the Bible so it will dry already pressed. The slacks we put between the mattress and the box springs. The next morning, they are creased to Army perfection.'

His chuckle widened her smile as Eden gathered up her cosmetics kit and carried it into the small bathroom. At least they had a private one and didn't have to share some community facility off the hallway.

'What's this?' Bubba's voice followed her. She came back into the room to find him standing by the bed, holding the .45-caliber pistol she carried in her briefcase. 'How come you're carrying a gun?'

'The planes we fly sometimes have sophisticated equipment aboard.' Eden took the loaded weapon from him and put it back in the briefcase with her manuals, charts, and orders. 'Gun sights, transmitters, and those IFF – If Friend or Foe – sensors. Some of them even have morphine in the medical packs.'

'But why the gun?' Bubba frowned. 'The Army doesn't expect you to shoot people, does it?'

'No,' she assured him with a faint laugh. 'But if we're forced down under "suspicious circumstances," the phrase they use, we're supposed to fire at a spot on the fuselage. Supposedly it will blow up the entire plane.'

He looked at her hard. 'That sounds dangerous.'

'And Camp Davis was a piece of cake, with artillery lobbing fifty-millimeter shells at a muslin sleeve towed behind a plane,' Eden reminded him ironically. She crossed to stand in front of him, then reached up and began unbuttoning his khaki shirt.

Halfway done with the task, she slipped her fingers inside to touch his warm, hard flesh. She felt the small tremor that shook him, and satisfaction ran hotly through her veins, smooth and fiery as aged Scotch whiskey – and just as intoxicating.

His long hands cupped her face, framing it. 'Do you love me, Eden?'

'Yes,' she whispered.

'No.' He shook his head, the strain of something else visible in the yearning of his look. 'Do you love me the way I am?'

'What nonsense is this?' Eden murmured. 'Are you talking about that jacket? Back there at the store –'

'I don't want you buying me things,' he said. 'I know you've got plenty of money, but I'll pay my own way. It isn't really that, though . . . it's just, I'm wondering if you're trying to change me. Eden, I'm a mechanic. I don't have any fancy houses or fancy cars or clothes.'

'Not now,' she said. 'How could you? The Army isn't exactly the place to get ahead.'

'What if I don't want to get ahead, Eden?' Bubba said. 'What if I like what I am? Can you be happy with that?'

She didn't like this talk. She didn't like the questions he was raising. She didn't want anything spoiling their precious time together.

'What does it matter?' she asked impatiently and pressed her body to his length. 'Does it change this?'

'No,' he admitted hoarsely and let his frustration be carried away by the roughening fire of a kiss.

A minute later, he was scooping her into his arms and depositing her on the bed. Wrinkled uniforms became the least of their concerns.

It was a balmy California afternoon, a fresh breeze was stirring, and the sky was high and blue. Mary Lynn didn't think a more perfect day could have been created. Even after the long flight she'd just completed, she felt revived and inwardly exuberant. Briefcase in hand, she moved away from the aircraft she'd just delivered to head for the operations building.

'Hey, Marty!' she called to the long-legged blonde in

her striking blue flying fatigues. This trip had been one of the rare occasions when their orders had taken them to the same destination, so they'd flown their planes tandem. 'Are you coming?'

Marty's hands were cupped to her mouth as she stood beside her plane with a mechanic. 'Gotta get my gear out of the plane.' Her megaphoned voice sounded even deeper and huskier. 'Go ahead without me. I'll be along.'

Mary Lynn waved an acknowledgment and crossed the wide flight line to the operations building. It seemed more crowded than usual, a lot more civilians milling around inside than she was accustomed to seeing. Most of them scowled at her with unconcealed dislike.

'What are you doing here?' one of them demanded, surprising Mary Lynn with the vehemence in his tone.

'I just flew a P-47 in –'

But he wasn't interested in her explanation. None of them were. 'Why don't you go home where you belong?' he challenged.

'No one needs you or the rest of your fancy-assed women. You aren't wanted here so why don't you clear out!'

'You got no business in the cockpit of an airplane!'

Unable to fight back against this barrage of verbal abuse, Mary Lynn tried to walk away from it, but the men crowded around her, not letting her by. Hostility swept from them in threatening waves, swamping her with the implied menace of their pressing bodies.

'Your organization is worthless. You're nothin' but a bunch of glamor gals.'

'Go home!'

Not knowing what to do, Mary Lynn looked at them in helpless confusion. She couldn't understand why they were attacking her.

An officer shouldered his way into their midst. 'Leave her alone,' a familiar voice snapped. In relief, Mary Lynn recognized Walker. 'Beat it. All of you,' he ordered, his low, hard voice commanding their attention and respect.

Reluctant and grumbling, they dispersed, moving slowly

away and leaving Mary Lynn standing there, shaken and confused by the experience.

'I don't understand. What did I do?' she asked.

'You didn't have to do anything.' With his usual disregard for the Army's uniform code, Walker's summer khaki shirt was unbuttoned at the throat, revealing a glimpse of the chain that held his dogtags. A cigarette dangled from a corner of his mouth while he squinted his eyes against the upward curl of smoke and stared at Mary Lynn. 'Don't let them get to you. They're just a bunch of former flight instructors, taking scheduled flight tests for Air Transport Command. I guess these guys didn't pass. Then you walked in and I suppose it was too much for their injured pride that a mere slip of a woman had made the grade and they didn't. You've got a job they want and can't qualify for.'

'I see.' She lowered her head, troubled by the venom that had been thrown at her so unjustifiably. 'That's why they said I didn't belong in those planes.'

'Hey.' His voice cajoled her while he touched a finger to the side of her mouth, trying to coax a smile from her. 'Not everyone feels like that. You can ride in the cockpit of my plane any time.'

His suggestive comment heated her skin. She turned away from the touch of his finger and made a move to leave, but his hand hooked her waist in a lightning reflex while he discarded the cigarette. She was stopped by the action, and turned of her own volition to face him. Indolent satisfaction darkened the gleam in his eyes as he traced her cheekbone and jaw with a caressing finger.

'Have dinner with me tonight,' he urged.

She lowered her glance, trying to elude his touch. 'No, thanks. You drink your dinner and I prefer to eat mine.'

With her head down, she walked quickly away from him, passing Marty just as she entered the building. Marty's glance flashed past her to strike at Walker. Ignoring her presence, he bent his head to light another cigarette, shaking out the match flame while he watched Mary Lynn walk away. Marty was rarely given to violent likes or dislikes, but she despised him.

'Why don't you keep your hands off her?' she snapped.

Without turning his head, Walker looked at her with amused scorn. 'What makes you think she wants to be protected from me?'

'What a ridiculous question.' Marty was angry. 'She's in love with her husband.'

The line of his mouth deepened its mocking slant. 'You . . . of all people . . . should know love has nothing to do with this.'

At a loss for a reply, Marty spun on her heel and marched out of the building after Mary Lynn. She caught up with her outside.

'Are you okay?' Marty peered at her.

'Of course.' Mary Lynn continued walking, head up and eyes to the front.

Marty matched the shorter stride of her friend. 'That guy is about as crude as you can get. Someone needs to teach him some manners and proper respect.'

'That's not quite true.' She defended him. 'Some pilots – men – were giving me a hard time because I was doing a job they felt should have been theirs. Captain Walker came along and sent them on their way.'

'Then *he* started bothering you.' Something about the man kept ringing more than alarm bells in her mind, but Marty couldn't place him. 'If I were you, I'd steer clear of him.'

'He knows Beau.' Mary Lynn mentioned it as if that gave him credibility.

'How?' Marty stopped, taken aback by the announcement.

Mary Lynn's dark eyes took on a lively, yet wistful quality. 'Captain Walker was a B-17 pilot in England with Beau. He knows all about him.'

'What's he doing here?' Marty didn't like the sound of any of this, and the graveled edge of her voice became rougher.

'Like Cappy, he's flying the C-47s to their embarkation

points when they come off the assembly lines at Douglas.'

'Why should the Army have a B-17 pilot doing that?' she asked, skeptical of his story.

'Look at what they have you doing.' The lilt in her voice said it all as Mary Lynn resumed walking, prompting Marty into motion.

But a bell had rung loudly in Marty's head. 'I've got it!' The declaration was made under her breath as all her attention was turned inward. 'That's where I saw him before. I'd swear to it.'

'What are you talking about?' Mary Lynn paused before they reached the jeep parked outside operations, waiting to transport them to their quarters.

'I'd bet a month's pay he's the bomber pilot I bumped into in Miami Beach. The scars on his face. The voice. I'd almost swear to it.' In an aside to Mary Lynn, she added, 'He was a coward – trying to drink himself brave when I saw him. More important, he doesn't know Beau. He is lying to you, Mary Lynn. I asked.'

Tired and worn by a series of long flights, Cappy sat in the post canteen on her old home base outside of Washington, DC, and pushed the food around on her plate. Her appetite had fallen off – along with a lot of other things, like contentment – since she'd been transferred. When she'd been assigned to the same ferry command where Eden was stationed, she had thought everything would be fine. Close to three months had passed and everything wasn't fine.

A new set of orders was in the sealed envelope lying on the table beside her plate. She hadn't looked at them yet, not particularly caring what she would be flying or where. Since leaving Long Beach nearly four days before, she had logged a prodigious number of hours. Cappy felt she had earned this break – and these few rare moments with her family, specifically her mother, who sat across the table from her.

Her mother was doing nearly all the talking, recounting to Cappy her visit to Capitol Hill. The House Civil Service

Committee had been meeting in regard to the WASP program, which they had concluded was a waste of money and effort.

'General Arnold argued with them for more than an hour,' her mother reported. 'He was most insistent that women pilots were necessary to the war effort. Jacqueline Cochran was there, sitting beside him, but she didn't say anything. The committee was all for disbanding the entire organization. They could do it just by refusing to fund it, since it is a civilian program. It's all that business about those flight instructors who lost their high-paying civilian contracts to train pilots for the Army. The committee made General Arnold give them his assurance that the services of these men would be utilized immediately.' A small smile touched her mouth. 'They're afraid of getting drafted in the "walking" Army.'

Cappy wanted nothing to do with the Army in any form. She just wanted to fly planes – and the Army could go to hell as far as she was concerned. Her throat got tight and some wrenching pain pushed at her chest. A raw unnamed emotion seemed to strangle her.

'Did I mention I saw Mitch at the committee meeting?' her mother inquired.

Cappy's eyes were the deep color of her blue flying suit and they burned. 'No, you didn't.' Her voice seemed to come from some hollow well inside her. 'How is he?' So casually.

'Oh, he's still the same handsome devil,' her mother declared with a laugh. 'It's a shame you won't be able to see him while you're here.'

'I hardly have the time –' Cappy began stiffly.

'Mitch isn't here,' her mother hastened to explain, then lowered her voice. 'He's in England with General Arnold . . . for the Allied invasion of France.'

'It's happening?'

'Soon,' her mother replied, then looked around to be certain no one had overheard.

Mitch. She had trouble keeping the tears out of her

eyes. He was staff so it was unlikely he'd be exposed to any danger. It wasn't that causing the ache, the clawing frustration, the near anger. She had done the right thing, Cappy insisted to herself. It wouldn't have worked between them. She pressed her fingertips to the bridge of her nose, trying to fight back the tears.

'Cappy, is something wrong?'

A silent shake of her head first dismissed the question, then Cappy dragged in a breath and forced a smile to her lips. 'I'm just tired,' she said, then attempted a laugh that came out brittle and false. 'Did I tell you a cleaning woman in the lavatory mistook me for a lady plumber in my flight suit? I don't know what all this fuss is about in Congress. Ninety percent of the people don't even know we exist.'

CHAPTER TWENTY-SIX

'Our sons, pride of our nation . . .' As president Franklin Delano Roosevelt began his prayer, Mary Lynn sat close to the radio and bowed her head. She, Marty and Eden were with their fellow WASPs, massed in the common room of the barracks to hear the latest report on the massive Allied invasion of France's Normandy beaches. The President was now praying for those fighting men. 'Lead them straight and true. Give strength to their arms, stoutness to their hearts, steadfastness in their faith. They will need Thy blessings. Their road will be long and hard. For the enemy is strong. He may hurl back our forces. Success may not come with rushing speed, but we shall return again and again . . .'

Early on the morning of June 6, Walter Winchell had announced the news of the invasion to the West Coast. He told of American armies fighting on Utah Beach and bloody Omaha, while the British battled on Sword, Gold, and Juno. Tense, Marty leaned toward the radio. She'd heard the reports of paratroop divisions dropping behind German lines before the first Marines stormed onto the beaches. Her brother was bound to have been part of it. At this moment, he was over there fighting with the rest.

'. . .Give us faith in Thee; faith in our sons; faith in each other; faith in our united crusade . . .' FDR prayed.

When he finished, the room echoed with Amens, and a rush of talk followed the guardedly optimistic report. Amidst all the fears and prayers, there was a need to celebrate. Marty, Eden, and Mary Lynn headed for the Officers' Club. Everyone else seemed to have the same idea. The place was packed with officers eager to talk, predicting victory.

'My brother David is over there,' Marty announced proudly. 'He's a paratrooper, so he was in the initial assault.'

An unhurried latecomer to their table was Captain Sam Walker. As he slowly approached, Mary Lynn lifted her head against the steady pressure of his presence. A drink was in his hand; there was always a drink in his hand. She tapped an unlit cigarette on the table, packing the tobacco.

'A vile habit.' A match flared and his long fingers held it out to her. Her eyes briefly met his, then fell away as she bent her head toward the match, letting the tip of her cigarette touch the flame.

'So is drinking.' Mary Lynn straightened from him, blowing smoke into the air in a strained attempt at nonchalance. 'But I notice you do both to excess.'

'I have fallen into sinful and wicked ways.' He dragged a chair around to sit angled towards her. 'Maybe you should try to reform me?' In a gesture of suppressed agitation, she turned her glass in half-circles within its damp table-ring. Sam Walker picked up her every little nuance of movement and expression. 'Or maybe I should lead you the rest of the way astray?'

Marty leaned an arm on the table, her posture carrying more of a warning than a challenge. 'Walker, why don't you lay off her for once.'

'Mind your own business, Rogers.' Walker didn't bother to look at Mary Lynn's defender.

'Keeping wolves like you away from her is my business.'

With a finger, he hooked a loose curl behind Mary Lynn's ear and noticed the way her dark eyes nearly closed under his feather-light touch.

'Do you think you need protection from me, Little One?' he drawled.

'No.' A tension remained about her expression as she kept her gaze downcast.

Marty changed tactics from direct to indirect confrontation. 'Aren't you lucky Ike ordered the invasion of France? Now everyone will think you're drinking to celebrate that and never guess it's where you find your courage.'

Such talk didn't faze Walker; instead, he used it. 'Does it bother you that I drink, Little One?'

With a rare display of cynicism, Mary Lynn retorted, 'Would you stop if I said it did?'

'No.' His taunting smile was slow and even.

But Mary Lynn didn't react as Walker had expected she would. She pushed her chair away from the table. 'Please, I'm not in the mood for this.'

'Don't leave.' He caught her hand, holding her with the small pressure. But he knew better than to use force to keep her; instead he let his intent gaze make inroads into her will. 'It isn't good for a man to drink alone.'

'You shouldn't drink at all.' There was a reluctance in her voice. She wanted nothing from him, yet found herself responding to him against her will.

'Then keep me away from that evil rum and dance with me instead.' He changed his hold on her hand, slipping under her fingers to curve them atop his.

A protesting sound came from Marty, but it seemed to goad Mary Lynn into action. That nervy restlessness could affect a person, push her into throwing aside caution. It was something he knew better than anyone there.

On the dance floor, he brought her inside his arms until her warm body was close to his. Her fragrance revived all his hungers. She was all things good and sweet – too good for him, but he wanted her all the same. And he'd have her, too. He knew that's where the wrong in himself lay. By taking her, he'd drag her down.

Her dark head came to his shoulder and her hand rested lightly on the muscled tip of it. Mary Lynn didn't lift her gaze higher than the silver captain's bars on his uniform. The sweet smell of her hair came to him.

'Do you think I'm a coward, Little One?' He asked gently.

'I try not to think about you.' She dodged his question.

'Do you succeed?' Walker tipped his head to the side, trying for a better view of her face.

'Most of the time.'

'At least you think of me once in a while. That's a beginning.' He smiled, but the look in his eyes was serious, completely sober despite the alcohol he'd already consumed. 'I think about you all the time.'

'In between the booze and the poker.'

'And the nightmares,' he added without thinking.

She looked at his face, striking him with the dark, earnest openness of her eyes. 'Why do you have nightmares?'

At that moment, he was careful not to shut his eyes, not to let in those images of fighter planes with black crosses painted on their wings tearing out of the sky, spewing rockets of death – or the sight of Flying Fortresses rearing out of formation as if clawing for life, with part of a wing or tail shot away, bleeding thick smoke from the wound – the crew of ten men inside, maybe friends and maybe strangers. More than anything, Walker shut out that sickening sense of helplessness when they went into their slow death spiral.

That bitterness came – that wretched, angry bitterness. 'Don't you know there's a war on?' There was cruelty in his voice.

Her head went down. 'Yes, I know,' she said softly.

The anger that welled in him took another course, deliberately seeking out sore spots and testing them to see if they were still tender – within himself and within her. 'Have you had a letter from your husband lately?'

She became stiff in his arms. 'Why? You don't know him.' Her glance rushed upwards to his face. 'Marty finally remembered where she had met you before. It was in Miami Beach. You told her that you didn't know him.'

'I did? Well, fancy that,' Walker murmured, untroubled. 'I must have made a mistake.'

'You deliberately lied to me, didn't you?' she said accusingly.

'You've had a long, lonely time of it, haven't you, Little One?' he murmured, ignoring her accusation. 'All that flying . . . and all that restless energy just has you taut as a drumskin. The ease of forgetfulness comes in the arms of a lover. That's what you need – someone to make love to you and untie those knots that have you all wound up inside.'

'Why did you lie to me?'

A rising energy made him impatient. 'You needed an excuse to be with me so I gave you one. We played a little game of pretend. You wanted to be able to say "He knows my husband" to explain why you spent so much time in my company. You use it as a reason to justify why we're dancing and why you're letting me hold you in my arms. The truth is it's what you want.'

Her feet ceased following the pattern of his steps as she halted in the middle of the dance floor. 'Marty was right about you. You're a liar and a coward. I must have been blind not to have seen it before.'

'You didn't want to see it,' Walker snapped. If it had been her intention to hurt him, she had done it well. For all his callous attitude, he had his pride.

'I love my husband,' she declared as if raising up a shield.

'Yeah? Well, he's not here and I am. That's the difference.'

Mary Lynn pulled out of his arms. 'You're a liar and a cheat and a coward.' Sensing how to hurt him, she struck deep to wound him and salvage some of her own self-respect in the process.

For a long minute he stood fast, then his mouth slanted

in a cruelly mocking line. 'Then what does that make you, Little One?'

It was a remark that struck low and hard. Mary Lynn whitened and swung away from him just as Eden danced right beside her, looking concerned. 'Are you all right, Mary Lynn?' she asked while her dance partner showed only mild interest.

'I . . . I have a headache. Tell Marty I'm leaving.' Mary Lynn left the dance floor, walking swiftly toward the exit with Walker following close behind.

Within seconds, Marty was pouncing on Walker, challenge glittering in her silvery-green eyes. 'Leave her alone, Walker.'

'What are you? Her keeper?'

'Yes. She's a decent kid, and I want to keep it that way,' she answered.

'Meaning what? That I'm not good enoough for her?' Walker taunted.

'You're a bastard, Walker,' she replied as if that explained it all. 'What did you say to her?'

Walker looked at her with hard, narrowed eyes. 'None of your damned business.' In a rank temper, he bulled his way to the bar.

A steady stream of reports came from the beaches of Normandy over the next few days, but most of the women pilots were in the skies. Marty hopscotched across the Southwest, gazed longingly at the B-17s in Las Vegas, and flew back to Long Beach on June 8. It never failed to amaze her how well the airfields on the Pacific Coast were camouflaged. Unless a pilot knew almost precisely where they were, she'd never see them.

Back at the WASP quarters after a three-day absence, she stuck her head inside Mary Lynn's doorway. 'Hi. I'm back.'

'How was your flight?' Mary Lynn set aside her letter-writing paraphernalia and swung off her cot to follow Marty down the hall to her own room.

'Not bad. I ran into some junk in southern Colorado, but I flew out of it before the weather got too rough.' She slung her briefcase onto the narrow bed and shuffled through the mail that had accumulated in her absence. She pulled out one envelope. 'Well, what do you know?' Marty said with surprise and curled a leg under her to sit on the cot. 'A telegram from my parents.' As she ran a finger under the flap, she looked at Mary Lynn. 'I haven't heard from them in weeks.' Marty took out the telegram to read it. 'No.' The soft word conveyed shock.

Mary Lynn started to speak, then saw Marty's whitened face and the glazed quality of her silvery-green eyes when she looked up from the telegram.

'My brother . . . David.' Confusion and disbelief swarmed through her roughly controlled voice. 'They've been notified . . .' Marty stared again at the telegram, as if needing to see it in writing. '. . . He was killed in action.'

The words, the finality of them, were silencing. Not David, not her brother – she kept thinking there must be some mistake. The shock seemed to suck all feeling out of her, draining her empty. He was her big brother, her idol and her rival; it was his feats she'd always tried to match or better. David couldn't die. He was supposed to come home the hero -- with decorations on his chest. It wasn't right that he should be killed. It wasn't fair.

Mary Lynn gazed at the telegram, the kind mothers and wives dreaded to receive. A twisting fear weaved through her. This was the first time the lightning had struck so close. It wasn't a neighbor's son down the block, or a third cousin's husband. This was Marty's brother.

'Marty.' Mary Lynn took a step toward the silent, staring figure on the bed, wanting to comfort and thus be comforted.

'No.' Marty swung off the bed and faced the corner, turning her back on Mary Lynn and hugging her arms tightly around her middle. 'I . . .' Her husky voice was choked with grief. 'Mom and Dad . . . they'll need me. I'd better . . . make arrangements to go home this weekend.'

'I'll help,' she offered.

'I think . . . I'd rather do it myself.' She needed the activity to release the spiraling tightness. Marty couldn't stay still as the phrase kept hitting at her: 'killed in action.' David Allen Rogers III had always played such a big role in her life; his death left a gaping hole. 'Do you mind? I'd like to be alone.'

But Mary Lynn couldn't stand the thought of being alone.

She needed to be around laughing, loving, living people. She left the nearly empty barracks. Most of the WASPs were on flights somewhere, and the few present were catching up on laundry or sleep.

The hustle of the flight line pulled her. For a while she stood outside, listening to the ebb and flow of voices and airplane engines, life recirculating. Impatient for something more to fill the hollow ache inside, Mary Lynn entered the operations building.

The jocular voices and the back-slapping camaraderie going on didn't include her, as pilots milled about the ready room, playing cards or chatting idly, puffing on endless cigarettes. She wanted to be part of the living world, not an onlooker.

Mary Lynn couldn't put a name to the force that made her turn around so that she saw Walker when he came in. The dark stubble of a day's beard growth shadowed his angled cheeks, concealing the scars. Tired lines creased his eye corners, but the hard, glinting mockery remained in their dark surfaces. His officer's cap was raked to the back of his head, showing the heavy brown hair that grew with such unruly thickness. His leather battle jacket hung open and the tails of the white scarf draped around his neck were dangling loose.

Walker paused to draw a match across the abrasive strip of its match cover and cup the flame to his cigarette. Over the fire, he caught sight of the small, silent woman watching him from a corner of the room. Her dark eyes were on him, rousing him fully.

For an instant, she became the only living thing in the room for him. Slowly, he lifted his head, staring at her as he shook out the match. Steadily, she returned his gaze, not looking away or showing reluctance.

There was a message in that – one he wanted to explore . . . to be sure of its meaning.

He moved toward her, crossing the room at a sauntering pace. 'Hello, Little One.'

She spoke, without preamble, her voice soft as a whisper yet urgent. 'A telegram came for Marty. Her brother was killed in action.'

He'd gotten from her the opening he wanted. With no sense of guilt, Walker followed through, gathering her into his arms and holding her there for an easy run of minutes until her stiffness and frigidity softened and melted.

Bending his head, he rubbed his mouth against the silken fineness of her raven hair. In tentative movements, she shifted, slowly lifting her head to look at him and the nearness of his mouth.

Walker needed no more than that. His driving kiss tasted her needs without restraint. She let him glimpse the deep and passionate core of her feelings. Walker wasn't sure whether she had willingly given him this entry, but she had returned his kiss with a full and heated response.

His breath was running deep when he dragged his mouth from hers. 'Tonight –' He needed the promise inherent in that kiss. '– I'll pick you up at nineteen hundred hours.'

There was a moment when he sensed her conflict, but her answer ultimately came with no reservation. 'Yes.'

In the hallway outside the hotel room Mary Lynn waited, clutching her purse, while Walker inserted the key the clerk had given him and unlocked the door. He led the way inside, making a quick survey of the room before turning to draw her in and close the door.

The room was small, with space for little besides the bed and chest of drawers. Its use was starkly limited and it pretended to little else. Rigidly she avoided looking at the bed as she crossed to the window, but the view was restricted to a seedy back street of Los Angeles.

A paper sack rattled and bottles were set on the bureau. Without looking, she could discern Walker's movements. Mary Lynn stayed at the window, listening to the sounds of glasses being righted and caps screwed off bottles.

'What will you have – rum and Coke or Coke and rum?' The lazy inflection of his voice didn't have its customary note of spiteful mockery.

'Neither, thank you.' She managed the response, letting a smile take any sting out of her rejection.

'Sorry I couldn't get you any whiskey. I know that's what you usually drink – when you drink,' he acknowledged, and liquid splashed in a glass, bubbles fizzing in a soft hiss.

Out of the corner of her eye she saw him drape his jacket around the lone straight-backed chair in the room, then she turned to watch him loosen the knot of his tie. Walker was talking to her, but none of his words registered as he crossed to the bed, taking a swig of his rum and Coke, then setting it on the nightstand.

Once the tie hung loose around his neck, he unfastened the collar button of his shirt, then pulled the shirttails out of his trousers and unbuttoned it the rest of the way. Soon the shirt was thrown over the end of the bed and the undershirt was being pulled over Walker's head to join it. His dogtags jingled briefly against their securing chain.

When bare to the waist, he stood up to loosen his pants. Walker noticed Mary Lynn standing silently by the window. He paused, searching her still features. He tipped his head to the side. 'Is something wrong?'

She looked toward the door, a drift of self-consciousness running across her face. 'That desk clerk knew when we registered that we weren't man and wife, didn't he?'

'I doubt that he cared one way or the other as long as we paid for the room.' His shoulder lifted in a vague shrug. 'What does it matter anyway?'

'I suppose it doesn't.' Her glance fell. 'But the way he

looked at us . . . it made this something . . . sordid and cheap.'

And the situation wasn't improved by his behavior, Walker realized – undressing as if he were bedding a common whore. He silently cursed his thoughtlessness and went to her, gently turning her from the window to face him.

'You're wrong, Little One.' He urgently pressed his feelings on her. 'You're much too beautiful and fine to be sullied by any of this.' He heard the high-sounding words as he spoke them, so deeply sincere. Coming from him, they seemed out of character. He chuckled in his throat and stroked the hollow below her ear lobe. 'I sound so damned noble, don't I? But it's the truth.'

She gazed at him, a hint of regret in her velvet dark eyes. 'I'm not as good as you think I am, Walker.'

Slowly he accepted these words as true; otherwise she wouldn't be in this hotel room with him. At the moment, it didn't matter whether she was sinking to his level or he was rising to hers. In some decent part of his mind, he realized she'd never done this before.

Gently, he led her away from the window and held her face in his hands while he kissed it with slow, seeking ardor. As her stiffness and discomfort melted, he began to undress her, taking time to caress the areas he uncovered before moving on to the next. There were hungers to be satisfied, the taste of her skin beneath his tongue and the feel of her hard nipples under his thumb. Her hands were splayed across his chest and the heavy thud of his heart beat against them.

Long-held desires heated their flesh and quickened their breathing. When she was stripped of clothes and all the restraints of society's conventions, Walker swung her feet off the floor and carried her to the bed.

Here they were merely participants in the most basic of all acts – no more than a man and a woman discovering ways they fit together that gave them pleasure, glimpsing old glories made new and sensing some of the wonder so fleetingly possessed – and always the straining for more.

Part Four

We wanted wings,
Then we got those goldarned things
They just darned near killed us,
That's for sure.
They taught us how to fly
Now they send us home to cry
'Cause they don't want us anymore.
You can save those AT-sixes
To be cracked up in the ditches,
For the way the Army flies
Really clears them out of the skies.
We earned our wings,
Now they'll clip the goldarned things
How will they ever win the war?

CHAPTER TWENTY-SEVEN

The bedsheet was drawn tightly across her breasts and firmly tucked under her arms to keep it in place. Mary Lynn couldn't explain it, even to herself, this need to hide her body. Surely not from Walker – his invasion of her had been most complete . . . and satisfying. Was that it? Had she wanted it not to be as good as it had been with Beau?

The raw sweet pleasure was all gone and her feelings were getting twisted inside. The cigarette she was smoking lost its flavor and she turned on her side to crush it in the ashtray on the bedstand. When she rolled back, Mary Lynn was conscious of Walker, his head turned on the pillow to look at her. A ravel of smoke from his cigarette drifted in the air above them. The hard and knowing mockery in his eyes was difficult to meet.

'You're thinking about him, aren't you?' A faint harshness crept into the edges of his voice.

'Who?' Mary Lynn pretended obtuseness.

'Don't play games, Little One.' Some kind of anger made him sit up and swing around to the side of the bed, where he reached for the rum bottle and poured some into a glass. 'Your husband, of course.' He bolted down a swallow of liquor, then made a study of the glass. 'That nagging sense of shame and guilt won't last. It'll pass like everything else, until the next time, when the urge strikes again.'

'How do you know?' she demanded, angry that he had somehow gotten into her head as well as her body.

Walker turned to look across his shoulder. His mouth

crooked in a humorless line. 'Because I've been there, my love.' He reached backwards to stroke her cheek and cup it in a gentle fashion before turning away. 'I've been there.' The glass was tipped again to his mouth.

One lamp illuminated the room, throwing out shadows from its single pool. When Walker lifted an arm, the dim light cast a rippling sheen over the bare flesh stretched tautly across the muscles in his back. His body was marked with scattered dull-red scars. Flesh wounds, she supposed they were called. They weren't old ones, but recently incurred. It would take a long time before the reddened scars would fade to rose-brown and finally to white.

'Don't lose any sleep over it,' Walker advised her. 'He won't. Many other things may rob him of sleep, but not the comfort of a body's arms. He might feel a twinge of guilt once in a while – maybe when she does something that reminds him of you. Is that what I did?' His head turned, his glance sliding to her. 'Remind you of him?'

At times she could despise him for his brutal honesty; no subject was sacred; no topic was discreetly avoided. Worse, perhaps, he preyed on her doubts about Beau.

'You're not like him.'

'Aren't I?' he mused, but let it pass.

'You don't even know Beau.' Mary Lynn didn't know why she persisted in the subject, unless it was some kind of punishment. 'You're only guessing about the women.'

'He's a man, isn't he?' There was a rising heat in his voice, impatient and hard. 'What's any man want when he's thirsty? If he's far from home, he'll drink from the well that's close by. Maybe he'll miss the taste of the sweet water back home but he'll drink to satisfy the craving inside. That's just the way it is. Maybe that's why we're made of clay, because the impulses that drive us are dirt-common.'

'I never guessed you were a philosopher.' She was calmed by the things he said, but it seemed strange to hear him speaking in Beau's defense, offering justification for his infidelity. Or was he giving reasons for her own? Or his?

'It must be the war.' Walker stared into the glass as if it held the answer. 'At first, you try to understand the whys of it, but it's such insanity that none of it will tolerate a close scrutiny. So you either go on with blind faith in the people supposedly leading you or else you turn to the bottle and drink until it's all a blur and none of it matters.'

'What's it like?' It had done things to him, things she didn't understand. And she wondered if all the bomber pilots returning home would be like Sam Walker.

'Hell.' A long silence followed the one-word reply while Walker was caught up in his own thoughts. Then he roused himself to go on, in a flat, emotionless voice. 'It isn't like what they write about or what they show you on the screen. In the movies, you *see* the enemy, whether he's a yellow-skinned Jap or a strong-jawed Jerry. Man fighting man is an honorable thing; there's glory in it. But you aren't fighting men; you're fighting machines. There lies the horror of this war. The side with more and better machines is going to win.'

'It can't be that simple.'

'Why?' He turned to challenge her with certainty. 'Because we've got "right" on our side? Because we're better than they are? Or braver or stronger? It will be because we've got raw material and factories that can throw out tanks and airplanes almost as fast as their machines can shoot them down.'

Looking away, she resisted the things he was saying. 'Don't you think we have a cause . . . a reason to fight?'

'Yes.' A sigh took the anger from him and left the bitterness. 'Yes, we have to fight, but do we have to lose so much? When we come back from raids over German territory, our generals don't count our losses in lives. It's planes – how many machines did we lose?

'They order us up there – maybe twenty formations of

397

sixty bombers each. They fill the sky.' He was staring sightlessly into the room, the drink clenched tightly in his hand. 'Overhead, the fighters ride escort, but not for long. Before their fuel runs low, they'll turn around and we're left at the mercy of . . . they have no mercy. They're waiting for you, though. They know you're coming and they wait – with their fighters and their flak. But you keep flying. When those German Focke-Wulfs pounce on you, you keep flying. There's no breaking off course to engage the enemy. You've got a target to reach and a bombload to drop and you just pray that none of those rockets flaming from their fighter planes hits your Fortress.

'And all the while, the intercom is alive with warnings – shoutings of the crew calling in your ears . . . your own voice among them . . . telling each other of planes diving toward your ship. Explosions all around you, and the thud of bullets tearing through metal . . . and the sickening feel of the ship when you know she's been hit, but you can't tell how bad. You just try to keep her in the air and on course for the target – always on course. You can't fall out of formation. A crippled bomber is a sitting duck, and the fighters will be on it like a pack of wolves.'

Beads of sweat were breaking out on his forehead but Mary Lynn felt chilled by the terror in his images. 'They come at you with black crosses painted on their wings, shooting their cannon shells. You see other bombers take hits, engines flame out, tiny lances of fire licking close to fuel tanks, black smoke pouring from an engine. A Fortress wings over and you'll watch the pilot fight to bring her out of the dive and back to straight and level so the crew can bail out before she blows. Maybe you know them, maybe you don't, but you'll count parachutes and yell for that tenth one to come out.

'Not always, though. Sometimes, nobody bails out. They ride her down, and you know why. One of the crew's hurt, or a parachute is shot to rags, and the guys won't leave one of their own behind, so all the fools will die.' His teeth were bared now, the words pushed through them while a wetness shimmered in his eyes, all hot and bitter. 'Then you watch the German fighters zero in on the parachutes, and you see guys jerking frantically on the shroud lines trying to dodge the bullets streaming at them. Or the ones whose parachutes are on fire and they have a mile to think about the way they're going to die.

'And that's just the fighters,' he said savagely. 'With them, the guys had something to shoot at. But the flak is different. The German artillery's got your range and altitude. They sit on the ground and throw fire at us, peppering the sky with their explosions until the air turns gray-black. Mile after mile, the deeper into Germany you fly, the thicker it gets. More bombers drop out of formation, some blowing up in an intense ball of light and others too damaged to fly on. But the rest of you go on to the target.

'Once you get there and drop the eggs in your bomb bays, you turn for home. And you've gotta fly through that hell again. Chances of coming through it without a scratch are nil. Your plane will have taken a hit, maybe not a bad one. Or one of your crew will be hurt, maybe a scratch or maybe serious. You wait for the fighter protection to pick you up on your way home, and maybe there'll be a little smile when you see the English Channel 'cause you've beat the odds again.'

Walker half turned to look at her lying on the soft, soft bed. She wanted to cry when she saw his stark expression, but fear had her by the throat. She was frightened by his brutal view of the war.

'But that isn't the real hell, Little One. It isn't the air raids, the flight to the target and back. No. The hell is knowing you have to do it again and again. It isn't just once that you go there. It's over and over and over. And your chances of coming back alive dwindle every time until finally you know you're a dead man. So how can they kill you when you're already dead?'

'No.' The awful coldness that came with fear drove Mary Lynn from beneath the covers and against the warmth of his body as she wrapped herself around him, hugging to the living fire.

His words made death seem close, and she wanted to live. It was this instinct that made their urges so strong. Mating was an integral part of procreation – and procreation promised survival. People could live on in their children. Thus, it was not so strange that fear created an aroused sexuality, that before battle, man sought out woman or woman sought out man.

And if two people also found solace and a measure of human warmth in each other's arms, they were that much luckier.

Later, while Mary Lynn slept, Walker stared at the ceiling, one muscled arm flung over his head. He dragged on a smoke and nursed another shot of rum. The pint bottle was nearly empty. His glance wandered to her, her face framed by the dark background of her hair. He remembered the soft black of her eyes, so bottomless and compelling.

He wondered what it was a man searched for in a woman's eyes – what did he hope to see? He'd wanted her, he'd had her, but he still wasn't satisfied. What was wrong with him that he couldn't be happy with what he had? Maybe there was nothing beyond the pleasure of her body for the short time it lasted. Or could they make something that would last longer?

Bitterly, he took another swallow of rum. Many times over Germany, he'd breathed the acrid smell of brimstone. He'd lived in that hell and brought it home with him. It had blackened him and left him thirsty for the good things. But when you lived in hell, how could you expect to hear angels sing?

Again, he looked at her, with a wanting so deep inside him that he wanted to cry. He'd known the rough and wonderful excitement of her giving passions, and his envy of the love she held in reserve for her husband grew immense. It was not easy to take what he could have without wanting more.

400

Tears ran down her cheeks as Marty stood on the front porch of her parents' Michigan home and stared at the gold star on the service flag in the window. A gold star for the death of a soldier son. Oddly, its presence seemed to make David's death more real.

Beyond the windowpane a figure moved; Marty wiped at the wetness on her face and crossed to the front door. She entered the house as her father walked into the foyer. Grief had aged him, bowing his shoulders and draining the life from his stern features. It took him a minute to recognize her in her official summer dress uniform of tailored jacket and skirt in Santiago blue.

'Martha,' he said, somewhat uncertainly.

'I came as soon as I could, Dad.' She hugged him, seeking solace and finding a mechanical response in the arms that went around her. 'I'm sorry, Dad.'

'There's nothing you can do.' He sounded so blank, like someone lost who didn't care about being found. 'There's nothing anyone can do.'

Despite the brilliant June sunshine, a dark gloom prevailed inside the house. Marty felt it as she drew back from her father. There was a suffocating stillness in the air as though nothing lived here anymore.

A small noise came from the living room and Marty turned to see her mother, dressed all in black, framed in its archway. 'Did you tell her?' Althea Rogers said to her husband. 'They aren't even sending his body home to us. They buried it in France. So far away.'

Without once looking at Marty, she turned and walked back into the living room. Marty was left standing alone as her father followed after her tragically forlorn mother. She trailed behind him. When she entered the living room, her attention was claimed by a black-draped photograph of David sitting by itself on a table. Marty felt immediately that she was standing before a shrine.

Her parents sat close together on the couch near the photograph. Her father had a consoling arm around her

401

mother's shoulders while they gazed at the picture. Marty had the awkward feeling that she was intruding as she sat in the armchair across from them. Everywhere she looked there were mementos of David – a photo album, a scrapbook, his bronzed baby shoes.

'Did we tell you what happened?' Tears shimmered in her father's eyes.

'No,' she said softly, huskily.

'He was killed trying to save a buddy who was wounded. He was trying to pull him to safety when a sniper shot him. He was killed instantly.' That seemed to comfort her physician father.

'Some place called Mézières.' Her mother picked up the world atlas lying on the table, opened to a map of France. 'It's located here.' She pointed to one of a hundred dots on the Cotentin Peninsula, and Marty dutifully looked. 'He was such a good boy – so brave.'

'We can be very proud of him, Althea,' her father stated. 'He's been recommended for decoration by his company.'

Marty looked at them, surrounded by the mementos and the black-draped photograph of David, and realized how wrong she had been to think they would need her. She had never been able to compete with her brother when he was alive; she could never hope to win against him now that he was a dead hero.

It was a lonely bitter weekend, during which Marty did her grieving for her brother in private. She would miss him, too, but her parents never seemed to consider that. She was glad when she climbed back onto the train to head back to California.

When she arrived at the WASPs' barracks, she noticed Mary Lynn's room was locked. 'Anybody know when Mary Lynn's due back?' she asked the handful of WASPs lounging about the common room.

There was a general shrugging of shoulders until one of them suggested, 'You could ask Captain Walker. He might know.'

Motionless, Marty asked challengingly, 'Why should he know?'

'They spent the weekend together, so I thought she might have mentioned to him when she'll be back in.' The information was indifferently offered. 'He was over at the Officers' Club if you want to ask him.'

'What makes you think they spent the weekend together?' Marty demanded.

'Hey, all I know is that Walker picked her up on Friday and didn't bring her back until Sunday. And I figure during that time they were together. That's all I know.'

Trouble, she knew the man was trouble the first time she laid eyes on him. Marty stood there a minute longer, then went slamming out of the barracks and headed for the Officers' Club.

At Marty's approach, the corporal on duty came to attention and cocked his arm in a rigid salute, as Army protocol demanded, but Marty ignored it – and him – as she charged up the steps of the Officers' Club. The truculent set of her features and the hard flash in her olive-gray eyes were warnings for those in her way to move.

Inside the club, she paused long enough to scan the room and locate the man with the captain's bars on his uniform, sitting alone at a corner table. The evening was early yet, but he looked well ensconced. Marty made a straight line for his table.

Walker saw her coming, neither surprised nor concerned by her arrival. Taking another drink of Coke-diluted rum, he noted with indifference the killing temper that had her energies all coiled for an explosion.

A careless smile indented the corners of his mouth when she stopped by his chair, battle-ready in her 'Ike' jacket and the ruffled honey curls of her Earhart haircut. 'Hello, Martha Jane.' Without looking up, Walker greeted her with her hated given name.

She batted the glass he held so loosely out of his hand to the table. Spilling booze and Coke, it rolled with a crash to the floor. 'You bloody bastard!' She made no attempt to keep her voice down, or to conceal her rage. 'You rotten, stinking son of a bitch! How could you do this to her?'

Walker used a cocktail napkin to push the excess spillage to the far edge of the table, away from himself, and signaled for another drink to be brought. 'Want anything?' He finally lifted his head to look at her.

When he did, the fist that had been cocked on a hair trigger swung at his face, slamming against the side of his jaw and splitting the soft inner flesh of his mouth on his teeth. The blow stung him and coated his tongue with the taste of his own blood. She had penetrated his outward cool and aroused a heat in him. The chair was kicked over as he came to his feet to face his female attacker.

As he took one threatening step toward her, someone grabbed his arms from behind. 'Hey, Walker, cool down,' the voice chided. But he seemed to be the only one who noticed Marty didn't back down an inch. In their locked glances, there was an iron message.

He flexed his muscles to shrug off the restraining hold. 'What you don't know about Martha Jane here,' he said to the officer behind him, 'is that she'd fight dirtier than most men.'

A trickle of blood made a red stain on his lips, coming from the cut in his mouth. Walker wiped at it with his finger, glancing at the bloody smudge briefly, then looked again at Marty. Amidst the raw animosity, there was a glimmer of satisfaction on her face – not enough perhaps, but some.

Uneasy in this atmosphere so charged with hostility, the officer looked from one to the other and backed away. The risk of further physical violence seemed to have passed, although the officer noticed he still hadn't been thanked for coming to Marty's rescue.

The minute they were left alone, Marty started her denunciations again. 'You're worse than scum. You are –'

'Save it.' Walker cut across her words. 'I'm sure you can swear better than a sailor, but I'm not interested in hearing the names you care to call me. If that's all you want, you might as well leave.'

A waiter came to pick up the broken glass and mop up the drink on the floor. His presence stilled Marty's tongue more than Walker's reprimand. He righted his chair and sat back down at the table. Another drink was brought to him. But Marty couldn't leave it at this. She yanked out a chair and sat heavily on it.

'Why?' she demanded to know. 'Why did you do it? Why couldn't you leave her alone?'

'If it hadn't been me, it would have been somebody else.' His forearms rested on the table, both hands closed around the glass.

'No.' Marty didn't accept that weak explanation. 'You were too persistent. You kept after her and after her.' She glared at him, hating him. 'I'll bet you're feeling very proud of yourself. You're drinking to celebrate, aren't you?'

'Celebrate.' He seemed to ponder the word. 'I have very little to celebrate, Martha Jane.'

'Don't tell me you're sorry,' she retorted scornfully, not buying it.

'No, I have no regrets.' He knew what Mary Lynn saw in him – her husband, the way he might be when he came home from the war. But Walker kept that piece of conjecture to himself. It was never wise to examine things too closely, especially relationships. Sometimes it hurt to learn what was below the surface.

'You're nothing but a drunken, used-up pilot who used to fly the big ones,' Marty scoffed. 'The Army's kicked you so far downstairs that you're flying safe, little two-engine passenger ships. You're not a man; you're a coward.'

'I've got my skin – no thanks to the Army – and I mean to keep it.' Walker saw it as survival, rather than cowardice. 'You can be the hot pilot. I just want to live through the war.'

'That's a terrific attitude. I guess it's because of men like you that women pilots are doing most of the dangerous work – the test flying, the target towing. When haven't the women gotten the shitty jobs?' Marty challenged.

'If you don't like it, get out.'

'I'm not a coward and a quitter like you,' she retorted stiffly. 'And a liar and a cheat and a rat – and all the other rotten things you are. I'll never understand' – an angry vehemence broke through – 'I'll never understand why someone like you is alive – and my brother is dead!'

'Look –' Walker lowered his gaze to his cigarette. 'I – I was sorry to hear about your brother.' The offhand offer of sympathy was a vague gesture.

'You shut up about him!' Her husky voice rumbled from deep in her chest, filled with grief. 'David was never afraid of anything in his whole life!'

Her hands were doubled into fists at her side, but Walker didn't say anything. He understood this resentment of the living, although it was seldom so openly admitted. Always, a vague sense of guilt clung to those who survived while their buddies fell.

Nearly finished, she pushed away from the table and stood up. 'Stay away from Mary Lynn while I'm gone, Walker. If you hurt her, I swear I'll get you for it.'

Walker smiled dryly. There was no going back to what had existed before. Always when he looked at Mary Lynn, there would be a sense of ownership. She had belonged to him – and would again. Each time their eyes would meet, a knowingness would be exchanged of the intimacy they had shared. It was a human weakness, this need to touch. And Walker had never claimed to be strong. He stared at his glass while Marty strode away.

Washington, DC, sweltered in the soaring summer temperatures while June officially ushered in the hot season. Major Mitch Ryan blotted the sweat beading on his upper lip. The air was close and stifling in the visitors' gallery of the House, and the heat made it difficult for him to concentrate on the endless debate being waged on the floor below.

406

His uniform clung damply to his skin and Mitch wished for the milder climate he'd so recently left in England. General Arnold, conferring with the Allied commanders as the combined armies battled inland, had yet to return. The air strategies that had come out of the Casablanca meeting more than a year before had proved successful. The bombing raids, by the US by day and the RAF by night prior to the invasion, had wreaked havoc with the enemy's transportation system, hampering the movement of Nazi reinforcements to Normandy, and their strikes on the aircraft plants had practically castrated the German Luftwaffe, rendering it impotent against the invading forces. The Allies had the superior air power.

So, while General Henry Harley Arnold remained in England, he had ordered Mitch back to the States to observe the House debate on the bill to militarize the WASPs. It seemed Mitch could not escape reminders of Cappy. In his job, it was too easy to keep tabs on her even if he hadn't seen her since they broke up – which was another reason he longed to be somewhere else.

The Washington *Post* had predicted a battle of the sexes over the legislation. Two days before, a Louisiana congressman, James Morrison, had fired the opening shot, critically referring to the WASPs as a glamorous and elite corps who wore stylish uniforms tailored by Neiman-Marcus and protesting the probable windshield-washing job the supposedly more qualified civilian male pilots were likely to get. From the outset, it was clear to Mitch the opposition to the bill was going to be as hot as the weather. He had his own problems being objective about the issue.

The second day, he had sat silently in the gallery while around him supporters of the civilian pilots' cause vocalized their objections to the WASP bill, constantly interrupting the member of the Rules Committee who was attempting to present the resolution and explain its provisions to the House. This turned into a forty-five-minute process. Once the rules had been adopted governing the debate and vote on the legislation, the House adjourned until the following morning, June 22, 1944, the first full day of summer.

Representative Charles Elston of Ohio, on the House Military Affairs Committee and a proponent of the bill, had the floor. '. . . Instructors are required to pass only the Class Two examination, which is the equivalent of the airline pilot test. On the other hand, a WASP must pass the combat examination . . .'

Mitch's attention drifted. All of the arguments for or against the bill were centered around the controversy regarding the civilian male pilots whose services were no longer required in the training of Army pilots. However, with the ground war in Europe beginning, the walking Army needed men. At issue was not whether the women were qualified pilots performing functions vital to the military, but whether they were taking jobs from men.

The thought triggered a flash of recall to the times he'd sat behind the pilot's seat while Cappy flew the plane – and he'd lean forward and kiss the curve of her neck, raising little shivers over her flesh. And the ache surfaced again, taunting and torturing him with images of her. Mitch wanted her – loved her no less than he did before – but the futility of it remained. She had allowed no room for compromise.

'What is it that these women are qualified to do that these CAA pilots cannot do?' Compton White, a congressman from Idaho, made this demand of the bill's sponsor, who had brought the matter to committee the past February.

John Costello, formerly a California lawyer, replied, 'The CAA pilots can qualify, probably for many of the same jobs, but what the Army needs now is fighting men.'

Mitch's glance sought out Costello's opponent in the House as he threw out the challenge, 'And the gentleman wants to take these men out of the flying corps and put them on the ground?'

'No.'

'That is the meat of the coconut, is it not?' White insisted.

To this, Representative Costello responded, 'No. If the men are qualified to fly planes, we want to put them in the Army flying planes. If they cannot qualify to fly planes we want to put them in as Army navigators and bombardiers. We want to use every man that is qualified.'

The heat, the debate, the prejudices of the gallery visitors, all combined to make Mitch impatient with the proceedings. White's reply was typical of other questioning comments that had gone before. So much of it was a repeat of arguments that had previously been expressed that Mitch's attention kept wandering.

Costello was speaking again. '. . .This should be done because these women, at present, are denied hospitalization; they are denied insurance benefits and things of that kind to which, as military personnel, they should be entitled. Because of the work they are doing, they should be receiving . . .'

Mitch glanced at his watch and wondered how much longer this would go on. While the debate droned on, he stepped out of the gallery to stretch his legs. When he returned, Karl Stefan was offering his opinion.

'No matter what this House feels about the women in our armed forces, Mr Chairman, I feel now that we are discussing them I cannot resist in some way championing their cause,' the Nebraska Representative said. 'My information is voluminous regarding the ability of these women in flying these monsters of the air through storms and clouds and making safe delivery after thousands of miles of flight. The knowledge of some of these women regarding the reading of maps and the handling of radio and their skill in emergencies are contained in many chapters of thrilling experiences of the Army Air Corps. It will be told more graphically when the war is over . . .'

They all spoke as if the end of the war were imminent, Mitch thought in disgust. The armies were only now entering Cherbourg to secure the Cotentin Peninsula, and in the Pacific, the Navy had engaged the Japanese fleet in the Philippine Sea near the Marianas.

The debate waged on until Representative Edward Izak brought the matter to a head, openly admitting his desire to kill the bill by striking the enacting clause from it. 'There are more than twenty-five hundred men sitting out on the beaches of California' – the state he represented – 'today, who have been instructing for four years, the finest aviators we have in this country. The Army says, "You cannot pass the examination so out you go, but we will uniform these women and let them take your places." Is that not a fine situation?'

That was the crux of it.

After nearly five hours of debate, Mitch was not surprised when the roll was called and 188 versus 169 representatives voted to kill House Resolution 4219 to commission women pilots in the Army Air Forces.

No doubt Cappy would be pleased to learn she would not be part of the Army.

On Monday, General Arnold was back in his Pentagon office, and meeting with his Director of Women pilots. Jacqueline Cochran interpreted the congressional defeat to mean Congress wanted no more women trained at the all-female Avenger Field base in Sweetwater, Texas. The general agreed. Telegrams were sent that morning to inform the class due to report June 30 that the training program was terminated. Those already in training would complete their courses, but no new classes would begin.

By the end of June 1944, twenty-three women pilots had been killed in crashes of their planes. Aircraft mechanical failures were the major cause, although a midair collision occurred when a tower controller negligently gave clearance to two pursuits to land. Some trainees at Avenger Field had been killed when their instructors were in the planes with them.

CHAPTER TWENTY-EIGHT

Jauntily swinging her briefcase and whistling a tuneless song, Marty ran up the steps to the barracks, and nearly bumped into Mary Lynn on her way out. They faced each other for tense, silent seconds while the July sun angled long afternoon rays at them, bathing them in its amber-tinged color.

During the two weeks since Marty had returned from Michigan, conflicting flight schedules had kept them apart – which was just as well because it gave Marty time to get over that first painful blast of anger and hurt at what she saw as Mary Lynn's fall from grace. She tried to put all the blame on Walker, certain that Mary Lynn simply couldn't see what a cad he was.

Irritation glittered in her silvery-green eyes as Marty noticed the raven-blue sheen on Mary Lynn's fresh-washed hair, silkily smoothed over its rat, then studied her face. Mascara blackened the heavy fringe of lashes around her dark eyes, her most striking feature, but the points of color on her round cheeks were not caused by rouge. Her glance dropped away from Marty's as she made a half-move to go around her.

'Going someplace?' Marty demanded, deliberately seeking to make Mary Lynn uncomfortable with her sins. 'With Walker, I presume.'

Mary Lynn attempted a stiff, but very quiet answer. 'I don't think it's any of your business where I'm going or with whom.'

'Is that right?' Hurt and angry, Marty hit her flash point. 'What about Beau? I suppose it isn't any of his business either! I thought you loved him!' She struck hard, trying to make Mary Lynn see sense and remember what she had.

'I do,' she insisted. Defensive and sensitive, she answered back with a protesting challenge. 'But I'm human, too. Don't you think I get lonely sometimes?'

'You've got us,' Marty retorted, meaning herself, Cappy, and Eden. In her opinion, that should have been sufficient company for a married woman.

'So do you,' Mary Lynn countered to refute the argument. 'Are you satisfied with our company alone?'

'It isn't the same.' She didn't want to know that Mary Lynn might have the same physical needs that she did – and if she did, it still didn't change anything. 'Nobody's going to get hurt by what I do. But you have a husband. How could you do this to him?'

Mary Lynn's only answers were selfish ones. She had needs and wants, the same as anyone else. Why was she denied the right to satisfy them? Why did she have to give up everything? But there was no real justification beyond the purely selfish reasons. So she walked by Marty without saying another word. She felt guilty about what she was doing, but she didn't know how to stop.

Marty watched her walk down the steps, knowing she hadn't accomplished anything. But she wasn't about to give up. More than ever before, Mary Lynn was going to need her. Turning, she started to enter the barracks, but Cappy was standing in the doorway, eyeing Marty with scorn.

'You've got a lot of nerve, Marty, throwing stones at her,' she said in low-voiced anger. 'Maybe you can tell me why sinners think they know so much more about morals than saints?'

Marty flushed darkly and pressed her way inside the barracks.

On an early August morning, the Douglas C-47 Skytrain made a sightseeing pass over Yellowstone National park in the northwestern. corner of Wyoming. Off the starboard wing, a clearing in the thick summer foliage revealed a log-walled lodge, a massive old giant of a structure that seemed in keeping with the mountain majesty around it. Not far from it, a blossoming fountain of steam and water shot into the air, a billowing spray of cloudy vapor and moisture.

'Did you see that?' Fran Davenport exclaimed excitedly from her copilot's seat, casting one glance at Cappy before turning back to the view. 'It was Old Faithful. What luck! Flying over it just as it erupted! We couldn't have timed that better if we had tried.'

Cappy smiled at Fran's contagious enthusiasm, the unabashed delight she took in things. This was the first time they'd been paired together as a flying team. The first leg wasn't over but Cappy could already tell Fran had the ability to turn a routine flight into a minor adventure.

'Do you plan your routes according to the points of interest along the way?' she asked in jest.

'When I can,' Fran Davenport admitted frankly while she continued to gaze out the cockpit window on the starboard side. Yellowstone Lake was a sapphire blue reflection of the late summer sky. 'Before I qualified for the WASPs and went to Texas for my training, I'd never been out of the state of Iowa in my life. Now I'm flying from one end of the country to the other. I may never get another chance to travel like this, and I'm going to see everything while I can.'

'I don't blame you.'

Climbing back to altitude, the twin-engined transport swung past Saddle Mountain and threaded between Windy Mountain and Sunlight peak, encountering only mild turbulence on the leeward side of the range. The thick forests of Yellowstone Park gave way to a barren stretch of rough Wyoming country.

'What's that?' Fran pointed out a collection of buildings grouped in the middle of nowhere. 'It looks like a town or a base of some sort, but my maps don't indicate anything here.'

Cappy tipped the plane so she could see over the wing. A large patch of green stood out in sharp contrast to the surrounding arid land and the bleak-looking structures near it, fenced by a barbed-wire enclosure.

'It must be the Japanese internment camp at Heart Mountain,' she guessed.

'Really?' Fran strained for a better look. 'I thought they were in prisons of some sort. That doesn't look like one.'

'It's fenced and guarded,' Cappy reminded her. 'I doubt if it's the most hospitable place to live.' A stiffness was beginning to settle into her shoulders from being in the same position. She arched them in a flexing shrug. 'You take the controls for a while, Fran,' she suggested.

They had a long way to go to their destination, Wright Field in Dayton, Ohio. There was no need to make it a tiring trip when they could spell each other along the way. Fran took over as pilot and Cappy leaned back.

Late in the afternoon they landed at Wright Field and taxied to the flight line to deliver their craft. The base was the center of Air Material Command, in charge of monitoring research, engineering, testing, and procuring equipment for the Army Air Force. Experiments and tests of new engines, instruments, and aircraft designs were constantly being conducted at the field.

As they walked from their parked plane to the operations building, Fran had to run backwards to keep up with Cappy and still look at the unusual array of planes on the flight line. 'That's a Japanese Zero,' she exclaimed. 'And look! There's a Messerschmitt.'

A sudden, high-pitched whine came loudly across the field, an unearthly howl that halted both Cappy and Fran. They stared, trying to pinpoint the source of it, as the eerie scream continued to drift through the air.

'What is that?' Fran wondered, frowning at the weird sound.

'I don't know,' Cappy murmured.

'They're testing a prototype jet engine.' The female voice startled both of them and they swung around to look at the woman pilot in her Santiago-blue flight suit. She smiled easily. 'Hi. Where are you from?'

414

'The Ferry Command out of Long Beach.' Cappy answered automatically, intrigued by the revelation. 'A jet. It's powered by that new propulsion system that pushes the plane through the air with its exhaust, instead of pulling it with a propeller. I'd heard about those jet-rocket attacks on England and wondered what those German buzz-bombs sounded like. Now I know.'

'Have you seen it?' Fran asked.

'Don't I wish,' the WASP replied. 'I've had glimpses of it, but that's it. I sure would love to climb into the cockpit of a jet, though.'

'Do you fly out of here?'

'I'm one of their test pilots for new oxygen systems, gun sights and other experimental equipment, or new engine designs.'

'Sounds exciting,' Cappy observed while the three of them started toward the operations building.

'It is,' she agreed. 'This place is real futuristic. When they say the sky's the limit, they mean it. Some engineers here are talking about going to the moon.'

At operations, they split up, Cappy and Fran going one way to file their papers and the female test pilot going another. When they were finlshed, they passed up the food at the canteen in favor of dinner at the Officers' Club.

When they walked in, the first person Cappy saw was Mitch Ryan. The ground seemed to rock under her and her pulse made a crazy leap. for an unsteady moment, she didn't know what to do. Unbidden, her feet carried her to him.

'Hello, Mitch.' She stopped beside his chair, smiling hesitantly, unsure of her welcome. But Cappy knew she wanted to see him – to speak to him.

With a turn of his head he looked up, into the startling blueness of her eyes. For a small second, he betrayed himself, then quickly the shutters came down to block out the glow of pleasure. The pain was still cruelly fresh.

Just for an instant, Cappy experienced that sweeping rush of excitement his smile had so often evoked in the past. Then his warmth was pulled away from her, and it was gone, and his expression was set in rugged, forbidding lines.

'Hello, Cappy.' His voice was flat.

'I was surprised to see you here when I walked in.'

'I don't know why you were.' Mitch rolled the ash off his cigarette on the edge of the ashtray. 'This is an Army base. You won't find me anywhere else.' His dark eyes gleamed with challenge.

Cappy drew back, belatedly noticing the woman in a WAC uniform sitting at the table with him. 'Mitch and I are old friends,' she said to quell the speculating look from the curly-headed blonde.

'Yes, we were good friends.' Mitch put it in the past tense.

'If you'll excuse me, my friend's waiting,' Cappy said abruptly. The scene had become too awkward. She backed away, hating him for making her feel like an unwanted outsider.

Fran was waiting for her at a table. 'Is he an old friend of yours?' Her admiring gaze strayed to Mitch.

'Was.' Cappy used his past tense.

'Ah,' Fran guessed. 'An old flame, eh?'

Without confirming or denying it, Cappy sat down and picked up the menu, but her eyes darted to the table where Mitch was sitting. She watched as he bent close to the woman, saying something and smiling. Her teeth came together on the sudden surge of jealousy.

During dinner, Cappy tried to ignore the pair, but it was difficult as she became conscious of Mitch's attention centering more and more on the woman with the flaxen hair. The WAC officer was every bit Mitch's age, if not on the high side of thirty, she thought cattily.

The more she tried not to watch them together, the more compelling it became to look. She hated the twisting jealousy she felt as she observed the intimate way Mitch watched the words form on that vividly red pair of lips.

Minutes later they were getting up from their table to

dance. It was almost more than Cappy could stand to see them twined so closely together and that slow, caressing movement of Mitch's hand on the woman's back.

'You're really a lot of fun tonight,' Fran murmured dryly.

'Excuse me.' Abruptly, Cappy pushed away from the table and walked blindly to the powder room to escape the sight of the dancing couple, nuzzling and kissing on the floor.

Splashes of cold water cooled her hot face, the shock of it driving away the tears that had burned the back of her eyes. Cappy managed to rationalize her reaction, convincing herself it was to be expected, but she'd get over it. She remained in the quiet of the powder room until her nerves felt steadier.

As she ventured outside, she met Mitch coming out of the men's facilities. A smudge of vibrant red was near the corner of his mouth and all the hot feelings she'd struggled to suppress came running back to the surface.

'You didn't get all the lipstick wiped off, Mitch,' she informed him, and angrily watched his hand move instinctively to his mouth.

His fingers came away with some of the telltale red on their tips. 'So I didn't.' Untroubled, he wiped the rest of it away with his handerchief.

'You wanted me to see it, didn't you?' Her teeth were held tightly together as Cappy struggled with the pain she felt, the wish to somehow strike back.

His aloof bearing didn't alter as he made slow work of folding his handkerchief and returning it to his pocket. 'Have you seen the report your illustrious director released to the press the first of the month?'

'I've seen articles on it, yes,' she admitted warily.

'In it, she made the same mistake you did. She virtually issued an ultimatum to General Arnold, by stating that if her WASPs can't be commissioned, then serious thought should be given to ending the program.' At his statement Cappy tensed, and Mitch smiled in a slow, unkind humor.

'Congress is in no mood to militarize a bunch of women pilots. And General Arnold is a pragmatic man. He isn't about to whip a dead horse. I'd wager my oak leaves that you won't be in the air much longer. But you shouldn't mind. After all, the alternative would have meant becoming part of the Army. And I know how violently opposed you are to that.'

'I don't really blame you for wanting to get back at me for hurting you,' Cappy declared tautly. 'But I hate you for this, Mitch Ryan.'

His hands caught her, stopping her and holding her by the shoulders. For a long minute, he simply looked down at her, his jaw clenched and angry. With reluctance, his gaze traveled over her features in a memorizing pattern.

'Do you?' he ground out bitterly. 'You have no idea how badly I want to say, "Frankly, my dear, I don't give a damn!" . . . But the hell of it is – I still do!'

He released her with a roughness that indicated a wish that he could rid himself of her memory just as easily. Torn and troubled, Cappy looked at the broad set of his shoulders, which was all she saw of him as he strode away.

Amid all the smarting hurt, the jealousy and the resentment, she felt a stab of fear at the thought of losing her wings, or being taken out of the skies and out of the uniform she wore with such pride. If they were disbanded, where would she go?

The sight of a B-17 bomber on the Long Beach flight line was not that common. When Marty spied the big bird with its hundred-foot-plus wingspan, she gravitated to it, gripped by nostalgia at the hours she'd flown in similar Fortresses.

'The Big Friend,' she said as she trailed her hand along the fuselage, caressing the metal skin. Her glance flickered to the plexiglas nose and three-bladed propellers of the heavy bomber. 'Losing you over a man,' she murmured wryly. 'He wasn't worth it, I promise you that.'

A ground man bent low to peer under the plane's belly

at the trousered legs on the other side. 'Are you talking to me?'

Marty bent down, previously unaware anyone else was around. 'Yes,' she lied. 'Is it all right if I take a look inside?'

'Sure. It's all right with me. You can have a whole party in there if you want,' he said magnanimously. It wasn't the first time one of these women pilots had asked to crawl into the cockpit of a plane. He'd long ago decided it was some kind of compulsion to have been in as many as possible.

Not needing a second invitation, Marty walked to the belly hatch and tossed her gear in, then pulled herself up to swing inside the fuselage. Slowly she moved forward, taking her time to look around and rediscover.

As she approached the cockpit, Marty spied an Army captain sitting in the pilot's seat. With a welling disappointment she started to back up, but the man caught the sound of her footfall and turned. She locked eyes with Walker and a fine anger ran smoothly through her veins.

'This is the last place I expected to see you, Walker.' She came forward and maneuvered into the unoccupied right seat. She looked over the familiar instrument panel, remembering all those blindfolded checks during training when they had to point out the location of instruments without being able to see them.

'Well, if it isn't Martha Jane,' he mused dryly.

'Where'd you find the nerve to get back in one of these?' Marty asked tauntingly.

'It's been a while since I was in the cockpit of one of these.' Walker absently rubbed his hand along the yoke, remembering, while he glanced over the array of gauges and switches. 'I wanted to see how it would feel again.' Then he turned to her. 'What's your excuse?'

'The same,' she admitted, with a qualification. 'Except it doesn't scare me. If those engines started up, I'll bet you'd shake in your boots.'

'You still despise me, don't you?' His hard and knowing

419

eyes looked her up and down. 'You still think I led Mary Lynn astray, don't you?'

Facing the front, Marty gripped the yoke, her fingers flexing and tightening their hold on it, suggesting a seething anger. 'I'd rather not talk about her.'

'You're a hard woman, Martha Jane. A real bitch. Don't you know yet why she sees me?' The challenge in his voice sounded bitter. 'She's afraid her husband might come home all twisted up inside like me. You were right a long time ago when you said she loved him.'

'I'm sure you're an expert on the subject,' she retorted sarcastically, 'but I'm really not interested in hearing your opinions.'

'What does interest you?'

'Flying.'

'Only flying?'

'Sometimes I think men aren't worth the trouble they cause,' she muttered. 'I never have had much patience with cowards and cheats, either way.'

'You know it all, don't you, Martha Jane?' Walker scoffed. 'You think you're a hot pilot, don't you?'

'I know I am.'

'Yeah? Well, I think I want to find out just how hot you are.' He started to rise.

'Meaning what?' Marty demanded.

Half out of the pilot's seat, he paused, bent over in a crouch. 'Meaning – that we're going to take this Big Friend for a ride. I want to find out how much of you is hot pilot – and how much is hot air.' He pressed a hand on her shoulder, pushing her more deeply into the copilot's seat. 'Wait here while I get permission to take this lady. If you're not here when I get back, I'll know you chickened out.'

Part of her didn't expect to see him again after he disappeared into the operations building, but Marty made a preliminary check of the cockpit gauges. She had no pride. She'd fly with the devil if it meant a chance to pilot a Flying Fortress again.

Twenty minutes later, Walker was crossing the flight

line at a running jog, giving Marty a thumbs-up sign to indicate permission granted. With a leap of anticipation and soaring spirits, Marty grinned to herself and pulled out the pre-takeoff checklist to prepare for the engine start-ups. From the underneath fuselage, she heard the small thuds of movement when Walker hauled himself into the plane.

Upon entering the cockpit, he tapped her on the shoulder and motioned her to take the pilot's seat. 'You fly,' he said, quickly taking the seat she vacated. 'But for God's sake, stay off the radio. You know how they feel about mixed crews. They think my second is "Martin" Rogers.'

'Hell, even if I got on the mike, they wouldn't know,' Marty declared in her man-gruff voice, flipping on the electrical switch that activated the hydraulic pump which gave oil pressure to the number-one engine. 'How did you wangle this?' She pushed the button to start the first 1,200-horsepower Wright engine.

'There are ways, Martha Jane,' Walker answered above the rumbling cough of the engine before it caught and thundered into a steady growl, the huge propellers spinning into a blur of metal.

Soon, all four engines reverberated in a deafening roar. The immense power, and the excitement of it, vibrated through the throttles as Marty advanced them to begin the roll. While she waited for takeoff clearance at the end of the runway, she gave Walker a wry glance.

'You look a little pale, Walker,' she chided. 'If you're going to lose your stomach, wait until we're airborne.'

'You just worry about yourself,' he replied.

With the underhanded grip she'd been taught, Marty moved the throttles forward and the big bomber lumbered down the runway gathering speed. As the airspeed indicator approached the 110-mile-an-hour mark, she could feel the long wings grabbing for the air and the controls become more responsive to her touch. When she pulled back on the control wheel, the B-17 broke free from the ground, acquiring grace as it soared into the air. The hydraulics system hummed to fold the landing gear and tail wheel into the belly of the plane with a locking thud.

The exhilaration of flight pounded through her veins. She angled the Fortress for the high clouds and banked it toward the empty desert. Everything came back to her. It was just as if she'd never been away from the cockpit of the Boeing B-17. At twelve thousand feet above the low desert, she leveled the bomber out. The September skies around them were free of traffic.

'Now, we'll put her through her paces,' she said to Walker. 'We'll see if you've got the stomach for some real flying.'

For the next twenty minutes, Marty had the massive four-engine bomber performing a circus act of aerial acrobactics, putting it through spins and loops and chandelles with flawless precision – all for the sheer joy of it. It ceased to matter that Walker was sitting in the right seat.

His low voice intruded. 'Are you through showing off?'

'Are you still here?' she returned mockingly.

'Yes. And it's my turn,' he announced.

Grudgingly, she surrendered the controls to him. Seconds later, she was treated to an exhibition of flying skill such as she had never seen. Walker more than matched her level of excellence. A lesser pilot would have felt like a rank amateur in his shadow.

After they landed back at Long Beach, Marty lowered herself out of the belly hatch and turned to wait for Walker. As he joined her on the ground, she studied him with a keen respect, however reluctantly given.

'You're a helluva pilot,' she admitted, even though she loathed finding something to admire about him.

'So are you.' He returned the compliment in the same reserved tone. 'Funny, isn't it?'

'What?' Marty stiffened.

'We both love the same things – those big bombers and Mary Lynn – but we can't stand each other,' Walker stated.

'Yeah. That's true,' she admitted. She started to swing

422

away, then hesitated. 'That was some ride up there.'

'It was.'

Her hand lifted in a kind of acknowledging salute, which Walker returned. With her hands shoved into the side pockets of her blue uniform slacks, Marty walked away from the big plane and the Army captain standing in its shadow.

CHAPTER TWENTY-NINE

The mimeographed letters swept through the barracks like a shock wave on that first Tuesday in October. The first was from the Director of Women pilots. After Marty had opened the official-looking envelope from the Army Air Force Headquarters in Washington, she didn't get beyond the cold, impersonal first lines.

To all WASP: General Arnold has directed that the WASP Program be deactivated on 20 December 1944. Attached is a letter from him to each of you and it explains the circumstances . . .

There was more, but Marty didn't bother reading it. She bolted from her room, the letters half-crumpled in her hand, and charged down the hall, coming to Eden's door first. Without knocking she swept inside.

'Have you –' Marty didn't have to say any more.

The redhead's posture as she sat on the cot and the stunned look on her face were all the answer Marty needed. Slowly, Eden looked up. Her reaction bordered on outrage. 'How can they do this?'

Mary Lynn appeared in the door opening, the letters drooping from her hand and tears making a black shimmer of her eyes. 'You got yours, too,' she said.

'Yes.' Eden stared again at the typewritten words that signaled the beginning of the end.

'Surely there's something we can do,' Marty protested, goaded by the way they seemed to accept the decision as final. 'Are we just going to let them pat us on the head and send us home? "Be a good girl and run along – we don't need you anymore." That's what they're saying!'

'If it's the money, I'll fly for nothing,' Eden stated.

'Their minds are made up,' Mary Lynn interjected to end their windmill-tilting. 'You aren't going to change them. The letters were very clear.' She looked down to hide the thickening tears in her eyes. 'We really should be glad the war is being won. The middle of December, Beau might be coming home with some of the pilots they expect to release from combat duty.'

One of the prime reasons they had gone to Sweetwater over a year and a half before was the desire to contribute to the war effort. But a subtle change had taken place.

Now that seemed of secondary importance. More than anything, they wanted to fly.

'Hey, van Valkenburg.' A head was stuck inside her room long enough for the woman to relay the message. 'You've got a visitor at the gate.'

'Tell whoever it is to go away!' Eden snapped.

'Tell 'em yourself.' And she was gone.

'I might as well go,' she muttered, rising from her cot. As she turned to drop the letters atop the Army blanket, Eden wondered aloud, 'Do you suppose Cappy has heard?' She'd left the week before on a ferry assignment and hadn't returned to Long Beach yet.

'Cappy knows everything,' Marty responded. 'She probably knew what the Army planned to do with us long before these letters were written.'

'She would have said something to me.' Eden dismissed the notion as she grabbed up her uniform jacket and slipped it on.

She was not interested in seeing any visitors, especially at this particular time. Eden had many 'acceptable' acquaintances in southern California, who thought it was a 'kick' that one of their own actually flew planes for the war effort. She supposed it was one of them wanting her to attend some social event.

At a distance, Eden saw the man standing with his hands folded behind him. It was obvious from his dress that he wasn't a Californian, accustomed to warm, sunny weather virtually year round. In addition to a dark suit, he wore a vest and tie – none of the open-collared, ascot-scarfed look for him. Sunlight flashed a reflection off his glasses.

'Ham!' Eden cried in surprise and rushed to greet him. 'What are you doing here?' She grabbed his hands. Suddenly, she was glad he had come. She needed the support and comfort he always gave her. In a rare demonstration of sincere affection toward him, Eden let go of his hands to wrap her arms around him and hug him tight while she pressed her cheek against his. 'It's good to see you.'

For a second, conservative Hamilton Steele was too startled to respond, then his arms loosely embraced her. 'If I'd known I would receive such a warm welcome, I would have come sooner.' His attempt at levity made Eden wonder if she was embarrassing him.

She pulled back, her head hanging slightly. 'Your timing couldn't have been better – or worse, depending on how you look at it.' A short sigh ran from her. 'The notice came today that we're being disbanded . . . as of December twentieth.'

'That's it.' Hamilton kept his disappointment to himself. 'In the face of that bad news, you need some cheering up. I recommend dinner at the Brown Derby . . . with me, of course.'

'And lots of Scotch so I can drown my sorrows.' A smile tugged wryly at her mouth. 'Dear Ham, you always know what I need.'

At the famed Hollywood club, over drinks and dinner, he told her about the business trip that had brought him to the West Coast. Eden listened, admittedly inattentively, although she knew he was trying to distract her from the unpleasant news. Her gaze wandered around the club's plush interior, the walls festooned with celebrity caricatures, but Eden was unable to rise to its atmosphere of sparkling sophistication.

'Would you care to talk about it?' he invited gently.

A second's pause, then she shook her head. 'It wouldn't do anything but make me more angry and depressed.' She held her after-dinner drink of Cointreau by the top of the glass as she swirled the liqueur and watched its play of amber and brown.

'Maybe this will help,' he suggested mysteriously, and he reached in his pocket to take something from it and lay it on the table in front of her.

When his hand came away, Eden saw bright, burning lights reflected off thousands of diamond facets. The brilliant in the center of the ring was a large carat-and-a-half American-cut diamond, surrounded by baguette diamonds to create a star-shaped design.

'I picked that up in Tiffany's the other day,' Ham said in the most casual manner. 'I thought you might like it.'

'It's stunning,' Eden admitted. But the proposal the diamond ring implied made her response reserved. 'Ham, I –'

He lifted a silencing hand. 'Don't say anything yet,' he requested. 'It comes as no surprise, I'm sure, that I would like to marry you. I believe I have mentioned it innumerable times in the past. I thought on this occasion I should make my presentation to you before that . . . uh . . . mechanic whisks you away.'

'But –'

'Eden.' Hamilton reached across the table to take her hand. 'You know I can give you the kind of life you want. You would be happy with me . . . perhaps never deliriously so . . . but you would be happy. The way I see it, your mechanic and I are playing for very high stakes – you.' He paused to smile faintly. 'It's my opinion that you are too rich for his blood.'

'I wish you hadn't done this,' Eden protested mildly.

426

'I don't want you to give me an answer now.' He went on as calmly as if he were discussing a business deal. 'I want you to regard this as one of the options available to you when you decide what you're going to do with your future. After all, the Army isn't going to let you fly for them after December, so you'll have to find something to keep you occupied.'

'True.' She couldn't help smiling at his dry wit. He made a practical appeal rather than a passionate one, which, coming from him, would have seemed ludicrous.

'In any event, I wish you to keep the ring.' He folded it into the palm of her hand and closed her fingers tightly around it. 'It's yours . . . as an engagement ring or a dowry for your marriage to someone else . . . or merely a pretty bauble for your finger.'

Subdued, Eden looked at the sparkling brilliance of the ring. 'Sometimes, Ham, I think you're too good for me.'

The deactivation notice started the base commanders scrambling to find male pilots and train them to fill the roles the women were being forced to vacate. Qualified pursuit pilots were in particularly short supply while the number of planes to be delivered to embarkation points hadn't dwindled. The WASP squadron at Long Beach sent telegrams to President Roosevelt, General Arnold, and others, volunteering to fly for the annual salary of one dollar to alleviate the problem. But their offer was politely turned down.

It left a bitter aftertaste as far as Marty and the others were concerned. Their skills were still needed, but they were being dismissed just because they were women. The war wasn't even over. By the end of October 1944, France was liberated, MacArthur had returned to the Philippines, and Russia was in Norway; but they were getting cheated out of being there at the end, when victory came. After the war was over, everyone would have to go home, but they had to go now – before the job was finished.

When they finally accepted the inevitable, they started to look for jobs. With their training, flying time, and experience in a variety of aircraft, they were uniquely qualified. Most combat pilots had flown one basic type of aircraft, and sometimes logging most of their hours in one individual plane, knowing every groan and cough it made like an old friend, while Marty had flown everything from a B-17 and a Mustang to a red-lined Dauntless dive-bomber, hopping from one strange plane to another, never knowing its idiosyncrasies.

In southern California, Lockheed, Douglas, North American, and Consolidated-Vultee all had aircraft plants. Marty applied for a flying job at each of them, but she was turned down cold. They didn't need pilots. Others received similar answers. It was the same all across the country.

All four of them – Marty, Cappy, Eden, and Mary Lynn – were crowded into Cappy's room, straining to read the job opportunities listed in a newsletter put together by some WASPs stationed in Alabama. Marty was the first to pull away.

'Nobody is going to hire us – not to fly,' she declared. 'The airlines have invited us to come to work for them – as stewardesses. The Civil Aeronautics Administration needs control tower operators. Or we could work as aircraft accident analysts or Link training instructors.'

'It doesn't look very promising, does it,' Cappy murmured.

'Maybe you can trade that Air Medal they're going to award you in for a flying job,' Marty suggested caustically. 'It would be more useful.'

Supposedly the Air Medal was being given to her in recognition of the feat she performed when she ferried a P-51, two P-47s, and a C-47 Skytrain to their destinations over a five-day period, forty hours of flying, covering eight thousand miles. Although she had been singled out, Cappy regarded it as a gesture of recognition for all the women pilots. The medal was to be presented to her at Avenger Field in Sweetwater, she'd been told, in conjunction with

428

the graduation of the last class of trainees, 44-W-10 . . . a visible sign of praise, a last pat on the head.

'The only thing I see interesting in this newsletter is the list of aviation companies in Alaska,' Eden remarked, then jested dryly, 'At least it would give me an excuse to buy a bunch of furs.'

'I didn't know you needed an excuse,' Marty countered.

'Do you think you could live in Alaska?' Mary Lynn sounded skeptical.

Eden shrugged. 'I haven't decided if I could live in Texas yet,' she said. 'Which reminds me – did I mention that Bubba's in Texas on furlough? I've got a job interview for a flight instructor's position in San Antonio. Command is letting me have a plane and three days' leave. Regardless of how the job turns out, I figured Bubba and I could at least have a day sunning on Padre Island.'

South of San Antonio, the countryside turned flat, studded with mesquite and prickly pear, thick brush-covered scrubland, good for a rangy bunch of cattle and little else – in Eden's opinion. They'd driven for miles along dusty roads, through half-deserted little towns and lonely junctions.

'If you don't want to stop and meet my folks, it's okay,' Bubba was yelling over the noise of the wind blowing through the open car windows, letting in the choking dust and a blessed stir of air. 'We'll go straight on to Padre.'

'I'd like to meet them,' Eden insisted, and tried to hide the reluctance she was actually feeling. 'What's Refugio like? That is the name of your home town, isn't it?'

'Yep.' A smile edged his wide mouth as he took his gaze from the long, straight road to glance at her. 'It's a small place . . . not much different from some of these towns we've gone through. Pretty quiet most of the time. 'Course, Saturday night is the big night in town.'

The wind blew her hair across her face and she turned into the fast rush of air while she lifted it away and held it aside. With a heaviness of spirit, Eden stared down the road, not speaking.

'You never did say how that interview turned out,' Bubba prompted after a silence had run long.

'It didn't.' But that wasn't what was weighing her down. 'They thought by hiring a female instructor they might attract more women to learn to fly, but it seems female students have more faith in male instructors. So they'd already hired a man for the position, and simply neglected to notify me that it had been filled.'

'That's too bad.'

'Bubba.' She dragged her gaze from the empty road ahead of them and the equally empty landscape around them to look at him. 'Were you planning to come back here to Texas after the war?'

'It's my home.'

Again Eden stared absently out the window, searching for something that she couldn't find. Finally, she sighed in defeat. 'I think you'd better stop the car, Bubba. It's time we stopped kidding ourselves.'

After one look at her very sober expression, Bubba pulled the car off to the side of the road. The trailing dust cloud caught up with them and swirled around the car before settling on a cactus bush. For a long second, he looked at her, then he ran his hands up the steering wheel, pulling his feelings inside.

'Yeah, I reckon you're right,' he said finally while the narrowed pinpoints of his eyes examined the rough land beyond the windshield. 'You don't belong here . . . and I don't fit in your world.'

'I love you, Bubba.' Pain and frustration vibrated through her voice.

'You know I love you,' he said and pulled in a deep breath, releasing it on a laughing note. 'I guess the poets were wrong when they said love conquers all.' He reached for the ignition key to start the car motor again. 'I'll drive you back to San Antonio.'

Eden wanted to stop him – to have these last two days with him, but what would they bring? Only more heartaches and regret. So she said nothing as he reversed the car to turn around in the middle of the road and go back the way they came.

At the airport, he carried her bag to the plane and loaded it aboard. They stood awkwardly in front of each other. Eden had tears in her eyes.

'My daddy is probably going to have to buy an airline so I can get a job flying from him,' she joked weakly. 'If he does, you can be the maintenance chief.'

'Yeah, sure.' But they both knew it would never come to pass.

'I'll never forget you, Bubba.' Her voice started shaking. 'I wish –'

'No.'

His hands touched her and she went into his arms. They kissed fiercely, aching with all the tomorrows that would never be for them. Then Eden pulled away and climbed into her plane. Bubba stood on the ground and watched her take off for the last time.

The new gymnasium at Avenger Field was crowded with Army officers, families, and friends, there to witness the pomp and ceremony of the graduation exercises for the last class of WASPs. While the sixty-eight graduates marched into the gym, the Big Spring Bombardier School Band played the 'Air Corps Song.' Cappy thought they played better at the graduation of her class, but perhaps the tune had been stronger, more inspiring then. 'Off we go into the wild blue yonder, climbing high into the sun . . .' With the end near, the words had a poignancy they had not had previously.

The brass had turned out in force for this occasion. An array of generals was present, as well as the WASP Director, Jacqueline Cochran, and General H. H. Arnold himself. Mitch was here, too. Cappy had caught sight of him earlier when the Commanding General of the Army Air Force arrived. Somewhere in the audience, her parents were seated, on hand to see their daughter awarded the flying medal. Naturally, the Army had notified them of the occasion, and Cappy had written her mother about it as well. She wasn't sure that her father would come but she'd seen both her parents at a distance before the ceremonies started.

Today was the third anniversary of Pearl Harbor. Cappy's thoughts wandered as General Yount of the Army Training Command addressed the throng. Avenger Field had changed since she had trained there. The construction was finished on all the runways; two new hangars had been built, and a swimming pool. A ground man told her they had electric runway lights, no more trucks racing out at dusk to set out the oil pots. But the painted rendition of Walt Disney's character, Fifinella, the WASP mascot, still sat atop the administration building and the Wishing Well was still there.

'. . . Well, now in 1944' – General Arnold was in the middle of the keynote address – 'more than two years since WASPs first started flying with the Air Forces, we can come to only one conclusion – the entire operation has been a success. It is on the record that women can fly as well as men. In training, in safety, in operations, your showing is comparable to the overall record of the AAF flying within the continental United States. That was what you were called upon to do – continental flying. If the need had developed for women to fly our aircraft overseas, I feel certain that the WASPs would have performed that job equally well.

'Certainly we haven't been able to build an airplane you can't handle. From AT-6s to B-29s, you have flown them around like veterans. One of the WASPs even flight-tested our new jet plane.'

At that announcement, Cappy wondered if it had been the girl they'd met on the flight line that day at Wright Field. She could still remember the scream of those jet engines.

'You have worked hard at your jobs,' the general said. 'Commendations from the generals to whose commands you have been assigned are constantly coming across my

432

desk. These commendations record how you have buckled down to the monotonous, the routine jobs which are not much desired by our hot-shot young men headed back to combat or just back from an overseas tour. In some of your jobs, I think they like you better than men . . .'

Cappy searched the crowd of faces for Mitch. There were so many things she hadn't seen – that she hadn't understood about herself the last time they'd met. She wanted the chance to tell him she'd been wrong – about the Army, about everything. She owed him that much.

The general had finished his speech and Jacqueline Cochran had taken the podium. After some opening remarks, she talked about the Air Medal and described how Cappy had earned it. When her name was called, Cappy came forward to receive the service medal. Distinguished, snowy-haired General 'Hap' Arnold pinned it over her breast, his round cheeks coloring slightly with embarrassment at the task.

After the ceremonies were over, the overflowing crowd spilled out the doors onto the base. Her mother waited to embrace her and proudly admire the medal she'd earned. Her father stood back, more silvered at the temples of his dark mane. Cappy noticed the shimmer in his eyes when she turned to him.

'You should be very proud,' he informed her with a military jut of his chin.

'I am.'

Lieutenant Colonel Robert Hayward tilted his head down and seemed to fumble awkwardly for the words he wanted to say, but they were difficult for him. 'Long ago . . . I used to wish for the day . . . a son of mine would . . . follow in the old man's footsteps, so to speak. But your mother and I weren't blessed with any sons. But today –' He lifted his head, and the tears glittering in his eyes were unmistakable. '– You made that wish come true. You, my daughter.'

Cappy hugged him. She knew he couldn't break that rigid discipline that frowned on emotional displays, so she did it for him. This day, she had gained his respect, a most precious thing. But Cappy also knew she had received it because the Army had acknowledged her worth, not because her father saw it. In these last couple of months since she had received the letter announcing the disbandment of the WASPs, she had mellowed and learned to accept the things she couldn't change and be grateful for the things she had, including her father's respect.

When she drew away, her father had managed to blink back the tears and display some military decorum again. 'When do you anticipate you'll be coming home after your mustering out?'

'I don't know.' But her glance went past him as Cappy spied Mitch standing near the generals. 'Excuse me, Dad. I'll only be a minute.'

So tall, so tan, lean, and muscular in his Army uniform, Mitch watched her approach with a blank expression. Her steps slowed as she drew near him, a thudding deep inside her.

'Hello, Mitch.'

'Congratulations.' He nodded at the Air Medal pinned to her jacket.

'Thank you.' Cappy hesitated only a moment, then asked with a false calm, 'Can we walk? I'd like to speak to you about something . . . privately, if it's all right.'

After a short glance at the generals to weigh how long they'd be, Mitch inclined his head in a nod of agreement and swung away to match her stride. As they made their way through the slowly dissipating crowd, she stole glances at his profile.

No one was around the Wishing Well. Cappy slowed her steps to stop beside the stone-walled reflecting pool. The fountain bubbled in the center and coins shimmered in the bottom. A plaque from General Arnold was mounted in the pool, inscribed: 'To the Best Women pilots in the World.' For no reason, she tossed a coin into the Wishing Well, without even making a wish. It made a plunking splash, sending out a small ripple.

'This brings back a lot of memories,' she said, then added wistfully, 'Soon that's all there will be.'

'Have you decided what you're going to do?' Mitch didn't sound interested, and when Cappy glanced at him, he didn't look interested either.

'I'm still looking for a flying job . . . without much luck.'

'I wouldn't feel too bad about it. Neither has Jacqueline Cochran. She's going aboard Northeast Airlines . . . as a director, in hopes of attracting more female passengers. And she's a flying ace with countless world records to her credit.'

'Like Earhart,' Cappy mused, but she didn't want to talk flying, at least not that aspect of it.

She sat down on the stone lip of the pool while Mitch remained standing. She let her fingers trail in the water. It seemed easier to talk if she didn't look at him.

'It isn't easy for anyone to swallow their pride and admit when they've made a mistake. I'm no different from anyone else in that respect,' Cappy said with a shrugging tilt of her head. 'When we were denied commissions in the Army, it took me a while to realize how much I had wanted it.'

Her gaze went to Mitch, needing to see his reaction to her words and discover whether they made any difference to him. His eyes were on her, watching, committing nothing.

'I don't want to turn in this uniform, Mitch.' Her voice was low and vibrant with the strength of her feelings. 'These girls are my sisters. I said I never had a home . . . family or friends. I was wrong. Home was every barracks I stayed in across this country for the last year and a half. The WASPs were my family and friends.' Cappy paused for a long second. 'I guess I'm trying to say that I had to be a part of it to understand. And I had to lose it to know it. I don't hate the Army any more, Mitch.'

'And?'

'That's all.' She looked again into the reflecting pool, a little ache starting inside.

'Is it supposed to make a difference to me?' Mitch asked.

She had hoped it would, but it obviously hadn't. With a quick move, she came to her feet, seeking to make her escape. Her head was up, held by that measure of pride that she wouldn't release.

'I wanted you to know, Mitch.' Cappy walked carefully around his question. 'Goodbye.'

His hand stopped her. 'Did you want it to make a difference to me, Cappy?' Mitch demanded. 'If you did, then dammit, say so!'

Her eyes were bluer than anything he'd ever seen, and her lips were trembling. She was the cool deeps and the fire, all the softness and the never-ending for a man.

'Yes. Yes, I did.' Her voice was a whisper, but a forceful one.

'I think I know where there's a place for you, if you want it,' Mitch said.

Her features were set in unbreakable lines, all the needing and wanting held inside while her gaze searched his face in near hope. 'Where?'

'Beside me,' he said.

'Mitch.' In his name was her answer.

Cappy came into his arms and her lips were hot and firm against his. It was all there. No one else would ever have as much from her as he did. She was proud and willful, her feelings and passions running as deep as his own. He'd heard the bitterness in her voice and seen the strain of hurt in her eyes. Now she was smiling, confident in herself and certain of him.

CHAPTER THIRTY

The slow, painful process of signing forms and turning in uniforms and flying gear was taking the bulk of Tuesday morning, the 19th day of December, the day before they were officially discharged. The four friends trooped to the various offices together, providing moral support for each other.

Marty rubbed a hand over the smooth leather of her fleece-lined flying jacket. 'I wish I could keep this.'

'Where would you wear it?' Eden wondered. For all its practicality, it was hardly the height of fashion. On her ring finger, the soon-to-be bride of Mr Hamilton Steele wore her diamond sparkler.

'Michigan winters are cold.' Marty shrugged vaguely.

'Then you've decided to go home,' Cappy surmised. Marty was the only one among them without any definite plans for the future, vacillating from one thing to another.

'I don't know. With David gone . . .' She still couldn't talk about her brother's death. 'I thought I might as well go back to Detroit. There's a bomber plant at Willow Run. If they won't let me fly them, maybe I can get a job building them.'

'Good luck.' But Eden was skeptical of her chances.

'Nobody's going to keep me grounded.' Her husky voice had a growl in it. 'I'll find a way to get back up in the air if it means ferrying war surplus airplanes from sale points to the homes of their new owners.'

'You know the kind of shape those planes are in,' Mary Lynn protested. 'They're all red-lined. How many have crashed just being ferried to the Army's sale depots? That's all you hear about.'

'So?' Marty countered. 'What do you think we flew at Camp Davis?'

With the roughly eighty WASPs stationed at Long Beach going through the discharge process, there was a lot of waiting in hallways and corridors. The four of them lounged along a corridor wall, part of a slow-moving line, supporting themselves with a shoulder against the wall, or sometimes their whole bodies slumped against it.

By day's end, they were divested of everything the Army had issued them – uniforms, parachutes, guns – but they kept their wings, those silver, shining insignias that had set them free for a little while. What was left of the time was spent packing their personal belongings and saying goodbyes to gals they'd flown with, strangers now in civilian clothes.

As they walked out of the barracks that last time with their suitcases under their arms, the California sun was shining as if the day were no different from any other. An awkward silence reigned, a self-consciousness claiming them.

Eden glanced at the two suitcases she carried and joked weakly, 'Two suitcases instead of the two trunks I brought with me to Sweetwater. I've learned something, I guess.'

Faint smiles were offered in response to the attempted joke, but not even Marty commented on it. Loosely walking abreast, they headed for the gate house, feeling oddly out of place in their traveling suits and dresses instead of the familiar Santiago-blue uniforms they had worn so proudly. Their route took them past the flight line and the numerous war planes parked on the ramp.

'I heard they have sixty planes on line, headed for embarkation points to the war zones,' Cappy remarked as they all looked at the aircraft, wings gleaming in the sunlight. '– And no pilots to fly them.'

The irony of it was not lost on any of them. A man in an officer's cap with his flight jacket unzipped left the flight line to approach their foursome. Marty recognized Walker and glanced quickly at Mary Lynn to discover if she had seen him.

Marty saw regret and reluctance mixed in Mary Lynn's expression. In the last two weeks, assignments had kept the two of them apart, one leaving while the other was returning. Marty's opinion of their affair hadn't altered. Now that Mary Lynn was going home, Marty didn't want Walker trying to change her mind.

She intercepted him before he reached Mary Lynn. 'Let her go.' Today his dark eyes were sobered by something, although his mouth quirked.

'You can relax, Martha Jane. I'm not here to steal her,' Walker said in lazy assurance. 'I just want to tell her goodbye.'

'We'll wait for you at the gate.' Eden and Cappy walked on, but Marty lingered, standing off to one side, watchful and wary of this last meeting between the couple.

His officer's cap sat on the back of his head, pushing forward his coffee-colored hair. A gentleness was in his eyes, a longing and a regret, but he made no move to touch her, his hands thrust deeply into the pockets of his jacket as if to prevent such an occurrence.

'You're on your way home, I guess.' His gaze traveled over her lively dark beauty. She was everything perfect and graceful and strong – things a man dreamed of and never expected to find.

'Yes.' The soft drawl of her voice was musical and warm. 'I'll be there by Christmas. My suitcase is filled with presents for my parents.'

'They'll be happy about that,' he said.

'Beau said in his last letter that they'll probably send him home after the first of the year.'

His mouth twisted. The subtle message hadn't really been necessary. 'I've always known you'd be going back to him, Little One. You know –' He paused, turning his head to squint into the sun and hide the stinging in his eyes. '– All my life I've always taken what I wanted. Life can trap a man. Because now I find myself wanting to give . . . and I have nothing to offer.'

'I'm sorry,' she said, so softly.

His head shook it away; he didn't want her pity. 'Goodbye, Little One.' He looked at her with moist eyes. 'Tell that husband of yours to take care of you.'

'Goodbye.' Mary Lynn walked quickly from him.

For a long, long time, Walker watched her, then he turned to Marty and tipped his head back, his mouth crooking at an angle. 'Well?' he taunted.

'Maybe you aren't as rotten as I thought, Walker,' Marty suggested.

'It looks like I'll be out in a few months,' he said. 'I've heard there's a market for surplus cargo planes in South America. I thought I might see if I could make some money. 'Course I'd need some good pilots to fly them down there. What do you think?'

'Look me up.'

'I'll do that.'

They shook hands to seal the agreement, then Marty was hefting her suitcase and striding after the others to the gate house.

The moment had been prolonged but the time finally came when the four of them had to say their goodbyes. Clinging and crying, they forced smiles into their expressions.

'We'll keep in touch,' they promised, but they all knew they wouldn't.

A big piece of their lives had been cut from them, leaving a hole. Until they found something to fill it – husbands, family, or career, it would hurt too much to see each other again and remember all that they had lost.

So they went home.

When Marty climbed the steps to the front porch of her parents' Detroit home, she saw the service flag hanging in the window. The gold star was there, signifying the loss of the family's soldier son. She walked into the house and went straight to the cabinet where her father kept the liquor.

Eden's hands burrowed under the collar of her sable coat, its dark, dark luster a contrast to the rich red of her hair. Her high-heeled and fur-trimmed boots crunched into the packed snow on the edge of the flight line as she hurried to keep up with a fast-walking Hamilton Steele.

'What are we doing here?' None of her questions had been answered, but still she tried as her breath made little puffs of vapor.

Behind his smug look was a mysterious smile. Hamilton

stopped to open the side door to a hangar and hold it for her, indicating with a sweep of his hand that she should enter. Eden walked through.

'Merry Christmas.'

A renovated AT-6 Texan glistened with fresh paint in a soft shade of sky blue. Lettered on it were the words 'A Lady's Wings.' Eden stared at it, then looked at Hamilton.

'Mine?' she whispered. At his affirmative nod, she threw her arms around him and hugged him. 'You are going to spoil me,' she declared, then she walked over to inspect her plane.

The skies above Mobile were a-hum with training aircraft. The drone of their powerful engines filtered into the front room where Mary Lynn was stringing the last of the tinsel on the Christmas tree. Planes would always be a part of her life, whether she flew them or Beau did. His presents were under the tree, waiting for him with bright, beribboned expectancy – just as she was.

'I simply don't see why you can't cook the meals for our boarders.' Her mother made wide, vigorous swipes with the dust cloth across the side bureau, the loose flab under her arm shaking with the action. Her small-built body had gone to plumpness, giving her a squatty look in the plain housedress she wore. 'You might as well help while you're here.'

'Mama, if you want to start providing meals for your boarders, that's your business, but don't expect me to do the work for you.' Mary Lynn turned away from the decorated tree to confront her mother, respectful but firm in her refusal.

'You haven't got anything else to do except wait for your husband to come home.' The sullen glitter of her small, dark eyes was turned on Mary Lynn. 'You might as well be doing something that will bring some money into this house.'

'I'm not going to be here that long, Mama,' she replied. 'As soon as Beau comes back, we're going to find us a place of our own. Wherever the Army sends him, I'm going.'

A Christmas tree, all decorated with shiny balls, colorful garlands, and wispy clouds of angel hair, stood in a corner of the Georgetown home. Gaily wrapped presents were crowded around its cotton-covered stand, waiting to be opened. But Cappy was standing at the window, gazing up at the beckoning clouds in the sky.

She didn't see Mitch enter the room or hear his approach. She wasn't aware he was there until she felt the touch of his hands sliding onto her arms. She half turned with a start, then smiled as he bent to brush her lips with a light kiss. No more than that, since her parents would be joining them in the living room at any moment.

'A penny for your thoughts,' Mitch said.

'They aren't worth it,' she answered.

His fingers curled under her left hand to lift it, as if needing to see the diamond engagement ring on her finger to reassure himself it was still there. He carried her hand to his lips. His dark eyes were warm and ardent.

'Happy?'

'Yes,' Cappy said, and she knew she would be – once she got used to the idea that all windows look out to the sky.

EPILOGUE

November 3, 1977
House of Representatives, Washington, DC

Time had healed many breaches. In a row, they sat in the seats of the House visitors' gallery. Eden Steele, the socially prominent wife of the financier Hamilton Steele, sat with her mink cape folded across her lap, still a strikingly attractive woman in her late fifties. A wide streak of snow white ran through her silvered red hair. On her right was Cappy Ryan, the wife of Air Force Colonel Mitch Ryan, the metallic gray of her hair somehow flattering when combined with the blue clarity of her eyes, darkly outlined with thick lashes. The petite, white-haired woman sitting next to her was Mary Lynn Palmer, the wife of the former Trans World Airlines pilot, Captain Beau Palmer, now retired.

They all led full, busy lives, involved in many activities outside the home. But none of the three was too busy not to be here on this day to witness another battle on the House floor over a bill which would grant military status to the WASPs, an act of recognition.

Over the years, countless such bills had been introduced to Congress, rarely ever being reported out of committee. This time they had hopes. Senator Barry Goldwater of Arizona had championed the legislation in the Senate, and the upper house version had been passed the 19th of October. The senator had firsthand knowledge of the role the WASPs played during World War II, having flown with them as a major general in the Air Force Reserve when he was based at New Castle, Delaware, as a pilot with the Air Transport Command.

Now the compromise version of the 'GI Bill Improvement Act' was to be voted on by the House. In the past, veterans had lobbied against any amendment giving military status and benefits to what they regarded as a civilian group of women pilots.

In the visitors' gallery, they waited tensely for the coming debate, for the battle on the House floor that they hoped would give them victory. They wanted to win. They had been 'Army.' Their discharge papers said as much: 'This is to certify that Eden van Valkenburg honorably served in active federal service in the Army of the United States.'

Outside, the sun was drifting lower in the early winter sky. Shifting, Eden thought she caught sight of a familiar, lanky figure on the House floor below and strained her eyes for a better look. William 'Bubba' Jackson was somewhere down there, she was sure. The representative from Texas was one of the ardent supporters of the amendment. With his silver-haired, down-home looks and country humor, he was a popular political figure in Washington. He'd married a pretty, freckle-faced Texas girl, who'd given him seven children. Eden had met his wife about six months before – the homespun type, exactly suited for Bubba. Congressman or not, he basically hadn't changed. During the committee hearings last May, she'd met him again for the first time in all these years. It had been outside, in the parking lot . . . and Bubba had grease all over his hands from tinkering with his car, which wouldn't start.

It was still there – the old magic – faded a little, as they were. But . . . Eden sighed. She and Ham had known many good years, and she had been happy with him. No, she had no regrets.

Congressman Olin E 'Tiger' Teague approached the table of the Speaker of the House. This Texas representative had long been a staunch opponent of any measure to militarize the WASPs and give their members veteran status. That afternoon, however, he requested a unanimous consent to pass HR 8701, as amended. According to parliamentary procedure, if there were no objections, it would be passed with no debate and no vote. No one objected. The ring of the gavel made it final.

It was over. The opposition had capitulated without a fight, robbing them of the glory of battle and victory.

Dazed by the anticlimax, they looked at one another, then stood to file quietly out of the gallery and down the stairs. The long, empty hallways of the Capitol were shadowed by the diminishing sunlight, and their footsteps echoed hollowly through the tall corridors.

'It was stolen from us again,' Cappy murmured.

'I don't know about you, but I need a cigarette.' Eden opened her Gucci handbag and took out a gold case.

'Did I tell you my youngest daughter, Lily Anne, is one of the women pilots taking part in the jet training program the Air Force just opened to females this past year?' Mary Lynn informed them in a musing tone. 'She's encountering the same prejudice and abuse that we did. Men still think the cockpit isn't any place for a woman.'

'During the war, we all found out there were a lot of jobs we could do that the men thought we couldn't,' Cappy said, then smiled, the corners of her mouth dimpling. 'And nothing has been the same since.'

'Yes, probably much to the men's regret,' Mary Lynn agreed, a smile almost lightening her low spirits.

The quick, heavy stride of a man disturbed the quietness of the congressional halls. As the footsteps came nearer, Eden turned to look idly over her shoulder while she expelled a trail of smoke. A trim-looking man in a dark wool overcoat approached them on his way to the stairs leading to the visitors' gallery. A very handsome man with distinguished silver tufts threading the temples of his jet-dark hair, he had blue, blue eyes. The contrast of dark hair and blue eyes brought a flicker of recognition. At almost the same instant, Eden noticed the man look at her and hesitate, as if trying to place her.

He paused, frowning slightly. 'Excuse me, but' – he almost laughed the cliché-riddled words – 'I believe we've met. My name is Zachary Jordan.'

'Eden –'

'Of course.' He interrupted with an expansive regret that he hadn't remembered. 'Eden van Valkenburg.'

'Married name is Steele, now,' she volunteered.

'Mrs Steele.' Zachary Jordan made a continental show of bowing over her hand, as charming and gallant as he was handsome. 'It isn't likely you'll remember me. We met only briefly . . . at the chapel where the Army held the memorial service for Rachel.'

'I do remember,' Eden assured him, all the vague memories clicking into place. 'How are you?'

'Fine. I'm with the Israeli Embassy here in Washington now.' After the war, he had immigrated to Israel – then Palestine – as he and Rachel had planned so very long ago.

'I . . . I still remember Rachel's plane crash.' It was an image she couldn't shake from her mind.

'I believe she mentioned to you that her grandmother was in one of the Polish death camps,' Zach said.

'Yes,' Eden nodded, curious. 'She did say something once.'

'Rachel's grandmother was one of the survivors of Oświę cim – Auschwitz,' he added, supplying the American-known name. 'After the war, I managed to find her. She had an interesting story to tell about Rachel coming to her in a dream, all surrounded by flames and assuring her grandmother that she would never know the fires. Her grandmother thought it was very odd . . . because Rachel had always spoken very bad Yiddish. In the dream, she had understood every word. I have often wondered . . .' Zach let his voice trail away and shrugged expressively. 'We shall never know.'

'I suppose not.'

His glance traveled up the stairs in the direction of the

visitors' gallery beyond. 'You are here for the debate? I heard it was scheduled for today's session and I thought I would sit in on part of it. Has it begun?'

'It's over,' Eden informed him, and smiled when she realized there was no elation or triumph in her voice. 'The bill was enacted, unanimously.'

'Good.' But the startled tone indicated that he, too, felt something was missing. 'Rachel would have been glad about that.' He looked around, somewhat lost, as if there was no more reason to be there. 'Congratulations . . . to all of you.' He included Mary Lynn and Cappy.

'Thank you.'

'In that case, I must get back to the embassy. Goodbye.' Again, he took her hand and kissed it with a European flair. 'Perhaps we'll meet again someday.'

'I hope so.'

The click of his shoes tapped loudly down the corridor as he walked swiftly away. Outside, it was growing darker. In mutual and silent consent, they started toward the exit doors. Eden slipped on her fur cape against the November briskness awaiting them. As they emerged from the Capitol building, they paused at the top of the steps.

A man stepped from the shadow of a column. 'Little One. It is you,' he murmured.

The lazy voice jolted her with recognition as Mary Lynn stared at Walker, an old Walker whose body had finally aged to match his eyes. But the glitter was still in those eyes, despite the lines of dissipation that jowled his face. The scars had faded until they had all but disappeared.

'Walker.' Her voice was warm and sad all at the same time. The years hadn't treated him kindly. He looked like a broken-down pilot in his worn leather flight jacket and crumpled officer's cap. His dark hair was shot with gray and his chest had fallen down around his middle. 'What are you doing here?'

'I've been reading all the publicity about this bill they're trying to pass to make you a veteran like me.' He smiled crookedly. 'I heard it went through.'

447

'Yes.'

'I wish Marty had been here,' Walker said absently.

'We don't know where she is,' Mary Lynn said. 'We tried to find her a few years ago when we were organizing our first reunion, but her parents had died and she hadn't kept in touch with any of us so –'

'I'm sorry,' he said, frowning. 'I thought you knew.'

'Knew what?'

'After the war, Martha . . . Marty and I had a little partnership going – buying surplus transports and flying them down to Central and South America. We were talking about setting up an air cargo business. Then . . . she had a C-47 . . . she lost power shortly after takeoff. She didn't have enough altitude to make it back to the field. The only open patch of ground was a playground full of children. Witnesses said it looked like she deliberately plowed into the side of a hill. She was killed outright, but nobody else was hurt. Noble damned fool, if you ask me.'

Tears slipped down Cappy's cheeks, while Mary Lynn had trouble accepting that bold, wild Marty wasn't somewhere out there.

'That was the end of the good times for me. At least now I can put an American flag on her grave. She'd like that, I think,' Walker murmured. 'It looks like you're doing fine, Little One. I suppose you're a grandmother now.'

'Yes. And you, Walker? What about you?'

'Same as before. You strip away the pride and there's nothing.' He shifted uncomfortably. 'I just wanted the chance to see you one last time, Little One. Guess I'd better go now.'

'Goodbye, Walker.'

He lifted a hand and sauntered away, a lonely figure.

They stood on the Capitol steps, looking out at the gray dusk. 'The three of us is all that's left,' Mary Lynn said.

'I don't know how you feel,' Eden said in a tight choked voice. 'But the two years that we flew in those skies were the best years of my life.' Neither of the others disagreed.